AUGU

by

C.D. Ward-Daniels

Copyright © C.D.Ward-Daniels 2013

All rights reserved

ISBN: 978-1-291-57908-6

This book is sold subject to the condition that it shall not, by way of trade or otherwise, be copied, lent, resold, hired out or otherwise circulated without the publisher's prior permission in any form of binding, cover or electronic means, and without a similar permission being imposed on any subsequent purchaser.

This book is a work of fiction. Names, characters, businesses, places and events are either the product of the author's imagination or are used fictitiously. Any resemblance to actual persons, living or dead, or events is entirely coincidental.

CHAPTER ONE
1986

There were twenty one empty lager cans in the pyramid Shaun had built on the window sill. He was proud of the fact he had drunk them all in one day, and as much as August nagged him, he would not let her take them down. Lying in bed she counted the cans and remembered how at twenty one she had taken the flat, her very own space, it wasn't very big, but bigger than having to live in a small bedroom and share a kitchen with others whose idea of a clean mug was that it didn't have the birth of penicillin growing in it. Now she had a lounge/bedroom, but also a separate small kitchen /diner and a bathroom, it was her territory, she paid the rent. Ten months later she had met Shaun, he had walked her home from a pub one night a year ago and never left. The flat had been a tip ever since.

Irritated by her own surroundings, she blew a sigh into the air which seemed to hang over her, and then settle down like an uncomfortable weight on the bed quilt. She pushed her head to one side bedding a fresh dimple in the pillow. The afternoon sun prodded her eyes and she felt like she was betraying a fine autumn day for what dismally was sex.

August now faced Shaun's redundant body, fat eyelids closed. Ten hairs heaved and sunk on his broad white chest, over shadowed by a huge rise of even whiter belly. His beery breath followed a grunt before he coughed and said, 'Gusty get me a fag will yer.'

She turned her head from his stale breath ignoring him. Facing her on the fireplace wall was a painting that had belonged to her late Mum, 'Bigshit bay', well that wasn't it's real title, but that's how August remembered it. When she was a small child, August would lay on that green cliff top overlooking the bay, watching the foaming crush of waves swamp the rocky toothed beach and listen to the voice of the sea. The waves would suck up such power and then strike the splintered cliff face, and as she lay motionless and listened she would hear the tide repeat 'Bigshit bay…. Bigshit bay', twice, every fourth wave.

Over the fireplace in a tarnished gilt frame was that bay. The painting was all that she owned that had belonged to her Mum. The painting reminded her of the nice times, the time before her Mum became sick, the time of picnics and sharing holidays and time together before the illness took all that and her Mum away .

'Get us a fag Gusty', Shaun's fat hand fumbled across her limp arm. A loud guttural belch from his mouth made her lip curl with revulsion and 'Bigshit bay' became distant. She moved herself away from the stale beer gas and out of bed to find his cigarettes.

'Give 'em 'ere', he was already coughing as he took the cigarettes. 'God I'm starved,'

he said lighting a cigarette, 'what's for dinner?'

'Not much.

'What do yer mean not much, it's Sunday, we always 'ave a late roast, what is it, pork? beef? lamb?'

'Mince.'

Shaun had a small coughing fit, 'Mince! you're joking me.'

'I'm not joking, so you can have cottage pie or Chilli.'

'Come on August, it's Sunday.'

'It's also near the end of the month and the rent is due and I haven't any money left, which reminds me , you owe me half the rent from last month and the month before, that's probably why I'm so broke. So Shaun Ratcliffe, it's your turn to pay this month and next month, and don't keep leaving the bathroom heater on and filling the kettle to the brim when you're only making one mug of coffee, I can't afford to keep feeding the meters'. August drew breath and could have gone on, but left it as Shaun stopped her saying, 'Alright, alright, but you know I'm skint.'

'Then you shouldn't have spent what you did in the Pub this lunch time.'

'But it's Sunday Gusty, we always 'ave a good time on a Sunday.'

'We're also skint Shaun.'

She stared at him, but his eyes closed, cigarette in his mouth. She waited for a response. With his short cropped hair and unshaven face, she thought he looked like a smoking tennis ball with ears.

August stormed off to the bathroom to shower and dress, she felt miserable because if this was having a good time she thought she could do without it.

CHAPTER TWO

August showered quickly aware of the meter running low and aware that everything seemed to have tripled in cost since Shaun had made himself at home. He must spend hours on the phone she moaned under her breath to herself, being as she hadn't managed to get that one out. Sometimes she walks into a warm flat and he's not even there. The gas fire left blazing, all the lights left on.

When she went back into the living room, Shaun was still in bed. There were his clothes strewn everywhere. She planted her fists on her ample hips and quite crossly said, 'Christ this flat is a mess, Shaun are you getting out of that bed!'

'Keep your hair on, I've been thinkin'.'

'So that's why you're still there then, wore yourself to a frazzle have you?'

'Shut up an' listen, about the rent' he said , August snapped back, 'yes it is due on Thursday.'

Shaun lit another cigarette and through a cloud of smoke said, 'couldn't you ask the bank again to let you 'ave an overdraft?'

August's mouth dropped open and her eyebrows elevated. 'Me ask for an overdraft!, it's your bloody turn to pay!'

'Alright…alright, I'll pay you back.'

August threw his huge jeans at him, which he took as a NO.

'Tell you what then,' he said getting out of bed and into his clothes, 'Let's have summat to eat and later on go t'pub' August threw him a threatening scowl and he held up a defensive hand saying, 'Listen…listen, if we go down t' Crown, Gerry Fallow will be in there and he owes me some money.'

'How come he owes you money?'

'I did this job for him right.'

'I hope you haven't been dealing in stolen stuff Shaun.

'Look I said he owes me money, so I'll collect it to pay the rent see.'

'And what do we buy a drink with while we wait for him?'

Shaun placed his chunky hands on her shoulders and bent forward to rest his forehead gently on hers, he kissed her nose and said in a soft voice,' Do you think you could call at that little hole in the wall with your plastic?'

'Aww…Shaun no.'

'Come on Gusty, you only need get a tenner or so, Gerry owes me two 'undred.'

August couldn't hide her disbelief and pulled away to look straight into his brown eyes, 'Two hundred!'

'Two 'undred.' Shaun assured her, 'now come on get that cottage pie on.'

August resigned herself to Shaun's plan of action, knowing there was nothing much of an alternative. She checked the time. Nearly 5 o' clock already, by the time she would have cooked the meal and they had eaten, it would be time to trail down to the pub and wash down some more calories, end up at the Chinese takeaway and sleep on an ever increasing belly. She wished to God that she could get out of this rut, but as much as she wanted to lose weight, preparing their meals made her so hungry, and … there was always tomorrow. Every Sunday she would drink and eat until she thought she would explode, but the more she ate, a few hours later she was really hungry again. Shaun was always hungry, and to him, eating was having a good time. So Sundays were always the reckoning day and every Monday was the day she was going to start a diet.

As she placed the heavily laden plates on the table, she looked down at her bulging figure, smelled the food, undid her skirt and sat down to eat. August enjoyed cooking, and it was nice to share a meal with someone. Before Shaun, the table lived pushed up against the wall and she would eat in lonely quiet staring at a boring calendar opposite.

As they left the flat, Shaun checked to make sure August had her credit card, he was concerned about things like that. 'Beats me how you remember the number,' he said.

'What number?'

'You know, the number you have to punch into the cash machine.'

'It's easy, it's the last four digits of our phone number, and that's another thing, can you try and stay off the phone, I'm dreading the next bill.'

After two hours, and three nursed drinks, it didn't look like Gerry was coming in, but Shaun insisted he never missed a Sunday night drinking session. He emptied his glass and said, 'Tell you what, let's have a walk up 'The dog and Duck', if he's not in 'ere, he's bound to be in there.'

'Oooh Shaun I don't feel like trudging up there.'

'I know he'll be in there' Shaun said hoping that August wouldn't go.

'Look I'll go back to the flat you go on your own.'

'I'll need some money for a drink though,' he looked serious and August thought it made him look vaguely intelligent. 'In my purse,' she said handing him her handbag. 'Take a fiver that's all, I'm going to the loo, wait till I get back, don't leave my handbag.'

They parted company outside the pub, August gave him a peck on the cheek, she felt better now that he was getting the money for the rent, and sorry that she had nagged him all afternoon. She tidied the kitchen up and placed two plates and forks ready, because she knew he would land with a bag full of Chinese food. She got comfortable in front of the TV.

A rasping snore buzzed in her throat waking August with a start. The TV was humming to a grey screen. She sleepily checked her watch, it was after twelve, she glanced over to the bed, no Shaun, she got up and went to the bathroom. There was no sign of Shaun. She reckoned he must have found Gerry, got drunk with his mates and crashed out somewhere, it wasn't unusual.

Before leaving for work the following morning, August left Shaun a note, not to spend the rent money.

CHAPTER THREE

August disliked Mondays. She failed to start a diet, having to take sandwiches of peanut butter and jam, because that's all there was apart from cheese, and she may need that to make a meal with. She also had a wafer biscuit at morning break time.

As she clopped up the stairway to the flat she was famished. She was hoping Shaun was back, hoping that he had fed the gas meter and that the fire would be on to take the chill off the flat.

August opened the door to a cold dark flat, the note and not much else. The TV and stereo were gone, the video, the radio and... 'Oh noo, Bigshit bay! No no, not Mums painting.' She burst into tears when she saw the empty hook framed by a clean rectangle over the fireplace. Staring at the space, tears rolled down her round flushed cheeks and seeped into her mouth. She was engulfed by a wave of emptiness, it was a feeling of utter loneliness, she had totally lost her Mum now, and where was Shaun now when she needed a shoulder to cry on. 'God you are so useless,' she said out loud.

The flat seemed unusually tidy to say they had been burgled, and some strange feeling propelled her toward the wardrobe. All of Shaun's clothes were gone, even the ones he was too fat for, all of them gone, hers were still there. August marched over to the phone to call the Police but stood stock still her finger hovering over the number 9.

She put the receiver down. Something had happened and she couldn't comprehend it. All she could do was to sink into the sofa and blubber out loud. She felt sick and crawled into bed, she felt like she did at seventeen when her Mum passed away and just cried herself to sleep.

When she woke the horrible living nightmare greeted her and she knew she couldn't face work and rang in sick. All day she drank endless mugs of coffee and ate slices of toast naively hoping that Shaun would turn up and everything would be sorted out. August knew Shaun was behind this, but she didn't want to accept it, she had no one to phone to trace him. Why would Shaun do this? She wanted to believe that some big fat burglar had raided their flat and he was the same size as Shaun and took his clothes. She mused with her tangled feelings, stared at the pyramid of cans and thought how it aggravated her, and then she thought back to the time before Shaun. The well of loneliness that her own space had created.

Her Mum had never rang the Police whenever her brother David had stolen the rent money, one day he even turned up with money that he had won betting the rent money on a horse. Her Mum had forgiven him in the relief that he had turned up good for once. But if Shaun had done the same, she would never forgive him if he didn't turn up with Bigshit bay.

For three days she slouched around in her dressing gown and ate everything left in the cupboard, waiting for Shaun to turn up and sort it all out. Thursday morning arrived and she knew she couldn't pay the rent, the larder was bare and she would have to supply work with a sick note to cover her time off. She couldn't get an appointment at the Doctors until the following week. It was now too stupid to ring the Police, she felt STUPID.

August had to make the effort to get dressed in order to go out and get some food. In the hall was some mail, it would keep until she got back.

She spent a little too much at the supermarket, but food was her soother. 'What the hell' she thought as she wrote the cheque.

With half a cream sponge gone, August took the time to read her mail. 'One from the bank,' she sighed,' wonder what they want.' She sucked the sticky sugar and cream from her fingers and opened it.

Dear Miss Jackson

I regret to have to instruct you to destroy your credit card, or immediately return it to the bank. Due to extensive use above your credit limit, I would like you to make an appointment to see me at your earliest convenience. Meanwhile do not attempt to use your card under any circumstances, the bank has blocked anymore transactions.

August had mouthed the words silently until her mouth was just agape, 'what the chuff are they on about, I'll bloody tell them where to shove their card, where is the bloody thing?'

Tugging and snatching at her purse, she emptied her plastic collection such as it was on the table. There was her cheque card she had just used, her Kidney donor card, library, video rental, but no VISA card. 'Oh no, where is the bloody thing!'

She searched all of her handbag, the zipper pockets, the mirror compartment, her purse, NOTHING. She thought to when she last used it. It was Sunday evening when she went to the cash machine and she knew she didn't drop it. She distinctly remembered placing it back behind her library card.

'Shaun, it has to be!' she said, but it couldn't be, she hadn't seen him since Sunday, when would he have had the chance to take it and even then he would have to know the pin number. 'What a Bastard,' she screamed as she realised. She knew in her heart of hearts that it had been him but she just didn't want to believe it. She cut a piece of cake and hurled it toward the pyramid, the cans skittled with a direct hit. Three loud knocks on the door made her jump to her feet. 'If that's you Shaun Ratcliffe, I'm gonna kill you so help me God.'

August opened the door that showed a face that could turn milk sour. A thin man shuffled backwards and forced a very weak smile.

'Err, rent Miss Jackson.'

August's anger turned to pain as she heard the request. 'Yes.....err .. no actually, I'm down with a virus .. and .. I'm not at work.'

'Oh I'm sorry to hear that,' he shuffled back out of germ shot. She did look rough as she had not showered for three days and neither had her hair been acquainted with a brush for as long.

'I'm getting over it slowly,' she said putting on a weak voice, hand cupping her nose and mouth, 'but I'm afraid I haven't been able to go to the bank to get the rent money.'

'I understand, maybe I could call next week then, will next Thursday be alright?'

'Yes, that'll be fine...sorry.'

'Not at all, one can't help being ill, I'll call next Thursday then, bye.'

August closed the door and closed her eyes to savour the relief. She had got one weeks' grace, but where would she find the money, she was in deep shit with the bank by the look of it and knew she had to face the music, but what could they say, it wasn't her fault.

August realised this is what her Mum used to go through when it was time to pay the rent and her purse was empty. The times that she had seen her Mum coppering up just to buy a pint of milk. Her Mum used to say the same thing, 'Some days we have butter moments, we have margarine months and when times are hard, there's always lard'. This would be followed by lots of washing and ironing, large white shirts hung from picture rails and door frames, other people's clothes lined the clothes horse. But it would be followed by temporary relief.

Now August had to do what her Mum had and tackle the problem, she made the call to the bank. She was nervous, the bank manager wanted to see her the very next day. What would he say? 'What a stupid thing to do, telling someone your PIN number, how irresponsible!'

CHAPTER FOUR

August hovered outside the bank. She felt sick and scared. When she walked through the large door, she felt she had GUILT written across her forehead in felt tip pen. Now she sat in the dull but charged atmosphere of the bank manager's office. A huge plain teak desk in front of her supported the elbows of the unhappy Mr Gordon. A creased thin face propped up by long pale fingers with clean nails. He was waiting for a response after his reading out of August's personal debt. She was silent, absolutely mortified and trying not to cry.

Her eyes became glazed as she stared at the paperwork in front of him. She blinked and both eyes spilled. Her cheeks were crimson and she could feel herself burning up. Pulling a ball of tissue from her pocket, she blew her nose before speaking.

'Are you quite sure you haven't got me mixed up with someone else.'

'Quite certain Miss Jackson.'

'But two thousand pounds, it can't be me.'

'Two thousand and ninety three to be precise,' he confirmed, 'And that doesn't include the three hundred pounds overdraft with the bank on your personal account.'

August just couldn't take it in and just sat there feeling ashamed, guilty and totally pissed off. 'Mr Gordon, believe me, I do not have the card and I honestly haven't used it for over a week, it's the honest truth.'

The bank manager eased his small frame into his large leather chair with a pompous authority giving a little side to side swivel of his chair just to show that he was in control. He felt even better when it was a large muscular man crying in the chair opposite, it gave him a power hit, a buzz, so much so that he would go home at lunch time and screw his large wife. He loved her big, he liked to thrash his puny torso into her and watch her body wobble. He loved feeling powerful.

He stared at August Jackson, her large breasts wobbled as she blew her nose again, and he drifted back from sexual fantasies.

'I believe you', he said in a matter of fact delivery.

'It is the truth,' she sniffed, 'I swear on my Mums grave. I have not seen that card since Sunday.'

'Do you think you may have lost it or misplaced it somewhere?'

'I.. I..think ..it may have been stolen,' she stammered. Mr Gordon raised his eyebrows and leaned back on the desk. August then blurted out the Shaun story. 'I can't prove anything though.'

'What are we going to do about this,' he said tapping the papers in front of him.'

Augusts' eyes fell to stare at the damp tissue she was tumbling around in her fingers. She didn't know what to say to him, didn't know why she felt so terribly guilty and ashamed, she knew she hadn't done anything wrong. She looked up at Mr Gordon and into his eyes as if he were God and she was pleading for help and forgiveness. He relished this. His hand fell to the desk with a slap which made August flinch and her cleavage sway.

'Let me see if I can help you out of this mess.'

August was so pleased for these words, she could have leapt over the desk and kissed him, and he knew it.

One hour later, August was back at home sipping a much needed black coffee and Mr Gordon was back at his home slapping his wife's fat thighs with his thin ones.

In the event of having her cheque book suspended and no money, she was pleased she'd stocked up at the supermarket. Sat in the quiet, dunking biscuits, she looked up at the pale rectangular space on the wall. 'BASTARD! ,' she yelled and threw a soggy custard cream at the bereft hook splattering wet and dry crumbs over the fireplace. She felt a tight pain rise in her throat, crammed a biscuit into her mouth urgently grinding it and swallowing. 'I will not cry,' she said aloud, and louder she chanted, 'I will not cry, I will not cry.'

The threat of a good sob didn't subside until half way down the packet of biscuits, then, she was pissed off with herself for eating so many. Within minutes she was aimlessly scanning the fridge for something to cloy her insatiable taste buds.

Whilst pushing pods of ravioli and buttered toast into her mouth, August tried to reason with what the bank manager had suggested.

The bank would suspend the use of a cheque book and of course her credit card, which was on stop. Her wages were already paid directly into her bank account, but now she wouldn't have access to it until the debt was repaid. Mr Gordon had set up another account for her in which he would transfer from her normal account a small allowance each week which she had to withdraw personally, but it wasn't enough to live on, it certainly wouldn't pay the rent.

CHAPTER FIVE

At four o' clock Friday afternoon, August rang the firm she worked for. She was going to ask Jayne, the typist who worked with her in the office if anyone had made any remarks about her absence.

'Hello, Ruban Co. how can I help you?'

August pinched her brow and pursed her lips. Just her luck, Slimy Simpson the company rep and all time twat. 'Could I speak to Jayne please?'

'She's just photocopying at the moment, is that August?'

'Err, yes.'

A smug grin crept across his face. 'Are you any better?' he said with almost accusation in his voice.

'No, I feel awful.'

'Oh dear,' he said mockingly, 'And there's a mountain of work piled up on your desk, poor Jayne here has been over loaded. Well here she is. You can spend time chatting to her yourself.' He pushed the phone toward the girl rushing toward the desk he was sitting on and August just caught the words, 'Fat friend to speak to you.'

'Hello, Jayne speaking.'

'Hi Jayne, what's the slime doing in on a Friday afternoon?'

'Oh floating about like a Lord, because he took a big order this week.'

'It is what he's paid for.'

'I know, anyway, how are you?'

' I feel crap, I can't tell you how crap.'

'Have you been to the Doctors?'

'Can't get in until next week.'

'Oh no August, you ought to see your desk, it's piled high and now with Slime getting this big order….'

'Don't worry Jayne, I shall be there first thing Monday morning, just let them know I phoned.'

'Okay, I'll tell Mrs Charlton. Look I'll have to go, Slime is on his way back, you know what he's like. Bye.'

Well at least she still had a job, now she needed to raise extra funds just like her Mum had to, but taking in washing wasn't an option. She stumbled around the flat to see if there was anything left worth selling. The furniture, what little there was came with the flat. The few things she had to her name had been stolen.

That weekend she scoffed herself stupid. She panicked Monday morning when she raked through her purse and realised she didn't have enough money for the bus fare into work. Frantic she plunged her hand down the back and sides of the sofa and still she hadn't enough.

It was embarrassing stood at the front of the bus asking the driver how far your spare change would take you. She was three stops short of the brick and concrete office block that four companies shared. Ruban Co., the box making firm that she worked for, had the ground floor and owned the building. Two small companies shared the first floor and the top floor was occupied by a company of graphic designers.

August arrived at the steps of the building totally breathless but on time, and took a minute to catch her breath. It worked in her favour, as she stood there clutching her chest and looking more than unfit, Mrs Charlton the secretary to the boss arrived.

'Oh my goodness August, are you alright? Are you sure you should be back yet?'

August nodded and nearly smiled when Slimy Simpson arrived and sprang up the steps pretending not to have noticed. 'Smug Bastard', thought August as Mrs Charlton helped her up the steps, and then felt a little foolish that at twenty three years old, she had to be helped by someone twice her age. Not that Mrs Charlton knew her condition was brought on by fast walking for less than one mile. She had just got her breath back when the sight of the stack of papers piled on her desk practically took the wind out of her.

Robert 'The Slime' Simpson was in his own small office which he generally used only on Mondays. There were several clusters of offices in one room, sectioned cubicles of half glass partitions with untidy memos stuck on the glass. The only private office was Don Holland's, the MD and big boss. Slimy was looking at August through his partition window. He was enjoying her shock. She saw him and put a smile on her face for show, just to annoy him and launched herself toward her desk.

Jayne arrived and breathed a sigh of relief when she saw the broad back of August Jackson. Although August didn't realise it she was the catalyst of the firm, the glue that kept everything together, the lubricant that smoothed the connection from orders in, through the factory floor and out through the doors to the paying customers. Jayne, Mrs Charlton and the blokes on the factory floor were the ones who knew her involvement was a key part to Ruban Co.

It wasn't long before Robert Simpson sauntered out of his office, looking impeccable in a new hand- tailored suit and expensive shoes. The after shave, no one within a ten foot radius could miss. He was not tall but wiry, which allowed him to more model clothes than to just wear them. He was handsome, kept a tan topped up, and with tousled blonde hair, at thirty one, was devilishly handsome sexy. He had everything. He came from a middle class family and had married into a wealthy one.

August was aware of him and wondered what his wife was like. He was standing in front of her desk now, looking straight at her with his striking blue eyes. 'Good morning August,' he smirked, 'Looks like you'll be working your lunch break'

August didn't answer, just smiled, wishing she had blonde hair instead of her straight mousey, just to the nape of the neck style.

'Like the suit girls?' he continued. 'Thought I'd splash out, I think I might be in for a bonus after this big order.'

Jayne pulled a particularly funny face behind his back which kept August smiling.

In fact,' he resumed, 'I think I might go to 'The Conservatory' for lunch to celebrate. Pity I can't take you August, but you have soooo much work to do. Well I must go and get my pat on the back from the guvnor.' He paraded away tugging at the margin of cuff linked shirt and straightening his silk tie.

'The Conservatory' was an expensive restaurant on the outskirts of town, servicing the well-heeled business men with the need to impress clients. August couldn't afford a starter there never mind a full course lunch. Lunch!, she didn't have any, and no money.

Searching the back of her desk drawer, she pulled out the old paper clip box. In it she found some change she had occasionally dropped in there. Coppering up she didn't have much, but enough for a sandwich or the bus fare home.

August's fat fingers rattled across the typewriter keys faster than the speed of light in an effort to clear her desk. She was so intent on moving the mountain she didn't realise it was time for the tea lady, until Hetty called from the corridor. 'Tea girls!, oh August, I thought you must still be off sick, you're normally outside this door before I am.'

August picked up just ten pence and handed it to Jayne as she went past. 'Will you just get me a black coffee, no sugar.'

Jayne feigned a slight heart attack. 'This I don't believe,' she said, 'Aren't you going to have a scone, a packet of crisps, a chocolate biscuit?'

'No, just the coffee.'

'My God, I know it's Monday, but are you serious?'

'Serious, and if I see it I'll buy it, so could you please just get coffee for me.'

There was much discussion outside in the corridor about Augusts' diet not breaking down by 10 o' clock. Undisturbed, August carried on ploughing through the paperwork, more to keep her mind off her grumbling stomach than anything. The heavy smell of strong aftershave announced the return of the Slime. Jayne handed him a list of return calls to make.

'I'll get back to these later,' he said, 'I'm just going down to Searson's to choose the colour of my new car,' he gloated, but got no reaction from the girls, so he continued. 'I told you I was in for a bonus, getting an SRI this time.' Still nothing. 'Maybe I'll take you both to lunch in it....or, would you rather wait until I get a BMW, I'm sure it won't be long.'

August rattled the waste paper bin with her drained paper cup. 'You know Robert,' she said not taking her eyes from the typewriter, 'It might be longer than you think, this order you've promised is really pushing it for this date, and we're in no hurry to go to lunch with you, are we Jayne?' Jayne put on a simpleton smile and shook her head, Robert Simpson marched away.

By eleven o' clock August was feeling sick with hunger, she complained so much that Jayne gave her an apple to shut her up. In less than an hour the Granny Smith had worn off, and at twelve she was feeling even more hungry.

Jayne pulled out her lunch box and as always gave a running commentary of what was in her sandwiches. August could have killed her for that cheese and pickle and hoped Jayne would decide that she didn't fancy them and give her some like she sometimes did.

'Just what I fancy today,' Jayne announced, 'nearly brought corned beef, but I'm enjoying this. I was going to go down to the park and eat but it's turning really cold now and it's only the beginning of October. I might pop out in a minute though, I fancy a big sticky cream bun. 'Jayne oblivious to teetering on the brink of being murdered carried on. 'Or do I fancy a Danish pastry, one of those with two fingers of chocolate in them. Mind you I like them warm and all the chocolate melts and … aren't you stopping for lunch August?'

'Err .. no, I had better shift some more of this, but if you're going to the shop, would you get me a sandwich please.'

'Don't you want a hot pasty and a bun?'

'No just a ham salad sandwich please.'

'Crikey, you are being good.'

August smiled weakly as she put some money on Jayne's desk. 'I think there's enough there, I'll owe you if not.' August worked on to take her mind off her hunger, though it was difficult preparing work sheets for boxes that she knew would be filled with thousands of chocolates.

Meanwhile back at the flat, Shaun was busy eating the last packet of biscuits while he replaced the bath panel. He'd almost forgotten the small stash of calculators he'd hidden there. A huge tyre of spotty flesh ballooned over his jeans, which were under much pressure and revealing four inches of bum cleavage. He was having difficulty squeezing his bulk by the toilet pan and his chunky fingers couldn't manipulate the small screws properly, so he left the bath panel hanging off. 'She can do that,' he said leaving the bathroom, 'she can't nag me now.'

He dragged a battered suitcase from the top of the wardrobe, threw the hand full of photographs out and a few other remnants of the past that August kept in there. He packed the calculators into the case, together with a four pack of beer from the fridge. He searched through the pockets of August's clothes and came across the full length black leather coat she had bought earlier that year. She had bought it back in May when she had found her size, it was unworn, waiting for winter. Shaun spread it across the bed. 'A lot of leather there,' he said to himself and packed the coat. He chased his hands around the sofa seats and came up empty. There was nothing more to check and nothing else to take, so he threw his keys on the bed with the photographs saying, 'I'm not payin' you any money, for you to pissin' nag me to death, you cow.' He left the door open and left with the suit case.

CHAPTER SIX

August was trying to devour the ham cob as slowly as possible to make it last. She was annoyed when the phone rang and she had to quickly chew and swallow a whole mouthful.

A well-spoken woman was asking in a soft manner if her husband Robert Simpson was in the office.

'I'm sorry he's out on the road today, he may ring in later would you like to leave a message for him?'

'If it's not too much trouble, could you ask him to let me know if he is going to be late home this evening.'

August took the message imagining a Barbie doll on the other end of the phone. August couldn't have been more wrong. Alicia Simpson wore her dark hair cropped quite short and had lots of silver and ash highlights in it. Robert hated it, said it made her look boyish as she had slender hips, a slender waist and not much of a bust. She often wondered why he had asked her to marry him, then again she often wondered why she had.

She had always blamed the fact that her parents were wealthy. That, she was positive was what attracted Robert to her far more than her 34A's. Her parents had also put pressure on her to wed a boy from a good background. All of them she met she declined.

Alicia and Robert had met at Art College. She had stayed the full vocational course, but Robert had buckled out after the foundation year. The fact that he could only draw naked stick people may have had something to do with it. He may have had no artistic talent, but he was charming and very good looking. She'd hooked him more like a prize, only wanting him because all the other girls were after him.

They were married on her twenty first birthday, Robert was a year younger than her. Their newly built detached house had been a present from Alicia's parents. Sadly her Father died two years later. Last year on her twenty fifth birthday, her trust fund was to be released but there had been a lot of red tape to sort out. Her Father had arranged her trust fund when she was born and it would return around two hundred and fifty thousand pounds.

This had caused frightful arguments in the Simpson household and Alicia had even resumed using her maiden name. Robert had wanted to squander the whole of the money on expensive holidays, designer suits and have a Porsche to play in at weekends. Alicia had kept him quiet with a new expensive wardrobe and they had settled their financial differences by Robert keeping his salary to himself, she keeping hers and they split the bills. They also had split bedrooms.

The love making she had half enjoyed for the first year of marriage had dwindled into a bi monthly sex session that lasted just longer than a commercial break. At first he would visit her bedroom and she allowed him because she needed some sexual stimulation, but he hadn't made one of his visits for three months. She knew he must be getting it somewhere else, but she didn't care, even when he stayed out all night.

The old photocopying machine was refusing to work so August would have to go up to the top floor to borrow a bit of copying from the Design Company. The stairs and lift were off the main reception area. She spoke briefly to June the communal receptionist who had a face like a bag of frogs and whose main purpose was to fend off any unwanted reps or reptiles as she called them. No one without an appointment got past her.

June was complaining about the décor, and she had got a point. What was once a plush reception area, designed when the building went up in 1976 was now dated. Ten years on and the teak panelling on the walls was as out of fashion as the purple box seating it surrounded. The smoked glass coffee table had dug it's chrome heels well and truly into the hog hair carpet tiles and the cheese plant was now touching the ceiling. The large pendant light in curls of stainless steel was positively vulgar.

As she waited for the lift, August played decorator in her mind. She was surprised Don Holland hadn't had it redecorated, he did collect a bundle of rent from the other companies, it didn't seem fair on them.

Soon armed with her copies of work sheets, she went to her favourite place, the factory floor. The box making unit was attached to the rear of the ground floor office block. August would spend one week out of every six working there, organising all work orders to tally with admin. She knew how the machines worked, and knew how many units any of the machines could turn out in an hour. When Fred the factory floor manager was away, August would cover. She didn't mind getting her hands dirty and the blokes that worked there ten in all liked her. She could work out order units to time schedules in minutes even when a test run had to be done on a new line. Fred was pleased to see her.

'Thank God you're back duckie,' Fred said in his broad Derbyshire lilt, 'a could 'ave done wi' you 'ere last week. That jumped up little bugger cum dahn 'ere shoutin abaht gerrin 'is bloody orders aht on time, an' we've gorra new line to set up an all!' Fred was all ruddy and pink in his soft lived in face. She smiled at him and made her way into his hutch of an office. 'Tell you what Fred, you make me a mug of black coffee and I'll sort out this box order.'

'You're on Lass, I won't be a jiffy,' and off he went to find a clean mug without a chip in it. August had finished the schedule sheets before her coffee had time to cool. She took it for a walk around the factory. At the loading bay, flat chocolate boxes were just arriving back from the printers for folding up.

'What a pity we can't print them here,' she said to Fred.

'We were allus supposed to be doin', but Mester Holland never got t'machines in, we got space an all.' Fred was nodding to the thick transparent plastic drapes that divided them from an empty section. August drained her mug and handed it to a Fred. 'Maybe he's still thinking about it, anyway, better get back to the office, buzz me if you need me.'

'Thanks Lass.'

CHAPTER SEVEN

August walked home against a cutting wind and her light weight jacket absorbed the cold drizzle like blotting paper. The bus droned past her and she wondered if she had enjoyed the ham sandwich enough. After the two mile walk August didn't think she could make it up the stairs to the flat, but the promise of warm food got her up to the landing and when she saw the flat door open she surged forward expecting Shaun to be waiting.

She didn't see the photographs at first, she was having a tantrum about the bath panel. When she did discover them her rage fuelled to volcanic proportions. The keys had landed on one of the photographs and warped the gloss. There was a sharp dent in her Mum's face which August couldn't smooth out. 'I'll fucking do him one day, sorry for swearing Mum,' she said to the dented photo, 'but he's a no good fat bastard!' She said it again when she found the biscuits and beer missing, and went ballistic when she discovered her leather coat that she now needed was gone too.

By Thursday the larder was bare. August couldn't pick up her measly fifteen pound allowance from the bank until Monday. The rent man would be coming that evening and she couldn't pay him. She was hungry and cold walking to and from work, and totally pissed off about the leather coat.

She borrowed a few pounds from Jayne, she didn't tell her of her predicament, she was too embarrassed. Shaun had caused her this embarrassment and she now detested him. August bought some cheap vegetables some that had been marked down for rabbit fodder. That evening as she stumbled into the hall with her tarnished sprouts, brown onions, bendy carrots and potatoes with white feelers starting to show, she met Mr Cruickshank, the rent collector. Knowing she had to come clean, she invited him up to the flat.

She asked him to sit down as she had something to tell him and made him a cup of coffee. Without crying she gave him the whole terrible tale. His balding head swayed from side to side as he tutted and sucked little gasps of air between his unruly teeth. She was just offering him a second cup of coffee when the lights went out and the fridge rumbled to a halt.

'Oh bugger, excuse me,' she apologised,' that's the last of the electric meter now.' In the dim borrowed light from the street lamp outside, Mr Cruickshank found his wallet and produced two fifty pence coins. August embarrassed again couldn't refuse and thanked him profusely.

She had a reminisce of being in front of the stern bank manager except that Mr Cruickshank was very sympathetic and strangely enthralled. Nothing exciting ever happened to him, and this was an incredible story. He knew he had to help her.

'So, I'm afraid,' August said, handing him his coffee, 'I haven't the money to pay the rent I owe now or the future.' She expected him to berate her stupidity, for not reporting the incident to the police. Instead he steadily took off the elastic band that bound his black rent book and flicked through the pages. 'Now let's see,' he mumbled, 'Ah here we are… mmm. In actual fact Miss Jackson, you are only in the agency's debt to one week. Remember you paid a month in advance when you first took up residence, so that's all you owe officially.'

August didn't know whether to smile or swear. Sure she was pleased because owing one weeks' rent was better than owing a months', but where was she going to go. Mr Cruickshank snapped the rent book shut. 'I have an idea,' he said with a dribble of excitement. August couldn't believe that his thin waxy face could blossom such a putative smile.

He had hutched himself to the front of the dining chair, knees pinched together. 'Now,' he said with some authority and pitching his hands as if to pray. 'I know that the agency have no bedsits or small flats empty because someone rang only yesterday and I checked, but there is something, not much I'm afraid, but if you're interested?'

'Where, what?' August was hopeful for any crumbs of comfort.

Cruickshank stood up and quickly walked over to the door. 'I'm not promising anything wonderful, I haven't been up there for years, but it may help you out temporarily. Now follow me.' Off he went with August waddling along the landing after him. He stopped in front of the dull hand dragged shellac door opposite the landing bathroom. August had often wondered what was behind that door.

The brass door knob waggled about loosely as he unlocked the door, the hinges moaned and the light switch lit up a lone dusty dim bulb at the top of a dingy bare staircase. This delighted Cruickshank and August was beginning to wonder about him. Should she be following him up there?. He was stood at the top of the staircase, just above his head, the stagnant light cast a shadow over his gaunt face and seemed absorbed into his long black coat. He waved her up, she shuddered, but slowly she went up trying not to wipe the dirty walls with her clothes. The staircase wasn't very wide. Cruickshank has now disappeared through a door to the right. The greying whitewash was peeling and loose chippings littered the step treads like dandruff. Slowly she stepped. There was a fusty smell and August felt her chest tighten and a pulse started to beat up in her throat. The door at the top was open but she couldn't see around it and although she could hear Cruickshank shuffling around, she felt lonely and scared. She was nearly there, her heart was in her throat now, three more steps. Cruickshank appeared, 'Come along Miss Jackson.' Miss Jackson nearly fell back down the stairs. 'Bleedin' hell!' she wheezed grabbing her own throat.

August took two short steps in through the door and squinted, 'What is it?'

'A room of course.'

'Well I can see that but ...'

'Don't you see,' he said with a kind of hushed excitement, 'this could be yours, temporarily of course. Isn't it wonderful!'

All August could see was a large, dim, empty room, save some broken pieces of furniture. There was an abundance of dust and other broken shapes which August couldn't pin an accurate identification on. A dormer window punched into the sloping ceiling tried very hard to let the fading light in. The glass was heavy with grime and cobwebs.

'The bulbs gone in here,' Cruickshank was clicking the brown light switch, then he trod over the bare floorboards, slid a pile of empty boxes to one side to reveal a small black cast iron fireplace. 'The only source of heat I'm afraid, but at least it's something.'

August stared at him as he cleared a circle in one of the window panes, her mouth half open like a gormless child. No plug sockets. What was she doing here? As Cruickshank rubbed, just like an magic lamp a warm orange glow lit up Cruickshank's smiling face. 'I can let you have a camping stove, my son doesn't use it anymore. There's ample room. I would say about twenty by fifteen feet wouldn't you?, the largest room in the whole building. I don't know why the agency haven't done something with it before. Well, what do you think?' His thin lips spread into a Stan Laurel smile.

'I think I'd like to get back to my coffee.' August said and hastily picked her way back down the dreadful stairway. Cruickshank was close behind, his excitement still bubbling. 'I'll tell you what Miss Jackson, you think about it this evening,' he chased after her, 'and I'll call tomorrow about six thirty.'

August didn't know what to say and just nodded, Cruickshank carried on. 'I will have to put a charge down for the room of course. Shall we say fifteen pounds a week?'

August flashed a disapproving look. 'Fifteen pounds!, it's filthy, needs decorating, no furniture, no .. no..plug sockets..'

'Alright, alright,' Cruickshank stammered, 'let's say ten, and I'll fix the books to say you left last week and forget the money you owe.'

August flopped down onto the sofa and dry washed her face with both hands. Her head was buzzing, the thought of having to move out hadn't occurred to her. She looked up at the parson like figure, his black rent book pinned under his arm like a bible. The bucket full of horrors he had just tipped over her, was in fact, her only way out, like a fire escape down to hell. August stood up. 'Thanks Mr Cruickshank, I will give it some thought and thank you for trying to help me. I will be here tomorrow at six thirty.'

Cruickshank half turned and turned back now holding his rent bible to his middle and his head slightly tipped to one side. 'Look,' he paused. 'There'll be no electricity to pay for it's on the main meter to the agency. You can use the bathroom facilities on the landing, it should be pretty much unoccupied as one of the bedsit tenants is a long distance lorry driver and the other tenant is away on a six month cruise contract.' He bid a soft farewell and left.

August just sat for a while when Cruickshank had left, wondering what her next move should or could be. Realising the flat had turned cold she checked the gas meter that had run out too. 'Bugger' she said to herself, and took the money she had put to one side for the bus fare to work to feed the meter. It was a treat she had decided to give herself on Friday.

She unloaded the few items of shopping and tutted as she emptied her pockets of toilet paper stolen from the loos at work. 'How low can you get,' she said, 'stealing bloody pieces of loo roll, and it's not even the soft stuff!, Jeeze if I owned the office block, I'd at least put soft tissue paper on there.' She spread the food out on the table. 'Now... what shall I have for dinner?,..brussel sprouts with cabbage. Brussel sprouts with carrots, or cabbage with carrots,

Oh August, go for colour and texture, oh yes and what do we have here? onions! ,just the job, it'll make you fart though, oh well!'

CHAPTER EIGHT

Friday morning was damp with a constant drizzle of rain. Alicia Simpson wiped the condensation from the front windows and was peeved to see Robert's car still on the drive. At the same time she heard the upstairs toilet flush, he was obviously just getting up and he was late. Alicia hoped he would be away early, she had a lot to do that day.

She stared at the litter of fraying leaves, shiny from the rain. Some had stuck to Robert's car and fluttered in the wind like tarnished butterflies. Alicia noticed how terribly dirty his new car was, a spray of sludge half way up the door panels and the wheels were caked.

A slow thudding told her he was on his way down stairs, she was shocked when she found him in the kitchen still in his bathrobe and unshaven.

'What's the matter with you? she said clocking his rough appearance. 'Are you ill or something?'

'No, I'm not ill, not that you'd care.'

She ignored him and began unloading the dishwasher. Robert carried on. 'I'm tired that's all. Is there any toast going?'

'There's the bread, and there's the toaster.' Alicia replied.

'Are there any eggs?' he said hoping she would cook for him.

'Plenty in the fridge.' She studied him for a moment. He looked really haggard, his blonde hair dull and greasy, crisscrossed like a hay stack. 'I'm not surprised you're tired,' she said placing the bread in the toaster. 'You're out so late.'

'So.' Robert snapped. 'That's got nothing to do with you!'

'I don't give a damn what time you come in Robert, and whatever our differences, I don't like to see you looking a mess, even your new cars filthy. Now you're late off to work, I really don't know what is the matter with you.'

'I don't know why you're so concerned all of a sudden, anyway I can do what the fucking hell I like!'

'Oh no, it's nothing to do with me, I spend all that money on clothes for you and you think it's fine to walk about like a tramp.'

'Ah ha, I knew it would come down to money, you selfish bitch!'

'Selfish! Alicia screeched, 'I wouldn't call three and a half thousand pounds selfish!'

Robert marched over to her and started prodding her hard on her breast bone. 'You've got more than enough, Daddy saw to that. A quarter of a million, so I don't think three and a half thousand is so generous darling!' The emphasis on 'darling' was as romantic as cat sick. Alicia's instinct was to take his legs from underneath him, but instead she tried to pull back. 'That was money I had worked for Robert, nothing to do with the trust fund, I've told you before but you won't listen!'

'Bullshit Alicia.'

'It's true! won't you get it into you're thick head that I had to wait for the money to be released. I didn't get a penny until two months ago!'

Robert took a few steps back. 'You mean we've been sleeping apart for nothing?'

Just then the toaster sprung two black crusts. Alicia snatched them and skimmed then straight at Robert. 'You Bastard!', she screamed as the burnt missiles smashed black crumbs all over his white robe. 'You mean we've been sleeping apart because you're so short sighted, stubborn, and YOU! you are selfish!'

Robert advanced again, Alicia flinched, her hands covering her bruised breast bone. He gently put his hands on her shoulders and stared into her grey eyes. She moved away.

'Alicia... what can I say?'

'Say what you always say Robert, shout 'selfish bitch, greedy cow! sexless dried up witch!', there's plenty more. I've had more than a year of it plus the odd bruise!' She rubbed her chest again, he looked on, pathetic, then made toward her. Alicia bolted, slamming the door behind her and Robert could only stand there looking and feeling a complete bastard.

CHAPTER NINE

At lunchtime August poured over the part time vacancies in the local newspaper she'd retrieved from the waste bin. For evenings only there were stacks of barmaids required which she didn't fancy. She rang about the three evenings a week usherette at the local cinema that was within walking distance of the flat. She secured an interview for the following day, after Saturday matinee.

August had on her mind the hovel of a room she knew she would have to take. The thought propelled her down to the factory floor to speak to Fred. She told him she was having to move flats and the new place needed a lick of paint. He found a large nearly full tin of white emulsion left over from painting the factory walls.

August was pleased with her free token until she had to carry the heavy tin all the way home. After the first half mile she was wishing she would meet Shaun and with her last ounce of strength she would enjoy wrapping the heavy tin around his fat head.

The thin metal handle dug into her flesh and with the biting cold she thought her fingers would break off. She couldn't slow down, Cruickshank would appear at half past six like the grim reaper.

As she quickened her step August thought about her predicament once again to try and put it into some kind of perspective. She went through all the bad things she had to face. Shaun had dumped her, plus not only had he stolen everything she owned, he had also got her into thousands of pounds of debt. She hadn't scored many team points at work for being off ill because of it. She was now being evicted out of her own home and she would have to use all of her bloody allowance to pay for a room that squatters would refuse. The rest of the depressing list took her all the way home and into the hallway where she found the telephone bill waiting. 'Oh bugger', she said under her breath, 'that's one more for the list.'

The flat was very cold and she daren't use up the bit of credit left on the gas meter. She made a mug of hot Oxo, not because she fancied it, but because she'd run out of tea and only had two teaspoons of coffee left, one to offer Mr Cruickshank and one for breakfast.

Nursing the hot mug, August tried to rationalise anything good about her life, like her Mum used to do to dredge up some kind of cheer. There was Mr Cruickshank. He did seem like an oddball, but he was being helpful, at least she would have a roof over her head. The she decided she was pleased that Shaun was out of her life. August had taken him into her life because she had been so desperately lonely. She had even preened at work taking the opportunity whenever she could to say, 'we did this, or we watched this programme last night,. The 'WE' word made her feel belonged to something. 'We are having this for dinner. We went out for a drink last night'. It was a sub culture that allowed her to be part of the same society as the others that she worked with.

Now, if she ever bumped into him again, before she killed him, she would tell him that she now had proof, that it must have been him that always squeezed the toothpaste from the top of the tube. That he always left the toilet seat up and left a dirty loo. Her list hadn't grown very much when the feeble rap of the rent mans' knuckles played on the door.

August was surprised to find Mr Cruickshank wearing overalls instead of his usual black coat, shirt and tie. He smiled at her as a greeting and bent down to pick up a large cardboard box at his feet.

'Come in, come in', August was slightly amused.

'I've bought you some bits and pieces', he grunted and puffed as he plonked the box down inside the flat doorway. 'I presume you have decided Miss Jackson?'

'Well I err… I don't seem to have much choice.'

'Oh I thought as much.' He was almost beside himself with mild excitement and plundered the box he had set down. 'Ah ha,' he said, holding up what appeared to be bits of a light fitting. 'Now all I need is my screwdriver, now then Miss Jackson.'

'Oh please call me August.'

'Excuse me?'

'August. That's my name.'

'August that is unusual.'

'Yes, it's not really me is it? to me August should be slim, tanned, have blonde hair and drive a sports car, and be able to model bikini's for a living.'

Cruickshank was busy planting wires and twiddling a screwdriver he hadn't listened to a word. 'What are you doing?' she asked him, the gormless expression revisited her face.

'I'm just rigging this, so that one of the light fittings up there can be used like a socket.' He held the plug aloft smiling like a child with a new toy. 'And here,' he said delving into the box again, 'we have a camping burner and gas canister, aaand,' he announced with a theatrical slur, 'I have some pieces of pipe and with these containers, I am going to try and rig up some kind of sink!' He looked like he had just made a brain out of Lego.

The words 'rig and rigging' didn't seem to August to really belong to this peculiar rent mans' persona, but all things being crazy, she looked at the pile of junk in his box of lame tricks and helped him cart his collection up to the hovel.

Mr Cruickshank had even brought new light bulbs with him, and August saw the room in its' true glory. It was a shit hole!

Cruickshank had brought some cleaning stuff and some oddments of emulsion paint and brushes. August could have kissed him when he produced chocolate biscuits and a flask of tea.

'Why are you helping me.? She asked as they took a break back down in the flat. There was an uncomfortable silence for a few seconds and the once excited rent man turned subdued. 'I had a daughter,' he said almost stumbling on the words, 'a lot like you. I was strict. Wouldn't let her stay out late, the usual things.. you know,?' August nodded and he carried on.

'Well… she got in with a bad bunch..and ..and, the more I said against them, the more time she would spend with them,.. well until ..she ran away. Her Mother, Janet, my wife, was so upset, frantic with worry..and so was I. I tried so hard to find her. Apparently she was sleeping rough… a ..daughter of mine.. sleeping rough!. I..I couldn't believe it.' His voice had taken to trembling and August warmed to him a little.

'Did you find her?' August was intrigued now.

'It was.. difficult.. she .. she had no forwarding address you see… so.. when I did finally find her.... It was too late. She had been saturated with drugs, heroin… She died August… Karen died before she was twenty one.. If only she would have had an address, I would have found her, and maybe Karen would have been here today.' His head had bowed slightly and he paused, then raised his solemn thin face and said, 'So you see August, how important it is to have an address.'

There was more shared silence, August didn't know what to say but, 'I'm sorry Mr Cruickshank, that's awful for you.'

'Oh it's all in the past now, but if I can help someone keep a roof over their head I will. Now let's go and see if this works, if you bring your hair dryer and I'll change the plug, then I must be off.'

'Thank you ever so much, when will I have to move out of the flat?'

'Oh yes, Miss Heyhott won't be taking up residence until Tuesday, so Monday evening will have to be it I'm afraid. I will come back tomorrow and rig up some kind of basin and take away any rubbish.'

'It's really good of you and I want you to know that I really appreciate your help.'

'There's no need to thank me August, I'm really quite enjoying myself. I'll be back tomorrow morning.'

CHAPTER TEN

August woke later than usual and was still tired. She pulled the warm quilt up around her ears and curled into foetal position. Her exposed nose told her it was cold in the flat. It was just turned eight o' clock, and from experience August knew it would half past before she could coax herself out of bed. When she finally did move, it was painful. Her shoulders, arms and thighs ached.

'Jeeesus Christ, so much for washing down walls' and Christ it's cold. Ouch ooh ouch.' She shuffled through to the kitchen and yelped again as her aching feet met the freezing kitchen floor. 'Hot coffee, hot coffee,' she chanted to herself as she made her brew. Then she spied the brown envelope she had discarded last night and opened it. 'Sixty quid phone bill, that's bloody Shaun again!'

It was warmer to go back to bed and drink her coffee and to try and figure out how to pay the phone bill. 'Right August, pull yourself together. Now the phone has to be disconnected and the meter re-read, that will do as a delay and then I'll ask the bank manager to pay it and I won't draw the fifteen pounds allowance unless absolutely necessary. I'll pay the rent with the money I get for the cinema job, well if I get it… then I've got to eat. Oh bugger, shit damn!'

Ten miles away in a warm pale pink bedroom at number 4 Hyland Way, Alicia Simpson was checking her bruises in the mirror. Three small purple dots and two additional shadows turning yellow were grouped just below her throat, ruling out 'V' neck sweaters for at least a week.

Alicia checked her swollen eyes, she had cried well into the early hours. Robert had been out all night and still wasn't home, but that wasn't why she was upset. She had been crying because she didn't care, there was nothing left of the marriage. She now knew there wasn't a thread of anything to be able to pull together.

So now Alicia gave herself a good talking to. 'Come on Alicia, pull yourself together,' Her lip started to tremble and she bit it, swallowed hard, took a deep breath, 'Damn it woman, your starting your new life, now take charge and carry on!' She reached for her rarely used makeup bag in desperate need of a cover up. She decided then that she would take herself into town and go to one of the large department stores with a makeup advisor. There would be lots of things she would be needing now and a shopping spree would do her good and define her new image.

It had been a tough weekend and working her notice hadn't been pleasant, not that people weren't sad to see her go, they were. It was when they found out she was setting up on her own that upset the applecart. She was now the competition and they knew how good she was at her job.

She consulted her diary as she did every morning. 'Today your all mine,' she smiled now as she spoke to herself. 'The sixteenth of October, nineteen eighty six, you are the first day of the rest of my new life, now! let's get off our arse and go!'

Mr Cruickshank was impressed at the much cleaner state of the hovel. August hugged her own aching shoulders. 'I really know about it too, I hurt everywhere. crickey! you've brought a sink.' He had nearly got it hung on the wall before she realised.

'It's only a basin… it's what I kept in the garage when I changed my bathroom, always knew it would come in handy.'

'It's brilliant.'

'Well now Miss Ja. August, don't get too excited, I can't get water supply to the taps, but I think I can rig up something of a small convenience and I believe I can get a boss into the soil stack so at least it will have a drain out.'

'I think you're a bit of a genius Mr Cruickshank.' His face flushed with a smile as if to thank her, nobody ever paid him a compliment. He was happy and disappeared through a small opening in the wall that accessed the roof space. August keen to help, tried to follow but her hips were refused entrance and she blocked out the light.

August decided on a hot bath to soothe her aching muscles and joints. The water had turned a dirty milk with all the dust from her hair, the bedding would certainly need laundering. She would have to do that Monday when she got the allowance from the bank to feed the electric meter. 'Oh bugger, that means I won't be able to do the washing until I get home from work, and I've got to move out that evening, I'll never get it dried in time for bed!' There was a huge rush of scummy water gushing through the narrow gap between the bath sides and her plump sides as August sat bolt upright. 'Bed! what bloody bed!'

Cruickshank came to her rescue again. He was to loan her his sons' redundant camping gear. One inflatable mattress, one sleeping bag, a box of matches, a tin plate, a small saucepan and some items of cutlery. August could now go off to her interview with one less worry. It turned out to be much less of an interview, more like, 'Can you be available for work 7pm to 10pm, Tuesdays, Wednesdays and Thursdays?'

So that was it, she had herself an extra job, but it still wasn't enough. It would only just cover the rent. She needed money for food, shampoo, soap, and now she would have to use a laundrette. As she strode home, it was difficult to keep the tears at bay. A familiar smell made her stop. A waft of warm air as someone entered the doors of The Crown pub. It was pungent of beer and cigarette smoke. It was as if something had attacked Augusts' nervous system. The tears that had welled up and rimmed her eyes dried up. The hard lump hurting her throat melted away. It was the scent of Shaun. Was he in there she wondered, and fuelled with a strong desire to murder, she marched in.

She found only a handful of regulars nursing their lunchtime drinks. She knew them only by sight, but she asked them if they had seen Shaun. They knew who she meant, but said he hadn't been around for a week. The landlord confirmed the story. 'Sorry Lass, I wish he were still coming in, he spent some money in here.'

'Huh, I think you mean my money!' August didn't hide her anger when she spoke.

'Oops,' Geoff the landlord pulled an exaggerated sympathetic face. 'Sorry my luv, tell you what. I've called time but why don't you have a brandy on me.'

'Thanks, but no thanks, not on an empty stomach, besides don't want to get used to it, I shall never be able to afford to drink brandy.'

'Oh dear, left you a bit short as he?'

'You could say that. Anyway, thanks for your help, I'll be off.'

'No wait a minute luv, how would you like to earn a bit of extra cash, if you're a bit skint an' all.'

Doing what?'

'A couple of nights a week behind the bar.'

August pulled a face. 'It's not really my thing. I..I don't really think I could do it.'

'Oh come on, you can add up can't you?'

'Well yes.'

'There you go then, the rest is easy. Now I'm desperate for staff Saturdays and Sundays, no bugger wants to work then, but there's a tenner a night plus tips.'

August scanned the rows of optics, bottles and glasses. To her it looked daunting, but the money was too much of a temptation.

'What do yer say lass, give it a try?'

'Okay I'll try it, but I warn you, I might not be able to cope.'

'Good lass, now here's a ham cob and I'll get you that brandy. Can you start tonight?'

August was so grateful for the cob, she said yes. By the time she got home, Cruickshank had rigged up an ingenious but simple system for running water. A large container was filled with water from the bathroom on the landing. A special tap with a short thin pipe was secured before being tipped upside down and fastened to brackets strapped above the basin. On the end of the pipe was a plastic nozzle with a lever and spout. This Cruickshank turned and they squealed like children as a thin jet of water flowed into the basin and gurgled down the drain.

'There you go, running water!'

'Mr Cruickshank, you're brilliant.'

'Only cold water I'm afraid, so now let's get the stove working. Would you like to sort anything out you would like removing and I'll take it to the tip.'

She scanned the piles of junk. 'Most of its useless, but I'll keep the newspapers and the bits of broken wood, for the fire. And that table will paint up, that's about it.'

'I'll take them with me then they're out of your way. I suppose you will want to decorate tonight.'

'Oh crikey, I forgot to tell you, I've got two more jobs.'

CHAPTER ELEVEN

Robert Simpson was miffed when Alicia wasn't home, he wanted to make up. 'Flowers,' he said out loud, 'she loves flowers.' He looked at his watch he would just catch the shops. He checked his wallet. 'Damn no cash. I shan't make it to the cash machine in time,' He remembered his emergency fiver in his Filofax and sprinted out to the car. In his haste, he slammed the car door on his trench coat and when he released it found a grease rimmed tear. 'Oh shit! still,' he consoled himself, 'when I get around Alicia, I'll be able to buy three more if I want .'

The Filofax wasn't anywhere in the car, he jumped out and his trench coat caught on the door and ripped even more. He didn't stall but ran back to the house where he searched in his briefcase. 'Oh no, where is it. Shit, must have left it at her place… damn. First things first, money,cash machine. Maybe I can still make it, must get Alicia back on side.'

Alicia saw the back end of the Robert's car pull out of Hyland way as she approached their drive from the other direction. 'Good', she said to the new image in the mirror, 'I wonder if he's coming back, better get a move on.'

The car was garaged in record time with the shopping left in the boot. By the time Robert returned, Alicia was soaking in the bath with the door locked. He knocked feebly, there was no reply. 'Alicia it's me Robert.'

'Bugger off.'

'Alicia, I want to talk to you.'

'Tough Robert, now bugger off, I'm soaking my bruises.'

He sauntered back downstairs, placed the flowers on the kitchen table where she would see them straight away and poured himself a gin and tonic. He listened to the bath water draining away and the whine of the hairdryer start up. He marched to the phone and punched in the number scrawled in biro on his comb wallet. In a quiet voice he spoke as soon as he heard the voice answer. 'Stella it's Robert'

'Well hello Mr Smooth, don't tell me this ..
'Stella listen, is my Filofax there?'
'You're what?'
'My Filofax, it's a tan leather case about seven inches.'
'The only tanned seven inches I can remember…'
'Stella I don't have time for that now, this is serious! Is it there?'
'All right, keep your hair on … yeah it looks like it, what's the big deal?'
'I need it for work it's got all my appointments in it. 'The hair dryer noise stopped and he could hear Alicia walking about. 'Look Stella I've got to go now, I'll pick it up tomorrow night.'
'I'll be at work.'
'Right I'll be there about eight, see you then.' He replaced the receiver and slugged back the gin. Another large double kept him company while he paced the kitchen floor waiting for Alicia to appear. She never did, and loaded with several more heavy doubles and the lack of sleep the previous night, Robert crashed out on the soft sofa.

Later in the Crown, August was getting to grips with the pumps and the till. Geoff the landlord had shown her the ropes and the other two barmaids were really helpful. Marian the Landlady was an attractive woman about forty and an old hand, who moved behind the bar like a cog in a machine. Stella, one of the barmaids was only nineteen, bubbly, and had a rapid quick fire patter with the customers. She had short cropped blonde hair and huge earrings that could have been car hub caps. Her tight leather dress showed off a striking figure that made August feel like a truck. She was talking to Marian about her new boyfriend. 'Oh Marian he's just gorgeous handsome, he's got blonde hair and brains. He's really smart and drives a lovely new car. Wait till you see him.'

'I can't wait.' Marian rolled her eyes and winked at August, she'd obviously heard it all before.

'You won't have to wait long he's coming in tomorrow night. Oooh August you'll love him. He talks ever so nicely, and he's got these gorgeous pale blue eyes.' And Stella drifted off to serve.

The walls of the Crown were adorned with pictures of various battles. There were shields and pieces of body armour together with a display of weaponry. August eyed up a couple of spears and a lethal looking ornament with spiked metal balls. Then she eyed the door and wished Shaun would walk in.

By ten o' clock her feet were throbbing and she knew the heels were a mistake. Not daring to take her shoes off for fear of not getting them back on again, she persevered. As it got later, it got busier and she was more than pleased when it was over. 'You did alright Luv,' Marian told her. 'We shall see you tomorrow night won't we?' It was just then Geoff handed her two crisp five pound notes. August took the money and nodded. Her feet were pulsating tight in her shoes, but she smiled as she took the cash. She could have the heating on now for the last couple of days she had left in the flat and she could pay Jayne back the three pounds she had borrowed.

Although her feet were crucifying her, she made a half mile detour, needing change for the meters, she could think of no better way of breaking up a fiver than a tray of chips and mushy peas. She could smell them cooking before she reached the Chippy. There was no way August could wait until she got home and decided to eat them open. It felt like a feast of a treat, she sat down on a low brick wall next to an overflowing litter bin. Upside down polystyrene trays and squashed chips were scattered around her feet. The night was cold and the wall was cold, but the chips were hot and warmed her hands and her insides.

Reflecting on the day, she decided it hadn't been so bad, like a new beginning, like starting a battle. The Chippy windows were blistered with steam and she struggled to make out the large red numbers on the calendar. The 16th of October, this would be a day to remember.

A queue was starting to grow from the door of the Chippy, along the wall. August decided it might be better to make a move. Just then two youths stumbled into the back of the queue causing a woman to drop her handbag. She picked it up and tutted at their behaviour, this amused the two lads and they mimicked her, just as schoolboys might, and giggled like school girls would. They were both in just their shirt sleeves which made August think they share a brain cell as well as a pair of earrings. In fact they could have been twins, an earring in one ear, both had an impression of a moustache and both were obnoxious and skinny. They might have been old enough to drink, but not experienced enough to be in charge of it.

'Hurry up and get that fuckin' fish fried, I'm fuckin' starvin', one of them shouted. The woman with the handbag tutted again. The other one started up on full volume. 'Oh you naughty boy, you swore. Don't you fuckin' swear again.' They both giggled again.

A huge chap in jeans and a leather jacket looked over to his mate leaning against a motorbike and mouthed 'little twats.'

August thought it better to move and she would have to finish her food on her aching feet. She was about to get up when one of the two lads made a revolting guttural sound and spat a gob of phlegm which landed on Augusts' shoe. This also seemed to amuse them. August stood up with her half eaten meal which she had suddenly gone off and with one quick move wiped her shoe up the back of the guilty ones' trousers. 'Hey what do you think your doin', you fat cow!'

That did it, Augusts' eyes glared at them. 'You're lucky I didn't wipe it on that bum fluff on your top lip.' Both boys shuffled uneasy, but tried to laugh it off. 'Ha ha , as if!' one sneered.

'Listen', she said baring her teeth, 'you have no idea what this meal cost me. Nothing could have put me off this meal, nothing, but you did. Yes, you managed it, especially you!' she said to the one who had gobbed on her shoe. 'So, for managing to do something so near impossible, I'm going to give you the rest! and she smacked the half full tray of chips and mushy peas on his chest. The tray fell away from his white shirt revealing a floral pattern in green lumps.

He stumbled back and squealed, the food was still hot and he whimpered. The queue clapped and cheered. August marched away, and two embarrassed but angry lads made to go after August, but the huge chap in leather stepped in front of them. His bearded face quietly growled, 'Don't even think about it.'

CHAPTER TWELVE

Sunday morning daylight and a noise roused Robert Simpson from sleep. A sharp pain brought him round a little more. He slowly sat upright a hand nursing the back of his collar. A large tumbler, empty except for a dehydrated slice of lemon that lolled on it's side next to him on the sofa. A dark circle indicated a damp patch and a scurfy stain trailed across his blazer sleeve. 'Oh shit, my favourite jacket!' Then he heard a car engine, it was Alicia pulling out of the garage. He stood up quick, felt groggy and fell down again. The garage door banged shut. Robert got up again and stumbled through the hall and outside. Alicia was reversing off the drive. He half ran across the wet lawn in his stocking feet calling out 'Alicia wait, Alicia!'

He made it to the car and banged on the window, it opened a little way down. 'Alicia, I want to talk to you.' She pulled back from his stale breath.

'Please Alicia, where are you going?'

'I'm going to Mothers'.'

Robert had a draining feeling like thousands of pounds about to bounce out of his reach.

'You're not leaving! We have to talk, please!'

'Robert, I'm not leaving my home, I'm going to Mothers', she wants me to go to church with her.'

'What time will you be back?'

Alicia didn't answer, but revved the car and a pall of exhaust fume expanded into a cloud next to him as the Golf GTi sped off. He took in a lung full of fumes and felt decidedly ill. He was shivering now, his feet were wet and cold and still he hadn't made up with Alicia. He'd already spoilt his chance for tonight having to fetch his Filofax. He had to make up with her before she did anything stupid with the money, like tie it up in stocks and shares, or long term investments.

Back inside he found the flowers still in the cellophane on the table. 'Huh, that one really worked better come up with something stronger than that. Maybe I should go over to her Mothers' and join them in church.' He immediately knew he couldn't go, not the way he felt. His body trembled, he felt sick, and knew he would have to sleep it off.

By lunchtime, August had painted the ceiling and one wall of the hovel. It was a delicate pastel blue she had mixed herself. Mr Cruickshank had brought a half empty tin of what looked like Co-op blue emulsion. Just a little stirred into the white tinted it into what reminded her of the pale blue summer sky that was the background on the painting 'Bigshit bay. She wondered where the painting might be, what would Shaun have done with it? Maybe she should visit the local junk shops, but even if she found it, she had nothing to buy it back with. She must try and put everything she can in the bank, the sooner this debt is cleared the better. 'But it will take forever to pay the bloody interest!' she said aloud.' Now think about this August', she went on, 'let's say the Sunday night shift will pay rent. Saturday nights' will buy food and stuff, that means the Usherette money can go toward the debt, that is after I buy a decent coat.'

Hunger got the better of her and she returned to the now warm flat. There was little to salvage from the vegetables. A half inch of spongy peel had to be taken off the potatoes to find anything of substance to boil. The two remaining carrots were no better and the brussel sprouts had given up altogether, turning black and yellow with a hint of slime.

With the potatoes and carrots on the boil, August set about organised the laundry. It would be the last chance to get it done today. She must finish painting the hovel as well before she went off to the Crown for the evening shift. Monday night she must move her clothes and herself into the hovel and clean the flat. She didn't want this Miss Heyhott to think she wasn't clean.

August decided she must have been more hungry than she thought, she actually enjoyed the naked potatoes and carrot. By eight o' clock that evening, August's feet, even in flat shoes were beginning to ache. She was just restocking packets of crisps in the tap room when Stella called to her from the lounge bar. 'He's here, I want you to meet him.'

'Who?'

'Robert, my boyfriend, c'mon.'

'I'll be through in a minute.' August had a deep desire to rip open six bags of smoky bacon crisps and stuff all the contents into her mouth at once. She had to buy a packet, not having eaten anything since her veggies. As she placed the money in the till, she could see Stella beckoning her over. Across the bar was the rear view of a blonde chap who looked familiar. As she approached, Stella said, 'C'mon August, this is Robert.'

As she said 'August', the blonde head shot round and August stopped dead. Robert Simpson flinched, the Filofax in his hand nudged the glass of orange juice and it tipped and flooded over the bar and down his trouser leg. Stella rushed to mop up. 'I'll get it.', she said, 'Cor, I thought you two knew each other then, have you met before?'

Robert looked from his wet trousers to August, to Stella and back to August. August smiled, finding the situation extremely amusing. 'I think we have met before haven't we?' she said. Robert flushed, she saw a kind of suffering on his face, she pretended to search for a time and place while enjoying Slime's horror. 'I know, 'she let the words out slowly, 'I think I met you at a party.' Robert looked awkward and gave a nod. 'Yes, yes', he stammered, 'that's probably it. Look I had better go and get out of these wet things.'

'Oh Rob don't go yet.' Stella implored, but he was already retreating. 'But you only just got here, when will I see you?'

'I'll ring you.' He said nervously, and left.

CHAPTER THIRTEEN

Monday morning arrived before August was ready for it. It had been such a hectic weekend, the last thing she felt was rested. She was so tempted to allow herself to take the bus to work now she had a little money, but talked herself out of it. Hadn't she felt fresher of a morning when she reached the office? didn't she feel healthier for it?. If she allowed herself to take the bus this morning, wouldn't she just get back into the habit, then all the money would go in bus fares and she would never pay off the debt. No, she would walk and save. 'The coat will have to be a priority though,' she sighed and her breath pearled the cold window. Outside skeletal trees braced a bitter wind. Few leaves clung to them and rattled like copper tinsel. Without thinking, August had written the word 'BASTARD' in the balloon of mist on the pane, then watched it fade away.

The walk to work had seemed to get shorter, and looking at her watch, August knew she had cut the time down by seven minutes and was only slightly out of breath. Those saved minutes were needed now the weather was turning even colder and wetter. It gave her time to get changed, so she could wrap up in jeans and heavy jumpers. Also her hair needed tidying, it was way past its' cutting date.

August bundled the carrier bags with her walking togs into a corner of the ladies cloak area and went back to the basin with the mirror over. Mrs Charlton came bristling in.

'Morning Mrs Charlton.'

'Good Morning August, isn't it cold?'

August watched as a very tired looking woman charged her lips with pale rose lipstick, smudged a finger of powder blue on her eyelids and patted a little rouge on to her sallow cheeks. She sighed at her own reflection. 'Tuh, that's not made much difference.'

August could see the makeup didn't hide her chrome pallor or the dark curves under her eyes. 'Are you alright?', August asked.

'I'll be fine, just didn't sleep well, and it's Monday, I'm finding Mondays less charming every week.' She snapped her handbag shut and sauntered out. As the outer door closed, August heard Slimes voice out in the corridor and she smiled to herself in the mirror. 'Well I'm finding Mondays more charming.' She couldn't wait to get into her office and when she did, made no attempt to look Slimy in the face. 'Let him sweat a bit', she thought. And sweat he did. For nearly an hour, he sat at his desk looking busy. All he could think about was would August tell anyone, would she tell Jayne. Would she tell Mrs Charlton, would Don Holland get to know, and worse still, what if it got back to Alicia.

Alicia had pointed the finger before, but this would be proof, then it would be final, and he would never get his hands on the money, goodbye Porsche. He couldn't think of an excuse to speak to August. Every time she and Jayne laughed, he thought they may be laughing at him. Then the tea lady arrived and he saw his chance. He would buy her a cup of coffee, both of them so it wouldn't look so obvious. August and Jayne were already at the trolley when he got there. 'Allow me,' he said pushing the money into the tea ladies' hand. 'My treat, and I'll have a tea.'

Jayne looked at August and then at him. 'Are you feeling well Robert, you know it's me and August you've just treated?'

He smiled rather awkwardly, knowing how extremely unlike him the gesture was. August looked at him for the first time that morning, she felt she had a sort of power over him and it was a rather becoming feeling. 'Thanks Robert,' she said, 'it's not quite lunch at 'The Conservatory', but it's nice of you all the same.'

'I told you August, you should go there in style, maybe when I get my Porsche.'

'We can all dream Robert, maybe I'll go before that in my own BMW.'

Robert smirked with less spite than usual, and August beamed as she returned to the office. Mrs Charlton came through with a pile of paperwork and August thought she looked worse than she did earlier. She whispered to Jayne, 'do you think she's alright?'

'Don't know, she does look a bit peaky.'

'I know she's not her usual self.'

'Well she's been in with him, Don Holland all morning. Hey you don't think they're .. you ..know?'

August nearly spat coffee all over her papers. 'Nooo... Don Holland! Never!'

Slimy sauntered up to her desk. 'Don Holland never what?' he asked. Jayne supressed a laugh and August composed herself and began work while she spoke. 'Oh Jayne was just supposing that all the time Mrs Charlton spends in the M.D.'s office, maybe their having an affair.'

Robert Simpson nearly dropped his drink. August carried on. 'And I was saying, no, I don't think he would be the sort of man who would let a married woman cheat on her spouse.'

Robert tipped his drink in his mouth rather too quickly, in a bid to hide his flush of colour, and tea dribbled down his chin and a random line of beige dots patterned his white shirt. 'Ooops,' said August, 'you've spilt your drink again.'

He dragged his handkerchief over his shirt and looked out of control from his normal smug self. Jayne was dumb with surprise. August ignored him and took the top paper from her work load. 'I reckon this is what they might have been discussing.' She read the information from the page. 'Representative required for Southern Counties and East Anglia.'

'What!' he snapped.

'That's what it says here.' She said handing him the sheet, 'And the instruction I have is to advertise for two weeks.'

'Well they might have bloody told me, that's part of my area!' He threw the paper down and sunk his hands deep into his trouser pockets, then ran a hand roughly through his hair, disturbing it to one side. 'What a bloody cheek,' he spat and began pacing the short distance between the two desks. 'I wonder what he's up to, he might have discussed it with me first, bloody cheek!'

Jayne looked at August and shrugged. August suggested he go and talk with the M.D. He ignored her and swearing under his breath, fetched his briefcase and stormed out.

The copier machine was on the blink again, August carted the work upstairs only to find that the designers had no copier. They had sent it back, was all they said. There was no whizz kid banter either, the atmosphere on the top floor was blank. On the next floor down, she called in at Darts, the express delivery firm. They didn't have a copier either. There was no point calling in at Judds. Judds Jewellery was just three women sat amongst cartons of coloured beads, threading bangles and carding up cheap earrings.

Back in the office, she dropped the pile of papers down on her desk. 'The designers said their copying machine got sent back and no mention of them getting another, you would have thought they couldn't be without one wouldn't you?'

'They must be getting another.'

'Strange atmosphere as well, everybody had long faces, hardly spoke to me. Must be something in the water, Slimy is not happy, Mrs Charlton looks ill. Don Holland hardly shows his face and when he does he's as miserable as sin.'

'Oh while you were out Slimy was summoned to Mr Holland's office, so if he rings in tell him.'

CHAPTER FOURTEEN

Robert was in his bedroom trying to find a clean shirt. 'There's got to be a clean one somewhere.' He growled stomping around, he was beginning to panic as every shelf and hanger in his wardrobe was empty. 'Shit! Don't tell me Alicia hasn't collected the bloody laundry!' He checked the drawers and then the dirty linen basket.' There were all his dirty shirts. 'The stupid bitch hasn't even taken it! Bloody wonderful!' he swat the crumpled shirts onto the floor in temper.

He picked each one up again inspecting them there wasn't one he could salvage. He sniffed the armpits of one of the shirts that didn't look too bad, then, he remembered he'd lost a button off it. Temper hit again and he screwed the shirt into a ball and threw it at the door. 'Bitch! bitch!, bitch!'

He went back to the wardrobe and took out a three piece suit, hoping the waistcoat would cover the tea stain on his shirt.

Half way along Hyland Way Alicia stopped her car. She could see Robert's car on the drive. 'Oh bugger.' She said under her breath, 'what's he doing home? I don't want him to know I've stopped working for Royd's.' Just as she was about to reverse, she saw Robert deposit a large plastic bag in the boot of his car, and by the way he slammed the boot down she guessed it must be his laundry. From a safe distance she watched him drive away, rubber screeching. 'Wait until he finds the larder bare and he's got to do his own shopping and cooking.'

Robert was smarting, he was really peeved, so he took himself to 'The Conservatory' for lunch and went back to the office a little calmer. 'Good afternoon girls, any messages for me?'

August ignored him, Jayne held out a sheet of paper, 'These are return calls and Mr Holland wants to see you.'

'I should think he does.' He said with an air of sarcasm. 'Ask Mrs Charlton if he's free.'

'Ask her yourself, she's only next door.' Jayne said without looking at him.

'Well that's nice, remember who treated you this morning.'

Jayne did look at him now. 'I'll give you the ten pence if you like, manners cost nothing.'

Robert could feel his temper start to rise again and walked away. Jayne and August smiled at each other.

Don Holland was stood at the window when Robert entered his large comfortable office. He was deep in thought and stroking his goat like beard. The daylight emphasised the freckle of dandruff on his collar which ruined the effect of the expensive pinstripe. He nodded at Robert to take a seat and sat down in his sumptuous leather swivel chair behind his large leather topped desk.

Don Holland still looked deep in thought. A deep row of furrows ran across the top of his bushy eyebrows and ebbed away when they reached the polished area left by a very receding hairline. 'Now Robert, I err.. meant to have a meeting with you last week, but there has been so many things happening, I didn't get chance to.'

Robert hutched uneasily in his seat, wanting to have the courage to say, 'what's all this about another bloody rep then?' but he wasn't that brave, just mad and a little nervous.

'I knew you would be in the office today, so it seemed the best time.'

Robert gripped his own hand, he wondered what he was about to say, best time for a chat, was he going to sack him or what. No it couldn't be that, he had just had a new car and didn't he just get a bloody good order? Don Holland leaned forward folding his forearms on the desk. He took a deep breath before continuing. 'Things haven't been too brilliant of late, the sales are down on last year.'

'But I've landed some big contracts this year.' Robert sprang to his own defence.

'You have Robert. In fact you have done exceptionally well gaining some new contracts.'

'Then I can't see why we would be doing so badly.'

'Well despite the new contracts, sales are down about fifteen per cent on last year.'

'I don't understand.' Robert was almost aggressive but scared at the same time. Don Holland half raised a hand as if to place calm in the air. 'Don't be alarmed Robert, I'm not blaming you, as I said, you've done exceptionally well. You've driven further afield and gained some very good business for us, but the fact remains we are fifteen per cent down, when we ought to be fifteen, twenty per cent up.'

'Well what's happened?'

'What has happened Robert is … we seem to have spread you too thin on the ground. Whilst you have been ambitious on new accounts, the old ones haven't been serviced, and consequently with no PR, no representation on a regular basis, gaps have opened for our competitors to move in.'

Robert could almost feel the hands of a new rep around his throat, he felt a little giddy. 'But I try to cover as much as I can,' Robert stammered, 'I mean there is only me to cover England and Wales.'

'Precisely' Don Holland half smiled now, showing his cigar stained teeth. 'so, I think the remedy is to bring in reinforcements.'

Robert almost sighed with relief. 'What do you have in mind?'

'Well, this is why I want to talk with you. I need to appoint another representative, but I would like to discuss with you, the best form of attack. We can do one of two things.' He paused to light up one of his fat cigars.

Robert hated cigars. The heavy pungent smoke lapped onto his clothes like an acrid wave, and he was wearing a three hundred pound suit.

'One,' Holland sucked another draw, 'We could divide your area into equal parts … or we could leave the area as it is, you covering new sales and another rep servicing existing accounts.'

Robert half frowned, thoughts zipping through his brain. Don Holland eased back into his chair now sucking and pouting a veil of smoke. Robert remained high and stiff backed on his chair, feeling a bit threatened, but he could see where Holland was coming from. What he didn't want was to lose his bonuses for new accounts, but neither did he want to sacrifice the soft option of the easy routine calls, lunching existing clients on the expenses of Ruban Co. 'Could … could I think about it.. the best possible way I mean?'

'Of course Robert, I'm advertising the position, so I would like to know your views before I interview the candidates. I would also like you to know that whatever you decide, I will abide by. On this occasion, you know more about this side of the business than I do. I've never been on the road as such.'

Robert smiled weakly he knew just that, Don Holland hadn't got a clue. The business had been handed to him on a plate when his father died. All he had done was to cramp the offices of Ruban Co. and rent out the rest of the building and use the revenue to supply himself with cigars, flash cars and a large house.

CHAPTER FIFTEEN

At ten o' clock Monday evening, August stood in the flat staring at the room, the room that had been the heart of her comfort once upon a time. The bed and bare mattress didn't hold any great memories, in fact she wasn't sad. She did though feel a sense of loss. Her eyes now focussed on the pale rectangular space above the fireplace. 'I don't know where you are.' She spoke to the empty rectangle, 'But I will get you back, and you will hang somewhere so much better, I swear.' She then placed the keys on the kitchen work surface, dropped the lock on the door of the flat that for her had been raped and plundered of any fondness she had felt.

She tramped heavy footed up the stairs to the hovel for the umpteenth time, this time after locking the shellac door at the bottom. Her legs were tired, her arms ached, and now there was no cosy sofa to embrace her, just bare floorboards, four large piles of old newspapers, and an inflatable mattress covered with her clothes. A carrier bag of ropey vegetables spilled onto the wonky table, next to the camping stove.

August stared at her new home and shivered at the cold she hadn't much noticed whilst being busy cleaning and decorating. She began making paper sticks out of the newspapers, just like she remembered her mum making. Making flat rolls and then platting them to last longer in flame. Mr Cruickshank, bless him, August thought, had even provided matches. Soon soft crackling away to flame she stared at the burning paper. Exhausted she sat on a bench of newspaper piles wondering why they were even there, but she was glad. Her ink blackened hands from the news print hugged a mug of hot coffee.

The warm orange glow of the street lamp stretched window shapes across the ceiling. At that moment August felt cosy. She couldn't remember the last time she had sat in front of a real fire. They had a coal fire at all the houses when she was a child. She remembered making toast, balancing the slice of bread on a twisted wire toasting fork. She would have to swap hands constantly when the fire was too harsh, but that was her only worry then. She had no responsibilities then. If she felt poorly, her Mum would make her better. August stared at the flames and longed for her childhood back and her Mum.

This was the time when she really missed the painting, her comforter. Her eye lids felt so heavy, she was now struggling to stay awake, and then she had to find some energy to pump up the airbed mattress.

Robert Simpson got up particularly early Friday morning in a bid to catch Alicia before she went to work. Every day that week she had been left before he had surfaced. He hadn't even seen her in the evenings, just notes left that she was off to karate training or one of the charities she supported.

Now he opened the fridge and still she hadn't been shopping. It was bare apart from two wrinkled tomatoes, an open carton of milk which was sour, an unpleasant smell and the light. It was just then that Alicia appeared in the kitchen and was surprised to see him.

'You're up early,' she said not looking at him.

'Yeah well, it seemed like the only time to catch you, you're about as scarce as food in this house.'

She ignored him and switched the kettle on.

'I'll have one while you're making it, better grab the coffee while we've got it,'

'Robert, you know where the shops are, I'm sure you can manage them by yourself.'

'I have been managing I've had to, the bloody larders been bare for a week!'

'Well if you're managing, why are you being sarcastic?'

Robert clenched his teeth, to stop himself from launching a verbal attack. He could feel the anger inside and wanted to shout and throw a tantrum because he had no clean shirts, and had to go to the laundry himself. He was sick of eating pizza out of a cardboard box, and he was angry because he wanted to take his angst out on Alicia but he knew he couldn't. He had to make up to her. 'Look,' he said softly, 'Alicia, let's not fall out. I got up early so we could talk.'

She planted a mug of coffee in front of him. 'You will have to drink it black, the milk's sour.'

That made him mad, but he swallowed his aggression and said, 'Alicia, just listen for a moment. Let me take you to dinner this evening and we can talk.'

'I've made other arrangements.'

'Surely you can cancel, it can't be that important, I suppose it's one of your poxy charities again?'

'No. I can't cancel, and don't start raising your voice just because I won't drop something that's been arranged for over a week, just because you make some last minute demands.'

'I could have made arrangements if I'd have seen you around. What do I have to do make a bloody appointment!?'

'There you go shouting again, is there any wonder I'm never around, when I see you , you shout!. That would be really wonderful in a restaurant wouldn't it?'

Robert's grip tightened around the mug, staving off the urge he had to throw it at her. He knew it wasn't going right, he must try again. He stared into the jet black coffee and mooched around while he readjusted his manner. He spoke gently now. 'Alright, alright... I'm sorry. I'm sorry for shouting. I didn't mean to. I'm sorry…. I've got a lot on my mind that's all. There are things happening at work and I..' He stopped as the door clicked and he turned to find Alicia gone. 'Bitch!' he spat, and this time the mug travelled across the kitchen leaving dark puddles all over the floor and table, and splashes up the new shirt he had bought whilst his laundry was being done.

CHAPTER SIXTEEN

August couldn't wait for lunch break to arrive, not because she was hungry, but because she was going to buy a coat. Tuesday, Wednesday and last night, she had done her usherette job and now her hard earned cash would just stretch to a thick Seamans' duffle coat from the Army Surplus store.

When she came back to the office in it, Jayne couldn't stop herself and giggled saying, 'Oh very chic.'

'Very warm.' August retorted.

'I'm only joking, I wasn't being catty.'

'I know. Anyway, one day I'll have an expensive wardrobe, real designer gear, clothes that would make Slimy look shabby.'

'That wouldn't take much at the moment, did you notice on Friday when he called in, the tear in his trench coat, and when he took it off there was a mark across his blazer.'

'Speak of the devil,' she whispered as Robert Simpson entered. 'Any messages?' he snapped.

August shook her head. As he disappeared into his office, she noticed the rip in the hemline of his coat. He reappeared minus his coat and immediately asked if there had been any applicants for the job. August tapped a pile of envelopes with her pen. 'Fourteen up to now.'

He reached over to nosey at the names and addresses and as he did, August noticed brown blotches on his white shirt. He saw them too and withdrew, slightly embarrassed tugging his jacket sleeve down to hide the stains. 'Look, I'm expecting a call from the buyer at Grants, if he rings tell him I'll call him back this afternoon. I'm just going in to see the guvnor, I shouldn't be too long.'

August looked up at a more nervous Slime than she had ever seen before and said, 'don't tell me you're getting a BMW so soon?'

He gave her a spiteful grin and marched off.

August wouldn't have minded the walk home so much, especially now that she had a decent coat, but she had to carry a huge bag of logs. She started out alright, nursing the sack like a huge baby, but the logs seemed to get heavier and heavier until she found that dragging the sack along was the only way to get them the last hundred yards. She reversed into the hall, where someone held the door for her. A woman's voice said, 'I'll get that.' August swivelled her head round but found herself looking at the inside of her duffle coat hood, which hadn't swivelled. She said a muffled thank you, but the woman had gone. 'Oh bugger,' she said dropping the sack, 'I bet that was Miss Heyhott, I've been dying to see what she's like.'

August caught her breath and hauled the logs up to the hovel, slightly mad at missing her new neighbour. It had been four days now since Heyhott had taken over the flat and that was the closest she had got to seeing her. She hadn't even heard her. There was never a sound came from the flat. August put it down to herself never being in, maybe she would see her over the weekend.

The weekend came and went and August didn't meet, see or hear anything from the new tenant. She was intrigued, even pausing to listen at the door when she passed by. The following Tuesday as August came home, she had just passed the flat door when it opened. She turned to see a woman coming out of the flat, carrying a parcel. She was mid-twenties with short hair. She wore a thick pale sheepskin coat, but underneath August reckoned she was slim. 'Hello, you must be Miss Heyhott.' The woman smiled back. 'I'm August Jackson, your neighbour,' she said pointing a finger to the ceiling. 'I hope you settled in ok.'

'Yes, thank you.' came a polished reply.

'Only if there's anything you need to know... you know, about the hot water, or heating or anything, just ask.. I used to live there.'

'Thanks, I think I have everything under control.'

'Well if you need anything, just ask.'

'The woman smiled and nodded. August retreated upstairs, inwardly laughing at what she'd just said. 'If you need anything, Ha, just ask! what could I bloody do, bloody nothing!'

As she got ready for work that evening, she remembered about the starter button on the gas fire. It had fell off and she had lodged it behind the pipe so she wouldn't lose it. She would tell Miss Heyhott tomorrow.

CHAPTER SEVENTEEN

Don Holland checked the time on his gold Rolex, then he strode over to the window and watched a car pull into the yard, it's headlights showing a deserted car park except for his own Mercedes. Everyone had gone home leaving just himself and the cleaners. It was a sod of a time to be interviewing, but it had to be done. He peered over the CV on his desk to remind him who was coming, then made his way down to reception to meet him.

Graham Topps was married with two small children. He did have a little excess on his girth at thirty years old. Don Holland would have described him as tubby rather than portly. A crown of brown wavy hair sat atop a round face which was clean shaven and almost cherubic.

Back in the office both men talked under a swirling canopy of smoke made by both of them. Graham soon twigged that the balding man opposite, didn't have a clue about being on the road, about sales pitch. He was just the boss.

'So you see Graham, it's not an expansion of area, but manning it properly. So I have decided to split the area into two. Our man Robert Simpson would cover one part and the other would be covered by our new representative.'

'Could you tell me which area is the available one?'

'Well I'm leaving the decision up to Simpson, I think he should choose, I do like to be fair about these things.'

'Oh sure.' Graham nodded.

'But either way Graham, it is still a considerable area to cover. I take it that staying away over-night doesn't bother you?'

'Oh no, I'm used to it, and so is the wife of course.' He lied. Pamela hated him staying away, there was usually an argument. But Graham loved his nights of freedom. Once a month he would take a night away and once a quarter he sometimes got laid.

When he had enthused enough about the job and Don Holland had run out of things to say, they shook hands. Graham Topps was quietly confident the job was his. As he sauntered back through the reception lobby, he thought how much it needed a decorating job.

August hated mornings more than ever now. It was like waking up in a fridge. It was necessary to have some paper sticks ready, made the evening before. She lit them in the small cast iron grate. It was still dark outside and she checked her watch, just gone half past six. She would have to be in the bathroom for quarter to seven to keep her time schedule. The bathroom too was cold, with just an inadequate heated towel warmer.

It was whilst August was getting dried, that she heard the flat door shut. She knew it would be Miss Heyhott and scrambled for her bathrobe. 'If you're quick, you'll catch her.' she hastened herself, 'Quick!' August could hear the clip clop of high heels descending the stairs and ran bare foot to the banister rail. Hanging over the banister, she caught sight of a slender woman in a smart skirt suit, carrying a briefcase and a large portfolio. August was just about to call after her, but the sight of the long blonde hair sweeping over the shoulders of the dark suit made her stop. 'Very early visitor.' She thought and knocked on the flat door. She knocked a second time. She put her ear to the door. Not a murmur.

As August left for work, she noticed the red BMW car that seemed to have been around circa Miss Heyhott was not there, but a long dry rectangle on the roadside suggested that it had not long been gone. Continuing her walk to work, she kicked the carcase of a spent firework along the pavement and decided the next project would have to be to buy a pair of boots. The frosty mornings really bit into her feet now and they didn't seem to thaw until midmorning. She paused at the first shoe shop on route, loving the soft leather fashion boots. Then she sighed at the clumpy fur lined clod hoppers that she knew were the practical ones she should have.

'One,' she informed herself, 'the soft leather ones would not zip up your fat calves. Two, those stiletto heels are not sensible for walking to and from work and , three, the clod hoppers are forty quid cheaper!'

By the time Hetty the tea lady arrived that morning, it was a wonder there was any staff to serve. Don Holland had been storming through offices threatening to sack time wasters and slackers. Jayne had been in deep shit for franking letters all first class, when half of them could have gone second class. As a penance, she was made to make note pads out of scrap paper to save money. All the phone calls, except those deemed urgent were to be made in the cheaper rate. August thought she was going to be burnt at the stake for throwing away three elastic bands that had arrived around the bundle of post. Anyone caught stealing so much as an envelope would be threatened with dismissal, and there was to be a staff meeting at lunchtime.

'Bloody lunchtime!' Jayne hissed, 'I was going shopping for Wayne's birthday present.'

'I was going shopping for some groceries. Still, with the mood he's in, the meeting shouldn't take long.'

August was right. Don Holland did an impression of his earlier act, which was to throw his arms about and shout about waste and large overheads, and trade being down. 'Shortly we will be taking on board another sales executive to increase turnover.' He was still bellowing unnecessarily. All the admin staff would have had no trouble hearing if he'd have whispered. You could have heard a fly fart when he paused.

'This does not mean more profit to be frittered away by senseless waste, unthinking members of staff and lack of efficiency, so I want you all to step up efficiency right now!, Ruban Co. spends too much money!' It was at this point the sun caught his gold Rolex and a shard of light almost blinded two staff, and they all watched him light a huge cigar to witness some company money go up in smoke.

'I have a little proposition for you all however,' his voice a lot calmer now as he sucked on his comforter.' This proposition applies to all staff, including you factory chaps,' he waved a smoking hand in the direction of the chaps he knew not one name of. 'I want an idea, a design for a presentation box for a new piece of confectionary. Our client is producing a mildly expensive truffle egg. They want something special, Mrs Charlton has the brief and a copy will be passed to each office. If someone comes up with a winning idea for us to get this contract, then the reward will be two weeks paid holiday off work, plus two hundred pounds.' The rest of his deliberations were a blur to August, all she could remember was 'two hundred pounds', could she do with that. The remainder of her lunch break she spent doodling ideas, on scrap paper of course.

The following days up to the weekend seemed to fly, even the walk to and from work. She was obsessed with the challenge and ran ideas through her head constantly, searching confectioners window displays for inspiration. All weekend, in between working at The Crown and trundling to the launderette, August sketched and crayoned and every idea turned out like a small version of a chocolate box.

'Oh bugger it!' she said and scored the page in temper. 'They want something different, exotic, posh!' she threw it off the table. It reminded her of the last temper tantrum when she threw something, an idea pinged into her head. She picked up the pad again and August knew what she was going to do.

CHAPTER EIGHTEEN

In a pale pink bedroom at 4 Hyland Way, Robert was carefully searching through Alicia's bedroom. He knew she kept all her important papers in an old tatty white handbag that had once belonged to her grandmother. It wasn't in the bureau downstairs where she normally kept it. He noticed that her wardrobe seemed less bulky and her drawers were half full. 'I bet the bitch is getting ready to spend her money on a new winter collection,'

He heard Alicia's car pull onto the drive and hurried out of the room straightening the duvet as he left. He made it downstairs in seconds, flicked on the television and draped himself on the sofa. It seemed an age before he heard the garage door close, and didn't stir when Alicia opened the lounge door. She smiled to herself when he saw his chest rise and fall quickly. She had seen her bedroom light on. 'God you are pathetic,' she thought.

'Is that you Alicia?' he called over his shoulder. She raised her eyebrows. 'Who else?' she replied. Robert slowly rubbed his eyes as if he'd been asleep.

'Sorry, I didn't mean to wake you,' she held back the want to laugh.

'Oh it's all right.'

'Have you been asleep long?'

'I don't know what time is it?'

'Just gone seven, I think I had better check upstairs, because I swear I saw my bedroom light on when I was driving down the street.'

Robert started, 'Oh er..,well I haven't heard anything. Look I'll go and see. I think you must be mixed up with next door though.'

She let him go. 'Pathetic.' She said under her breath.

The evening was cold and August counted the early fireworks spraying the sky with coloured lights as she walked to The Crown. She didn't feel like working at all, she was so tired. She thought about the two hundred pounds, but besides that she could do with two weeks off. But to shift that debt, that's all she would think about when her feet became leaden and hurt, when her eyes smarted from cigarette smoke. When she had to clean half eaten toffees from cinema seats and empty stinking ashtrays, that's what she thought about, getting rid of the debt, having no black mark against her name.

On Monday evening, August stoked up her fire in the hovel and began work on her miniature chocolate box design. She would make a box making pattern up first in cardboard, then she would make a mock up out of a clear plastic cigar carton she had collared from the bin at The Crown. A clear plastic pyramid to carry the truffle egg, wrapped in a gold foil like a jewel. The clear plastic would carry the makers name in gold, simple and classy. It was a difficult shape, but she knew the capabilities of the machines in the factory. She worked nonstop all evening, even forgetting to eat. She finally had the finished piece. It was ten minutes past one when the last sliver of plastic was cut, and the one piece peculiar in shape folded about itself and clasped together underneath. There it was equal and perfect for packaging. You clever bugger August!' she congratulated herself and yawned, 'I reckon you've just earned yourself two hundred quid.'

Her eyes were sore and she knew she couldn't keep them open much longer, the fire was almost spent, and she shivered at the thought of using the cold bathroom. Instead she lay on the air mattress, scooped the duvet and sleeping bag on top of herself, still dressed and went to sleep.

It wasn't the alarm that woke August the next morning but a strong desire to use the toilet. She half screamed when she saw the time, 'Half past eight! ... NO..NO Don Holland will fire me for sure!' Her heart thumped hard in her chest as she chased to and fro from the bathroom. She scooped the pyramid and patterns into her bag and hurtled noisily down stairs, stamping across the landing and furiously clattering down the main staircase, missing the last two treads, landing on all fours. She had dropped her bag and the pyramid and sketches went skidding across the floor towards the door which was opening. August threw herself forward and flicked the pyramid from the path of the fashion boots just stepping in.

'Good Lord! whatever has happened, are you alright?' came the soft plummy voice.

August sat ungainly on the floor. 'Oh Miss Heyhott..yes, but I won't be if I don't get to work in the next few minutes!'

'Oh you're running late, I thought the place was on fire.'

'It may as well be, because I might as well be in hell fire when I lose my job.'

'Have you far to go?'

'Town, but it takes me seventeen minutes, and that's when I'm not crippled.' She said rubbing her knees.

'Oh come on, I'll take you. It's August isn't it?'

'I don't want to put you out.' She looked up at the manicured hand offered her, and then to the smiling face, with kind blue grey eyes.

'Not at all, now come along, I'll have you there inside five minutes.' With the help of a surprisingly strong arm August was up and collecting her pyramid and drawings.

The car was warm and smart inside.

'What's so special about that plastic carton?'

'Oh this?' she pulled out the pyramid and drawings. 'This is the cause of me over sleeping, oh left here and first right.'

August then explained basically about the design of her creation and the two hundred pounds reward. 'I think it's a fabulous idea August, but I think your M.D. s being rather cheap, he would have to pay a design studio hundreds more, if not thousands.'

'Oh just pull up here, I can just nip through Rope walk. Thanks ever so much Miss Heyhott.'

'You are very welcome and do call me Ali.'

August hid her drawings and pyramid in the back of her desk drawer. All ideas had to be handed in by Friday and August wanted to choose the right moment.

Don Holland called Robert Simpson in to his office for a meeting to inform him that his new work colleague would be Graham Topps. He made him sound so successful and perfect for the job, Robert felt threatened and a kind of hatred for this stranger who was to join them Monday next. There was a spite burning inside him, he wanted to know that this new guy wouldn't be getting paid any more than him. That he wasn't better than him in the Guvnor's eyes. He was though too much of a coward to ask Don Holland these questions, so had to leave screwed up with childish jealousy. His thoughts ran rapid, 'What if his salary and bonuses are bigger than mine? What if the Guvnor has had to bait this great sales executive with a better car than mine? What if the bastard gets a BMW! No he couldn't, not before me!' He now hovered in front of August's unmanned desk and turned to Jayne.

'Where's August today?, took another sicky?'

'She's down in the factory all morning, so would you mind listening for the phone a minute, I've got to nip to the loo.'

He tutted, but agreed seizing the opportunity to search for an order for a new company car. As soon as the door closed behind Jayne, he shuffled through the pile of papers on August's tray, then, hastily pulled out her desk drawer. A clear plastic pyramid slid forward, coming to rest on sheets of sketches and drawings. Robert picked up the pyramid and glossed over the paperwork, a sly smile un-pursed his lips. 'Perfect,' he whispered, 'just the job for a few team points.' He closed the drawer and slipped his prize into his briefcase and made off before Jayne came back.

Robert drove out of town and pulled up in a layby. There he took time to examine the sketch proposals and the carefully constructed pyramid. It certainly looked a winner. 'Fancy little fat August coming up with a gem like this.' He laughed aloud. 'This should put me in favour with the Guvnor Mr Topps even before you step through the door. Now then these drawings could do with a bit of professional help. There's no way Alicia would help me out, but I know just the fella.' He checked the time. 'just right to take him out to lunch.'

By 10am the following morning, Robert had the proposals for the pyramid all drawn up in his briefcase. He chuckled at his own cunning. 'Buck shee, free, well a good lunch paid for by the company,' He chuckled again. 'You smart boy.'

CHAPTER NINETEEN

August was exhausted when she reached home and swore at every stair tread. The thought of her shift at the cinema was torturous and she had to take a rest at the landing. Ali appeared from the flat. 'Hello August, I was hoping to catch you on your way in, about the gas fire.'

Oh yes, the button, I'm sorry, I meant to leave you a note. Should I show you where it is?'

'Please, would you?'

August went into the familiar flat. 'Cor, do you need the fire on? it's red hot in here.'

'Oh yes, I need to dry some colour washes, I have had my hair dryer on for ages trying to dry them.'

As August moved toward the fireplace, she noticed the window blurred with condensation and the word 'BASTARD' still showed up as she had written it. 'I'm sorry about that.' She said looking at the script and blushed a little. Ali burst out laughing when she saw it. 'I hadn't noticed, someone you know?'

'Used to, anyway that's another story, here's your button. Hey have you done these?' August bent over four pictures taped to separate boards.

'Yes, they are what I need to dry.'

'They're very good, whose houses are they?'

'Oh, it's a job I'm doing, they are marketing pictures for a builder, that should be what they look like when he's built them'

'You're an artist?'

'Yes, a graphic designer. I say, would you like a cup of tea? you look absolutely bushed.'

'I'd love one thanks, but I don't have the time, got to get ready for work.'

'Work? are you on a night shift or something?'

'Yeah, I do three evenings a week at a cinema, it's a long story.' she said making her familiar way to the door.

'How did your pyramid design go down?'

August perked up now, her face blossomed. Alicia thought how innocently excited she looked.

'We'll see tomorrow, I can't wait if I'm honest, I'm quite pleased with myself.'

'I should think so, that's some really innovative design there.'

That was the shot in the arm that August needed to propel her onward.

Robert Simpson stood in a stinking telephone box, feet astride the unidentified pool on the floor. He checked the ear and mouth piece of the receiver for spit and second hand chewing gum before phoning Stella. He needed to screw so badly. He was so full of himself, of mad and bad, and he had not had a lay for over a week. It rang and rang. He drummed his fingers on the graffiti smeared glass. The smell was unbearable. 'C'mon, you silly bitch ans…'

'Hello.'

'Stella it's Robert.'

'Hi.' She said flatly.

'Hi. Look, are you doing anything tonight?' There was a pause.

'Robert, you were supposed to be calling me early this week. It's Thursday you know?' There was a blunt edge to her voice.

'I know, I've been… away on business darling, I'm sorry. How about I make it up to you now? There was no response. Robert couldn't believe all the adoration had disappeared.

'Stella, are you there?'

'Yes.'

'Well, how about it. I'll pick up some hot Indian food, bring it round and we can have a really hot night.'

'I don't know if I really fancy that.'

'Okay… Chinese then?'

'No. It's not the food, it's the other… you hurt me last time Robert.'

The words took him by surprise, he shuffled uneasily, forgetting the puddle. He knew he'd hurt her, and he knew he relished it and feeling a bit of a shit but not really caring, thumped the kiosk door with bitter frustration. There was a pregnant silence whilst he collected his thoughts, he was semi stiff in his pants.

'Stella, baby, darling, I didn't mean to hurt you, it..it was pure passion, sheer passion baby. Oh Stella, come on darling, let me take you out for a meal... yeah. I'll come round now and later I'll take you to an expensive restaurant.'

'Can we go to the French one you know, the place on Station street?' There was a more cheerful note to her voice now.

'Sure we can, anywhere you like baby, see you in five minutes.' Robert slammed down the receiver before she could change her mind. He then swore at the piss pool he was stood in. He was stiff in his pants before he reached Stella's small flat. He hated that small cheap furnished box of hers, but he needed to be in it now, in that bed and inside Stella. As soon as he saw her, he knew she was going to hurt, but he liked it more when they suffered a bit. Anyway he thought if she wanted to eat rich, she ought to pay.

Alicia Simpson was having better sex alone in the shower, she knew there were Stellas' out there, but she didn't envy them.

CHAPTER TWENTY

As August shone her torch along the dim cinema seats, she spotlighted an open zipper, and a girls' hand slithering inside, like a snake about to snare a turkey. It was when the turkey's head popped out, August dropped the torch and she felt her cheeks fire up. She was so pleased it was dark. She needed a shock to keep her awake, being so, so tired and tempted to rest her aching feet, she knew though to sit down for a few seconds, she would surely fall straight to sleep,

When the welcomed end of the shift arrived though, it was slinging it down with rain. Cold drenching rain, which seeped into her thin shoes, but on the upside half soothing momentarily her leaden feet. August knew she couldn't hold on much longer for the boots, both shoes now had sprung a leak.

August was always in a hurry to get back home until she actually got there. It was so cold and bare, she wondered why. She also had something else on her mind. Mr Cruickshank and her, had a hiding place where the rent money would be deposited for him to collect. Her money was so hard earned she needed to check that the money was still there. It was. The money she had put there that evening before going to work. Also the last week's money was still there. Mr Cruickshank hadn't picked it up, maybe he's ill she thought. She left it in the old servant bell box over the door just inside the hovel.

The heavy Seamans' duffle-coat was cumbersome but she left it on until the fire had took hold of the logs. She sat close to the heat, her bench of newspapers getting quite low now. August held a hot mug of coffee up to her chin and let the steam thaw her nose and cheeks. Hooping her skirt up over her knees, she let the fire warm her thighs and fanny. Small pleasures don't cost anything she mused. August eased the tight elastic of her knickers, her thighs felt balloon like, then a dull ache in her lower back made her understand why.

'Oh shit, not the monthly curse, no wonder I've been craving chocolate all day.' She decided on a soak in the bath, knowing she wouldn't feel like it in the morning. The bath warmed her through.

She lay motionless, hot water tickling her earlobes. She daydreamed. The old sash window with stick on plastic to obscure the glass, became a tall multi paned framework of arched glass. The crazed milky green tiles that lapped halfway up the wall, topped by a black line of ceramic dado trim became panels of cream marble, veined with warm peach and smoked violet. The cracked ceiling would be smooth and hemmed with a fresco of egg and dart moulding. A huge gold swan spouted water through an elegant mouth at the turn of a gold hand wheel.

A charge of water blocked her nostrils and made her jump. She was shocked awake, spluttering and tried to clear her nose, creating a horrible sensation somewhere in her nasal cavity. August cursed herself for falling to sleep, and stepped out onto a very real, very cold black and white chequered lino floor. It was like standing on a derelict chessboard. One day she thought picking up on her day dream, she would have a deep pile carpet, something that oozed around her feet, suckling into her toes, and a warm bathroom.

Now this is what she hated, getting dried in a cold ugly room. The warmth evaporated from her skin, leaving her covered with hen flesh. Cold droplets ran from her wet hair and she rubbed her head furiously to dry her hair, but the towel was sodden and cold. 'God, this is a blooming punishment… I can't ever remember shooting a flock of robins.' She shivered. There was a loud banging outside on the landing, followed by shouting. A man's voice. August stood still listening.

'Open up sis…open thish door,.. C'mon.'

August dragged her robe around her. 'Oh no a bloody drunk, somebody must have left the door unlocked.' She put her ear to the door, the banging was either Ali's door or the bedsit next door.

'C'mon,' the drunk persisted, I can't stay 'ere all shodding night.'

August had the same thoughts as the cold crept up her legs. The dull ache in her lower back was growing and hurting more and she felt she was about to give birth to an anvil.

'Open the door August. I've come all thish way to vi ..vis.. to see ya.'

Hearing her own name, the existing goose bumps grew. She closed her eyes and whispered in to the door frame. 'Oh no please God, not David now…not now!'

Her brother was making a terrible racket and she knew he wouldn't go away before doing some damage. She had to get out there before poor Ali. August opened the door, and there was her brother David, crumpled on the floor outside Ali's flat. A pile of untidy black leather and tatty frayed jeans. He had a cheap bottle of sherry which he now waved toward her.

'There ya are.. God did I get it wrong..the wrong door gal?.. I could 'ave sworn ya lives 'ere.'

'Come on David you can't stay here, where the bloody hell have you come from?'

He waved the bottle at her. 'The Offi'..do yer want a jrinck?'

'No. Now get up.' She tugged at his leather jacket, pulling his puny body up with it. He staggered to his feet. She was pissed off at him for coming to the flat, pissed off at him at being so thin when she was fat, and pissed off at him for being so pissed. August tried to trundle him towards the staircase to make him leave. His gangling arms and legs wouldn't co-operate.

'But sissy..I've come to shee ya.'

'So, now you've seen me..bugger off.'

'Oh be nice…I've come a long way.'

'You must have , it's took you two bloody years!'

'Don't push me away Gussy.' He started to slide down the wall, she caught him and he started to cry. Loudly.

'Don't you chuck me out as well, don't..dowen't!'

She could have smacked his dirty face, but instead hauled him upstairs to the hovel. Her back and stomach ached. She balanced him on her only chair, while she boiled some water. David started to unscrew the bottle top, she took it from him. 'You take another sip,' she shouted, 'and I'll wrap it around your skull! you bloody waste of space!'

'Ohhh.. Gussy, don't be angry wiv me..cos nuffins goin' right..nuffin..please be nice.'

'Give me one good reason why I should be nice to a shit who leaves his young sister on the streets with nowhere to go. The big brother shit! that never bothered to make sure she was okay, but who turned up years later to sponge off her and then steal my bloody rent money. I bet Mum is turning in her grave.

'Don't shtart bringin' Mam into it you always were her fuckin favourite.'

'I didn't have much competition did I! you were always bringing trouble home, shoplifting, stealing from Mum's purse!' August cringed with stomach cramps and realised she had no pain killers. She decided to go and apologise to Ali, for the noise and ask if she had anything for period pain. There was no reply. August went downstairs, no BMW. She made sure the latch was on, this kind of visitor she could do without.

When she got back to the hovel, David was sprawled out on her bed. She pushed him with her foot. 'Get up! you're not bloody sleeping there!'. She pushed him again, he moaned but didn't move, in his unconscious state, he was a dead weight. 'You bastard.' She grunted over and over again as she tried to drag him off the airbed. When she finally managed to move him to the floor, her insides were at war. Her body flushed hot and cold and she felt like death. August could feel the colour drain from her cheeks and she took a swig from the sherry bottle. The rest she emptied down the sink, a cheap pungent smell made her pull a face.

She half-filled the empty bottle with very warm water and used it to ease the twisting pain in her belly.

CHAPTER TWENTY ONE

Robert Simpson breathed a sigh of relief when he pulled onto his own drive, he had had rather more than his quota of alcohol to have been driving. He wondered if Alicia was home, if she was, she was obviously in bed, the house was in darkness. He felt the kettle when he got into the kitchen, still warm, she must not long since gone to bed.

He made himself a coffee and pondered on whether it would be a good idea to creep into her bed and try it on. No, he'd been drinking and she hated that, maybe tomorrow night. He might buy her a little present with his two hundred pounds bonus, then again he had wanted a new silk shirt and some Italian leather shoes. No bugger her he thought, she'll want it sooner or later. The thought that she might be getting it somewhere else, crossed his mind. 'No she wouldn't,' he whispered to himself. 'Not Alicia. She wouldn't go out with anybody who she didn't know might have been screwing around.'

He paused outside her bedroom door, then smirked to himself as he swayed into his own room. 'She'll come begging soon.' He grinned.

Friday morning, August awoke with some discomfort. It wasn't so much the cramps, but the sherry bottle digging into her ribs. She turned over and was relieved to see no David. 'Thank Christ for that.' she sighed, her breath white grey in the cold air. Then a horrible thought struck her, and she scrambled from her bed and yanked her purse from her bag. 'You bastard David,' she cursed into an empty purse, just like she had witnessed her Mum do so many times. She now placed her brother on the same status as Shaun, Death Row. Her wages for the last three nights work, gone.

She had hated every minute of those shifts, and it was all for nothing. August had to take out of the rent money, she needed to buy some food today, but it was goodbye boots for a while. She might have let herself have a bus ride to work today if she hadn't have had this set back. She felt washed out. She forced herself every step of the way, thinking all the time about the 'pyramid'. Two hundred pounds, she would encourage herself through the spiteful cold. 'Today's the day.'

August decided she would present her idea to Don Holland at break time. She had only just managed to take off her coat, pop a couple of pain killers from the first aid box when Mrs Charlton had her running down to the factory floor checking card stocks.

At five minutes to ten, she dashed back upstairs, passing the tea lady. She couldn't resist any longer. 'Hetty, give us a Kit Kat and a coffee please.'

'Oooh and you were doing so well Luv,' Hetty said.

'Just this once,' August smiled. She thought she would deserve a treat today. Making her way into the office, her heart stepped up a beat. She felt excited all the way through herself. Opening the desk drawer, she pushed her hand into the back. She pulled the drawer all the way open, then slammed it shut, yanking the bottom drawer open. She pawed at the few papers in one drawer, then again in the other. 'It can't be,' she said, 'I left it in here.'

Jayne looked across at her bewildered expression as she raked through the drawers yet again. 'What's the matter, you lost something?'

August didn't answer, but plonked herself down on her chair. 'I can't believe it!'

'What, what is it?', Jayne was intrigued.

'Has anyone been near my desk while I was downstairs? Did anyone go in my desk drawers?'

It was Jayne's turn to look blank. 'Not that I know of, just tell me what you're looking for and I'll tell you if I've seen it.'

August remained silent, her heart pounding and her mind charged up with accusations of who might have stolen her design. Still, she would find out soon enough. If it was a winning design, the winner would get more than they bargained for.

'August, are you alright?' Jayne was staring at her. August returned her stare, but with tired eyes, swollen underneath with a crescent of dark shadow.

'Have you lost something?' Jayne persisted.

'Only my temper,' August replied and ripped the wrapper from the Kit-Kat and much to Jayne's disgust, crammed the whole four fingers in her mouth with the etiquette of a piranha.

By three o' clock in the afternoon, nothing had been said about a winner or anything. August decided that the-someone that had stolen it had found out it wasn't good enough. Mrs Charlton came through with the mail to be franked. 'Mrs Charlton,' August caught her attention, 'Has there been a winning design brought in yet?'

'We're not quite sure yet, the proposals have to be put to the client, but I must say that we do think we have a winner in there, quite an extraordinary entry. I didn't think we had such talent in our employ.' She turned to go. August stopped her. 'What's it like Mrs Charlton?'

'Now that would be telling.' She smiled.

'Oh pleeease.' August begged.

'No..no..well, let's just say it's rather Egyptian in origin.'

August was struck dumb. It was her design. She needed to get into Don Holland's office it must be on show somewhere. She had an idea. Waiting until Mrs Charlton went to the loo, she then launched herself to the M.D.'s office door and knocked lightly. Jayne thought August had flipped, as she spied bemused as the chubby figure slipped into Don Holland's office. 'Yes, what is it?' he boomed without looking up. August scanned the office. 'I was just wondering Mr Holland, if any of the design entries needed calculations for the briefing, you know, costings and man hour quantities?'

He looked up at her now, and without speaking, walked over to a small rose wood cabinet. From it he took a folded dyeline print and on top balanced her pyramid. The same one only with gold lettering on it.

August stomped her way through puddles on her way home. She normally played the game of not stepping on the gaps between the paving slabs, the curse of bad luck to befall you if you did. This spitefully cold evening, August took the course of stepping on as many cracks as she could, thinking, 'I've obviously been doing it wrong all these bleeding years.'

She was so mad at not finding out who had stolen her design. The cheeky buggers had drawn it up again properly, and there she had to work out all the figures for making it, and couldn't say a word. Well she could have, but what proof had she got, who would have believed her, only the shit that had stolen it. Don Holland couldn't praise the thief enough, but wouldn't let on who it was. 'The person wishes to remain anonymous.' He said when she asked him. 'Ha of course,' she thought, 'I'll just have to wait to see who had more holidays than anyone else.'

August was so mad, the twisting cramps inside hardly bothered her for a mile and she stamped noisily up the staircase. Ali met her at the top. 'Hello, I've been waiting for you to come home.'

August pushed off her heavy hood, the dark welts under her eyes showing up against her chalky pallor. She hadn't really heard what Ali had said and just said 'Hi.'

'Good heavens August, you really don't look well. Come on inside, I'll get you a drink.'

'Oh it's okay, it's just the curse you know.'

'Sorry?'

'Period pains.'

'I know just the thing. Now come on in, don't argue.' Ali took Augusts' bag from her and led her into the flat and over to the fire. The warmth inside enveloped her and her stiff limbs eased into the comfy sofa. 'Cor, it seems like a year since I sat this comfortable.' she said to no one but herself. Ali was clattering around in the kitchen, but she soon appeared, carrying a tray with a tall glass beaker sat in a lovely silver holder, which August knew had definitely not been on the inventory of the flat she had left.

'Oh do take your coat off darling, now get this inside you.'

'Aren't you having one?'

'I haven't got the cramps, besides, I'm driving and there is a few tots of bourbon in that.'

'I'm not sure if I like bourbon.'

'Get it drunk, you will feel much better. Now I wanted to see you before I went.'

August didn't know what she was talking about, but noticed there was a huge drawing board where the bed used to be, the bed was pushed right up against the wall. There was no duvet on it.

'Are you going away somewhere?'

'I shall be gone over the weekend, I'm going to stay with some friends down south. It's their annual ball, always throw one Guy Fawkes night. Mind you they put on a marvellous firework display. It is rather worth the journey just for that.'

August gulped some of the hot toddy. 'A ball,' she thought to herself, she had never met anyone before that went to balls.' She sipped her drink, liking the taste and the warm sensation inside her. Ali's slim body stretched to reach the top of the wardrobe, she had beautiful poise, almost ballerina like. She dragged off a canvas bag. 'I've been having a sort out,' she said handing the bag to August. 'I thought you could make use of these.'

'What is it?' August said fumbling with the tied strings.

'There are some tubes of paint, designer gouache. I thought you might like to use them up. I'll sort some brushes out for you.'

August unrolled the canvass bag to reveal a row of pockets, each filled with different coloured tubes of paint. She didn't understand why Ali had given her these. As if reading her blank expression, Ali explained. 'For your designs, it really is a good medium to work with.'

'What designs?'

'Don't be silly the pyramid package!, I mean , that's awfully clever. And of course you must tell me how you got on.'

A thin ribbon of salt water collected on August's lower eyelid, but she managed to stare it out until it subsided and blinked it away. Ali felt the emotion. 'August what happened?'

'Someone stole it.'

'Stole what, your model?'

'All of it. The paperwork, the pyramid.'

'Never!' Ali was horror struck.

'Well, they did the paperwork better. Dyeline prints, the works. Little proper gold letters on the model, it looks great. Oh yeah, the M.D. thinks it's brilliant, but he thinks someone else designed it.'

'Did he say who?'

'They wish to remain anonymous.' August mimicked Don Holland.

'That's hardly surprising. Oh dear, I'm so sorry August. It really is abominable. You'll find out who it is I'm sure.' Ali glanced at her watch. August drained her beaker. 'I had better let you get off.' She said standing up.

'Sorry to be in a rush darling, we must have a little get together another time.',she dashed off into the kitchen while August hauled on her heavy coat. Ali returned with a jug.

'Here take this with you, I made up a pint. All you need to do is warm it up as soon as the cramps start, prepare yourself a mug full.'

'Thanks ever so much Ali, oh and thank you very much for the paints.'

'You are very welcome, and I will see you after the weekend some time.'

August was so pleased she didn't have to work that evening. She was pleased for Ali to be her friend too. Well not her friend exactly, but a friendly neighbour. August realised then that she didn't have any friends. Not proper friends. There was Carol that came in The Crown on a Saturday nights, but she was only a face she knew from the past, they had nothing in common. There was Jayne at work, but they had never socialised. Once, Jayne had taken her home to show off her house when she first married. August called it the 'Wendy house syndrome'. Jayne had teetered around the house introducing August to all the new furniture.

'And this is the new three piece suite we got from Jameson's in town. Wayne's Mum and Dad bought us this cabinet, 'Do you like it? And this is the table and chairs I told you about. This is the Kitchen.'

August decided that if that's what being married did to you, she would rather stay single.

CHAPTER TWENTY TWO

Robert Simpson, on Friday evening, was in a bad mood. He was angry that Alicia hadn't been home. There was no food in the house, except muesli and there was no milk. He repeatedly turned the thought over in his mind that maybe Alicia was seeing someone else. The crackle of fireworks aggravated him. Then as a rocket fizzed into his view through the window, he realised where Alicia would be. He sprung off the sofa. A grin spread across his unshaven face as he padded into the pink bedroom. He knew he had all weekend to find that old handbag.

It was an uneventful, wet blanket of a weekend for August. Drained of energy, she slept through most of it. Her reckoning, that while she was asleep, she was neither hungry nor felt the cold. Her shifts behind the bar were robotic and seemingly endless. As she made it home and to the top of the main staircase she also reckoned she'd passed through the pain barrier. Glancing at the door of the flat, August groaned at the thought of the vacant soft sofa and empty proper bed. Sloth like she ascended to the polar regions of the hovel.

'I wonder,' she thought, 'if in my life, I will ever go to a ball?' She felt like Cinderella and an Ugly sister rolled into one. A fat Cinderella. No, she had given up on Fairy Godmothers before bellbottom trousers were in fashion.

Robert Simpson made a collection of the dirty foil cartons that stank with remains of Chinese food. He grimaced at the acid burn in his throat, and with one thump to his chest released a loud belch which was also visible in the cold night air. He blamed Alicia for him having to live on takeaway food. The he wondered if you could die from too much monosodium glutamate. 'I bet that's what the bitch is hoping,' he said and crammed the smelly rubbish into the dustbin. The lid crashed down as he vented his anger. 'For Christ sake, if I wanted to look after myself, I would never have got bloody married!' He kicked the dustbin and stormed back inside. In the light he saw that he had scuffed his eighty pound shoes, and a corrugated line of soy sauce decorated his shirt sleeve. 'Shit! shit! shit!, I'm nearly out of shirts again! God, no food, no cooking, no laundry! so now we may as well be divorced.' He checked his watch, nearly eleven, Alicia should be home anytime now she had work the following day.

Robert poured himself a gin and tonic and thought about divorce, not for the first time. Still the same objectives came to the fore. If he divorced her now, what grounds could he claim, because if he walked out, he wouldn't get a penny of her money. The big factor was, Alicia was heading to be much, much wealthier when her Mother dies. He sipped his drink. The answer was for his Mother in law to kick the bucket, followed shortly by Alicia. Then he would get the whole of the treasure. A grotesque thought captured his thoughts. He took a large gulp of his drink, 'Could he make it happen.'

Twenty minutes later, Alicia stumbled through the door with a large suitcase. Robert rushed to help, taking her by surprise. 'You're late, I was beginning to worry.'

Alicia didn't respond, apart from a frown of disbelief.

'I was just about to pour a drink, can I get you one?'

'I'll have a small brandy, thank you. The traffic has been horrendous, break downs all over the place.'

'Here you are.' Robert handed the brandy glass in a way that she would have to touch his fingers. He hesitated letting go. 'As I was saying, I was beginning to worry.'

'No need, I'm back now.'

'Well I thought you would have been earlier, you know... Monday morning ..work and all that.'

'I'm taking the day off tomorrow.'

They became silent. It was the first time in ages they had sat down together in the same room. Robert wanted to ask if she would be sorting the laundry with her day off, or maybe doing some food shopping, but he knew that would kill any further conversation dead. His mind raced before saying, 'Err..actually, I was contemplating staying home tomorrow, clear up some paperwork, too many interruptions in the office.' He smiled weakly. 'Maybe we could do lunch together?'

Alicia swallowed the brandy, and looked at Robert. She loved his blonde hair, his pale blue eyes and sexy smile, but she loathed what was inside of him. It was like admiring a wind sculpted desert, knowing it was cruel and cold at night and harboured deadly scorpions. He was such a shallow shit, but she was tired of fighting him and reluctantly agreed to lunch.

Monday morning, August marched briskly to work, leaving a vapour trail of breath in the cold air. She hadn't so much a desire to get to work, but an eagerness to meet the new rep, Graham Topps. She imagined a six-footer, very dark wavy hair, and such burning good looks, Slimy would pale in his shadow. In the Ladies cloakroom, August paid extra attention to her hair and plucked a couple of unruly eyebrow hairs in readiness to meet this rep with the film star good looks.

By the time Alicia had got up and made it into the kitchen, Robert was pouring coffee. 'Last of the coffee,' he announced, 'shall we do a bit of shopping later, perhaps after lunch?'

Alicia nodded remembering their date. Robert began moving files from his briefcase and placed them in an orderly fashion across the table. He consulted his Filofax. 'Oh bloody hell, I forgot!' he said jumping up from the table. 'Bloody Graham Topps, I've got to take him to pick up his car.'

'Who's Graham Topps?'

'The new rep, he starts today. Look I won't be long…just an hour or so.'

'Robert, I don't mind skipping lunch..'

'No..no..look, it won't take me long, in fact I'll leave my paperwork here, I shall be back in plenty of time to sort them out before lunch.' He hurriedly dragged on his jacket and smiled at Alicia, as if promising his speedy return was a gift all precious. As the door closed behind him, Alicia sighed, feeling that she had just missed the escape route, why did she agree to having damn lunch together.

August hid her disappointment when the rotund figure, as smart as he was, came in and stood in front of her desk. She smiled, it was a relief really, she would have felt all inferior if he had been the handsome hunk. 'Hello Love,' he said offering his hand, 'I'm Graham Topps.'

'Oh well she thought, at least he's not stuck up like Slime.' It was at that moment that Robert strode into the office, totally ignoring August and stole the handshake. She glanced at Graham, who was a bit put out, and his hamster cheeks flushed with embarrassment. August ignored Slimy and butted in. 'Here is the paperwork you'll need when you pick up the car.' She said with a smile.

'Oh yes,' Robert said dismissively, 'August here will sort your paperwork out.'

'Not today though,' August said, 'I'm on the factory floor for the rest of the day, see you later.'

CHAPTER TWENTY THREE

Alicia laid her briefcase on the top of Robert's tidy files and set herself a desk to work on some accounts. 'Oh bugger it.' She said as her calculator refused to read out. She had just resigned herself to use her brain instead of the silicon chip, when the initials R.S. gold embossed on Robert's tan briefcase caught her eye. 'Of course, he'll have a calculator.'

The briefcase was unlocked and she flipped the collection of papers inside. Robert always liked to have the best, it would have far too many buttons that he couldn't understand. The video recorder was still alien to him after eighteen months. Yes there it was. As she grabbed it, she also pulled out a dyeline print. She unfolded it, having no guilt of sniping, knowing that in her absence, Robert would have rifled her belongings looking for the handbag.

Now she was looking at the design details of a small pyramid. A single chocolate truffle box. Alicia sauntered over to the phone and picked out the familiar numbers. A female voice answered. ' Ruban Co, can I help you?'

'Err.. who is that speaking?'

'Jayne Stockwell, can I help you?'

'Oh sorry, yes, it's just that I normally speak to another girl.'

'Oh, that will be August, she's not in the office right now, would you like to leave a message?'

'No..no, it's not that I need to speak to her or anything..no..err..I do want to leave a message though for Robert Simpson. If you could tell him his lunch date would like to take a rain check.'

Alicia didn't listen to Jayne's reply but replaced the receiver as she looked back to the kitchen table, the briefcase, the initials. A taut muscle spasm embraced and shrunk the pit of her stomach. 'You..you,' she struggled for words to match the sick anger that ripped through her insides. 'Bastard! heinous .. hedonistic, BASTARD!' she spat.

Fred stood in the doorway of his office. It was just a timber framed kiosk clad with chipboard that the factory lads had covered with nude pin ups and saucy calendars. The pictures used to embarrass August, but apart from Miss July, she coped with all of them now. Fred saw August approaching, his smile showing an untidy row of tobacco stained teeth. 'Aye up lass, let me get thee a cup o' coffee. Am reight pleased to see yo'. Only 'ave made a bit of a mess wi' lads' time sheets, an a was 'opin' you'd sort um fo' me'

'Well, only if I can have a mug with a handle.'

Fred shuffled off, wiping his dirty hands down the front of his grey overall coat in a bid to look hygienic. He always shuffled around the factory, August thought it was because the funny sandals he wore didn't fit him properly. The truth was, that he started shuffling when he'd had some bunions treated. The lads always heard him coming and stopped doing anything they shouldn't, so he kept it up. That way he never had to tell anybody off. August made herself comfortable in the beaten up leather chair. The smell of machine oil hung in the background. Pillars of stacked cardboard piled high added a malty aroma that reminded her of a nice feeling from the past. It was the smell of a freshly opened corn flake box. She was a small child elbow deep inside the new carton fishing for the free plastic toy.

'Ere we are then.' Fred returned with her drink. 'Ave yo' 'ad time to look at them time sheets?', he was nodding his flat capped head at the time sheets in front of her. She scanned down the neat grids, pock marked with blue biro, the crossings out were carved practically right through the paper. 'Can yer fix 'em lass?' he asked hopefully.

'Not even with a gallon of Tippex.' she answered looking up at his anxious ruddy face. She knew all too well that his academic skills were limited, and she was always having to bale him out. But, put him in front of a broken down machine and he could strip it down and get it working in record time.

'Oooh lass, Mester Holland 'ull give me a bollockin' fo' sure, you know what e's like!'

'Don't panic Fred, I'll go up later and sneak some new sheets and fill them in for you.'

'You are a good lass. There's summat else mind.' He went over to the plan chest where all the patterns were kept. He pulled out and held up a really elaborate pattern, smothered in cut and fold markers on both sides.

'Don't tell me,' she said peering at it, 'It's the first of the Easter egg cartons.'

'How did you know?'

'It couldn't be anything else, look at it.'

'Looks more like a bloody doyley, 'ave you seen 'ow many cuts there are?'

'I don't suppose you've got the marketing pictures?'

'Oh aye. It's one of Simpson's jobs o' course, he always brings in awkward ones.'

August always liked to try and make out what the finished carton would look like just by studying the cut and fold marks, but Fred was right, this one was complex. The marketing picture revealed the carrier carton for the Easter egg was to be a rocket. Fred tutted and shook his head. He always did this at weird and wonderful packaging, even in supermarkets.

'Look at the bloody thing lass, I don't know which Easter they think they're gerrin it fo' am sure, it'll 'ave to go through creaser at least twice each side an' me an' Reg think it's got to go through t'cutter three times!'

'Is Reg busy?'

'I'll go an' find 'im lass.'

Don Holland had just dictated a letter to Mrs Charlton that would start a series of events likened to that of a knotted fuse on a stick of dynamite. Mrs Charlton would like to have changed some of the narrative in the letter least not send them at all. Some ten years ago when he took over from his late Father, she thought him dynamic and fancied him a little.

She had overlooked the dandruff, the cigar breath and the thinning hair. She even fantasised about him making a pass at her. The ten years working for him had changed her view of him. Now all she could see was a pin striped arrogant man full of greed. His Father would be turning in his grave if he could see how he manipulated the business to benefit himself and him alone. Without looking at her, he dealt his orders. 'Tell that Jepson girl I want to see her.'

'Err.. Jepson?' She questioned. He looked up at her puzzled face. 'You know, the girl that does the costings for the briefs.'

'Oh, you mean Jackson, August Jackson.'

'Whoever, I want her to go to the trade show with me on Friday. There are some new machines I would like her to look over to see if they will be beneficial to us, don't want to spend money if we can cope with what we've got.'

Patricia Charlton wanted to say, 'We haven't got any money.' But she quietly left his office.

August was still studying the pattern when Fred returned with Reg, a stocky chap just short of fifty years old, fifteen of them working for Ruban Co. 'Now then Miss Jackson,' Reg smiled, 'What can Reggy do for you?'

August giggled. Reg always called her Miss Jackson, always played that she was the real boss and called Don Holland 'Donkey Brains', behind his back of course. 'It's this Rocket Reg, Fred reckons it's got to go through the cutter three times'

'That's right. It's these windows here, can you see how close they are to this cut?' August followed his finger travelling along the red markers. 'Can't fix the blade that close to another one,' he continued.

All three of them bent over the pattern in silence, except Fred who sighed at regular intervals. August clicked her fingers. 'I've got it!' she said, 'all they have to do is change the design and shift the windows onto this flat instead, it will still look the same.'

'She's got it Fred.'

Fred sighed again. 'But what if they don't want the windows there?'

August was used to Fred being a problem monger when it came to a package he didn't like. I'll tell you what.' She said setting her hands to pray and axing the air as she spoke. 'We'll cost it out like they've designed it, and we'll cost it out with the alternative window position. Both proposals can be returned with the brief, then it's up to them.'

Fred loved a solution and exposed his mustard coloured teeth again in a smile, although he wished she would have said 'I'll' cost instead of 'we'. He knew August would do it, it's just that the words always made him uncomfortable. August let her praying fingers slip in between each other to cover each knuckle. She bounced her double fist on the desk. 'Right then Reg will use his expertise to work out how long it will take to change the sets of cutters and Fred can tell us how long a sweep through will take with an allowance for any breakdowns, which I know he will fix with his usual brilliant speed.'

Both men puffed up with the compliments and she carried on. 'I can then work out the man hours and cost them up. Together we'll sort it out.' Both men left when the phone rang, Fred especially hated the phone apart from being able to reach August in times of trouble.

'Hello August Jackson speaking.'

'Hello August, it's Mrs Charlton, Mr Holland would like to see you in his office.'

'Me!'

'Yes, he's free at the moment, if you want to come up.'

As August put the phone down, the events of the previous week occupied her mind. She was only late one day by five minutes as far as she could remember. Only half armed with confidence she ascended the few concrete steps that led from the factory corridor up to the carpeted floors. She stopped off at the toilets to tidy her hair. Her brown locks were at that awkward length when the ends touched the shoulders and sprung the hair out of shape. The cuffs of her white blouse were a little grubby, so she unbuttoned them and tucked them up her jumper sleeves.

Don Holland had the rude habit of looking at paperwork on his desk when he spoke to anyone. August didn't mind, she couldn't stand his dark beady eyes viewing her as some lower life.

'Now then Miss Jipton.'

She didn't correct him, she didn't particularly want him to remember who she was, just in case she had been late.

'There's a trade exhibition taking place at Birmingham this week. I would like you to go with me.'

August swallowed audibly, wondering what the hell was happening. He looked at her on and off, but mostly stared out of the window. 'There will be on show new cutters, packers and various machines allied to our trade. I'm being pestered every week by damn reps selling me their benefits.' He glanced up at her and she nodded, being as it seemed the right thing to do and she was still in a state of shock.

'I don't believe most reps,' he said sharply, 'And I think you will be able to tell me if the new machines would have any advantage over the machines we already have, cost effectiveness and things like that.'

August didn't say anything, but was scanning the room for the pyramid.

'Well,..that is your forte', isn't it costing?'

'Err..yes.'

'So I'll pick you up at seven fifteen Friday morning, be waiting in the car park, we'll get an early start.'

'August gripped the seat she was perched on the edge of. She was already panicking about being able to get up early enough without an alarm clock.

'That's it then Miss Jepson,' he said with a dismissive air. August was in a hurry to get out, just before she escaped he added. 'Oh and smart dress for the occasion, see you Friday.'

That was the other thing she was worried about.

Robert was thoroughly pissed off at Alicia for cancelling their lunch date, but then again he didn't mind showing off to Graham Topps. He took him to 'The Conservatory', and ordered the most expensive dishes on the menu.

Over dinner that evening, Graham gave an account of his new work colleague to his wife Pamela. 'Oh he's got a watch that tells the time in different countries, he has shoes that cost more for one pair than all ours put together. He says he's got a wife that's more attractive than most, got a better figure than most and is richer than most. I would say that he's more of a twat than most.'

CHAPTER TWENTY FOUR

As the week dragged on it got more chilly. A crisp frost regularly sugared the ground, night till morning. August make believed that it was the sight of Christmas dressed shop windows that just made it feel colder, I'm sure they get earlier she mused. Then she saw the sensible boots displayed on a cloud of cotton wool which was sprinkled all over the window bottom as pretend snow. As the temperature had dropped, the price had risen. 'Two bloody pounds more!' she cursed to herself, 'the winter is here and the boots are getting further out of reach.'

She stamped a couple of times to encourage the circulation in her freezing feet before heading home. It was Wednesday evening. She must sort some clothes out before she went to work ready for Friday. She had solved the problem about getting up, Fred had given her an alarm clock he didn't use. August was disappointed again when there was no BMW parked outside. She hadn't seen Ali since before the weekend and she was dying to find out all about the ball. She also wanted to ask if she had seen Mr Cruickshank, because he still hadn't collected the rent money.

For the rest of her journey her thoughts turned back to work. Harry Cohen from Darts Deliveries upstairs had been raving, wanting to see Don Holland. Mrs Charlton had been trying to calm him down. He was waving a letter and shouting about extortionate rents. Then a woman from Judds Jewellery had been sent down to hand deliver a letter that made Don Holland shout. The gist of it seemed to be that Judds would be vacating the premises at the end of the month.

Within five minutes of entering the hovel, a fire was crackling in the grate and the gas burner was alight under a pan for a hot cuppa. When she had warmed through, her plan was to find something to wear on Friday. August unloaded the newspapers she had collected from work and put them to the bottom of her dwindling pile. If she did have a little spare time she liked to read them, so keeping the latest at the bottom meant she would burn old news first. Then again it was all old news by the time she got around to reading it.

August thought she would have missed the TV, but she had hardly given it a second thought. If anything, it was her stereo and music that she missed. Strangely enough, it was this time that she enjoyed now. The getting home, such as it was. Sitting quiet and feeling the cold move out warming her insides and her skin. She was in charge again, it might be that she was in charge of a shithole, and she was waist deep, but at least she was standing up for herself.

Her wardrobe had never been very grand, and she slid back several hangers loaded with clothes that had become too tight. Then sticking a thumb easily in the waistband of the skirt she was wearing, decided to try some on. 'I can't believe it.' She said trying a third skirt on. 'I haven't been able to get in this since last Easter.' She stood on the chair to catch her reflection in the darkened windows. 'Cor I've actually lost weight!'

August was so delighted she didn't have time to eat, but tried every item of clothes she thought had been redundant. She didn't mind going to work that evening.

Robert Simpson unloaded his clean laundry from his car, and the shopping he was forced to do. Alicia had left a note on Monday to say she had to go and stay with her Mother, but didn't say for how long. Robert hated shopping more than cooking, but his consolation was that his Mother in law maybe ill. He reckoned that the longer Alicia stayed there, the worse her Mother must be. He could be quite a rich boy soon.

At 5.30 Friday morning the alarm clock wailed, August fumbled around and then remembered she had put the clock out of reach to force her out of bed. It was so cold, she pulled on her heavy dufflecoat rather than her bathrobe until she got a fire started on top of last nights' ashes. The bitter cold pinched her feet, even through her bed socks. August moved the chair draped with the clothes she had got ready last evening close enough to the fire to warm a little. She gathered her toiletries ready for the chilly bathroom run.

August now had a routine, she would run just hot water in the bath while she brushed her teeth. She would let it sit there while she used the toilet. That was enough time for the cold cast iron bath to take some of the heat out of the water, so when she sat in it her bum wasn't cold. She had only taken three steps out onto the landing to go back to the bathroom when a giddy rush swam inside her and she padded straight back to the toilet. She did feel nervous, she supposed it was because she had to accompany Don Holland. She had always wanted to go to the big trade show, she wondered what it was like. Slime had told her bits and pieces but had, in a round-about way, said it wasn't really for her, it was mainly executives like himself who went. 'I wonder what he thinks about me going,' she thought, smiled and relieved herself.

The bath water warmed her and she was quite enjoying getting ready until she got conditioner in her eye. Rubbing it with the towel made it worse. She rinsed the rest from her hair. As the water swept across her ears and thundered back into the bath, she though she heard someone try the door. She stopped still to listen, and shuddered as the cold draped her bare shoulders. The door handle rattled.

'Hello,' she called. 'I won't be long.'

The dented brass knob turned a quarter and back again. 'Who's there?' she called. There was no reply and August got out of the bath, annoyed because she was certain no one would surely want to use the bath that early. She was also confident no other tenants entitled to the bathroom were in residence. She hitched a bath towel in front of her pinning it under her armpits. She pressed her face up to the door edge and spoke through the thin crack. 'Whose there…who is it, I won't be long.' There still was no reply. She stood firmly behind the door as she slid back the brass bolt. She decided if it was David again, she would punch his face in before throwing him out.

Through the narrow gap August saw a painfully thin man in a dark suit stood along the landing at the top of the main staircase. Cold air was rushing through the narrow gap and August was just about to shut the door when the man turned around. To her relief it was Mr Cruickshank, but he didn't look well, gaunt and grey in the face. August opened the door a little more and called to him. 'Mr Cruickshank. I wondered where you'd been, just give me a couple of minutes and I'll be out.'

Cruickshank raised a pale hand and spoke in a broken whisper as if he'd lost his voice. 'Can't stay, I have Karen's address now, you must keep yours.'

'Just two minutes Mr Cruickshank, I'll be with you,' She closed the door and hurriedly dried herself. She was concerned that Mr Cruickshank looked ill. 'A bit early for calling though.' She thought. 'Well he probably feels a bit off it, finding his daughters' address too late and all that. Poor man.'

The poor man wasn't on the landing when she opened the door again, and neither was he upstairs in the hovel. She checked the bell box over the door. 'Flippin 'eck, he's still not taken the rent money, he's certainly not with it lately.'

August didn't dwell on the visit, she had too much to do and think about today. She managed to put a decent face on with the dregs of what was left in her makeup bag, noticing her cheeks weren't as chubby. The calf length black skirt would have looked better with boots, but the shoes had cleaned up quite well, they would have to do. August felt that the white blouse and black cardigan made her look like a waitress, but she was just pleased that they fitted her and she looked smart. The coat though was a problem. Would she go in the smarter light weight jacket, or the warm duffle-coat and the leave it in the M.D.'s car. The latter seemed the more sensible if not flattering. Indeed, when Don Holland pulled into the car park at nearer to quarter to eight than quarter past seven, it had been the better choice, but his face distorted into horror at the bulky hooded figure waiting for him.

August opened the car door and said hello to the stern face, the warmth emitted from the car interior. ' There's a map on the back seat, can you get it, are you any good at map reading?.

'I'll try, is it ok if I put my coat in the back?'

A wave of his hand August translated to, 'Yes, and pick up the map'

Although August wasn't enjoying close company with her boss, she enjoyed the comfy seat and the heater. The car was more sumptuous than the flat never mind the hovel. He had pointed out their destination and where they were now. 'Can you watch out for the road numbers and make sure we turn off at the right time.'

August truthfully had never had a need to look at a map, never mind read one, but she accustomed herself with it. Ten mile into the journey up the M1, her stomach gurgled. Don Holland actually offered her a mint sweet, which she was grateful for, and then he pushed a tape cassette into the player which at first she was grateful for, ' Elvis crying in the chapel' to cover further rumblings, but when he was still crying in the chapel when they came off the M1 and was putting on his blue suede shoes for the second time, she was all Elvis'd out.

She was relieved to be able to announce 'The Exhibition Centre next turn off.'

Don Holland ejected the tape. August thanked God silently.

Men in fluorescent orange jackets waved the traffic this way and that and there were bollards for different exhibitions. Finally they parked in what seemed a city of car parks. August was amazed at the sheer size of the place. It even had it's own buses to take people from the car parks to the many halls.

At first when they walked in. the M.D. handed a ticket in and they both were handed name badges to pin in their clothes. August felt quite important, the most important she had felt since being in the presence of her mum. They entered the first hall, it was massive. It was obvious from the start that Don Holland didn't want her with him, but as much as she hated his company, she tagged along close by his side. The hall with its' many stands was buzzing with suits, briefcases, shiny shoes, men shaking hands, smart attractive women talking to the men with briefcases and shiny shoes. After less than three minutes Don Holland halted. He stuffed his hand into his breast pocket, withdrawing his wallet. 'I want you to meet me here at 3.30.' August waited for the money for her lunch, but instead he placed four business cards in her hand. He poked the top one, 'That's the company. I want you to meet me there at half past three.'

'Where is it?.. their stand?'

'You'll find it, there's a plan layout at the entrance. The other business cards are from companies that are trying to sell me their machines. Go and find out all you need to know.' With that, he strode off and on to the nearest stand, bearing his directors badge and received a wonderful arse licking welcome, a cup of coffee which

August could have snatched from his hands. She stood there for a few deathless seconds, feeling bewildered and small in this huge place. She was ravenous hungry and felt sick inside, staring down at the business cards in her hand.

CHAPTER TWENTY FIVE

August sauntered aimlessly along the many aisles in this massive cavernous hall. It was a labyrinth of stands with a busy hum of business, mainly men. This hustle of business seemed to show few females. When she did observe one of her own kind, it seemed she was a species apart. The rare birds she spotted were above average on the beauty scale and woven into this workaday world of efficient and smart suits. She felt like a zeppelin sized waitress who was lost.

It took August an age to find the first of her mission. Tastic Ltd. had an impressive stand, all decked out in white, lemon and pale grey. August was totally ignored at first. She didn't know if that made her mad or glad. She helped herself to leaflets spread out on grey tables. A balding man in a pale grey suit, a lemon tie and crisp white shirt approached her.

'Can I be of assistance?' he said in a more questioning her presence than wanting to be of help. August had spotted a large diagram of a cutting machine. 'Err..yes..I was wanting some information on your cutters and folders.'

'I believe you have the information in your hands.' He said almost dismissing her. Then gave her one of his cards and walked away. 'Right. Thank you.' She said to an empty space, and sauntered off the stand not knowing where to aim herself.

August got the same cold shoulder treatment at Supa Box Co. She was so miserable, so hungry, and when she saw a welcome sign of the Ladies loo, she bolted inside needing a pee and refuge. She emerged from the cubicle before she was ready, she was on the verge of bursting into tears, but there was a woman at the wash basins, and she realised she would look just plain stupid. Still that's how she felt, stupid. Slimy was right, it was no place for her. Clumsily she fumbled about in her handbag searching for her comb. Her bag left her hands and crashed onto the floor. The business cards scattered together with an emergency tampon, a biro and two spent tissues. August pounced on her belongings as if they were the crown jewels.

The woman crouched down to help, her bob of blonde hair swung like a short curtain, so smooth and perfect.

August panicked, snatching at the crushed tissues. 'Oh my God, what an idiot, what a fool I am.' She was calling herself all manner of self-derision, finding it hard to catch her breath in between. The woman grabbed her wrist. 'Hey steady on.' The woman said softly. Elegantly the woman stood up, gently pulling August up to her feet. 'Whatever is the matter?' she asked feeling August tremble.

'Oh, I just shouldn't be here, our rep was right, this place is for the executives, not for idiots like me. I should never have agreed to come.'

'Now hold on, just wait a minute.'

August looked directly at this woman now holding her hand. August had never seen eyes so emerald green. This woman had a rare beauty, which made August feel more out of place. She realised that those green eyes were showing concern for her.

'I'm sorry, I really, really feel out of place.'

'Good heavens why?'

'Talk about a fish out of water.'

'How come you're here?'

'The boss asked me to come.'

'Well, there you are then.' The woman looked at August's badge. 'You are August?'

August nodded and half smiled now allowing her shoulders to drop a little. The woman continued. 'You have a trade badge, and on that badge it tells me you are a representative of your company, so in what capacity are you here?'

'Pardon?' The shoulders tightened up again.

'Why did your boss ask you to come?, Look, do you want a coffee?'

The expression on Augusts' face said it all.

'Come on let's get out of the loos. By the way, I'm Samantha Dowles, call me Sammy.'

August followed Sammy very closely, not daring to lose her. As they walked, Sammy chatted. 'What company are you with?'

'Ruban Co.'

'Aah yes, I know that name. I've called on the design company in the same building.' She pulled August into one of the coffee bar tables and went to the counter to get coffees.

As soon as Sammy left her at the table, she felt immediately lonely, she hated this feeling. She played around in her handbag, she felt so self-conscious. She watched the men in the bar watch Sammy, she was a head turner. August wished for even just a little of that confidence that Sammy effused. She planted the welcome coffee in front of August and elegantly sat down opposite.

'Now then August, tell me, why did your boss send you?'

'Oh he brought me actually he wants me to have a look at the new box making machines. He doesn't know whether it would be worth investing in the new technology stuff. He doesn't know much actually.'

Sammy laughed. 'Typical. Where is he then? in here?'

'Yes, he sent me off. I have to meet him at half past three.'

'Well that's very nice of him just to dump you like that. Listen to me August. For a start stop pulling yourself down. You see all these rattlesnakes in their three piece suits' they are here to get your business. You are a very important person to them. Half of them are jumped up little wankers that carry their brains in their briefcases. The other half wear their balls on their sleeves of expensive suits, they will be pissed by lunchtime, and trying to get their hands up some girls' skirt.

August smiled, this whole new ocean she felt out of depth in was becoming more shallow in more ways than one.

'It's a cattle market August, where the Reps and the Directors come out to play. It's even worse in the hotels in the evening, much worse, that's why I travel all the way home every night and drive all the way back in the morning.'

'But everyone looks…you know…so important.'

'Ha, self-importance August. C'mon, I'll take you to a decent Company we'll get ourselves a free lunch.' As they were leaving the coffee bar, they passed a table with four blokes around it, the loudest, facing them touched Sammy's arm and said, 'Will you marry me?'

Sammy just quickly said 'No.' then turned to August and said, 'See what I mean.'

August followed Sammy down to the other end of the long hall and on to a large stand with some models of machines on it. A smart man of about forty gushed toward them. 'Sammy da.a.rling,' he said kissing her on the cheek.

'Roger, I have bought you a present. This is Miss Jackson, the buyer from Ruban Co.'

August flushed at her introduction and felt at ease when Roger took her hand in both of his, it was a kind hand shake. 'Pleased to meet you, I won't be a minute, I'll get you a drink, white wine? Red?'

'Oh I daren't, not on an empty stomach.'

'Me neither Roger, I shall be driving later.'

'Would you ladies like some lunch?'

Both ladies smiled and Roger spun around like a dancer and minced his way over to a door marked 'Private' He went through the door and reappeared within seconds waving them over. August liked Rogers' pleasant smiley face. He had a moustache that was immaculately groomed as well were his eyebrows. He held the 'Private' door open for them, a wonderful aroma of cooking food met them. August was amazed that there was a miniature restaurant tucked away on the stand. Roger escorted them to the one out of four free tables. His voice was happy and plummy as if he were about to break into laughter all the time.

There was a small counter and kitchen, where two women were working like bees wings cooking meals. Before she knew it August was being wined and dined and talking business with two total strangers who treated her like 'a somebody'. She felt like she was with friends.

CHAPTER TWENTY SIX

Roger made August feel welcomed. Sammy was so laid back and honest, she gave August the confidence to talk. There was not a moments' pause. August joined in, giving a good account of herself, even she was surprised at how much she knew and understood. Every word that was said about this business over that small table, August drank it in. The graphic design companies, the cowboys', who was spending money, who was not. Which company employed the biggest wanker. August thought Ruban Co. could be well up in the running for that title. August was fascinated. She had always thought that if you found the very heart of a maze, there should be a prize, and August reckoned she had got there.

After lunch, Sammy left August with Roger and he gave her his undivided attention, and imparted a great deal of knowledge. Not only did he know what he was talking about, he showed the sort of passion for the machinery, like Fred, Reg and herself had.

'Now this little baby,' Roger said, patting a model. 'This may look Neanderthal darling, but I don't give a flying fanny what anyone else says, this little girl is so reliable and efficient, and at nearly half the price of the pretty things they're flogging over there.'

August could have listened to his patter all day long, he gave her facts and figures, explained the data in a clear reliable manner. She didn't leave his 'Northern Box' stand until two thirty. He kissed her sweetly on the cheek as they parted company, and she thought how lovely he was. If he hadn't been so obviously gay, she could have fallen for him.

She set off in search of the other two companies with much more confidence. She received the same dismissive air on the next stand as she had done earlier, but it didn't bother her this time. When the chap on that stand jabbed a handful of leaflets toward her and said. 'Take these, I'm sure you'll find them really interesting.' August took them, and with a set face, looked him straight in the eye and said, 'well thank you for all your help, maybe, I will try and find time in my busy schedule to read them.'

The man looked stunned and offered her his card. 'Oh no thank you,' she said, 'I think I have enough to read don't you?' and with that she left him stood there holding his own card.

Trudging around the outer run of the hall, she passed what appeared to be a pub. The smoke filled room was an extension of the perimeter aisle, partly separated by floor to ceiling glass panels. August spotted Don Holland perched on a stool at the bar. His tie was askew and his cheeks looked like ripe plums. He was talking to a woman swaying at the side of him. She had a heap of frizzy carrot coloured hair, and as she turned to face her boss, August could see she was showing more bust than could ever have been left in her bra. Huge pendulum earrings swung either side of a heavily made up face.

August watched bemused as the woman walked her fingers up the front of Don Holland's shirt and playfully tugged his tie. Then to August's astonishment, he planted a hairy hand on the woman's behind. 'Well, Sammy was right', she whispered, and trudged onward.

She couldn't resist nipping into the graphics section, where she could have spent a whole day just learning where the whole process began, on the drawing board. It was like viewing a technical art gallery. The designers displayed their arty talents, and the suppliers showed off their art materials. It was on one of these stands that she bumped into Sammy again, who loaded her up with a carrier bag of free samples. Pens, colour markers, note pads and stencils. 'Have these,' Sammy said, 'We'll be clearing away the stand in half an hour.'

'Why is that?'

'It's the end of the show, the last day.'

'Oh crickey, I'd better shoot off then, I have one more company to find.'

'Well August Jackson, remember what I told you.'

August thanked Sammy all over again and set off to find what was the largest stand in the hall. There, four chaps grouped together, laughing loudly and drinking wine out of plastic tumblers. The name on the card was Colin Crosby. And she, against her will approached the mob to find which one he was. It was the most drunk out of all of them. 'Aah ha ha, now then,' his pink face announced, 'I'm afraid I won't be able to give you my expertise, as I won't be covering that area for the next few months.' He then winked at the others. 'It will be my colleague who is our new special agent.' The other chaps found this statement amusing, and Colin Crosby called to a young man stacking catalogues into neat piles. 'Hey double o seven, here's a special mission for you.' All four blokes found this especially funny.

August was pleased to leave their company and walked toward the dark haired chap that had turned in response. Colin called over,' Don't forget, you're licensed to thrill.' And behind her she heard the mob guffaw. August was getting annoyed, especially when the young man blushed at the last statement. She introduced herself and this lovely square jawed, dimpled chinned, blue eyed shy young man firmly shook her hand. She decided there and then that she wanted to bear his children.

He retrieved his hand and in a surprisingly deep voice said. 'Can I be of service to you?'

August couldn't say what was really in her thoughts at that moment, but just asked for the same information as before. While he was putting together some brochures, she asked him what the other blokes were making jibes at.

'Oh that, just ignore them, they're just letting their hair down we pack up today.'

'Yes, I know, but what's with the double o seven business?'

'My card,' he said handing her the explanation, 'My parents had a strange sense of humour I think.'

August smiled as she read the small business card. 'James Blonde.'

He shrugged and said. 'At least you won't forget my name.'

'Never.' She said as she slipped the card into her handbag.

At twenty five minutes past three, August wandered around the stand where she had to meet Don Holland. She stood for about ten minutes before someone approached her.

'Can I help you?' a young man asked.

'Oh no thanks, I'm just waiting for my boss. I have to meet him here at half past.'

'You must be Miss Jepson.'

'Jackson,' she corrected.

'Would you be waiting for Mr Holland of Ruban Co.?'

'Yes, that's him.'

'He left a message for you, he said to tell you that he had met up with a business colleague, and had to stay over, and for you to take the train home.'

August nearly dropped her bags. 'He said what? take a train, wonderful! I don't suppose this business colleague had fizzy orange hair and had her boobs spilling out?'

The weak upside down smile from the messenger said it all, and August rushed off to see if she could catch Don Holland. Her coat was in his car and she had no money for the train fare home. When she reached the right car park, there was no Mercedes, just a dark oblong shape in the frosted tarmac. 'You Bastard,' August spat, 'I'll get you too!' Without thinking, she caught a now empty bus back to the main entrance. Her feet were now banging sore and the icy cold easily found its' way through her cardigan and flimsy blouse. She shivered and cursed at the same time, she was pissed off mad.

The only thing she could think to do was to try and find Sammy or Roger. Everybody was rushing in the opposite direction. Someone stopped in front of her, a rather wide bloke, and she side stepped to get around him, and he side stepped with her. She had no patience left and went to shoulder her way past, he grabbed her. August looked up to a face she had seen before, but in her fury couldn't place him. Her face was one big frown. 'Do you mind?' she snapped.

'It is August isn't it?'

She stopped pushing and he let go.

'I thought I'd seen you in there,' he said.

Her head tipped to one side, she still couldn't place him, her eyes were questioning.

'You've forgotten me already…it's Graham. Graham Topps, your new rep.'

CHAPTER TWENTY SEVEN

August was so pleased to get home and thanked God for Graham, she could have hugged him for being there. He was good to talk to as well, and even offered to loan her the money to buy the boots she needed.

August tumbled that around in her mind. She desperately needed to establish for herself some credence. Loathing the fact that she had lost all credibility with the bank, she felt she had lost part of her soul. The thing her Mum used to strive for, to be above poverty, to have respect. The respect part that makes you feel wholesome. Even when she reflected on the good parts of the day, she knew that she had this dark secret that made her feel not as good as anybody else.

So she decided to work out, how to get back her credibility. If she carried on her frugal way of life and kept the extra jobs, she would be able to pay Graham back the money for the boots almost straight away and then gain trust from him. She was overall pleased, and awarded herself an evening off, building up the fire with logs, and swathing herself for a comfy evening of newspaper reading.

August filched out the latest newspaper she had, it was Wednesday's 'Evening Post', and set out to read it from front to back. When she read the obituaries, a prickly heat washed over her skin turning it to hen flesh.

'Jesus Christ!' She was staring at a picture of Mr Cruickshank. She read the column.

Joseph Arnold Cruickshank passed away suddenly Monday 7th November.

'Monday!' she shouted and physically shivered. 'The funeral,' she read aloud, 'will be held on F.Friday .. Jesus.. Oh Jesus Christ… I bloody well saw you!' She looked at the picture again, surely she must be mistaken. Her goose bumps rose again. August slapped the newspaper down and pulled the sleeping bag and duvet up under her chin. She stared into the fire recalling the visit that morning. 'Oh my God.. it wasn't really him, he was already dead. Shit! It was his ghost!' She remembered what he had said that morning.'I have Karen's address now.'

August rubbed her face. 'Holy shit, it was his chuffin' ghost, I've seen a ghost! But he can't be gone?' she said not wanting to believe, and stared into the fire and the flames blurred as she allowed herself to cry.

Graham Topps kissed his wife on the cheek and apologised for being late.

'As if I'm not used to it.' Pam said.

'You will never guess why though, what's for dinner?'

'Steak, do you want salad with it or chips?'

'Both, but we might not be having much more steak.'

'And why is that?'

Graham slid his jacket off and his tie. 'Well the reason for me being late..I had to give one of the girls from work a lift.'

'Oh yes,' Pam said suspiciously and smacked his thieving hand from the salad bowl. 'Ouch, I'm starving.'

'You're late. You'll wait.'

'But let me tell you why, this girl, August.'

'August, is that her name?'

'Yep…she'd been taken to the trade show by the M.D. today, and then the bastard had dumped her, without any money, just left her to find her own way back.'

'She should have asked him for some money.'

'Poor little bugger didn't have a chance, she went to meet him at an arranged place and he'd left a message, like' find your own way home' .and he took off with her coat that she'd left in his car! Can you believe it?'

'So..you came to the rescue did you?.. pretty is she?'

'No not really,' he said and laughed. 'Well she's not ugly, I suppose she could be quite attractive, if she had her hair done, and lost some weight.'

'Ha, look who's talking.'

Graham slapped his own guts, trying unsuccessfully to hold his stomach in. Pam gave him one of those resigned looks and turned the huge slab of red meat over and a loud hiss made him release his flab.

'Smells good,' he said, 'but I tell you, I don't think my moving to Ruban Co. was a good idea.'

'Oh Graham, don't say they're in trouble?'

'I'm not quite sure, August was telling me that Don Holland had just put all the rents up in the building and all the tenants were leaving.'

'So, surely that's nothing to do with this boxing trade, and he can always rent spaces to other companies.'

'Yeah, I suppose you're right.'

August slept with the light on all night, Cruickshank had really spooked her. Despite having suffered weird dreams, her first thoughts on waking, was to visit Cruickshank's grave. She still needed to see for herself some kind of proof, not only so she could reckon with seeing things that were not really there, but also to counter her grief.

August leaned against the green painted railings of the cemetery, and cursed Don Holland for having her warm coat. She watched the half dozen people, mainly elderly ladies tending the graves of their loved ones. Bending, kneeling, arranging flowers that never will be seen, or the fragrance smelled by the ones for whom they were for. August shivered again as she remembered Mr Cruickshank's visit. 'Maybe they do see them.' She whispered, as she made her way up the central path, washed pebbles crunching under foot. At the top of the graveyard, there were two new graves heaped with fresh wreaths, and she guessed, one of them had to be Mr Cruickshank. August decided to make a detour down a soft grass aisle that led straight toward a clump of rhododendron shrubs. A huge branch of cedar stretched a flat canopy over a garden wall and cut out the weak November sun. In this sheltered cove, where the tumbled stone wall grew fat with moss, there stood two lichen scarred headstones, of the darkest dampest green. The sunken bellied plots still crusted with frost, belonged to a husband and wife who must have chosen this spot together, to be side by side forever.

'I wonder if you knew how cold a plot this would be when you chose it.' August thought, 'well I suppose you can't feel the cold now.'

August thought that it was easier to realise proper that her Mum had gone, more so because she had been cremated. There was no life size patch of earth entombing a box of crumbling features. Just a rose bush, planted over her Mum's ashes. It could have been sherbet or cosmic dust, but it wasn't a decaying body. In the middle of the cemetery, the headstones were cleaner and their dates more recent. The latest section, the headstones were fashioned mainly in shiny black speckled granite, with gold inlaid letters collectively adoring and cherishing and not forgetting loved ones. It was at the end of this aisle that the two floral mounds cloaked the new turned sod.

JOSEPH ARNOLD CRUICKSHANK
LEAVES LOVING WIFE AND SON
TO JOIN LOVING DAUGHTER
KAREN IN EVERLASTING SLEEP.

CHAPTER TWENTY EIGHT

Robert Simpson swore at the breakfast in front of him. It was bad enough he had to cook for himself, but the sight of undercooked egg wobbling like warm snot on black cinders. 'I bet that bitch is alright, Mummies little helpers will see to that! In fact I think I'll pay them a visit. Yes, I'll go over, check the old dear out. See how close I am to becoming wealthy.' Robert was seething out loud, and his fist thudded into the yellow dome and poached slime shot across his sweater, suckling into the cabled wool.

Alicia struggled into her jodhpurs, Nancy's cooking was certainly taking its' toll. She found her hacking jacket exactly where she had last hung it six months ago. She thought how strange it was to have clothes deposited at several addresses. She inwardly smiled at the change in fashion and the person she became. Downstairs her Mother was taking breakfast in the drawing room, in front of a roaring fire that Tom had been stoking since six this morning. It was now eight thirty and her Mother sat there immaculate, her pewter silver hair gathered and pinned into a neat French roll at the back. Her delicate face dusted with powder and a light frost of blue eye shadow matched her eyes. A newspaper lay on her lap, keeping croissant crumbs from her tweed skirt.

'Morning Mother.'

'Good morning darling, the tea is still hot, would you like a croissant?'

Alicia conscious of her thigh hugging jodhpurs refused.

'You'll need a good breakfast if you're going riding, where are you riding by the way?'

'Caroline's.'

'Caroline Standish?'

'Yes, her brother's polo horses are there while he's on holiday.'

Her Mother clasped her hands together and Alicia clenched her teeth, she knew what was coming.

'Oh Gerald Standish. Alicia why couldn't you have married that young man, such good stock, and now look at you, I knew you wouldn't be happy.'

'Mothe.e.er, please don't say I told you so.'

'Well we did…I know you're not telling me all dear, but something is wrong, otherwise you wouldn't be here.'

A light knock on the door preceded Nancy. Nancy was smiling, she was always smiling. She was always busy. She cleaned, she washed linen, baked, cooked and went shopping. 'Tom would like to know if the fire is to be made up yet, and I want to know if Miss Alicia would like crispy smoked bacon, scrambled eggs and grilled cherry tomatoes for breakfast?' Alicia playfully collapsed into a chair, wishing Nancy wouldn't make it sound so nice.

'Tell Tom to leave the fire, I'm popping out, so if you could ask him to warm the Rover up please.'

Nancy looked at Alicia, waiting for her reply.

'I'll settle for a slice of toast please.'

'Would you like a poached egg on it?'

'Oh I give in. I'll come and eat it in the kitchen if that's alright Nancy.'

'Of course, love to have you with us, five minutes.' She smiled and hummed her way back through the chilly hallway. Her sandals clip clapped along the cold stone slabs. She was happy to cook for someone, especially Alicia, she was so appreciative like her Mother. Not like that husband of hers. Tom and Nancy had been more disappointed than Alicia's parents when the marriage was announced. They both saw the other side of Robert. The pernicious rude youth who spoke at them like underdogs when no one else was around. Nancy knew they were servants, but the family had always treated them with respect.

Alicia made to follow Nancy before her Mother picked up on the discussion of her marriage.

'Alicia dear, why don't you stay a little longer?'

'I can't, you know I have my work.'

'Alicia, you don't have to work at all.'

'Oh yes I do, because I want to, anyway why are you still lumbering around in that old massive coupe'? Daddy bought you that little Metro. I bet you haven't put a thousand miles on the clock.'

'That old coupe' has class, and leather upholstery, the Queen drove one you know. Anyway young lady, don't change the subject, at least stay another few days.'

Alicia sighed, it was so tempting. 'Mother I am going home as soon as I get back from riding.'

'Oh dear, and there is so much I need to talk to you about.'

'But I've been here a week, and tonight you have your bridge clan to keep you company.'

'Alicia, I do wish you wouldn't refer to them as a clan, they are highly respected ladies.'

'I'd better go and get my poached egg, don't want to upset Nancy.'

'Wait. If you won't stay longer, I would like to speak to you before you go, I'm off to see Bradley in a moment.'

'What has the solicitor got to do with me staying?'

'We're having a private meeting to discuss turning the estate over to you now.'

'Now!' Alicia said sitting down again. 'Why now?'

'I know it's sudden, but Bradley and I think it would be a good idea to reduce the capital gains tax.'

'Oh my God, you're not ill are you?' Alicia was on her feet again, but her Mother laughed and waved away her concern. 'I am as fit as the coupe' dear, but one never knows.'

'But you're only fifty six!'

'Your Father was only sixty one!'

Alicia glanced at the photograph of him on the mantel piece and a lump grazed her throat inside. Her Mother continued. 'There is this damn seven year after death term to recognise. So, I am going to discuss the matter privately, but I don't want to make any arrangements if…if your marriage is on loose footings.' She looked at her daughter who was still staring at the photograph. 'We'll talk later,' Alicia said and left the room.

The telephone rang and echoed shrill in the shamelessly baron hall. Nancy clip clapped her way to answer it. Before she had finished confirming the number, Robert butted in.

'Is my wife there?'

'If you mean Miss Alicia, she's..'

'Of course I mean her, and it's Mrs Simpson, remember! how many wives do you think I have?'

Nancy had the urge to spit into the mouthpiece but didn't, she would only have to clean it anyway.

'Well woman, is she there?'

'I was about to say that Miss Alicia is not back from riding yet.'

Robert tutted loudly and Nancy pulled a face.

'Will she be back for dinner?'

'Miss Alicia informed me that she would not be staying for dinner, but will be returning home.'

This took Robert by surprise and enquired about the patient.

'There is no patient.' Nancy was quite sharp.

'You mean..she's dead?'

Nancy thought he had gone quite mad, especially as the gravity of the words didn't match the song in his voice.

'Who's dead?'

'Alicia's Mother, she's ill isn't she?'

'Oooh!' Nancy growled, 'I'll Miss Alicia you rang when she gets in.'

Robert listened to the buzz of the empty line when Nancy put the phone down. If his Mother in law wasn't sick, he may have to hatch a plot to make her ill, he thought.

Alicia didn't bother to phone Robert, but reluctantly set off in his direction. She sang along to the music and through habit went to tap her ringed finger against the steering wheel and remembered she had taken her wedding band off as she set off for her house, it wasn't so much home. It was a decision she had been shying away from, but hadn't completely known why. She didn't love Robert, but then again who would welcome the upset of a divorce, but then, why prolong the agony. It was her Mother who had jolted her to make the decision, and she was right.

Alicia had always relied on her Mother to do that, they understood each other. It was like going to the dentist as a child. Alicia would suffer toothache, until her Mother made the appointment and pushed her through the door. She remembered her Mother's words, 'what is the point of carrying on with a marriage of broken arches, you have nothing to build on. If he's been unfaithful Alicia, he does not get paid half of your Father's hard earned wealth.'

She was definitely right, and she thought of how well off Robert would be for an adulterer. She reckoned she would give him the house and everything in it. It should be quite tidy, she began to sing again. The lit clock on the dashboard read 6.10. and she was beginning to feel hungry. That was Nancy's fault for charging her metabolism, she had never eaten so much and still have an appetite. Still, all the exercise she had kept up, the riding, the karate, jogging around the huge garden every morning had helped burn it off.

Driving along Hyland Way, she stopped singing as her headlights picked up Robert's car parked in front of the garage. A feeling of gloom and dread swam through her, and goose bumps peppered her arms as she pulled up behind his car. With the music off and the engine stopped, it was so quiet. She slumped and closed her eyes. 'You have got to do it,' she whispered, 'he's got nothing to lose.'

Her thoughts were muddled with anxiety.' Why had she married him in the first place? Had she ever loved him?' Well if there was any love there, Robert had destroyed it. Even the dregs of decent memories were clouded with sediment. Alicia didn't think she liked him anymore.

Robert was nursing a gin and tonic, and studying a Chinese take away menu when she walked in. Alicia was repulsed by his appearance. His unshaven face looked dirty. Greasy hair criss crossed in every direction, and it was very obvious it wasn't his first drink. A yellow scab of dried egg yolk shone leather like in the weave of his Aran sweater.

'Ahh you're back. I was just about to order some Chinese, want some?'

Alicia was about to shake her head, somehow the thought of dining with him had chased away her hunger. Then she thought this was a good vehicle as any to travel toward a conversation she had to make. 'Yes,,order me a chicken foo yung.'

CHAPTER TWENTY NINE

Robert stumbled to the phone in the lounge. Alicia surveyed the kitchen, it didn't look as if it had been in use much, but the evidence of when it was, was still there. A spirographic pattern of mug rings adorned the table top, and all around the waste bin and the sink lay dirty turds of rice. Robert appeared. 'I don't suppose you mind nipping for it,,only I've had a drink.

Alicia nodded and examined the past weeks' mail.

'There's nothing much,' Robert said waving his glass. 'do you want a drink?'

Alicia shook her head, Robert tutted and said, 'Not very talkative are we?'

'Sorry, I was miles away.'

'You have been lit... literally, for a week. I mean..how is your Mother?'

'Fine Robert, she's fine.'

'I thought she might be ill or something?'

'Whatever gave you that idea?'

'We..ell I just thought that when you disappeared for a week, there was something drastically wrong.'

There were some pregnant moments of silence as Alicia remembered why she had upped and gone. Robert unsteadily plonked himself down at the table, spilling the rest of his drink, which lifted the coffee circles into a dirty puddle, which found his dry sleeves.

'I mean,' he went on, 'One minute we are about to have lunch together, the ..the next.. you've disappeared.'

Alicia looked at him now, his tone was beginning to match the coarseness of his appearance. She didn't want things to turn that ugly.

'Yes. I'm sorry about that, Mother was ill, a touch of flu I think, but she's fine now.'

She thought Robert mumbled something into his empty glass, but ignored it. 'Anyway, I'm back and we are having dinner together, in fact I had better go and fetch it, which Chinese is it?'

Robert held out a ten pound note. 'Fortune House on Gorman Street, I'm paying, I err was buying lunch..remember?'

Alicia plucked the money from his hand, not wanting their flesh to touch. She snatched up her car keys wanting to get away from him.

'Bitch!' Robert whispered as the door closed, then he spied Alicia's handbag. As soon as he heard her car pull away, he grabbed it. Inside, folded papers clipped together with a hand written note, signed Bradley.

'Bradley! that's the family solicitor,' he was euphoric in his discovery. He had to force his drunken eyes to focus, picking up words to the effect that Alicia had an early inheritance, he became giddy. He did a little unstable dance and sang, 'Yes oh yes, she's got it. I am so fucking rich, yee..e.es.' He was nearly wetting himself putting the papers back, making sure they were as he had found them.

August pulled her first pint of the evening. That one always smelled strong. The smell would wane as the evening wore on, the glasses charged, over and over, and a veil of smoke hung three feet from the ceiling. By nine o' clock, 'The Crown' was packed solid and August was tempted to take off her pinching shoes. Geoff stood at the pump next to her. 'Saw that fella of yours the other day.' He said, not taking his eyes off the pint he was pulling.

'What fella?'

'That boyfriend you were lookin' for.'

'Shaun?'

'Big bloke, short hair..was in 'ere.. ooh, be Thursday lunchtime, trying to sell somebody a calculator.'

'Sounds like him,' she seethed, 'did you speak to him?'

Geoff shook his head, not taking his eyes off the steady head of the pint he was perfecting. 'One of the girls served him.'

'He doesn't know I work here then?'

'Don't think so Lass.'

August carried on serving, but for the rest of the evening, kept an eye on the door, just in case he came in. Her distraction apart from punters was Stella, introducing her latest boyfriend Spud. Spud was clad in metal studded black leather, had untidy long dark hair and a chain tattooed on his neck.

'What do you think?' Stella asked, 'isn't he macho?'

August sucked air between her teeth. 'You can say that again Stella, he looks a bit wild.'

Stella smiled and bent forwards to August's ear as if to share a great confidence. 'A big softy,' she whispered, 'Aren't looks deceiving, now, take that blonde Robert...perfect gentleman you would have thought,'

August couldn't wait, her eyes widened and she encouraged Stella to spill the details.

'Huh..gentleman..gentleman!..an animal more like.. a bastard.'

August's eyes were like wagon wheels, and she wanted to laugh but didn't, Stella was on a roll. 'He was,' she continued, so bloody rough..well I never want to see him again, he's an animal!'

At the take away, Alicia sat on a box seat that was far too high. The smell and hiss of Chinese cooking made her feel more hungry. The meal wasn't ready and she stared at the television hung on a wall above the counter. She wasn't really watching the programme, but thinking about what her Mother had discussed with her. There was a lot to think about before she signed the agreement. Still she had the draught to read through. It was then she realised she had left her handbag with the draft in that she had to read through. She didn't want Robert to know anything about it, or at least until she had made her mind up about him.

Robert was busy shaving, he had showered in record time and wanted to sober up as much as he could before Alicia returned. He slapped expensive after shave all over himself and put on a clean white shirt and pulled on some pale grey trousers.

Alicia rushed through the door and was relieved to see the handbag where she had left it and no Robert. She heard him padding downstairs and was surprised to see him fresh and smart. Alicia zipped the handbag into her holdall. Robert smirked to himself, then he watched her bend over the table to wipe it. Her riding breeches were tight on her slender thighs and small bottom and stretched high into her crotch. He fancied taking her there and then, she would be unprepared and dry and he could imagine her cry out in pain. A bulge formed in his trousers and he was tempted to carry it through, then the bulge in the holdall caught his attention and he knew he would jeopardise it's rich contents. 'I'll get the plates.' he offered, 'I must say it will be nice to sit down and share a meal together.'

Alicia nodded in agreement, but didn't mean it. Robert continued talking as they each served themselves. 'We ought to do this more often, spend a little time together, don't you think?'

Alicia filled her mouth with food so she didn't have to answer out loud, and slightly nodded again.

'You're hair looks nice,' he said. Alicia was pleased that the change had worked. More blonde highlights and a soft feather cut. She smiled at the compliment, but didn't know if she was comfortable with it, coming from him.

'That's better,' he said, 'you should smile more often, it's ages since I saw those dimples.'

Alicia wanted to say, 'that's because you've been a complete and utter bastard,' but didn't. If she had to live with him for a while, she preferred him like this. He rested his fork on his food, and his chin on a cradle of fingers. He stared at his wife who was preoccupied with her meal rather than his glowing blue eyes that he used on a regular basis to come on to the female kind. 'Alicia,' he spoke soberly now, 'Alicia,' he repeated and she gave in and glanced at him. 'Yes Robert.'

'I've been thinking…maybe we should get away from here, take a holiday together, let's..let's go skiing.. or if you want the sun, let's do Florida for Christmas.'

Alicia half smiled again and Robert went on, excited like a child. 'We could go to Bali..it's warm there at Christmas, ..or..what about an African Safari?, that would be different..no no wait..a cruise down the Nile.'

Alicia laughed a little and said, 'A little expensive don't you think?'

Robert rammed a whole pork ball into his mouth to stop himself from shouting, he would normally lose his temper when Alicia came up short on money. His temperament was still a little gin infused. 'Cunning bitch,' He thought, 'doesn't want me to know.' 'I'll take out a loan,' he said, quite flippant.

Alicia couldn't quite believe what she was hearing.

'We could go next week, I've got holidays owing, I'm sure you could arrange yours.' He looked at her for an answer. 'Well,' he continued, 'what do you think? a nice log cabin in the Swiss Alps...twin beds, even separate rooms if you like.'

Alicia swallowed hard, she didn't know her answer, so just said, 'I'll think about it.'

'Good girl.'

That night, knowing that the garlic would mask his boozy breath, Robert crept into Alicia's bed, and she allowed the access to mute her frustration. Robert didn't take long before he was through, he laid on his back and taken with deep sleep. Alicia didn't mind, at least she'd made it this time, and she put that down to a long sitting trot on neglected parts that had been aching for attention. She didn't need any arousing, which was just as well, as Robert's style was more likened to rape than sex. It was definitely sex, not making love. She went to sleep, pondering the difference. She had always thought that for sex, two people weren't necessarily required, but, for love making it had to be a couple. What she had just experienced could have been achieved by herself, Robert had just been a labour saving device. Maybe, she thought, that's why it got the nick name 'tool'.

CHAPTER THIRTY

Don Holland sat in his burgundy leather wing chair, smoking his breakfast cigar and studied the busty girl on display in the Sunday paper. The phone started up a double barrelled ring. 'Don Holland speaking.'

'Hello Don, it's Henry. Wondered if you fancied a round of golf this lunchtime?'

'In this weather! You must be mad old chap.'

'Alright then, how about a few rounds in the club bar?'

'Sounds a lot more agreeable, oh by the way Henry, did you manage to find anyone interested in buying the Bentley?, I'm sick of seeing it in the garage, I hate money just tied up you know?'

'What you could do with, is a rich widow.'

'Ha ha, you could say that again old boy.'

'Well actually Don, you might be able to kill two birds with one stone. Priscilla and I are having some supper guests over this evening and I think one such guest might fit the bill.'

'Hmm, tell me more,' Don Holland rolled his fat cigar in his teeth and stroked his goatee beard.

'Well,' said Henry,' do you want to come out for a lunchtime round, or supper?'

'Both of course, you can tell me more about this rich widow before I meet her.'

Alicia was up early and left Robert to sleep with his own bad breath. She took the draft of the agreement into the bath with her, where she read through it carefully. Yes, she agreed her Mother would stay in the house for however long she wanted or until she died. She agreed that Tom and Nancy upon their chosen retirement, could stay in their tied bungalow until they passed on. Alicia smiled now as she remembered their faces yesterday, when her Mother had given them the little red Metro. Nancy had hugged them and Tom's voice had warbled with emotion as he said thank you. Alicia had to swallow a lump in her throat as tears made the long trip around Nancy's cheeks. She didn't agree with her Mother retaining fifty thousand pounds and made a mental note to change it to one hundred thousand. Alicia jumped then as the door shuddered on it's lock.

'Alicia I need to pee.'

'You'll have to use the down stairs, I'm in the bath.'

She heard a groan and then a muffled clatter as Robert descended the stairs. Alicia immediately got out of the bath and hid the papers under the padded jacket on the hot water cylinder.

When they met up in the kitchen, Robert was looking drawn, and was making a mess of making coffee. He was whimpering for sympathy, and although Alicia reminded him it was a self-inflicted illness, she did make him breakfast. It was the first decent breakfast he'd had in weeks. He felt much better after eating and went upstairs to shower. He reflected on their evening together. He had made progress he thought, she had actually allowed him into her bed, better not push it though he cautioned himself. Robert stood and let the water rinse away his dirge and the soap as he tried to remember what the papers had said. He could recall thinking what a greedy bitch the old lady was, keeping fifty thousand, and he smirked at the part saying that the housekeepers could live in the tied bungalow. 'Not a bloody chance', he thought, 'That place would be great for a private party or two or three, a games room, bar, perfect. It would be more practical for his needs to have a nymphomaniac au-pair living there.'

August snuggled back into her sleeping bag, pulling the duvet over her and a cup of coffee at hand. She had got up, made the fire, pumped some more air into the ever deflating mattress, and tried to enjoy not being at work. It wasn't a total day off, she still had the shift behind the bar that evening. She wasn't too bothered as there now may be a chance of Shaun walking in. The sour seeds of anger were spawning greater inside her and the need for vengeance was immense. She really didn't know what she could do if he walked in. if he spotted her first, he would escape before she could get the police there. Even if he was caught, she probably couldn't prove enough to get him a good telling off. She needed to punish him though, he can't go and do this to someone else. If she clouted him, it wouldn't make much of an impression in such a mass of lard. The best she could do was to pull an ear off. Somehow she would have to humiliate him, he couldn't bear that. She wasn't very good at that though. August looked at the bare pale walls of the hovel and her thoughts turned to the painting. 'Where are you 'Bigshit bay? you are about the only thing that could brighten this place and my life!'

A tickle fizzed in her nostrils and her lungs snatched lumps of breath until a huge sneeze touched orgasm, and then blast, and another..and another.' Yes Don Holland thanks for the near hypothermia, you are another bastard, you'll get yours, you just better not have thrown my coat out!'

CHAPTER THIRTY ONE

Don Holland decided to drive the Bentley to Henry's, the engine needed turning over. It was so beautiful to drive and he felt so important behind the wheel. It had been a big mistake. He had bought it with money he had salted away from the rents and then not dared drive around in it, not because he felt guilty, but in case someone got suspicious of his burst of wealth.

His decision was to get rid of the Bentley, and with the fifty thousand he should get from the sale, buy a piece of property abroad. His money would be safely invested, and he would always have a bolt hole if the Inland Revenue ever got on to him.

He drove up Henry's broad driveway, he squeezed a finger between his Adam's apple and the top of his collar, he hated wearing a bow tie, but he wanted to make a good impression to this rich widow, Henry had told him about. He parked between an old Rover and a gleaming Bristol.

Henry took him directly to meet the widow. 'Brigitte, meet Don Holland, Don is into real estate aren't you old boy? I'll get you a drink Don.' Henry sneaked a wink to Don.

'Thank you, a small brandy I think.' The elegant lady in front of him half smiled, and Don thought that Henry had under sold her attractiveness.

'Real estate?' the lady asked politely.

'Err, umm, yes,' Don lied, 'I'm considering purchasing abroad actually.'

'Commercial?'

'Oh no, not just now just somewhere to use as a retreat, holiday retreat.'

'Very nice.' Brigitte smiled again.

Don didn't know how to follow so offered to get her a drink. Brigitte covered her glass with her hand, and he noticed the aggregate of diamonds on one of her rings.

'No thank you, I'm driving, 'she said with her plummy soft voice.

Don Holland seized the opportunity of cars in the conversation. 'I don't suppose that lovely Bristol out there is yours?'

'No, I still lumber around in the old Rover coupe', much to my daughters chagrin.'

Don forced a polite titter into his brandy. 'Maybe you ought to change it then.'

'I know ..but well it's just that Peter, my late husband loved it so, and we went so many places in it together. Even when we bought the Rolls, we would go out in the Rover and have a picnic out in the country.'

'Do you still have the Rolls Royce?'

'No, I sold it after he passed, I regret it a little but it was his car, not mine.'

'Sometimes Brigitte, a change is needed,' he encouraged her.

'You're right of course, I do have lots of other things to remind me of him, like his paintings.'

'A bit of an artist was he?'

'Oh my word no, he was a collector, another of his many investments.'

Don Holland now had an overwhelming desire to know the measure of her wealth. He made light of his probing. 'Got a couple of Picassos' on the wall have we?'

'Only a couple of signed prints, Peter didn't care for modern art, his favourites were the 'Munnings'. He used to say, 'now Sir Alfred knows how to paint a horse.' She laughed at this memory, 'He once bought a portrait by Gainsborough, and then sold it within a year, he couldn't understand why he'd tied so much money in a painting of someone who wasn't related.'

Don Holland tittered along, he was stung because he understood how famously expensive a Gainsborough would be, but he had no idea about this Munnings chap, so ploughed on with his investigative discourse. 'How many Munnings do you have?'

'Just three now.'

'Err any of the impressionists?' Don was getting excited now and he could really have done with unbuttoning his collar.

'Peter loved the impressionists, especially Degas, but he mostly always maintained a ceiling price of forty thousand. He said more than that it would definitely have to be somewhere secure and that no one would see it regularly enough, and that was what art was all about.'

When Don Holland drove home that evening his bow tie hung bat like from his open shirt collar. He was happy that he had managed to secure a dinner date with the widow Brigitte for the following weekend. He wondered if she had really liked him. She had agreed to the dinner date, but then again had taken a little persuading.

He garaged the Bentley and thought how nice it would be to sell the car to Brigitte, then talk her into marriage and get it back again. This could be his lifeline, being as he would be losing the rent money income for a while. He chuckled at his own good fortune.

CHAPTER THIRTY TWO

Monday morning was freezing and August had dawdled too long in the cosy warmth of the sleeping bag. There was no duffle-coat to keep her warm on the way to work, so being as she was running late, she caught the bus. She managed to get a window seat and rubbed a clear porthole to see out. The bus was packed, most people sniffling and coughing, August made a mental note to scrub her hand, the window must have been misted up with germs. The bus route was different from the way she walked, taking the main roads lined with shops. As the bus crawled away from one of it's stops, August stared into the dark shop window of the 'Curios and Collectables'. She pushed her face flat to the porthole, there hanging in the gloom she swore she could see 'Bigshit bay'. August would walk back that way home to check.

The phone was ringing as she entered the office. She dashed to pick up. 'Ruban Co., how can I help you?'

'A bit out of breath aren't you?' a man's voice. August gave a little laugh she didn't know who it was.

'It's Graham…don't tell me you've forgotten me again?'

'How could I forget my knight in shining armour, hey thanks again, I don't know what I would have done without you.'

'It's ok, anyway that's what I'm ringing about, listen, I've got a mate who works at the railway, he's going to sort out a ticket stub so you can claim the fare, I'll get it to you tomorrow.'

'Can I do that?' August felt glad and guilty all at once.

'Look August, that bastard left you high and dry, what do you think he reaps in expenses that don't exist, more than you earn I shouldn't wonder…well?'

'Well, alright then.' She was convinced and Graham laughed. 'See it's easy. Now I'm spending the day in the office tomorrow, and at lunchtime I am going to take you out to eat, and on the way back, we are going to buy the boots you need, I'll lend you the money.'

'You can't do that!'

'Oh yes I can, I've just got my back holiday pay from my last firm.'

August didn't know what to say, and Jayne had just walked in, Graham was still waiting on the end of the line. 'Alright?' he asked

'Err, yeah.. yes please…thanks.'

She had just put the phone down when it rang again. 'Ruban Co. can I help you?'

'Hello, could I speak to Miss Jackson please?' It was a deep voice on the end of the phone and August was taken aback with the formality.

'Err..speaking.'

'This is James, James Blonde, we met at the trade fair, remember?'

A pink glow crept up August's cheeks and she sat down. 'Yes I remember.' She did so remember, she had a vivid picture of him. The long dark eye lashes, blue, grey eyes and the deep dimple in his chin. James cleared his throat and sounded nervous as he spoke. 'Would I be able to.. I mean could I make an appointment to see you?, did you manage to have a look at the brochures?'

'I haven't actually, but it's probably Mr Holland who you would have to see.'

'But I thought you were the buyer?'

'I am, I mean I was, but only to report back to Mr Holland, it was him that asked me to look at new machines.'

'Then I have the right person.'

'I suppose you have.' August felt quite giddy at the prospect of seeing him again.

'So, when can I make an appointment for?'

August had never had an appointment made to see her before and said awkwardly, 'I don't know, when are you free?'

'I'll tell you what shall we make it a lunch date tomorrow?'

'Oh I can't tomorrow, I'm out with Graham.'

'Ohh,' James sighed.

August noticed Jayne staring at her and she blushed to red. The deep voice went on. 'What about the day after then, Wednesday?'

August was so rinsed through with excitement. 'Yes, that's fine, I take twelve till one.'

'I'll pick you up at twelve then, Wednesday,'

August managed to get her jacket off at last and swanned across the office to hang it up.

'Well, well,' Jayne said, 'you're in demand.'

August didn't blush now, she decided, she liked all this attention.

Jayne's ears were burning for more information. 'Who's this Graham?'

'The new rep, Graham Topps.'

Jayne tutted, and August mocked her. 'It's not what you think!'

The face that Jayne pulled suggested disbelief.

'And if you're going to pull faces like that, I will not tell you the latest gossip.'

August would not tell Jayne a thing, and for one hour she pestered. August didn't break, her mind full of wonderful daydreams. She found herself writing James Blonde all over her scrap pad. She was reliving their meeting and then she remembered the lousy bits that followed, and thought about her missing coat. Mrs Charlton bustled in and August ripped off the top page of scrap and binned it.

'Morning Mrs Charlton, is Mr Holland in yet?'

'He is, but he's expecting someone any minute. Is it something I can help you with?'

'It was just that I left my coat in his car after the exhibition and I really need to get it back.'

Patricia Charlton was silent for a moment wondering why August Jackson's coat would be in the M.D.'s car.

'I didn't actually leave it, he left me.'

Both Jayne and Mrs Charlton stared at her now, waiting for more information.

'I was supposed to meet him at a certain stand at half past three, and well, he got off, I mean he got tied up with a business colleague and left a message for me to find my way home.'

Jayne and Mrs Charlton both tutted at the same time.

'My coat was in his car, hopefully it still is.'

'Oh my dear,' Patricia Charlton frowned, 'you must have been perished.'

'I was until I got home, had to fork out for a train though.' She bit her lip, she hated lying. Mrs Charlton was shaking her head, realising what a total shit Don Holland really was. 'You must give me your ticket, and I'll make sure you get reimbursed.'

'Oh, I forgot it today, I'll give it to you tomorrow, I do need my coat today though.'

'I'll get his car keys.'

Jayne could hardly contain herself and begged August to tell her more.

When Mrs Charlton placed the car keys on August's desk, she didn't hesitate, leaving Jayne craving for gossip. This time when August stepped out in the cold, she hardly felt it. As she place the key in the lock, she couldn't see her coat through the window, only a black briefcase yawning open, it's chrome catches hanging like fangs.

A turn of the key and all four door locks clunked open. August opened a rear door, and there on the floor was her scrunched up beige duffle-coat. She leaned over to retrieve it and caught the lolling jaw of the briefcase, and it slid from the seat, she grabbed at it. Some papers escaped and she picked them up. As she gathered them together, she recognised some of the names in Don Holland's hand writing. They were all the company names that rented the other parts of the building. There was a cheque clipped to a letter. It was from the design company on the top floor, made out to Don Holland. The cheque was for seven hundred pounds.

A sudden feeling of guilt swept over her and she put the papers back in the case. She noticed some photographs of property stuck to typed sheets labelled with prices. One was a small farmhouse in France. 'One, an apartment in an exclusive development in the southern region'. There were several sheets featuring white painted villas in Costa Del everywhere.

August straightened out her coat and locked up the Mercedes. 'Some expenses.' she said to herself.

A dirty Vauxhall stood parked outside a travel agents' on the high street. Robert Simpson was inside making a collection of brochures. He leafed through them and asked someone what they had in available short notice flights. There was a lot of choice because of the time of year, and he loaded the front seat of his car. As he idled through the town traffic, he flicked at the pages wondering which one would be the easiest place to cover a fatal accident. Skiing seemed to be a good idea, but then again Alicia could ski a damn sight better than him.

August swanned through the rest of the day. It was the best she had felt for ages. At lunch time she treated herself to a couple of items of makeup on the strength that tomorrow she would get money for the train fare. Then, when Jayne told her that she had lost a fair amount of weight, August could have dusted the ceiling, she felt so good. Then again, she didn't know if the compliment was to gain access to gossip. August had noticed a considerable difference herself though, she did feel better for losing a few pounds, apart from she felt extremely tired, but that she guessed was due to the extra work she had took on. Thankfully Monday was a free evening, but she needed to iron some clothes, especially for her lunch dates.

August had just finished her ironing when she remembered the painting. 'Oh bugger I forgot to check on 'Bigshit bay', I must go that way tomorrow. She sang as she tidied the hovel. She sang as she bathed, and she hummed as she drifted into sleep.

CHAPTER THIRTY THREE

Alicia had gone to bed early, she had, had enough of pictures of snow topped mountains, log cabins and lists of flight schedules. Robert had been relentless, until she had made a decision. She smiled into her pillow as she remembered the look on his face when she had pushed the brochures away and said, 'China. If I am going away on holiday, I would want to go to China.'

This had miffed Robert as he hadn't any brochures on China, didn't know if they could get a flight at short notice, and he knew it would be bloody expensive.

As he sat nursing a gin and tonic, he warmed to the idea, fancying that he would come across some old back street merchant who made potions. A poison that would be undetectable, a powder he could sprinkle on her muesli, or some tasteless drug to add to a drink. 'It would be worth the investment,' he smirked.

The case clock in Don Holland's study gonged once. He poured himself a large brandy and lit another cigar. He hadn't been sleeping well and paced the short run of the hearth. 'Damn Alfred Dickenson for retiring.' He spat out loud, taking a huge slug of his drink. 'Some bloody notice, two months, shit!' He poured a deep brandy, drank half of it and topped it up. 'Damn him, he isn't even sixty five yet, bloody accountant, paid him too much money..that's what!' He ranted to himself often as he had no one else around to tell. He dropped into the leather wing chair and drained his glass. He rubbed his forehead as if to remove the deep frown, then combed his beard with trembling fingers.

Alfred Dickenson was retiring his accountancy. There were no partners to pick up where he left off, no one to pass delicate information onto like, don't ask the Managing Director of Ruban Co. what happens to the rent monies from the three companies upstairs. Don't ask about the Bentley he drives up to the golf club.

Alfred Dickenson had never liked Don Holland. He inherited him as a client, when the previous M.D. had passed on. Old Mr Holland was so different from his son it was hard to believe they were really related. Alfred's sophism was to turn a blind eye and charge Don Holland a hefty fee, which he knew wouldn't be queried. He could only enjoy taking money from him. He had enjoyed the pained expression on Don Holland's face when he told him of his retirement plans. It had made up for all those years of scanning columns and columns of figures. The tedium, the boredom, the days and months of prodding calculator buttons. The minor tantrum that Holland had performed, made Alfred's working life complete.

Another brandy coloured the glass and Don Holland cursed again. 'I need another Alfred, bloody hell, if someone else.. God! I don't need anyone probing about, anyone straight and proper!' He harshly sucked on his fat cigar, inhaled and burnt the back of his throat, and doused it with brandy. He refilled his glass, emptying the decanter.

'How long could I get inside for a hundred and sixty thousand?' he swayed back to the chair and wondered where it had all gone. All he seemed to have out of it was the Bentley, a piece or two with antique value, a Rolex and seven grand in the safe. He had frittered most of it away, expensive meals, champagne, holidays and the best hotels. He'd had is fair share of costly prostitutes and private V.D. checks

'One hundred and sixty thousand pounds, gone..gone..gone' he whispered, 'I should think it will buy me a few years lock up that's for sure. Why did I buy that bloody car!. It's got to go!' He rambled on through a couple of glasses of bourbon and then slumped unconscious in his chair.

CHAPTER THIRTY FOUR

The hovel was bright with firelight soft crackling in the grate, she had made it up at five thirty that morning. There had been no dawdling, no wanting to cling to the inside of the sleeping bag, just the urge to make the most of today. When August returned from the chilly bathroom, the hovel was nice and warm. Her clothes were neatly pressed and aired. And she had found yet another skirt that fitted her properly. No stressed crease across the front no extreme knicker lines or guillotine waistline.

August was a few minutes early to work and spent the time applying a little makeup. She had never used much makeup and the bruised copper eye shadow she had chosen had to be applied cautiously. She didn't want to look like she had trod on a garden rake. It wasn't until she was applying the blusher that she realised that the hamster pouches had shrunk away. August looked at herself, she felt good for the first time and smiled at her own reflection, she was just about to have a conversation with herself, when the door swung open with the entrance of Mrs Charlton. 'Good morning August, my, my isn't it cold,' she paused taking a good look at August 'You look well today, have you been on a diet?'

'You could say that.'

'Yes, you certainly look a lot better than you have recently, got over that chesty cold?'

'I think so.' August smiled and smoothed her hands over her thinner but still wide hips.

The deep buttoned burgundy leather chair squeaked in Don Holland's ear as he jacked himself up against the bulge of the wing his head had been party to for the night. He moaned as he came to, his body hurt as it unbuckled. His head throbbed, a sickly drum pounded behind his bloodshot eyes. Tar lined lungs rattled and his guts gargled with acid. He rang Patricia Charlton to say, not to expect him in to the office that day, and then dragged his tortured body up the stairs and collapsed into bed.

Graham slipped the ticket stub onto August's desk while Jayne was hanging up her coat. As Jayne took her seat, she did a double take of August, she looked different. She stared at her. She didn't have much makeup on and yet she appeared so different. Right up until morning tea break Jayne observed August. When Hetty, the tea lady commented on how much weight August had lost, she dumbly realised the development.

At twelve o' clock, Graham silently signalled through the glass partition for August to be ready to go. Jayne pouted a wry smile when August and Graham left together. August smiled too, at Jayne's suspicion.

The sun had fought hard to thaw the frost and had won. The pavements were now dry. August steered them, at Grahams' request to the shoe shop. With the boots still firmly on her calves, Graham steered her to the closest pub with a hot food sign. August couldn't remember when her feet had felt this cosy, and as the fur lining cosseted her from the floor upwards, she relaxed in Graham's company. She found him very easy to talk to, but, didn't let on about her total predicament with the bank.

'Thanks Graham,' she said as he placed their drinks on the table.

'My pleasure.'

'For everything I mean, lending me the money, I'll pay you back as soon as I can.'

'You pay me back when you can, don't worry about it.'

'And thanks for saving me from the Trade show.. and for the ticket stub, and for lunch, for…'

'Hey I told you, it's my pleasure, you can be my mate.'

August laughed. 'your mate?'

'Yeah, I need a mate at work.'

'What about Robert Simpson?'

'What about Robert Simpson?'

'I just thought..you know..you chaps..would be mates.'

Graham leaned over the table, closing the gap between them. He looked serious for a moment, and then half whispered, 'The man is a prat.'

This made August giggle. 'We have a name for him in the office.'

'What might that be?'

'Slimy.'

'You're right!'

The smart young woman in the blue blazer studied the list in front of her, then without looking at Robert Simpson read out cost of ten days in China for two, and was pleased to inform him that there was a vacancy in two weeks' time. Robert felt the sweat dampen his armpits', but expert at playing the rich boy, managed to stammer, 'Is that all?' He smiled at her and said he would confirm a booking by the end of the week. Smiling back with her pen still hovering over the booking form, she said, 'I'm afraid we're not able to keep a short notice vacancy unless you pay a non-returnable fifty per cent deposit.'

The sweat had now wet Robert's shirt and it clung cold and clammy under his jacket. He leaned against the counter like he would casually use a bar. In reality, he wanted to scream at the woman, 'Fifty per cent!', but apart from not wanting to fracture his image, he knew the trigger on Alicia's gun was cocked. 'I'll take it.' He announced.

Alicia had spent half the morning preparing a dish for their evening meal, before setting off for work. She had placed the casserole in the oven and set the automatic timer. She felt fairly content as she sped along the now familiar route. Her black Golf pulled up outside a pair of tall timber gates that were in need of a coat of paint. After unlocking the padlock, she pushed the heavy gates open and drove into the puddle pocked yard. A brick warehouse of a building, much in need of mortar, made up part of a perimeter wall. Another building was of worn stone and might have been a barn at some time in it's life. Some Gerry builder had filled in the rotten framed windows with grey breeze blocks.

Both buildings had double doors which could have been made by the same person that had botched up the block making. Alicia un-padlocked both sets of doors. In one building, she garaged the Golf and from the other, she drove out a red BMW. The routine was so very familiar to Alicia now, but the feeling of freedom still had the same fresh unchained sensation. It was the sensation that made her feel she didn't need Robert in her life. He was the bumps in her new road, the toast crumbs in the bed, he was the pubic hair on the soap.

She would wait and see if he came up with this trip. If he could find a holiday in China at short notice and finance it, he must be trying to make amends.

The flat was cold and had the frowzy air that reminded her that it had been empty for a week. Alicia checked her diary, the appointment she had was one o' clock, not two as she had thought. 'Christ, I had better get a move on.' She said slamming the diary shut. Her portfolio was ready, and inside an hour, she had nearly completed her transition. 'Thank God for wigs,' she said fluffing out the long blonde tress, that corkscrewing about her collar. She checked her makeup and added a touch more lip liner. 'Well Darling,' she said to the mirror, 'you've certainly mastered the change, even I don't recognise you.'

As Alicia sped through town, she spotted August going into a pub accompanied by a large but smart fellow. They were laughing and she was pleased for her. Alicia decided she would call in and see her later, she liked August Jackson.

When August got home that night, she cursed for forgetting to check out the painting in the curio shop. She decided to grab something to eat and go to the cinema early. Then she could make the detour. She daydreamed as she made a fire. Her thoughts of the day stole away the misery of a cold hovel as she sipped her hot soup. James visited her heart as she did the washing up. She couldn't wait to see if she had found 'Bigshit bay' and raced off at ten minutes to six. She even forgot to lock the hovel door as she rushed out, halfway down the stairs, she realised, but decided there was nothing worth stealing anyway, apart from the rent money and that was well hidden, so she went on her way.

At five minutes to six, the red BMW pulled up outside the flats. Alicia reminded herself that the casserole would be cooked for seven, which would give her time to visit August Jackson. She quickly got changed and took off all her makeup. She went along the landing to the right where she found a shellac door. She knocked hard, waited and then knocked again. She tried the wobbly brass knob, the door was unlocked. It was very dark, and she found a light switch. She pulled a face at the naked stairs and peeling walls. 'August,' she called, 'August, it's me Ali.' Alicia slowly took the bare treads, keeping her sleeves away from the walls. She called again, focussing on the closed panelled door at the top. She knocked on that, still nothing. Worried that something might be wrong, Alicia tried that door. A deep orange glow greeted her and she quietly repeated August's name. Alicia found the light switch there and was shocked at what she lit up. She stood in silence and surveyed the pale blue room. A table with it's skeletal cooking facilities, the lone chair. A contraption of plastic that dangled like an intravenous drip to a small chipped basin caught her attention. On close examination, Alicia found that the rig was the only source of running water. She sat down on the chair and stared bewildered. The heap of bedding on the floor, a horizontal broom handle supporting hangers of clothes. The carrots on the table were so bendy she could have tied bows with them. There was a crackle in the fire grate, and a wisp of dead smoke left a log as it slumped into grey ash. It was then she shuddered, realising how cold it was. The question that bombarded her, was, why would August leave a comfortable flat to live in an awful place like this? Why was she living like this? Was she so poor? But she worked all the time. Who was the 'BASTARD', she had left reference to on the window? Her head swivelled from side to side, tears welled up in her eyes and she remembered the pyramid. August Jackson needed that money so bad. Alicia marched noisily across the bare floorboards, paused at the door took another look around the barren room before switching off the light. She clattered down the stairs and raced off to swap cars.

CHAPTER THIRTY FIVE

When Alicia walked into the kitchen, the smell of beef bourginoine greeted her. Robert was testing the casserole straight from the pot. 'Oh hello darling, I take it this is ready?'

Alicia nodded.

'Shall I dish up then,' he said waving the ladle.

'I don't want any,.. you eat.'

'Have some, it's lovely.'

'I'm not hungry.'

Robert shrugged and spooned a large serving for himself. Alicia made herself a coffee and sat down at the table opposite Robert. She watched him eat, wishing that every mouthful might choke him. He smiled at her, swallowed his food and said, 'I've got something to tell you.'

Alicia didn't reply. 'You'll love it.' He said.

'Robert, the other day, I borrowed your calculator…out of your briefcase.'

'That's ok.'

'I noticed some drawings in your case, design details, it was of a carton, shaped like a pyramid.'

'Oh yes, did you like it?'

'Impressed, who did it?'

'What, the drawing?'

'No the design.'

'Ah, I'm not just a pretty face you know, and wait till you hear what else I've done.' He fumbled in his breast pocket while he spoke. 'Guess what these are?' he waved a small red and blue envelope in the air and then let it fall on the table. He sniggered like a small boy and filled his mouth. When Alicia ignored the packet, he flicked it toward her. 'Go on..open it.'

'Are you saying that you designed the pyramid?' There was a silence except for the rattle of Robert's spoon against the plate. 'Alicia,' he sang, 'open the packet.'

She stared at him. He stared back.

'Are you saying that you designed the pyramid carton?' she repeated.

Robert put down his spoon, picked up the packet and opened it, he held up the airline tickets and waved them like a flag in the tense atmosphere.

'Did you?' Alicia raised her voice.

'What?' he snapped.

'Design the pyramid!'

'Yes!'

'Liar!'

Robert leaned over waving the tickets. 'Alicia.' He was almost shouting she got up and started walking away. 'Alicia! He yelled, 'these are bloody tickets for China!'

She turned to him. 'I hope you bloody enjoy it.'

'Alicia, this is what you wanted!'

'No Robert, it's what you wanted.'

'China…you said China.'

'I said, if I was to go on holiday, I would choose China.'

Robert caught her arm and yanked her around to face him, Alicia saw the rage in his eyes. He pushed the tickets into her face, keeping hold of her so he could scream at close range. 'You said China! and I've got the tickets!'

'Then cancel.'

'I've fucking paid for them!'

'Then you go!'

'You're coming.'

'Oh no, I'm not going anywhere with you! you're a lying bastard Robert, a cheating lying bastard!'

He drew back his hand and swung it towards Alicia's face, she moved her head to one side and he caught her ear, as he drew back for another slap, she thumped him hard in the gut. He doubled over in agony gasping for breath, she bolted to the door, he lurched after her and grabbed her sweater. She rammed him with the door, shunting his foot and sending him off balance. Her heart was racing and she slammed the door and ran, fumbling for her keys in her pocket. She heard the door open and Robert shouting. 'Alicia bitch I'll kill you!'

She saw him launch out of the door, she grabbed the metal dustbin lid and skimmed it with all her might in his direction, he jumped out of it's path. There was a loud smash as it took out the glass pane in the door. Alicia had then grabbed the near empty dustbin and with a fierce angry strength skimmed that at her target. It hit him across his shins and he dropped to his knees, swearing death threats. That gave Alicia enough time to get to the car and drive off, he saw her screech away and ran back to the house for his car keys.

Alicia drove anywhere, her vision blurred with tears. She took this turn and that, frantically checking her rear view mirror. Her thinking was muddled but she knew not to aim herself toward her Mother's, that's where Robert will think she's going, he may catch her then. Headlights in her mirror made her curse and put her foot down. 'Must swap the car.' she instructed herself. After a few more turns she lost the following headlights. She turned out of the suburban maze and found herself on a country road. The only traffic here was a stationary car in a lay by. Just as she was feeling relieved she had to slam the brakes on. Her heart was in full beat again as she screeched to a stop. 'Oh my God, someone's dead on the road!' She got out and ran to the front of the car, and raised her hands in horror at the dark shape. She crouched down and patted the coated body. It felt strange, her heart seemed to be booming in her ears, she pulled at the coat and found that it was just a coat with bags of rubbish under it. Alicia breathed a sigh of relief and then jumped up as she heard a car approaching, honking it's horn. 'OH NOOO' ,she screamed as she jumped back in her still running car. She screeched off again bumping over the lumpy coat. She snatched at the gears and stamped on the throttle, but the car behind came just as fast, flashing it's lights, beeping it's horn. Alicia saw a light further up the road, as she got closer there were more lights. 'Thank God a country Inn'. She slid to a halt at the entrance and ran into the car park. She heard the car slide to a halt behind her, it's headlights showing her running shadow. She felt sick inside and then heard a woman's voice shouting. 'Stop! Wait, I'm not after you!'

Alicia slowed and looked back. A blonde woman was running toward her. Alicia stood panting, the woman ran up to her, waving, half calming, half distressed. 'Wait…are you alright?, did he do anything?'

'What?'

'Did you see?' the woman raved, looking at Alicia's blank expression. 'You didn't see,' the blonde woman went on, 'the man, when you stopped and went to the front of your car, a man got in the back, ..of your car, I saw him, I was just in the lay by. And now you've just stopped, he got out and ran off!'

Alicia stood bewildered and gulped in the cold air. Her heart seemed to be pumping outside of her chest now, up in her throat and in her ears. A woozy blank moment made her stumble, the blonde woman caught Alicia by the arm and steadied her toward a low stone wall and sat her down. 'Stay there,' the woman was saying to her, 'I'm going to park the cars.'

Alicia heard the heels clip clop away from her, she tried to breath more calmly, half crying, half laughing now and taken to violent shivering. Her head was buzzing and she was pleased when the blonde woman came back. 'Come on love,' she said gently, 'we both need a drink.'

Without any more words between them, they strolled out of the cold air and into the warmth of the half empty lounge and found vacant stools at the bar. 'Two brandies please,' the woman ordered. 'Are you okay?' she turned to Alicia and in the light of the bar, Alicia found herself staring into the most beautiful green eyes she had ever seen. 'Thanks.' Alicia nodded.

The blonde woman slid a brandy toward Alicia then offered her hand. 'Samantha..Samantha Dowles..call me Sammy.'

Alicia introduced herself and swallowed the brandy, the warming sensation trickled down her insides and she ordered two more. Sammy put her hand up. 'No more for me, I have to drive.'

Alicia felt a slight panic, she didn't want her to leave. 'Please don't go yet.' Alicia placed her hand on Sammy's arm. Sammy smiled saying, 'I've got a hotel room booked I'm afraid,' looking at her watch she said, 'I've got time for another though, I'll have a soda. Look I'm sorry if I frightened you.'

'Oh it wasn't you..it was my darling husband.'

'You're married?' Sammy looked at Alicia's left hand, no rings.

'Not any more as far as I'm concerned, just got to sort the paperwork out. We had a fight... he was after me, I believe he wanted to kill me.'

'Why? Did you do something terrible?'

'I found him out.'

'Ah another woman?'

Alicia shook her head. Sammy smiled and asked if the cheating was another man.

'No. He did cheat, he always has, but I kind of knew about that.'

The green eyes looked intrigued now and Alicia carried on. 'I think he always screwed around, and we sort of went our separate ways for a while, just meeting up for the odd argument. Then just recently he seemed to want to change.' Alicia stared into her glass, slightly puzzled herself at what she had just said. 'Yes, he seemed to...oh, I don't know, he seemed to be trying to make it work, and...well I don't know. I think I clung on to that as a last ditch attempt even though I didn't really want to...and then I got the evidence that confirmed he was a louse. A liar, a total shit who is probably capable of anything underhand. I loathe him for what he's done.'

Alicia seemed close to tears and Sammy lay a comforting hand on her shoulder. 'Whatever has he done to you?'

'It's not what he's done to me really, it's just him, he has no regard for people. This poor girl I know had done this design for a competition at her work, the prize was money which I found out she is in desperate need of. My bloody husband took it, he actually stole her design and poor August, she had worked so hard on it.'

'Did you say August?'

'Yes, that's her name, unusual isn't it?'

'There can only be one, what's her surname?'

'Jackson..August Jackson, do you know her?'

'Yes, well not know her, we've met, works for a box forming company around here.'

'The same one as my husband..Ruban Co..'

'That's the one.'

This mutual acquaintance gave them a familiar bond. Alicia had stopped trembling and they moved to a more private table.

'Where did you meet August?' Alicia asked.

'At the Exhibition Centre., the company I work for had a stand there, we supply drafting equipment.'

Alicia fumbled in her purse and produced a business card. Sammy took it and read it out loud. 'Alicia Heyhott, Graphic Designer', would you believe it, we're in the same trade. Do you know August well?'

'No. August used to have a flat, the flat I have taken to use as an office, she lives in the same block.'

Sammy smiled at the memory of her first meeting with August. 'You know, when I first bumped into her at the show, she was a nervous wreck, poor little sod. She had been wandering around all on her own with about as much confidence as a hedgehog on the M6 on a Friday afternoon.'

'You know Sammy, I'm quite worried about August, I've just seen where she lives.'

'I thought you said she lives in the same block of flats?'

'She does, but it's not a flat. It's more like an attic, and it's not actually where she lives that bothers me, but how she's living, something is not right. Do you know she was so sweet, she tried to be so helpful when I first moved in. She said, ' if you need anything, just ask', and do you know Sammy, she hasn't got anything.'

Sammy looked at her watch. 'I've got to get going I'm afraid, it's one of those, if you don't check in before a certain time, they're liable to let your room. Can I take your card?'

'Sure, that's the number for the flat, maybe you'll call me, try and sell me some of your wares. I think I'll try and check in here for the night, it is a hotel, I'm certainly not going home.'

CHAPTER THIRTY SIX

August was angry that the curio shop was closed by the time she got there, but over the moon when she saw the painting. There had been an embarrassing moment though, when she first recognised the picture, the elderly couple also looking in the window had hurried away when she yelled 'Bigshit!' at the painting. August didn't care, she had found her Mum's picture. There was a small white tag dangling from the frame, but it was too small to make out the price. She wondered if it would be rude to drag James there tomorrow lunch.

August was even happy to do her shift at the cinema, but felt a little giddy, she put it down to the fact that she had a date with James the following day. She knew it wasn't a romantic date, but she just wanted to be with him.

When the lights came on in the cinema, August felt quite light headed and couldn't wait to get out into the fresh air. With every step on the way home, the energy she seemed to have earlier drained away like a bomb dropping. By the time she arrived home, August found it a real trial to climb the stairs. When she walked into the hovel she sniffed the air, there seemed to be a trace of perfume in the air, she had smelt the same perfume before. She shuddered, wondering if Mr Cruickshank had paid another visit.

Robert had given up the chase nearly as soon as it had started. He was hot with temper and hurting with the unbelievable punch Alicia had delivered and cold in just his shirt. He hadn't a clue where Alicia had headed when he couldn't find her en-route to her Mother's. He now sat in the kitchen staring at the shards of broken glass spread all over the floor. He was inspecting his bruised shins and was swearing in between sipping gin. On the work surface lay the tickets. Robert hurled his tumbler at the wall and it smashed into many pieces and joined the other brittle litter. He crossed his arms flat on the table, buried his face and cried into his sleeves. 'I hate you Alicia,' he sobbed, 'just look at what you've done to me, you've broken me in pieces you bitch, well I'll get you!' He reared up now, snivelling then laughing. 'I will so get you, oh I will get you!' He danced in the broken glass, kicked the door and then poured himself another drink.

The following day August took the bus to work, the lethargy she had experienced the previous evening had not left her. She yawned as she ripped yesterday's date from the desk calendar. Jayne swept into the office. 'I don't know where November's gone, it'll soon be Christmas.'

August was still staring at the date. She realised that it had been a month since she had moved into the hovel. She sneezed and then thought how lucky she was not to have suffered hypothermia. The sneeze was the first of many that morning and Mrs Charlton suggested that August go home. August refused profusely insisting that she was alright. There was absolutely no way she would have missed that lunch date with James. The morning dragged by. Her nose grew pink and sore from constant wiping, and when she spoke, she sounded like she had her nostrils stapled together.

At one minute past twelve, August stepped out of the building and a blue car pipped and stopped in front of her. The handsome face of James Blonde smiled and he pushed the passenger door open for her. This was the moment August had been waiting for since Monday morning and she wished she felt better for the occasion. She had even wore her thin jacket instead of the unflattering duffle-coat. His deep brown voice made her go all wobbly inside.

'Hello.' August squeaked, hiding her nose behind a tissue.

'I've just passed a nice place on the way in. Let me just turn around and we're off.'

'Fine,' August croaked.

'Oh dear, have you caught a cold?'

'I'm afraid so, I hope I don't give it to you.'

James made a short journey, and to her surprise, pulled up at 'The Conservatory'.

'It looks a nice place doesn't it?' he said, 'is it?'

'I wouldn't know personally, I do know it's expensive.'

'Don't worry about that, I'm paying.'

August couldn't believe she was walking through The Conservatory foyer, she wished she felt better to enjoy it. James was holding the door open for her to the dining room. It was too good to be true. The menu was the most exciting thing she had read in ages, and to her disbelief, she had no appetite. 'I think I'll have a salad, just something and salad.' She muttered running her finger down the page. 'Prawn salad,' she said, knowing she didn't really want it. August watched James as he poured over the menu. He flashed his long lashes at her. 'You'll have to excuse me, I can never make up my mind, my parents have a restaurant like this and get I a little picky. I can just embrace what the poor cooks are going through from the head chef. My Father wanted me to follow in his footsteps, but I don't think a Father and Son relationship can survive that shouting and commanding discipline. I don't think that's how a relationship should be.'

They made polite conversation over lunch. August was terribly pissed off because she felt so rough, and couldn't even eat her prawn salad. When the sweet trolley rolled by, what normally would have been a vision of ecstasy to her, had no effect. They covered the subject of cutting forms and creasers and then went on to a more personal conversation.

'So, your boyfriends name is Graham?'

The question took August by surprise and it showed. 'Graham.' James repeated the name and kept his eye on August's expression. 'You said you were out with Graham Tuesday?'

'Oh yes, but he's not my boyfriend, he's our rep, one of them that is, he's nice.'

'Does he take you out to lunch regularly?' His eyes were fixed on hers.

'Noo.. he has just started with us.'

James smiled and nodded as if it was the answer he wanted to hear. They fell silent and August wondered if she dare ask James to stop off at the curio shop.

'Would you like more coffee?' he asked, 'we still have time.'

'No thanks, actually I wondered if I may be cheeky and..well?'

'Go on.' He urged.

'There's a curio shop, just on the Derby road, and there's a painting in there. It was my Mums', and I would really like it back, and I would like to know how much it is.' She had just wished she hadn't said the last bit, and was looking at a very puzzled face. 'It was stolen from me.' She tried to explain.

'Shouldn't you inform the Police?'

'It's a long story.' She glanced down, and he guessed she didn't want to say anymore.

'Hey, let's go,' he said, 'we've got time to spare.'

When August stood, she felt dizzy, she swayed a little and caught hold of the table. James took hold of her arm. August felt ill and embarrassed.

'I say, are you all right? Look, I had better get you back, you should probably go home, shall I take you home?'

'Oh no, I'm okay, honestly, I will be fine, probably the stuffy cold, could we please go to the shop?'

'Of course, it obviously means a lot to you.'

'It does.'

August was livid inside. The date she wanted to enjoy, the day she wanted to look her best, the day she is taken to The Conservatory by the man of her dreams! , and she blows it!. James was concerned and kind and she felt such a fool. When they reached the shop it was closed.

'Oh no, it's half day closing.' August closed her eyes and placed her hot forehead on the cold window. This day of all days had turned into a nightmare. She was hot and cold at the same time. Her nose and cheeks glowed like a beacon, and if it wasn't for showing herself up, she could have collapsed on the spot.

'August, come on, there will be other days.' James tried to be sympathetic, 'I really think I should take you home.'

She shook her head and persuaded James to leave her there and said she needed to walk back. After putting up a good argument, James lost. August slowly trundled back, through the park, feeling quite faint. She sat down on a bench. It took her a while to gather her strength to move on, but having to stop for a rest along the way.

James had driven for five minutes and turned around, he felt such a prick leaving August like that she looked so ill and vulnerable. He felt an overwhelming desire to look after her.

At ten minutes past one, August trudged through the car park, observed by Don Holland from his office window. Her reward for making it back to camp was a reprimand from the M.D., passed on reluctantly by Mrs Charlton. August felt so poorly, she couldn't be bothered to argue that she was out discussing Ruban Co. business. Jayne could see how ill August was and brought her some aspirin and water.

CHAPTER THIRTY SEVEN

Robert had surfaced very late and was in no fit state to go to work. He thought his tongue had died and festered in his mouth. He groaned as his brain cramped behind his eyes. It was a death defying act just to get upright and mobile. As he descended the stairs, he shivered at the unwelcoming cold, and wanted to weep when he saw the mess in the kitchen. He hadn't cleaned up last night, but made it worse. He swore as he recalled his drunken tantrum, hurling everything he could lay his hands on around the kitchen, tipping the waste bin into the sink, and the one he'd enjoyed most of all, throwing eggs at the window. The freezing cold blasted in through the shattered back door, and Robert limped away unable to handle any of it. He submerged himself in his duvet and slept until miafternoon. Not until then could he face the wreckage downstairs.

A slice of toast helped line his stomach. He attempted a few business phone calls, putting them down on his work sheet rota as visits. He was tempted to phone Brockley to find Alicia, but he wouldn't know what to say. He needed some fresh air, and couldn't face anything more to do with work. He decided to take a drive out, away from the house, he needed a distraction.

The tablets August had taken didn't seem to make any difference to her aching snotty state. She had cleared out Jayne's box of tissues. 'Sorry I've used all your tissues.' August sniffled, 'but you want to try using that shiny stuff in the toilets, it slides..well it's useless.'

Patricia Charlton came to the rescue with a handy pack of tissues and insisted that now Don Holland had gone, August should go home too. This time she didn't resist. She took the bus home, made up a roaring fire and wrapped the duvet up over the sleeping bag around her shoulders. Just as the duvet shawled her, so did the thought of the debt. She would have to feel better for her shift at the cinema tonight, she needed every penny. She wanted to slay the debt and never feel beholden to anyone ever again. She wondered when someone would turn up to collect the rent. Until someone did, she would have to find a better place to hide the money. August decided the roof space would be the safest place, but it would have to wait. Right now she had several hours she could use to sleep off this horrible cold bug. August set the alarm clock in fear of overlaying for her shift at the cinema. It was the last thing she felt like doing, but hoped that when she woke, her batteries would be recharged.

She was wrong. When the alarm wailed, August could do no more than lay there and let it exhaust itself. The battle was on, her body would not respond to her orders. There was no evidence that a scrap of energy was present and she was sure that her veins had sagged and her nervous system was only delivering messages of pain. She lay motionless, fighting to keep her leaden eyelids open. Audibly, August tried to make a deal with a God she questioned existed. 'If you would just take this crap out of my body and let me be well. I will never eat chocolate again. I will be kind to everyone…even Slime. I might even pop into church one Sunday.' Her appeal was stopped by a surge of sneezes and a bilious twist in her stomach. 'Well, she continued, remember this, you kept me from the fold, I did offer.'

August took a few deep breaths and her chest hurt. It was a torment to even think about getting up, but she had to. She also had to revive the fire before getting ready to go to work.

August forced herself every step of the way. She willed the film to end. In the dark interior, she sat down as often as she dared. When the lights went up, she was relieved, that was until she saw Slime. She didn't want him to see her working there, and joined the punters shuffling through to the foyer. No sooner had she set foot in the corridor, the manager sent her back in. Surveying the many faces making their way out, she was anxious to spot him, that way she could avoid him. There was not a glimpse of him anywhere.

Robert sat in his car eating fish and chips and was wondering what August Jackson was doing, playing at being an usherette. 'Maybe,' he thought, 'she's been sacked from work.'

The thought of Ruban Co. niggled him, he knew he had let his work slide this last week, and now he had the Topps guy as competition, he couldn't get away with what he used to. Slumming it a few days and putting false calls down on his work sheet. He might have just earned a few team points, but he would have to be on his toes now. Robert hadn't been in the office at all this last week, but he would put it right tomorrow. Just then a lump of batter fell from the tiny spatula of a wooden fork and zig-zagged a greasy trail down the lapel of his trench coat and came to rest in the nest of his crotch. Normally this would have brought on a temper tantrum, but Robert simply picked up the loose food and popped it into his mouth. As he continued eating with his fingers, the car windows steamed up with greasy vapour. His thoughts turned to Alicia. She would definitely be at Brockley.

Alicia was definitely not at Brockley, but at the flat. She felt much safer having changed the car over to the BMW. She had spent most of the day shopping, she needed bedding for the flat and she also needed to stock it with food. Alicia had taken no chances though, dressing in her disguise to go into town, she could take no chances of Robert spotting her. She felt a great need to go running back to the safe surround of the family home, and to her Mother. There was though the need to have some of her own space, to be able to cope on her own. Alicia decided it would be good therapy to stay at the flat, and cook and clean for herself, rather than be cossetted by her Mother, Nancy and Tom.

The flat was quiet, unknown to Robert, and with the car hidden and her disguise, she had the anonymity that would allow her that breathing space she craved and needed. She was looking forward to cooking again and she would invite August down for evening meals, she certainly could do with it. Earlier Alicia had tried the shellac door that led to that dreadful room, but it was locked. She had obviously missed August off on one of her evening shifts. The phone rang. Alicia was delighted it was Sammy.

'I thought I had better ring and see if you were alright.'

'That's awfully thoughtful of you Sammy, thank you. I didn't really thank you properly for last night.'

'Oh don't mention it.'

'No really. It was afterwards I realised how dreadful the situation could have been if you hadn't intervened. I would like to treat you to lunch, how are you fixed?'

'Well I'm staying over at the east coast tonight, travelling back down tomorrow. I shall pass through your area, and then I won't be back up there for about three weeks.'

'How about tomorrow then?' Alicia really wanted to meet Sammy again.

Sammy was also pleased with the opportunity to meet Alicia. 'Okay'

'Do you know a restaurant here called 'The Conservatory'?'

'Yes. I've been there before.'

'Could you meet me there tomorrow at twelve thirty?' Alicia found she had involuntary crossed her fingers.

'Yes I would be delighted.' Sammy had the biggest smile on her face.

CHAPTER THIRTY EIGHT

August couldn't wait to get home. When she saw the BMW outside she felt glad, but in no state to make a social call. Besides it was late and all she needed to do was to lie down and sleep. Her chest felt tight, as if a belt was strapped around her ribs. By the time she reached the summit of the hovel, her lungs ached. The room was barely aired, the fire almost dead. As poorly as she felt, August knew in her state it would be sensible to mend the fire.

Suffering all night, August tossed and turned. Her legs ached, her chest hurt, and even her backside ached. A discomfort drilled into every joint and she prayed for sleep. It came too late and too deep. The alarm wailed unheard, and when August eventually woke midmorning, she knew that Ruban co. would have to do without her that day. At twelve thirty, she dragged herself to the payphone downstairs in the hall and confirmed to Mrs Charlton what she already knew. When Patricia Charlton put the phone down, she then went into Don Holland's office with the memo she had scribbled. He was at the time being bull shitted by Robert Simpson, whom she thought looked a little dishevelled, so different from his normal impeccable turn out. It was obvious from the conversation that Robert was after some time off.

'I wouldn't ask, but it is a rather desperate family matter.' He was saying.

Don Holland was only half listening he had problems of his own. He was also reading the memo in front of him and stopped Patricia Charlton. 'Isn't that the Jackson girl, who was late back from lunch?'

'Yes, she was off colour yesterday.'

Robert reading into the situation hutched himself forward in his seat and butted in, with a grin of a smile he said, 'Surely you don't mean August Jackson, I saw her working at the cinema last night.'

Patricia looked narrow eyed at Robert and shook her head. 'Oh no, you must have been mistaken.'

'Nooo it was definitely her, working as an usherette.'

Don Holland's brow collected deep lines, his lips tightly pouted sticking from his whiskers like a group of haemorrhoids. 'Mrs Charlton, see me in five minutes, a letter to Miss Jackson, cause for instant dismissal I think.'

Robert was laughing inside, Mrs Charlton protesting, 'she really did look poorly yesterday.'

'Obviously a good actress.' Don Holland growled, dismissing his secretary and satisfied he'd given a five minute warning to Simpson. He couldn't be bothered with him until he heard him say. 'Of course, I wouldn't expect to be paid while I was off, short notice and all that.' Robert hadn't wanted to say that, especially as he had waived the two weeks holiday prize for the pyramid design. It struck him then that 'the pyramid' is what Alicia had freaked out at, but how did she know. He began to fidget uncomfortable in his seat, panicking because he didn't want to waste the great expense that super bitch had cost him. Having to ask the guvnor for a favour, when he himself knew he hadn't been putting the hours in. Don Holland seized on the magic words. He could certainly do with lessening his wages bill. His thoughts were brief and calculating. He was about to sack one employee and then to save half a months' salary from his area sales manager not have to give two weeks free holiday would all help his own purse.

'Without pay?' Don Holland unfurled his furrowed brow. Robert hooked onto the bait of hope. 'Err..yes..well I know I have a weeks..'

'Well,' Don Holland took the advantage, 'if you're prepared to forgo two weeks wages, I think I can authorise it, but I do not expect the figures to suffer, I'm sure you'll make up for it.'

Robert was verbally grateful, inwardly thinking he had sold himself far too cheaply, but blamed Alicia for his short comings as he always did. He was thoroughly pissed off at Don Holland and decided he would blow some company expenses and lunch at 'The Conservatory'.

Sammy Dowles sat alone at her table staring at the car park through the Arcadian glass wall. She nursed a fruit juice, whilst waiting for the arrival of a black Golf. Several cars drove in, one a red BMW. A slim woman with bouncy blonde hair got out of the car. Sammy felt a pang of heartache as the woman reminded her of her last girlfriend, the pale tress of hair, the long legs and the confident strides. Sammy checked her watch, nearly twenty to, where was Alicia? Her manicured nails drummed the pastel pink table cloth, she sipped her juice and scanned the car park again. She was aware though that the blonde woman had entered the restaurant. Sammy couldn't help but glance up at the gorgeous female. The woman was smiling at Sammy and to her surprise, sat herself down opposite. Sammy began to apologise that the seat was taken, and the woman smiled even more broadly. Sammy smiled awkwardly in return. The other blonde spoke. 'Sammy it's me.'

Still Sammy looked pleasantly bewildered.

'It's me..Alicia.'

Sammy's mouth dropped open.

'Oh I'm so pleased you didn't recognise me, that *is* the idea.'

'But such a difference..why?'

'A long story, I hope you have time.'

' I'll make time.' Sammy Dowles meant what she said.

Over lunch the words spilled out. Alicia telling someone for the first time of her unhappiness. For so long she had guarded her misery, as if her own wellbeing would suffer even more, if anyone else knew about her puppet existence. Unable to change the situation, break up the so called marriage, to the effect of creating a bigger monster of Robert. Every-one told her not to marry him, and she believed that she would release some of her own cheerlessness on her Mother. Now as she sat exchanging glances into the deep green eyes, she felt a hunger inside that pecked at a gaping desire that was both strange and refreshing, but she didn't know what it was.

Sammy listened and silently adored the woman opposite, just as she had done when the met on that bizarre evening. The urge to give her a comforting hug was almost unbearable, and there was such an electric feedback coming from those grey eyes. Neither of them ate very much, there was a near tangible fizz between them. They also seemed to attract far too much attention from the waiters. Alicia knew that the lunch was coming to an end, and was suddenly charged with a remote feeling that seemed like being stranded. It was a lame panic inside of her, and as yet another waiter intruded and they both refused deserts, the feeling of panic grew stronger. Alicia felt the need to prolong the conversation, to keep Sammy there. 'Gosh, your face when I sat down here.' She giggled, and with impulse touched Sammy's hand. A tingle coursed through her fingers and her pulse doubled. The responding coupling of fingers sent a huge bolt of excitement to her brain. 'Look,' Alicia said, 'shall we get away from here and have coffee at the flat.'

Sammy glanced at her watch, Alicia felt a disappointing blow coming, but then Sammy smiled encouragingly and said, 'It sounds good to me, I'll just have to make a couple of phone calls from the phone in the foyer.'

'Make them from the flat if you like.'

'If you don't mind.' Sammy wanted to go back to this flat with Alicia, she didn't care where she made the phone calls from that she would invent a story that would 'prevent' her from getting to her appointments, this was electric.

Robert Simpson had been lecherously admiring the two blonde females across the dining hall. He couldn't make up his mind which of the two he fancied most. Which one would he most like to be beneath him, watching her face as he rammed into her. He was contemplating that he might offer to buy them a drink when he saw them get up to leave.

As Alicia swung round, she caught sight of Robert. She turned back to Sammy, who gathered from the worry scribbled across her face, something was wrong. 'What is it? Are you alright?'

'It's Robert, oh my God, get me out of here!'

'Just walk on and talk to me.' Sammy led Alicia through the maze of diners, but couldn't resist in a whisper asking which one was Robert. She had to have a look, just to see what a total shit loser looked like.

CHAPTER THIRTY NINE

The hovel was the warmest it had ever been. August stoked up the fire even though she kept ripping through fever hot flushes she knew she had to stay warm. She wrapped the rent money in a sheet of newspaper making a thin parcel. After removing the panel to the roof space, she grimaced at the entrance. The thought of crawling along cobwebbed joists made her go hen fleshy. She felt lousy inside and out, and very slowly she forced herself forward, her reward being that her hips went through the gap that only a month ago refused fattly and flatly.

Sammy Dowles stood at the large drawing board upon which some of Alicia's work was laid. She was admiring it when Alicia came in with coffee. Placing the tray down, she went over to explain the design format. They were stood very close to each other, closer than necessary, their perfumes mingling. Their fingers pointing to various elements on the drawings until their fingers touched. Alicia feeling an overwhelming electricity stumbled through a graphic account of her work, but Sammy wasn't listening. Alicia felt those green eyes drawing her attention, each time they held her glance a little longer. Her pulse was rapacious, and she felt a vaulting yearning that she had never had the paradise of before. Her voice faltered as Sammy placed her hand over hers. Alicia was stumbling 'and..and..the..that's what I'm er..working on..I don't really know what I'm doing,' she finished in a whisper leaning toward Sammy. 'I do.' said Sammy, and slowly and gently covered Alicia's mouth with her's.

August was happy to leave the thin parcel underneath the redundant cold water tank. Slowly she reversed back along the thin timber joists, hands on one, knees on another. A spoke of light made her look down. A small hole the size of a pea in the plaster lathes caused the thin beam. August reckoned it was the tiny hole in the ceiling she used to stare at when she was laid in bed in the flat. Closing in on the hole, she could see she was right. 'Cher.r.ist,' she whispered as she spied the blonde heads entwined. 'It's that blonde friend of Ali's kissing..a..oh bugger..another woman..she's a lesbian.' August blinked and looked again. 'Oh my God, they're stripping each other.' She lost sight of them as they moved over to the bed. Then seeing just two pair of feet, mixing, August nearly overbalanced and had to calm herself down, the last thing she wanted was to go through the ceiling and become a threesome.

She huddled back in her sleeping bag, unable to think of anything but what was going on downstairs. 'I bet Ali doesn't know what's going on, God the cheek of it.' August tutted, 'She lets her use the flat and her car, and this is how she repays her. What a carry on, I wonder if she's one of those high class prostitutes. Good God, I've got to let Ali know what's going on as soon as possible.'

Her shocking discovery filled her thoughts all through the shift at the cinema. Again she sat down as often as she could while the film was showing. Her chest was tight and her head becoming more and more stuffed up. She could feel beads of sweat gathering on her top lip, but she felt cold, then burned so hot her hair dampened with sweat. At the interval she managed to swap jobs with Gillian on the confectionary counter. There she could sit until everyone came out, she wouldn't have much to do.

Don Holland pushed the button to move the car window down. The Mercedes wheels slowly followed the double yellow lines that ran the kerb outside The Odeon cinema. Now level with the doors he stopped the car. There in the interior behind the counter he saw August. The row of mustard coloured teeth bared a smile, 'so Simpson was right.' He stuffed his half spent cigar back into his mouth and drove off.

August really couldn't cope with the smell of the hotdogs, she felt sick. She wiped her sweaty palms down the front of her overall. Feeling close to passing out, she found the manager, excused herself and headed back home. She stumbled along the street resting frequently on garden walls, litter bins and when nothing was available, she sank down on the pavement with her feet in the gutter. 'How low can you get,' her voice croaked inside the great hood. Then came the pit pat thud, slowly at first and then in fast, smacking, splashing strobes of cold unrelenting rain. Against her own rule, August sobbed, she raised her head, her face distorted with her own galling weary grief. The rain ran with mascara stained tears and she cried to the dark heavens. 'Why me!' she half expected a reply to boom back 'because I fucking hate you!', but the fizz of the downpour was all she got. Shivering she dragged herself up, the duffle-coat flapped open, the front of her clothes wet through. She could no more hurry than fly.

As August dropped the catch on the entrance door, she heard the door to Ali's flat, she wondered if it was the lesbian hooker or Ali. She could really do with a friend right now, and she had to let Ali know what was going on. A quick glance from under the brim of the dripping hood, her heart sank. The woman was coming downstairs and calling back to someone, it must be the other lesbian August guessed, and stood hunched like a sack clothed monk, her head down. The hood and coat dripping rain water waiting for her turn to use the stairs. 'Just drop the lock when you come out, I have the key.' The woman was calling up the stairs. August was dying to collapse onto her bed, a feverish heat swamped her, and she screwed up her eyes with impatience. Anticipating the woman's last couple of treads, August moved ready for the uphill assault. She could have sworn the coat had got heavier. To her surprise and annoyance, the woman stopped, lingering on the last tread. August was never rude or pushy, but now feeling so lousy, she made to go past the woman.

'Hello August.'

August stepped back, snatched a glance at the blonde woman and tried to embark again, her mind a rush of all thoughts. 'God she knows my name, the cow's trying to chat me up!'

She tried to push past the woman. The woman stopped her by the arm. 'August it's me. Look.'

The familiar voice made August obey, the woman was giggling, until she saw the tear stained red cheeks, swollen eyes and scarlet nose. 'Oh my goodness darling, are you alright?'

August pulled away from the woman's clutch, a frown grew deep over questioning eyes, August pushed past and tried with leaden feet to rush up the stairs. It was easy for Alicia to catch her up. On the landing August gasped for breath and was fighting a massive dizzy spell. Alicia stood in front of her. 'August, it's me..Ali.'

August knew it was Ali's voice, but shook her head in disbelief.

'It's true darling, why don't.'

'Don't you darling me.'

'August what's the matter, gosh you really don't look well, come in, let me get you something.'

'I don't want anything from you.'

'But sweetheart, look here's another friend of yours.'

Sammy stepped onto the landing, August couldn't believe it, maybe she was hallucinating with this fever, she involuntary whispered Sammy's name. Sammy lost her smile to a worried concern. 'Are you okay August?' Sammy asked glancing across at Alicia who was looking very alarmed. Alicia stepped toward August and August backed away. 'Don't come near me.' cried August reversing down the landing, Sammy then made toward her. 'Any of you.' August snapped. Both women stood motionless, their benevolence shot to pieces. August backed up to the bathroom door, she felt blindly, finding the knob and before opening the door she cried at them, 'You're not my friends, I know what you are, I've seen you, you dirty bitches!' Alicia made another move, August turned, Sammy caught Alicia by the arm. The bathroom door slammed shut and the bolt slammed across.

August leaned against door gasping for air as her body heat soared with a volcanic torrent and she slid down in a soft duffle-coated heap on the chequered lino floor. Alicia ran to the door slapping the painted panels with the palm of her hand. 'August..August, please come out,' she turned to Sammy, 'something's really wrong, she's ill.'

Sammy took her turn trying to raise a response through the door. Resigned to the fact that August wasn't going to come out whilst they were there, they went back into the flat, where Alicia began to cry. Sammy put her arms around her, 'we'll see her later.' She consoled.

August didn't come round for some fifteen minutes. She had crumpled down with one leg under the other thigh and it had lost circulation and mobility. She had to manually lift her dead lower leg into position to try to stand up. She was like a hobbled horse. What had happened was vague, she could remember Ali and even Sammy Dowles, and she could remember wanting to reach out to them but they couldn't get to her. August wondered if she had dreamt it all as she limped pathetically across the landing to the shellac door. The stairs might as well have been Mount Everest, it took every gram of energy she could muster to make it to the top. Never had she wanted to see that airbed so much. The fire was dead in the grate but she was beyond caring. She completely drained, her vision blanked and she swooned with thudding grace half across the airbed.

Alicia and Sammy heard the heavy thud above them and scrambled out of the flat. Alicia rattled the wobbly brass door knob on the shellac door and bounced her body against the door. 'It's no good Alicia, she's locked it.' Alicia slipped off her stilettos', hauled her pencil skirt right up to her waist, took a few steps back and seriously composed herself.

'What on earth are you doing?' Sammy was bemused.

'Please move out of the way,' she said, not taking her eyes off somewhere beyond the door, 'it's about time I put this to use.'

Sammy moved away from the door and watched as Alicia made a strange stance, her vision locked on what appeared to be the other side of the door. Seconds later, the door splintered from it's lock as the ball of Alicia's foot struck like a missile. Sammy stood speechless and obeyed Alicia's commands. 'Oh my God, she's unconscious! let's get her on this mattress, first go and ring for a doctor, the number is in my diary.'

August was rambling, it was mostly unintelligible. Alicia picked up the words, 'money must pay, and something about 'bigshit bay'. By the time Sammy reappeared, August was flaying her arms around and Alicia nearly caught a left hook. Things were calmer by the time the Doctor arrived, but he didn't hesitate organising an ambulance. Alicia insisted on travelling with August and Sammy followed by car.

CHAPTER FORTY

In the bleached primrose corridor of the hospital, Alicia paced in front of the neat row of plastic chairs where Sammy sat cradling a styrene cup of coffee.

'God she looked ill.' Alicia repeated. Sammy pleaded with her to sit down. The same act went on until just before midnight when a young ginger haired Doctor strode toward them. Alicia was sorry to not be able to offer much information. The best she could do was name and address and clue him up on her living conditions. 'She overworks too,' she added, 'she has a full time job and she goes to work in the evenings.'

'Well she won't be doing that now.'

'What! she is going to be alright isn't she?'

Alicia sat down now and listened to the Doctor. He was concerned that in her state of exhaustion she would be able to fight off what may be influenza or pneumonia.

On Friday morning Patricia Charlton reluctantly typed out the formal letter to August Jackson. She thought she might take it round personally, but decided against it. Jayne was very upset when she found out and Fred was beside himself. Now what would he do, he had always expected for August to be there, to help him out. Patricia had tried one last protest that Robert could have been mistaken, and lost the argument to the other eye witness.

Don Holland felt good, he liked to be able to enforce his power, and tonight he also had a date with a very rich widow. He would take her out of town and take her in the Bentley. When Patricia brought him the letter to sign, he demanded some petty cash.

'There is only twenty pounds.' She informed him.

'Get some more, send somebody to the bank, I need one hundred and twenty!'

Patricia once again wanted to protest, she knew as the company secretary, that the business was thin heeled at the moment. She also knew that the money was for personal frivolous activities.

Alicia was back at the hospital before 9 am. When she wasn't allowed to go in to see August, she went into town. She bought a huge basket of fruit, a glorious spray of flowers and the most expensive chocolates the shop had. She returned to visit August, laying the flowers on the bedside cabinet like a wreath, She stared down at the sleeping face of August Jackson. Her hair lay untidy about the pillow, Alicia smoothed it into place. 'I'm not allowed to stay for long, but I will come back later. Sammy sends her love, she's going to try to get up and see you tomorrow.' She stroked August's lifeless hand and left.

When Alicia got back to the flat, she went up to the hovel and searched for any scrap of information that August may have of any relatives. There was nothing. She could not believe that someone could have so little. She fretted the afternoon away unable to do any work. She rang the hospital twice for reports, and motored down again that evening. All she could do was stare until a nurse would usher her away. At nine o' clock, she decided to call her Mother, and was surprised to find out that she had gone out on a date. Nancy had announced it as if it was a big secret. 'Anyone I know?' Alicia asked.

'I don't think so, I haven't seen the gentleman before…I think I heard your Mother call him Donald. Came in a big posh car.'

'No, I don't know a Donald, anyway what are you still doing there, go home and put your feet up.'

'I'm just preparing a little cold supper, in case they want something when they get back.'

'Go home you fusser..oh Nancy I don't suppose Robert phoned there asking for me?'

'Well not as far as I know, would you like me to ask Tom?'

'No..no, just between you and me and Tom, if he does ring, could you just say that I'm out at a friends'.'

Nancy agreed without hesitation, she loved it if she thought she was part of a conspiracy against that husband of hers.

Alicia didn't know if she was sad or glad that her Mother had a date. It would be selfish of her not to want happiness again for her Mother, but all the same, she felt a sort of mourning for her Father. Everything seemed topsy-turvy and not for the better, to cheer herself up she rang Sammy.

Brigitte Heyhott stretched her legs in the roomy car.

'You like the Bentley then?' Don asked as he pulled out of the restaurant car park.

'Yes, very comfortable.'
'It could be yours.'
'You're selling?'
'I'm afraid so, it is a beautiful motor.'
'Then why?'
'Oh I have a Mercedes, for when I'm in this country, and a car like this, well she doesn't really get the attention she deserves.'

Brigitte fell silent and he was scared to lose the thread of the conversation. 'Now you could give her that attention.'

'Oh I don't know, besides I'm happy with the coupe'.'

Don knew he would have to leave it there and try again later. 'Did you enjoy your meal Brigitte?' he said looking for team points.

When the Bentley crunched to a halt in front of Brockley House, Brigitte would have preferred to have got out alone and gone straight to bed. For his charm and because he was polite she invited him in for coffee. She was pleased when he didn't outstay his welcome, but did decline another date in the week. She did change her mind the following morning though when three dozen pink roses were delivered, with a card saying 'thank you for a pleasant evening.'

The attention was welcomed, it was the bouquet of flowers that made Brigitte realise how long it had been since she had received any. She arranged the flowers herself smiling at the flattery. Maybe it was time that she allowed herself a little dating. Besides Donald was quite charming and was obviously wealthy, so he wasn't pursuing her for her money. Yes she would enjoy getting out and enjoying male company once again.

When Don replaced the handset of the phone, he rubbed his hands together. 'Always, always, flowers work every time.' He laughed. He had taken a thousand pounds from his safe, and divided it into one hundred pound wads. He lay them separated along the keys of the piano in his study and before closing the lid, he counted them aloud. 'Now each one of you, are an investment. You are each dedicated to wining and dining Brigitte.' To the last wad he said, 'And when I get to use you, I must have either my Brogues firmly under the table, or Brigitte's toes under the Bentley's dash board.'

CHAPTER FORTY ONE

The remainder of the glass tinkled into the dustbin, and Robert begrudgingly prepared to pay the glazier for repairing the back door. Saturday morning had gone and he was left to himself. Twice he went to the phone and picked up the receiver to phone Brockley, twice he had put it down before punching in the last digit. He paced from the kitchen to the hall and back, then the third time he picked up the receiver and punched all the numbers in and waited. After four rings he was about to put it down when Nancy answered. 'Heyhott residence.'

'It's Mr Simpson, is my wife there?'

Nancy hugged the mouthpiece close to her double chins, and turned to the wall guarding her conversation. 'I'm afraid Miss Alicia is out with her friend.'

'Which friend?'

'I'm afraid she didn't say, I'll tell her you called.'

'What time will she be back?'

'Miss Alicia didn't say.' Nancy heard an exasperated blow of air and was pleased she'd experienced Robert slightly out of sorts.

'When did she get there?' he persisted.

'I'm sorry, I have to go now, I have a pan on the boil, I will tell her you rang, goodbye.'

Robert slammed the phone down. He had no control over the situation, he had got only nine days to sell the tickets or make use of them. He still needed to make up with Alicia, now she was really loaded, ..or favourite, the bitch should die before a divorce could be effected, then he would have it all. The thought of being rich free and single gave him a buzz, and he celebrated with a huge tumbler of gin.

Alicia didn't sleep too well, uncomfortable with worry for August. She tried to remember what she had yelled at them, what she had rambled. Those thoughts would wax and wane with the anticipation of sleep and looking forward to her next meet with Sammy. Concern for her Mother would also butt in, and then she remembered the draft papers she had hidden in the cylinder jacket. She must get them back.

By midmorning Alicia couldn't think straight, so she went up to the hovel where the cold nakedness bared it's teeth. As her breath misted in front of her, so did her head become clear. 'Good God,' she said into the barren room, 'if I had, had to live like this.' Her problems became insignificant by comparison. She wanted to cry again, then, in the morbid quiet, she heard the faint sound of the doorbell. Her emotions were acrobatic, excitement rinsed her insides, and she raced down the two flights of stairs to let Sammy in. When she saw her, the feeling was exotic.

At the hospital, the same ritual played a silent but sad scene. August still in a deep sleep. Alicia stroking her hand. This time Sammy was there to support her. 'At least' Sammy comforted, 'whilst she's asleep , she is not suffering darling.'

'She may be free of physical hurt, but God knows what nightmares she might be going through.'

'I thought you said, you didn't know her that well.'

'She needs me Sammy, I just know she does. I don't think she has anyone else, besides, no one has ever needed me before.'

On Monday morning when Graham Topps strode into the office, he was surprised to find no August, and completely shocked when he was told she had been sacked. He couldn't get any information out of Mrs Charlton, but did manage to wheedle a little out of a very upset Jayne. 'I know Mrs Charlton didn't agree with August being sacked, but I do know it was more than her just being late and being off sick.'

'Jayne, do you know where she lives?'

'I've never been, I think she has a flat, the other side of town somewhere.'

'There must be something in the office with her address on it, could you find it for me?'

'I'll try.'

'Please.'

When Robert walked in to the office Graham felt a shudder of 'I wish he wasn't here' rattle through him. Then when he sat on

August's chair and swivelled round, announcing, 'Good heavens, there seems to be a lot more space in here today.'

Graham wanted to rip his blonde hair from his scalp. 'You knew then?' Graham said to Robert.

'Knew what old boy? knew what?'

Graham gave him a direct and disturbing look. Robert recognised a warning glare and sloped away from the desk saying, 'I merely said 'what!'

'I know what you said.' Graham said to Robert's back.

'I suppose she's late again.' Robert laughed as he hung up his coat. There was an ugly silence that made Jayne scoop a collection of papers together, for the want of making some kind of noise. Robert marched away into the rep's small office, with Graham hot on his heels. Jayne now didn't need any noise, there was a kind of jousting going on and besides wanting to hear the feud, she wanted to throw a handkerchief to Graham. Her ears scrutinised the air like radar.

Robert was opening his briefcase on one of the desks'. Graham firmly planted his brick like fists on the same to carry the broad shoulders that confronted Robert.

'You knew.' Graham said in a threatening whisper, then a little louder, 'you bloody well knew.'

Robert felt uncomfortable in Graham's huge shadow, but continued to unpack his paperwork. 'Knew what?' Robert said soberly.

'You knew that August had been sacked!'

'So!'

'So!, how could you know?' Graham's voice was quiet but firm. Robert closed his briefcase, not wanting to engage Graham's eyes, sat back in his chair and casually crossed his legs. His eyes not his head raised to Graham, blue eyes under a blonde hood. 'Look old chap, you're new around here, me and the guvnor are..well..quite close. There are a lot of things the guvnor consults me on. I am a senior executive in this company.'

Jayne listening curled her top lip and screwed up her face, listening harder in case she had heard wrong. The Slime continued. 'So yes I knew, of course I knew,' Robert smirked now, 'I know everything old boy. I even had the say in your position, so if I were you, I would be careful what you say.'

Graham's knuckles were white pressed against the desk, he wanted to plant them in Slime's face, but stayed put. It was Robert who had the uncomfortable feeling around his bowel area, and made an exit as smoothly as he possibly could. He worried all the way to the Gents that Graham would follow him.

Jayne urgently frisked the filing cabinet in Mrs Charlton's office whilst she was in with Don Holland. She found August's address and scribbled it on a piece of paper. Patricia Charlton was in Don Holland's office translating gruff barking noises into shorthand notes. None of the notes reflected letters, but orders of work duties, mainly hers, audit, V.A.T., profit margins and overheads. Sales input, sales output, sales forecasts. Her pen shuddered across the pad, her nerves adding zig-zags' that would have made Pittman wince. The MD strode about his office grunting orders and stroking his goatee beard. He paused to open the cigar box. The sight of only two cigars silenced him for a moment. 'Err have we any petty cash Patricia?'

Her heart froze, she hated that question, and hated having to tell him no.

'Get some.' He barked.

That she despised even more. Patricia had already done the toward the month end on the books, this being the twentieth of the month. She knew things weren't looking good, especially with the wages due to go out. She did smile inside though when he informed her that Robert Simpson would be docked two weeks from his salary this pay day. It would almost make the redoing of the figures worthwhile she thought. It was having to cook the books for the MD. that made her fret. Don Holland wasn't concerned that she would have to balance the accounts with the disappearance of petty cash that had leapt into his pocket without receipts to cover it. He hadn't mentioned the rents from the building and she knew she would have to pick up where the accountant had left off.

CHAPTER FORTY TWO

Alicia had visited the hospital again to find no change in the patient. She took herself into town and purchased an answer phone, that way she wouldn't miss any news about August from the hospital, and she wanted to keep in touch with her work, and she did not want to miss a call from Sammy.

Her next call was to Hyland Way. The new putty smudged glass in the back door reminded her of her last encounter here. The house certainly didn't hold any good memories for her, she wouldn't miss it. Robert was welcome to it as a settlement, she decided. Alicia marched swiftly through the house, her mission was to retrieve the draft papers from the cylinder jacket. This she did with no other interest and marched straight out again. Her next port of call was to see Bradley, the solicitor. There was more to sort out with her Mother's estate and most definitely before that.

Bradley could hardly contain his delight when Alicia announced her intention to divorce Robert. He couldn't stand the hedonistic little prick as he would himself refer to him.

'Let me have him watched Alicia, we could catch him with his pants down as it were, you wouldn't have to pay a penny.'

Alicia sighed heavily, thinking she might have her own infidelity caution, and the thought of Sammy in her life extolled her in her road to happiness. 'No, no Bradley, just get the ball rolling, if I leave him without a payoff, he will just make my life a murderous hell!. I would rather be free of him.'

'As you please,' Bradley resigned himself, 'I suppose you know him best. Would you like to join me for lunch?'

'Awfully nice of you Bradley, but, I have a million things to sort out today. Would you though go through the changes I have made to the estate papers with my Mother, I will speak to her later this week.'

Alicia's head buzzed with ideas as she motored back to the flat. What she really needed was a town centre position for her business. She also needed large business premises with a staff of good designers that could handle a steady stream of work, especially from the larger clients. Alicia knew the kind of turnover she wanted couldn't be achieved alone. She would get changed and go hunting at the estate agents.

Just as the wig had been satisfactory positioned over her fully made up face, the door buzzer sentry went off. She wasn't expecting a caller so she ignored it. On the third buzz, which seemed to go on forever, she went down to the front door. She found a large chap with curly hair, who she thought she had seen before. 'Can I help you?'

The bloke offered the small crumpled paper toward Alicia. 'Is this?, this address?, I'm looking for a girl called August Jackson.'

Alicia took a good look at him and asked. 'Are you a relative of her's.'

'No a friend, well a work colleague really.'

There was a pregnant pause as Alicia surveyed him narrow eyed before saying.

'Didn't I see you going into a pub with August the other day?'

'That's right, I took her to lunch, Err..she does live here then?'

Alicia thought she had found a corner to a jig saw puzzle. 'I think you had better come in.' Graham easily followed this attractive female inside. They introduced themselves in the hallway and Alicia told Graham that August was in hospital.

'Oh my God, is it serious?'

'It is serious, but the doctor seems to think, fingers crossed that the worst is passed.'

'Of what?'

'Look, let me make you a cup of coffee, maybe between us we can form some kind of picture.'

Alicia took Graham on a tour of the hovel, he couldn't believe the destitution.

'Pitiful isn't it? I have sat here several times and cried. I just can't understand it, she works somewhere most evenings besides having a full time job.'

'Had a full time job.'

'What do you mean?'

'They sacked her Friday apparently.'

Alicia was horrified. 'Why! what for?'

'I don't know. Has she had any mail today?'

'Yes I have it in the flat, let's go and see.'

There were two envelopes, the faint red franked stamp of Ruban Co. identified the offending letter. Alicia picked it up. 'I know I shouldn't do this, but.' She ripped it open and read the letter aloud.

Your appointment at Ruban Co. has been immediately terminated as from date above. We have two witnesses to your working at The Odeon Cinema, Station Road whilst being absent from work claiming to be ill. Any monies due to you in wages will be forwarded minus any days that you were absent.

'Oh bloody wonderful, this is all she needs!' Alicia was incensed and slammed the letter down hard. Graham seemed to be somewhere else and under his breath repeated 'two witnesses, two witnesses, I knew he had something to do with it, I knew it, it's got to be him!'

'Who what?'

'Oh this little shit back at the office, I'm sure he's behind August getting sacked, the slimy bastard!'

'It wouldn't be Robert Simpson by any chance would it?'

'You know him?'

'Let's just say, I've heard about him, look, do you want to follow me to the hospital?'

Graham nodded thinking I would follow this gorgeous, confident woman anywhere.

At the hospital Graham followed the figure of this caramel coloured suede trouser suited glamorous perfectly formed female through the maze of corridors. She went at such speed that Graham knew she had travelled this pale grey floor lots of times. He thought that all the millions of dimples may have been caused by her high heels alone. Alicia headed straight for a nurse she called by name. 'Angie, is there any change in August?'

The nurse shook her head. 'Her temperature has stabilised though so that's good news we're all keeping our fingers crossed.' Alicia introduced Graham and politely asked for permission for him to visit. 'I have to leave you now Graham, here's my card, please call me, and I will keep you informed too on how our patient is doing. I'll be calling back later to check on her.'

Graham witnessed for the first time a vulnerable state in this woman, it was her concern for August. He followed the nurse into the room where August lay. A drip feed trailing into her arm, compounding how seriously ill she was. There were flowers everywhere, and on the bedside table a staircase of expensive boxes of chocolates. 'I didn't think she had any relatives.' Graham whispered.

'There's no need to whisper, we can't wait for her to come round, and no she doesn't seem to have any relatives.'

'But all these.' He motioned at the array of gifts.

'All from Alicia, she comes twice a day.'

Graham stood at the side of the bed, looking down on the pale motionless face of August's.

'I'm afraid this is how she's been since Thursday night, well she is a lot better than she was, believe me. You might try talking to her, oh and there's a drinks machine just over the corridor.'

Graham took advantage of the vending machine first, and sipped at a coffee whilst trying to think of something to say to the lame August. He did the weather speech, made a joke about her boots and not being able to wear them in bed. He found it strange talking to someone so asleep. There was no response, he rumbled on some more. 'I met your friend today, she's very nice, says she is going to come in later. I called by your place and she let me in. She has taken care of your mail by the way. Mind you it's not all good news. Christ that slimy little creep of a man, he's such a..a a Bigshit!' Graham swore he saw August's lips move. 'August..August..it's me..Graham! oh shit.' Her mouth moved again. 'Come on girl, come on, oh nurse!, ..doctor, anybody..Angie!' he called.

Angie came in.

Graham was excited. 'She moved her lips!'

'Are you sure, sometimes you can stare for so long, and want them to move so bad, you think you see a movement.'

'I honestly did, I swear ! no bullshit!'

A sound came from August and Graham and Angie held hands.

CHAPTER FORTY THREE

It was early evening before Graham got through to Alicia to tell her the good news.

Graham was still excited. 'She wasn't fully awake, but rambling a bit, it was laughable really. I remember saying the chap at work was a big shit and that's what she kept repeating.'

'You didn't tell her she had got the sack did you?'

'No no, not that she would have understood, she didn't really come around fully before I had to leave.'

'Well thanks Graham, thank you so much, I will get down there right away.'

There was panic at the flat, Alicia darting around to get changed, and then nearly left without her wig on, not that it mattered, it would have confused the nurses though. She was really now having to think about her two persons. She thought about the night August collapsed. August didn't know it was her. She had backed away from her, from Sammy as well. She had looked angry, frightened and confused. When she was rambling and flaying her arms around, Alicia remembered her say 'bigshit'.

The hospital corridors seemed never ending this evening as Alicia sped on her way. She bumped into Angie on her way out. 'Hi, heard the good news then?'

'Yes, I'm sorry I can see you are on your way home, but could you please tell me how she is?'

'She's not upright yet, but she is awake, I haven't seen her the last hour, Sandra is the duty nurse, she'll tell you the latest.'

When Sandra took Alicia into the familiar room, she could see August still had her eyes closed and whispered. 'I thought she was awake.'

'Go and see,' Sandra said with a smile, 'I'll be back in a while.'

Alicia made her way to the bedside that August was facing and softly called her name. Slowly, August narrowly opened her eyes, it was a moment Alicia had watched for, for hours. She said her name again and August opened her eyes some more, and steadily her gaze travelled to meet her visitor's. Her pupils dilated some and then became small. There was a frozen demeanour about her face which chilled the air between them like an invisible claw, Alicia felt uncomfortable.

'August, it's me Ali, oh thank God you're alright.'

August slowly turned her head away.

'August…it is really me.' Alicia took hold of August's hand like she had done countless times before, this time, August dragged it from her, leaving Alicia open pawed and intensely wounded.

'It is me,' Alicia raced around to the other side of the bed, August turned her head again.

Alicia raised her voice, trying to hold back the tremble in her throat. 'Look at me, look it is me.'

August turned to look at her as Alicia untidily pulled off her blonde wig. 'See..it's me!'

There were tears brimming on the bottom lids of Alicia's grey eyes.

August also was close to tears, but she said in a croaky whisper, 'Go away from me, I don't want you near me.'

'Why?' Alicia wailed.

'Get out, get away from me.'

Alicia took her hand again, but August snatched it away. 'Don't touch me, get away from me.'

The nurse came in, paralysed for a few moments at the scene. August raising her up till now empty voice telling this visitor, the bringer of many gifts and concern to go. The visitor, crying, holding a wig in her hand, looking totally bewildered.

'Get her out of here!' August screamed at Sandra. The nurse was embarrassed and looked at Alicia, who said, 'she doesn't understand, I'm her friend.'

Sandra beckoned Alicia, and she followed her out of the room.

'I don't understand, what's the matter with her?'

Sandra said, 'It must be down to the illness,' and convinced Alicia to go home. Stood in the corridor where she had paced so many hours wishing for redemption for August, a good life. She had admired this stranger, who had been dealt a discouraging hand, from a bloody bad deck. She had witnessed someone who had nothing, but obviously worked all the hours God sent, and had even offered her help. Now the hospital scent seemed morose, she grew nauseous, and left. She couldn't remember the drive back to the flat. Her head was full of questions and crooked answers. She shivered at the cold, and at the icy discord running through her veins.

When she got in, she poured herself a brandy and tried to thaw the cold jangle inside. She sat and sipped, sipped and poured, poured over her thoughts and poured more brandy. Why was she so upset, she negotiated with herself. Who was this girl anyway!..she's just a stranger, really for God's sake! So, then why get so upset?, forget her, have another brandy. 'But why does she hate me!' she said aloud, and began to cry.

Alicia wanted to go to the safe haven of Brockley, through the tall stone gateposts, the high embracing walls, the large lush gardens, the safe house. There her Mother would reassure her, Nancy would hug her and Tom would swear that everything would be alright. But because of the brandy, she couldn't, so she poured another, and decided that she must stand on her own two feet. She picked up the pile of leaflets she had collected of commercial properties for sale. She was surprised at who was selling. It was difficult for her to concentrate, her thoughts still wandering back to August. Her eyed scanned the pages far too fast to pick up the information properly. She flicked from one property to another until she flung them up in the air with frustration. She settled her busy head against the cream sofa staring into the crate of orange flame hissing quietly in the gas fire. Her eyes became glazed again and the flames distorted into a spangle of orange and yellow. She looked up and the pale rectangle on the chimney breast stole her thoughts. Would she ever find out what picture hung there, would she ever be able to ask August. Would she ever know why the poor girl lived like she did, worked like she had. The phone rang and Alicia jumped nearly spilling her drink. After saying hello to Sammy, all Alicia could do was to blubber uncontrollably for five minutes, until Sammy decided to drive the eighty miles to be with her.

August Jackson had refused to eat breakfast and despite advice and reprimand had curled up to go to sleep. She didn't want to be awake and secreted her head under the covers to kill the light and fall drowsy with her own breath. The world beyond that bed was a barbed path to nowhere good and she didn't want to tread it. She wanted to desert life as she knew it. Maybe if she didn't eat anything, soon she would meet up with her Mum and Cruickshank, and he would sort her out a settled address. It would have to be better than that ice box she had been squatting in. Even if it was hell, at least she would be warm. August tried to close down her mind, release her turmoil from it's moorings, to float free into a hopeful calm. Her limbs were stiff and ached she did not want to move a muscle. She could hear the nurses' whisper, but she didn't care, maybe she was dying already. It was only a matter of time, and she would help to speed it up. When they brought in lunch, she dozily refused it.

'We will have to feed you by other means if you don't eat yourself', they chastised. August thought she knew what they meant and decided that it would be easy to pull a needle out of her arm.

CHAPTER FORTY FOUR

Sammy was trying to persuade Alicia to have something to eat.

'I couldn't really, you get something.'

'I'll wait to eat with you. Ooh Jesus Alicia, why don't you just phone the hospital?'

'No.'

'Then I'll drive you there.'

'No. I can't go. Would you phone?..please.'

When Sammy had replaced the receiver, she had only time enough to endorse the conversation when the phone rang again. Alicia shook her head unable to speak and gestured to Sammy to answer.

'Hello.'

'Hello Alicia it's Graham, I'm just phoning to see how August is.'

'Oh hello Graham,' Sammy answered more to announce who it was, 'it's not Alicia, but I have just phoned the hospital and I'm afraid August is refusing to eat,'

'Did she say anything to Alicia? I know things seem pretty wrought, August's circumstances and everything.'

'It seems she didn't say much really..err..nothing really.' Sammy was struggling for words when Alicia took the phone from her. 'Hello Graham, it's Alicia, I know you care about what's happening to August, and I do too, but I have to tell you…she wouldn't speak to me. She wouldn't have anything to do with me.'

Graham was put out. 'I don't understand.' He said

'Neither do I, she even demanded I leave, so I haven't seen her today,' her voice started to break emotionally. Graham heard the falter in her and wanted to help. ' I tell you what my love, I'm not far away from there tomorrow, I'll make a detour and call in to see her, do you think I would be allowed in around lunch time?'

'Yes, yes, I'm sure, I've been there at all hours, even close to midnight when she was comatose.'

'Alright then, will you be around at lunchtime, for me to get in touch?'

Alicia fumbled with her diary. 'Well I shouldn't be, but I will, I'll change my appointments, and in fact if you do that, I will treat you to lunch. Do you know 'The Conservatory' on the edge of town?' Alicia was just regretting that remembering her last trip when Robert was there, but when Graham said yes, she carried on. 'Meet us there at twelve.'

Sammy looked up when she heard the 'us', but resigned herself to having to cancel tomorrows calls, Alicia being so upset was more important to her than everything. She loved the woman, and couldn't even help herself.

There Alicia stood blurting on about this girl she didn't even know that well, even she had a silly softness for her, but Alicia had most of her time, thoughts and feelings for August's wellbeing. Sammy just honestly understood. Now she cradled her in her arms and she kissed the tears from her beautiful face, she knew she would do anything for Alicia. If anyone would ever hurt her, she would swing for them, she would die for her.

Alicia clung to Sammy, this was the first person in her life that truly loved her passionately, who apart from her parents, Nancy and Tom wanted nothing from her but love. This was a lover who came running when she was upset. The lover that took her on a trip to a place where she could forget all things and just have unadulterated pleasure. Alicia looked at Sammy now, pouring her a drink, attentive for her, fussing over her wellbeing. She was so beautiful, so exact, this girl could have anyone she wanted. What was she doing hanging around somebody so fractured she was trying to be two people, both of them going to pieces, and be so..so.. together. Alicia watched Sammy, every move so precise, in charge of the situation. 'I love you Sammy.' She blurted out.

'Not as much as I love you.' Sammy smiled.

'You don't know.' Alicia smiled back.

Wednesday morning announced itself with a sleet that attacked the window of Robert's bedroom. He woke believing he was happy, but he soon put that down to a dream he'd been having. Rich, free of work, nothing but good, hedonistic rewards. Surrounded with bronzed beauties in very little clothing serving him chilled champagne as he lazed around a cliff top swimming pool in one of the top hotels in the universe. He had woken with his hand around his own stiff cock and realised he was a lonely married man, with only the future in his hands. After taking care of that matter, he felt empty, unrewarded and angry. He would have to make himself breakfast again, go to work and still hadn't got Alicia in his grip. There was this expensive trip too that was not going to pay the investment back. He lay in his untidy and sex sprayed bed and thought about nubile oriental girls. He decided he would go on his own anyway.

CHAPTER FORTY FIVE

August refused breakfast again, but the nurse left it in front of her. She lay propped up by pillows and stared over and above the breakfast tray on the over bed table. She blew a sigh of discontent into the clinical air and glanced over to her left. There on the bedside table piled a wonderful stepped assortment of boxes of chocolates. She wondered first, why they were there and then tripped back to the pyramid. The trip was bad, the barbed path tightened it's grip in her head and she slumped down against the stacked pillows until her chin touched the covers. She was surprised that her belly didn't push against the tray table. Feeling her midriff, she found she didn't have a belly. Her hand involuntary moved across the flat flesh. It was tender, anything more than flat was just swollen. She pushed against it and it hurt some. She felt she should have been happy about that, but the prickly non future reared it's negative bribe. She lay her head to one side, slid the covers over her head and decided she would be better off dead. Definitely.

The nurses gently ranted when they retrieved the untouched breakfast, but August just faded back into her own oblivion, blocking out 'what the Doctors would say', and hoped they wouldn't come.

She was still trying to squeeze herself into sleep when, without any introduction from a nurse she heard an un-medicated voice announce himself. 'Are you awake?..August..are you awake?'

Vague but familiar the voice carried on, and she wanted to look, but the battle within was trying hard to make her lapse into a final sleep, and was losing.

'Well if you're not up to it,' the voice continued, 'but I don't quite know when I can make it again…probably Monday I expect.'

August realised then that she didn't know what day it was, she didn't care though, but who was it?, she knew it was friendly.

'They said you were awake.'

There was an empty pregnant silence and Graham wanted to fill it. August, under the cloak of hospital covers and a turmoil of decisions was overwhelmed. Graham continued, 'Don't tell me you're going to send me away, mind you, you're always forgetting me.'

August heard the scrawl of a chair being dragged to her bedside. She hung on to the words and the voice, but lay in another motive silence thinking so many thoughts at one time. The thoughts she had conditioned herself to behold, now had a difficult direction. The minutes that had dragged on became hours. The hours that she had tried to harness to sleep seemed useless as an egotistic almost cynical claw pulled her head from the grey sublime of what she wanted to believe was comfort. Surfacing she looked straight into the challenged round face of Graham Topps.

He smiled, forgiving August thought, feeling a pang of unseasoned guilt.

'Hi there,' Graham was still smiling, 'I was beginning to think you had had a relapse.'

August didn't say anything, but drooped her focus down to the bed sheets, and slowly turned her head from side to side.

'It's strange you know,' he said seriously, 'they told me you were much better, you look pretty miserable to me.'

August stared blankly at the bed sheet. There was that silence again. Graham stood up now and said, 'Well, if this is a visit, I guess you don't need me in it.' He started to walk to the door. August said panicky, 'No don't go..I'm sorry.' Still her eyes were downcast. Graham resumed his seat, and now August didn't know what to say. Graham tried to look relaxed, leaning forward, placing praying hands on the bed. 'I was speaking to one of your friends yesterday.'

August looked at him now, and then restored her doomed look at the sheets, which she nervously rubbed at with her thumb. 'I haven't got any friends.' She mumbled.

'Oh yes you have.'

'I haven't got any friends,' she repeated emphasising 'any'.

'Well thanks, should I really go now.'

'Oh no....I didn't mean..oh I'm sorry.'

'August, do you really believe that no one cares about you? I mean, who bought you all these?' Graham gestured to the bedside piled with a staircase of chocolate boxes, flowers and fruit. August pulled a frown.

'You do know who bought them don't you?'

'She's not my friend, I don't know who she is, someone who lives in the flat I used to live in, I don't know her.'

Graham watched as August rubbed the sheet faster and harder, her thumb nail flicking over the rim of the hem, like his youngest child did with her comforter.

'She is very upset, she told me that you wouldn't have anything to do with her.'

'I don't know why she should be so upset.'

'She cares about you.'

August looked at the window as if not to care.

'She cares about you a lot, and she is very hurt that you won't speak to her, why won't.'..

'She's not my friend.' August raised her voice now and repeated over again, 'she's not my friend, she's not my friend!' Tears started streaming down her face and her mouth contorted and she couldn't speak for crying. Graham moved to sit on the bed and put his arm around August, pulling a squeeze hoping to stop the erratic rubbing and picking and the tears.

'I think, August Jackson, you ought to tell me what's the matter.'

CHAPTER FORTY SIX

Don Holland was happy, he had secured another date with the rich widow, but his money on the piano keyboard was getting toward the lower notes. He would have to step up the charm, spend a little bit more to impress her. Even he knew you had to speculate to accumulate. At least he had two irons in the fire. If he sold the business, he could afford to disappear, even though he may have to look over his shoulder to evade the tax man. If he snared Brigitte, he wouldn't really have to sell up, but, if he did, he would be able to have both his own pocket money and Brigitte's wealth to play with.

Graham drove without concentration, his head full of what August had just reeled off, and imagined what she told him, or because she was suffering maybe had got her story mixed up. Her story certainly sounded a sensational muddle. Ranting on about someone called Sammy who was a woman she knew that turned out to be a lesbian, and there was Ali, who turned out to be a high class whore. He squeezed a finger into his collar as if to release the pressure around his neck, he wasn't going to enjoy this. He pulled into the car park and saw Alicia getting out of a red BMW. He was thinking that he could really fancy her, then, out of the passenger side another equally attractive woman took his fancy. Realising that this could be Sammy, whom August had just told him about, he forced two fingers into his collar. 'This is hot stuff.' he told himself.

Within seconds, they all met in the foyer. It was Sammy, and what a gorgeous pair of bookends, these two made Graham lecherous. If what August said was true, the thoughts he had made him hot. His complexion involuntary became more ruddy than usual. The three of them followed a young chap to an empty table. As they sat Graham noticed an envious gleam in the waiter's eyes, which made him feel good. It was Alicia who spoke first. 'Did you see her?, is she alright,? Did she say anything?'

'Alicia!' Sammy stopped her, 'give Graham a chance, we might even order first, save lots of pestering.'

'She did have a lot to say actually,' Graham said sticking a finger in his collar again, 'but it might be an idea to order, it could be a long lunch.'

Throughout the formalities of menu discussion, Graham noticed the closeness between the two beautiful women across from him, it was more than a buddy relationship for sure. He now knew, August might not have been as mixed up after all. He now thought, even doubting himself that he wouldn't be as nervous broaching the subject, or would he be.

Alicia couldn't contain herself, and as soon as the waiter had taken the order, she began her questions again. Graham held up an arresting hand and said. 'August is okay under the circumstances. She is still not eating, and the Doctors are very concerned about that. She is however extremely upset and I think a little muddled.'

'Muddled? Sammy said, looking puzzled.

'Would you mind if I loosened my tie? I feel more comfortable eating without this restriction.'

The girls silently shook their heads in unison, Alicia asking what August was upset about.

'Eerr ..well,' Graham swallowed hard, 'you will have to help me on this one, this is the muddled bit.' Just then a waiter appeared and placed bread roll at their elbows, and Graham busied himself with a knife and butter, watching for the waiters return with the soup.

'Go on.' Alicia urged. Graham's exaggerated glance to her rear announced the waiter's delivery of their dishes. Before Graham had dunked his first piece of bread, Alicia pestered him again.

'We,e.ll,' Graham started nervously, 'August said some strange things, well not strange, really but, well more sensational I suppose.' He crammed more bread into his mouth, not really wanting to carry on, but he looked at the two waiting faces, politely sipping from their spoons. Alicia now using hers' as a wand to wind him on.

'She ranted a bit about a friend of hers called Ali, who turned out to be a high class whore.'

'What!' Alicia reeled with shock, amused Sammy nearly choked laughing.

Feeling some relief at the amusement, Graham carried on, 'Do you know her as well?'

Sammy was now incapable of finishing her soup to save spraying it across the table.

'Ignore her Graham.' Alicia smiled, 'do carry on.'

'She also mentioned you Sammy,' he took a mouthful of hot soup, which should have been blown cool first, it trickled down his throat like hot lava, his neck was now crimson.

'What did she say about me? don't tell me, she said I was a stripper.' Sammy laughed.

'No…nooo, she didn't say that exactly, she did mention strip though,' He took a slug of water in a bid to cool his nerves and his throat. The two females were now incredulous, silent and waiting for him to speak.

'August said she saw you stripping,..err well stripping her friend, the one that turned out to be a high class whore.'

Graham witnessed Alicia turn a shade of rouge now, Sammy remained calm but puzzled. The clatter of Alicia's spoon hitting the floor broke the silence. A waiter appeared at the sound of the silver gong, and Alicia decided they had all finished their soup, and were ready for the main course. Graham politely made no resistance, though he was hungry and found eating was preferable to talking at this charged moment. Left with nothing to fill his mouth, he carried on.

'A lot of words got washed away in garbled sobbing, but I still don't understand what this has to do with you.' He said, looking at Alicia, who was still warm with embarrassment. It was Sammy who spoke. 'What I can't understand is, how did she see us?' Alicia elbowed Sammy, it was Grahams turn to look puzzled.

'Alicia', Sammy chastised, 'just tell Graham that you are that high class whore.'

Alicia elbowed Sammy again, who was infected with giggles.

'Graham, I am not a high class whore.'

It was at this moment the waiter arrived with the plates. Sammy muffled a goster of laughter into a serviette, Graham had to smirk as the waiter obviously took his time, lingering for the next snippet, and Alicia played with the newly laid cutlery. When the waiter had idled away, Alicia dared herself to explain. 'Oh dear Graham, it is complicated, well it's not, 'it's more..Oh God help me,..I am Ali..and

Alicia, but I am not a prostitute. Good Lord where did she get that story from.'

A long half whispered explanation took them through lunch and Graham listened, fascinated and incredulous that this was in fact Robert Simpson's wife. He was beside himself at the finale, that she was a lesbian. Slime's wife was a lesbian, his marriage had collapsed, and he had done the most despicable thieving act against August, earning him the total bastard of the decade award. It couldn't have happened to a more deserving person he thought.

Graham did consider not telling them about the hole in the ceiling because he fancied to try the view himself, but he did want to help all three girls get back together again. August would need their friendship more than ever now, and this was the best entertainment he had had in ages.

CHAPTER FORTY SEVEN

Robert didn't like the small, grim, stinking office of Dennis Roebuck. He didn't care for Roebuck himself, but he didn't have time to shop around for a Private Detective. He thought Roebuck looked as if he had remained in the seventies. His wide lapelled black leather jacket had certainly been dragged from there. His woolly polo neck probably had as well. A droopy dark moustache was an echo of his hairline, collar length and sideburns. Robert was curious to know if he was wearing flared trousers, but he had not yet ventured from behind his untidy desk. Roebuck chain smoked too, which aggravated Robert. He watched as his nicotine slicked fingers fanned out the photographs of Alicia.

'These recent Mr Simpson?'

'About a year ago, she hasn't changed.'

'Attractive.' Roebuck said releasing a pall of smoke. Robert didn't reply, but tried not to breathe in what Roebuck had exhaled. 'So Mr Simpson, you would like your wife followed?'

Robert nodded.

'Hyland Way is your home, but Mrs Simpson doesn't live there, she has left you?'

'Not exactly, I believe she is at her Mothers.'

Roebuck looked at the notes. 'And that is Brockley House, and the name you have beside that is Heyhott, is that correct?'

Robert nodded again, 'what I want you to do is find out if she is there and where else she goes. I've also written down the registration of her car, it's a black Golf GTi., the address of her Karate club, a couple of her friends, her place of work and her hairdressers.'

Roebuck now blew another lung full of cigarette smoke toward Robert and he couldn't wait to get out. He stood up to leave, took out his wallet and handed fifty pounds to Roebuck. 'That is the initial fee you asked for?'

'Yes thank you, I'll bill you for the remainder, when I deliver the information.'

'I will be away until the tenth of December, so don't try to contact me, I shall be in touch with you when I return.'

Roebuck stood up to reveal he was wearing faded jeans. The two men shook hands and Robert clunked down the uncarpeted stairs and out into the fume filled street. He was feeling hungry. A sharp wind buffeted him and whipped up a few spots of rain into harsh wet bullets. The 'Hot food' sign in the pub window over the road drew him, and soon he was sat nursing a pint of lager, while he waited for his lunch. A fat youth came over and pestered him to buy a gold cigarette lighter.

'No thanks, I don't smoke.'

'What about one o' these then?' the fat man produced a watch, two slim calculators and another small cased object. He brought his fat head close to Robert and lowered his voice. 'This watch..two 'undred quid in the shops, this last one I'm letting go for fifty quid. Need a calculator? a fiver that's all, a fiver.'

Robert shook his head, wanting fat man to leave him alone. But fat man picked up the other case and started fumbling with it. 'Now this, just what a gentleman of your ..err.. wotsits needs. A dictaphone..a little tape thingy..see just press it 'ere…speak look 'the fat brown cow jumped over the lazy dog'. Robert listened as the little machine played back fat man's voice. He was mildly impressed and handled the little black box.

'It's yours for twenty.'

Robert's meal was called out for him to collect, fat man followed him to the bar and got excited when a twenty pound note came out of Robert's wallet but put out when it went straight over the counter. 'My last twenty,' Robert said, handing back the Dictaphone. Fat man watched the change being handed back. 'Tell you what sir, to you, just fifteen notes, 'ow's that?' Robert was tempted. He was also tempted by the hot food in front of him. Just then a scruffy thin youth joined fat man. Fat man winked at him, Robert saw the gesture and took his plate to the table.

''Ere, don't you want it?'

Robert shook his head. The two youths followed their target. Robert looked up at them and said, 'I'll give you a tenner.'

'A tenner! but it's worth thirty five.'

Robert shrugged and started on his meal.

'Go on then.' Fat man slid the gadget onto the table and Robert shoved over a ten pound note in exchange. Robert felt smug with his deal and thought he could now enjoy his meal in peace, but fat man spread himself heavily onto the adjacent bench seat. Robert pulled his plate a little closer to him, like an animal wishing to share no more. He looked intently at his food and at adopting the same defence, hoping fat man would take the hint. But instead the huge denim clad arm waved over the stick insect mate.

'This is Dave, between us we can get anythin', 'ain't that right mate?'

Robert glanced an acknowledgment at Dave saying, 'okay, I'll remember that.'

'We've got contacts' 'aven't we Dave?' Dave nodded and sat down opposite Robert, who found himself rushing his food in an attempt to control his own activity of being on his own. He failed. His half eaten meal and drink was left on the table went he excused himself and left. Fat man picked up the chips and stick insect downed the lager.

CHAPTER FORTY EIGHT

It was 6.30pm, Tom had just sauntered into the kitchen and the warmth eased his bones. The smell of freshly turned out meat and potato pie filled the room and his nostrils. Nancy was humming her own tunes as she swished about the sink. He sidled up to the familiar table, the evening paper waiting for him. He picked it up and drifted over to the well worn green leather wing chair near the fireplace, and planted his slim frame deep into it's cosiness.

'Lady is out tonight.' Nancy called over her shoulder. Tom grunted, to let her know that he had heard her.

'Out with that man again.'

Tom turned a page and grunted 'Umm' again

'You know, that man with the pointy beard, balding. Don't like a man with a pointy beard.'

Another newspaper page rustled over the air. 'It's damn cold out there.' Tom said.

'Some people don't like folk because their eyebrows or eyes are too close together, I don't like pointy beards. I don't like his beady eyes much either.'

Tom settled on the sports page, he had though taken in what Nancy was saying because he thought the same.

'Have you locked up Tom because we'll be off straight after dinner?'

'Yes, the cars are garaged, the back door is locked, can't lock the front until Mrs Heyhott is away, what time is she away?'

'He's coming to pick her up at eight. She says they have a table booked for half past. It'll be somewhere posh I expect.'

'Yes I suppose, but they'll not be getting meat 'n potato pie like yours love.'

'No, likely be some fancy mousse and a frogs leg. This will be on the table in ten minutes, so just go and see if Mrs Heyhott has got her key and remind her how to set the burglar alarm.'

'But I've just sat down with my paper.'

Well make sure you do it after dinner. You know she forgot to set the alarm last time. I know I wouldn't like coming home to this big place on my own at night.'

'Aah, but will she be coming in on her own?'

Nancy gave Tom a stare, her eyes narrowed. 'she whispered, 'You don't think she would….with ..him do you?'

Tom shrugged. 'Who knows, they've been out a few times together.'

'Nooo..he's not right for her, there's something about him…you mark my words.' Nancy waved a serving spoon like a baton to emphasise her words of warning. Tom smiled an acknowledgment, knowing that she was always right. On matters such as these, she was always right.

'He drives a nice motor.' Tom said volunteering the only good point he could.

'So did Hitler.' Nancy snapped.

CHAPTER FORTY NINE

The teatime trolley clattered along the shiny hospital floor and August heard it stop outside her room. Angie, the nurse she liked, held the door open for an older woman who carried in the tray. The tray was placed over the bed table, which Angie manoeuvred toward August.

'Come on, sit up, you must eat some of this one.'

'I'm not hungry.' said August pulling a face.

'If you don't eat some of this meal, you will have something to pull a face about.'

August didn't like the tone of Angie's voice and stared at her silently asking for an explanation. Angie slid the plate closer to the patient and whispered, 'Just a bit of inside information, I know if you don't start eating now, the Doctor is going to sanction a different method and believe me, you won't have an appetite for that!'

August blew a disgruntled sigh, took up the fork and slowly ate a couple of mouthfuls of potato. Angie watched and encouraged. 'Just have a little bit more, a little of the fish now. You don't have to clear your plate. I can tell the Doctor that you have started eating.'

August did as she was told, but chewing seemed too much like an effort. She did clear the semolina pudding though and enjoyed a cup of tea. Angie was beside herself with curiosity at what had happened with her visitor, but didn't want to say anything to upset August. 'Sandra said you had a visitor this morning?'

August nodded.

'Boyfriend was he?'

'Just a friend, a work mate.'

'That was nice of him to come and see you.' Angie was disappointed at the lack of information. 'You all work together then, all four of you?'

'Four?'

'The two blonde ladies that have been visiting?'

August stayed quiet, Angie was getting warm, but didn't want to over-heat the conversation.

'No we don't all work together.' August said firmly.

'Oh it's just that he came here with one of them one day, Alicia, the one with.'

'I don't know her.' August cut Angie off short and the nurse knew not to push any further, but now was even more intrigued. She took her time plumping up the pillows just in case August offered more talk on the subject, but not one more word came out. Angie retreated with the tray and a smile.

So August was alone again, alone with noises that had become so familiar, so regular. The train like chatter of the trolley wheels, the clip clop of footsteps and distant thuds of doors opening and closing. So many doors August thought. There were voices, some clear, some just a drone. It was a never ending patter, like a ticking clock, sometimes it annoys you, mostly you forget it's there, whether you are aware or not, it was monotonous. August stared at the framed print on the wall opposite like she had done before. It was a picture of a vase of red and yellow tulips. August decided, she did not want to see another tulip, she wanted that picture to be 'Bigshit bay' and tried to imagine it. The red cupped heads of the tulips spoiled her imagination, so she closed her eyes and pictured the green cliff top. She saw herself lying there, peeping over the edge. The sea was very rough and pounded angrily below. Her Mum's voice came sweet and sound, 'I wish you wouldn't get so close to the edge, if you fell over I would never forgive myself.'

August meandered back through conversations she had with her Mum. She would say to August, 'We haven't got much money, but we're clean and tidy. I'm always proud of you when we're out. You remember your manners and I'm sure you always will, and always let me be proud of you.'

The door opened just then and Angie came in with the Doctor. August swallowed the hard hurting lump in her throat. The Doctor picked up the clipboard from the bottom of the bed. 'The nurse tells me you ate some of your dinner.'

August pushed herself to sit up straight. 'Does that mean I can go now?' she asked.

The Doctor and nurse looked surprised.

'It seems that you have regained more than just your appetite. But it's not total recovery by any means. We need to make sure that you are fit and well before we set you free.' He gave a grimace of a smile. August pushed herself up some more and said, 'I'm feeling much better now.'

'Good, I'm glad to hear that,' the Doctor spoke monotone as he simultaneously read the chart clipped to the board. 'You're temperature is a little up and down, we need to stabilize that amongst other things. The nurse will take your blood pressure and tomorrow we will do the same. We also need to see if your appetite improves.'

'But how long before I can go?'

The Doctor hated that question. He knew full well that his patient could not be allowed out yet, and you could never say the right thing. He opened the door before saying, 'We will see what the patient is like tomorrow, nurse will report back to me and I will be able to give you a better idea.' With that he left. Angie followed him saying she would be back later.

The bed that had been a warm cocoon for her, now felt like a shackle. She slumped with her thoughts. Her Mum had worked so hard to keep her and her brother clothed decent. She had wanted so much for them to make something of themselves. Well August thought, she had a nonstarter in David, but she wouldn't fail her Mum. As soon as she could get out of the hospital, she would. She would work harder than before, pay off that bloody debt to the bank and start afresh.

CHAPTER FIFTY

Brigitte Heyhott was surprised to find Don holding open the passenger door of a Mercedes. 'A change of chariot Donald?' she said as he settled into the driver's seat.

'Having the Bentley valeted,' He lied, 'got to keep her smart to sell.'

'Pity, I was getting quite fond of her.'

'She could be yours you know.'

Brigitte made a sound that he thought quite encouraging. 'It would be nice if you were to have her, I would know she had gone to a good home.'

'Oh I have a few things to sort out before I make any large purchases.'

Don didn't know if that was good or bad news. 'Anything I can help you with my dear?' he tried to sound casual, but was itching for information.

'No, no it's just some trusts and funds you know?'

Don didn't know but needed to know so bad, he wanted more. 'Ah well, if ever I can be of any help to you, but I'm sure a very capable lady like yourself will have everything under control.' he said hoping his speech would allow Brigitte to empty more of the subject. He liked the sound of trusts and funds and the only help he wanted to give Brigitte was how to spend it. He really wanted more details but was pleased with the bullshit he had added at the end. Besides, there was time to find out all he needed to know of her chattels.

Brigitte had begun to enjoy the getting ready to go out, she used to enjoy going out with her husband, and after his death she dismissed any activity that related to enjoyment. Her mourning was a year of sadness. She had been in limbo, no art galleries, no dinner parties, no trips abroad. No glitter or glamour, no smiles. Out came the drab tweed suits, and Brigitte Heyhott had thrown herself into charity work. It was her only socialising for a year, then gradually she began playing bridge again, and turning up for the odd social get together. Now she was choosing the evening wear for the occasion, visiting the hairdressers more often and thoroughly enjoying the attention. Donald did know some lovely restaurants and did seem to be a welcomed visitor. She did wonder about him as a conversationalist though. It is nice she thought that someone wanted to know about oneself. When he did talk it was more about restaurants, good food and wines more than anything. He always seemed to be probing her to do the talking and she supposed it wasn't a bad trait, she thought, but he asked about her late husband and the recent past. She still felt precious about that, and always steered the discussion along another route.

Don desperately wanted to know more. He had ordered Champagne with their meal and insisted that Brigitte had a vintage port to round it off. He hoped the alcohol would loosen her tongue. He was wrong. He did get the idea though that the old mare was getting a little frisky on the booze. He certainly wasn't ready for that!. It suited him to play the honourable gentleman for once. For God sake he liked the buxom tarts, he wanted prostitutes. He didn't have to hold his stomach in, having to perform for his partner's pleasure. The prostitutes took care of his pleasure and they didn't give a flying shit what he looked like with his clothes off and he didn't have to care about them. He paid for his pleasure. As he pulled to a halt in front of the porch of Brockley House, Brigitte paused as she opened the car door, 'you are coming in aren't you Donald?'

He tapped the dashboard. 'Look at the time my dear, I do have to run a company tomorrow.'

Brigitte didn't like the endearment 'Dear', she was a widow, not a national treasure, but he was paying her such attention, and taking her out to nice restaurants, plus she felt an argument of frisky in her being. 'Donald, come along and have a night cap, there's no one else at home.'

'I can't have any more to drink, I'm driving.'

She placed her hand over his on the gearstick. She lowered her eyes and her voice, 'You don't have to drive, you could stay here, if you wish.'

Don was feeling decidedly nervous. He couldn't run away from his treasure trove, but if she was intent on sex, he didn't know if he could get it up with her. That would be burying the treasure and him without a shovel. 'Oh my darling Brigitte,' he said kissing her hand to give him a few precious seconds to think, 'A little white lie I'm afraid, I will see you inside safe and sound, but then I must leave for I have to pack my case for a journey to Manchester airport tonight, I have to take the shuttle flight to London from Manchester first thing in the morning.'

Brigitte was mildly disappointed, she didn't actually know if she was ready to handle a more intimate relationship, but, the attention would have been nice. Don turned on the charm by getting out of the car and opening the door for her.

'Oh Donald, would you please switch the burglar alarm off for me?'

This aggravated him, he wanted to drop her off and get away. 'Certainly my dear, where will I find it?'

'Under the stairs, you have 40 seconds. 'she said fumbling for the door key.

'Where is the alarm key?' he said stopping her from unlocking the door.

'Oh that's in it.'

'You shouldn't leave it in the alarm,'

'I know, but I can never get it in the right hole. Just turn it anti clockwise.' She said pushing open the door. He found the alarm box and stopped the flashing light. Brigitte floated past him and went into the drawing room. He followed. She was hovering by a set of crystal decanters, one of which she had picked up, 'Are you sure you wouldn't like a night cap Donald?' She was pouring a drink into a brandy glass when he sauntered in. 'Not another drop Brigitte, and I really must bid you good night.'

Brigitte was now stood in front of the grand fireplace. The mantelpiece was as tall as her shoulders, carved stone and elegant, just as she was. She had switched on the table lamps which showed off her beautiful features. She had poise, she was polished and cultured, and would be described as attractive, with high cheek bones, slight arched eyebrows framed pale blue eyes. Although Don Holland would have classed her as an old mare, he knew she was a thorough bred. He stepped forward to kiss her on the cheek, hoping that would be his goodnight bidding. When her hands slid up the lapels of his jacket, he knew he wouldn't be getting away so lightly. Brigitte pressed herself close to him and he knew he was in trouble.

It was the closest she had been to a man since Peter. A long time since any sensations of arousal moved within her. Although she felt the need to be touched, she really didn't know if she was ready. It had been an age ago and she didn't want to mix up feelings of lust with love. Just then she caught sight of Peter's portrait and the flickering desires went out. She drew gently away. 'Thank you for a wonderful evening Donald, I mustn't be rude and repay you by keeping you when you have such a busy schedule.'

Don Holland couldn't believe his luck. 'Oh my darling Brigitte, the pleasure is all mine. It is a pity but, tomorrow is a heavy day for me, and I'm not as young as I used to be.'

They smiled at one another, both relieved now. He kissed her hand and then just to keep the hotter stuff warm, gave her a lingering peck on the lips. 'Keep the weekend free,' he said as he left.

CHAPTER FIFTY ONE

The hole in the ceiling wasn't so noticeable, being on the perimeter of the plaster rose in the centre of the room, but now Alicia knew it was there, she couldn't help but stare at it. 'Thank God I moved the bed over here,' she thought. Sammy had gone to the bathroom. Alicia lay naked under the duvet, relaxed and spent after nearly two hours of pleasure. She lay with a smile on her face, not believing this small box of a flat could have held so many changes for her. It had been her escape, a closet for her masquerade. It was like opening a door to a new life when she entered this little place. In such a short space of time so many changes had happened. She was so content here, and when Sammy reappeared, Alicia knew who was most responsible for her happiness.

'Come here you high class whore!' Sammy said jumping into bed. They both collapsed into fits of giggles. 'Oh my God Alicia, you looked so embarrassed.'

'I was embarrassed my darling little stripper.'

'Are you still?'

'Why should I be, I have never been so happy in my entire life.'

Robert Simpson stumbled upstairs while speaking into the dictaphone and downing his seventh gin. He sat on the toilet as a seat and carried on his ramble into the machine. 'Razor, soap, flannel, toothpaste..and brush. Deodorant, oh..aftershave and nice smellies,' he scanned the bathroom, 'what else will I need, towels? No they'll be there, bloody ought to be trimmed with gold the money it's costing. Christ you're a bitch Alicia…ahh yes condoms, get yourself some condoms Robert old boy.' He rocked his way along the landing and into his bedroom. He opened the wardrobe and examined all the drawer contents too, speaking into the dictaphone all the time.

'Boxers, get some new and some briefs, go to laundry, make sure you get silk shirts back in time. Oh yes trunks, ties, better take a dicky I suppose. Condoms, yes yes, got to get them, mustn't forget though. Socks, shoes, suits, hey wait a minute, I bet the cow's taken all the bloody suitcases. He took a large mouthful of gin and charged to the spare bedroom. Robert opened the door to the cupboard over the stairs. There were two suitcases still there, he dragged them out, a thud came from inside the smaller one and he opened it. It was the handbag. He clenched his fist, threw back his head, 'Yes!' he shouted as if he had found treasure. His excitement turned sour as the bank statements he found in there were prehistoric ones from Alicia's student days. The bag contained nothing more than a collection of what was once important. Then he found something resembling treasure, a current credit card, still in the envelope it was sent in, unsigned, then in another envelope, the PIN number.

'Who's a lucky boy then, I bet she forgot about this since she got her gold card.' He snatched up the Dictaphone and recorded the card details and PIN. 'China should be much more fun now.'

CHAPTER FIFTY TWO

A week went by before anyone visited August, it had been Graham's idea. He told Sammy and Alicia that it might do August good to have some space to think. Now she was getting better, she may be able to put things into perspective. He was to be the first visitor. Graham didn't know what to expect and decided to ask the Nurse how she was.

'She did pick up,' the Sister explained, 'started eating a little, and then when she was told she was too weak to leave yet, she dipped into a lethargic state again.'

'Oh good,' Graham thought, 'another jolly visit.' He spotted a newspaper trolley down the corridor and bought a 'girly' magazine. He delivered it to a less than happy August. Her face didn't brighten when he walked in.

'Hiya, thought you might like something to read.' He placed the magazine in front of her.

'Thank you.'

'It's alright, am I the first visitor of the day then?'

'You're the only visitor since you last came.'

Graham didn't react, but then again she wasn't looking at him, but flicked aimlessly through the magazine.

'Don't your relatives know you're ill?'

'I haven't got any, well apart from a brother and I've disowned him. I don't know anyone else. I don't have any friends.'

'Oh but you do.' Graham said tapping the unopened chocolates. August flicked the pages faster. 'What were you doing with that prostitute?' she said snapping the magazine shut.

'What prostitute?'

'You know? the one from the flat.'

'August, I think we need to have a little chat,' he said drawing up a chair. 'Now I want you to begin with..why aren't you living at the flat anymore?'

August began turning the pages again. 'Because I moved,' she said sarcastically.

'I know you moved and I know you moved upstairs, I've been there.'

She looked at him horrified. 'How did you get in? you don't know my address!'

'I got your address from work.'

'It's only temporary..just..just for a while, until..until I find somewhere closer to work,' She stammered, 'I'm looking for a nicer place.'

'You moved out of a nicer place, why?' Graham gently took hold of her wrist, 'Now, come on, you've got something to tell me, and I've got something to tell you.'

August took some getting started, but when she did, it all came flooding out.

'And, that's why I couldn't afford the boots, and that's why I can't stay in here, I'm losing money from 'The Crown' and the Cinema, still at least I get sick pay.'

A tell-tale grimace travelled across Graham's face, August saw it. 'I do get sick pay, don't I?' She looked worried. Graham didn't know quite what to say, she had to know. 'Oh shit,' he thought, 'why me!' August seemed to go whiter than her already pale pallor. 'Please tell me I'm entitled to sick pay, or I might as well stay here and die.'

'August,' he didn't know how to put it and clenched his teeth together, 'August, you..would get sick pay…if you ..had a job.'

'What do you mean?'

'I'm sorry to be the bearer of bad news sweetheart, but apparently you were spotted working at the Odeon, and you had apparently been off work sick.'

'But I can explain what happened!, I thought I would be better.' August was getting terribly upset and Graham didn't know if he had done the right thing telling her. August began to cry and he sat right beside and hugged her shoulders.

'I can't believe it,' she sobbed, 'I may as well be dead.'

'Hey, we'll have none of that talk, now you can cry it all out, and while you're doing that, I'm going to do the talking, and I don't want any interruptions.' He began with Alicia's story of moving into the flat, 'because she was married to a horrible man.' He could see that August wasn't paying much attention, so he asked her, 'do you know who that horrible man is August?, that man is the man who stole your pyramid design.' Graham felt August stop her panting sniffle and tense up. Now he had her attention. She raised her head, her amber eyes looked alive and questioning.

'Do you know who that man is?'

She shook her head slowly, but deliberately, her eyes never leaving his.. Now he had the fish hooked, he paused just as a salesman does, making sure he has the punter before he reels them in.

'Tell me, tell me who he is.'

Sold, he thought and withdrew his comforting arm and sat back on the chair very close to the bed.

'Tell me Graham.'

'Okay, but first promise me that you'll hear me out.'

August nodded and pushed herself more upright.

'The man…is.. our very own 'Slime', Robert Simpson.' August clenched her teeth so tight, she nearly split a filling. She drew a surge of air through her nose that flared her nostrils.

'So, August, we all have something in common. We all hate the bastard!'

'Not as much as me.' She spat.

'I don't know about that, you see Alicia, shall we say Ali.' August threw him a look that made him raise a correcting finger. 'Ah ah,' he said before carrying on, 'that man has done some pretty awful things to that woman, but she was beginning to handle that, but, the one thing that pisses her off more than anything that he's done, is what he's done to you.'

August produced a puzzled frown, trying to connect up her image of Ali and Slime.

'But how did she know? I don't understand.' August was bewildered now. She knew Ali knew about the pyramid. Then August remembered her interest in the project, the gift of paints, the hot toddy. She had a pang of how she thought she had a friend when no one else was there.

'She found out somehow,' Graham said, 'and apparently, every time she tried to see you, you weren't there, obviously because you were working. And the blonde..err prostitute, is not a prostitute August. That is Ali.'

August was stunned, and Graham realised how complex the whole thing was just trying to explain it. But he tried the best he could with the information he had been blasted with himself. August remained silent and listened to the story. She stared at the tulip picture not seeing the red cups of petals, but the images from Graham's words. When Sammy came into the story, she remembered the despair she had felt, that Sammy had taken away. Graham paused, and August said, 'But I saw them together, it wasn't Ali.'

'Yes it was,' Graham said firmly, 'I've just explained all that.'

'But they were kissing and…and then they were…well..they must have been..doing..'

'It doesn't matter what they 'must' have been doing August, that doesn't matter at all.'

'But I saw them!'

'Yes, you saw them, but you weren't supposed to see them.'

August had a sharp pang of guilty spy stick her. Graham saw her reaction and said, 'What I mean is…they weren't putting on a show for you.'

August swallowed hard.

'Well, they thought they were doing whatever they were doing in privacy, just imagine…well you have got to err..imagine,' Graham stood up now like a lawyer in front of the bar. 'You have got to get out of your head, what you think you saw.'

'But I did see it.'

'I know, I know, I mean, you have to get it straight that, there is no blonde prostitute, or stripper!'

'Stripper?' August looked more than confused.

'No..no, forget the stripper,' 'God this is hard,' thought Graham, striding about the foot of the bed. 'Now. There is this one person called Ali, who is also Alicia, married to Slime. She is your friend and so is Sammy. What they do in privacy does not affect you or I,' he said pushing a finger behind his tie and collar. 'All I know and all you need to know is this August Jackson. You are up shit canal without a canoe, never mind a paddle, and you hardly have the strength to swim. And with a work colleague like Slime, a brother like David and a tosser of a boyfriend like Shaun, you sure as fucking hell don't need any enemies sweetheart.'

He paused standing at the bottom of the bed, he bent forward gripping the metal frame, he had said his piece except, he added, 'So if I were you, I wouldn't let your friends go so easily.'

August was taken up with rubbing the sheet hem, her eyes glazed with tears. She swallowed hard before trying to speak. 'But I really don't have any friends.'

'Now, that sweetheart is up to you.' He walked up to her, kissed her on the forehead and went to the door. 'This friend will see you next week.' He then left. On the other side of the door, he met Angie. 'Do you think you could leave her on her own for five minutes,' he said gently and winked, 'I think it will do her good.' Angie smiled and walked away looking at her watch, five minutes would be all she could bear before getting in there.

CHAPTER FIFTY THREE

Graham drove out of the car park feeling really sharp, it had been the best sell he had ever done. His ego switch was on trip and he went onto the rest of his calls with so much positive, he could have surged the national grid. He made sales and he was late home again. Pamela was beginning to ask questions, and he told her this incredulous tale. He felt good that he could talk about it all with his wife. He felt even better when she understood, and felt truly knackered and happy after the most exciting sex romp they had had in ages. He also knew that he would never stray again.

The following morning, Pamela prepared him his favourite full English breakfast. She was still interested in the story he had told her, intrigued even, and she suggested he rang Alicia. 'I think you ought to tell her to try a visit to August now.' Graham finished his breakfast and phoned Alicia, and told her just that.

'Do you really think so?' Alicia said, gripping the receiver so tight her knuckles were white.

'We both think so, my wife as well.'

'You told your wife!' Alicia broke into a whisper.

'Yes, she understands perfectly.' Graham looked at Pamela who advanced and took the receiver from him. 'Alicia, go and see her my love, you have nothing to lose, but August has.'

With this aspiration from a stranger, Alicia began to converse with this faceless person.

'I don't know what to do.' Alicia burbled on.

'Do what's in your heart, I think that's taken you to the right place, don't you?'

Alicia blushed and was please the conversation was by phone. 'Yes,' Alicia said, 'thank you err..I don't know your name.'

'Pamela, I'll pass you back to Graham now.' Graham was looking at his wife with a new perception. He realised that he was married to a very understanding person, not what his Mother had said at all. It had never crossed his mind that she might be interested in what happened to him at work. Albeit, this was an incredible case, but he had never really talked to her about anything to do with work, apart from being threatened with redundancy, things that would extremely affect them. He watched her now as he spoke, systematically clearing the breakfast things away, cleaning porridge debris from a six foot radius of the baby. She was smiling through her chores, wiping the table, entertaining the baby and toddler and she was pretty. Graham put the phone down, August's predicament in his head, he kissed the kids and took hold of his wife in a bear hug. 'God, I'm a lucky man.' He whispered into her hair.

CHAPTER FIFTY FOUR

It took three attempts for Sammy to find a phone in working order on the outskirts of Birmingham. She checked her watch it was just before 10am. Sammy punched the numbers hoping Alicia would be at the other end. She was shivering, not just from the November cold, but she had just received a tough bollocking from her sales director, as her figures were down for the month. She cursed when she heard the engaged tone, and began the routine again. Still engaged, she punched the numbers harder knowing it wouldn't make any difference, but her temper was up. Then she wondered who was on the phone talking to Alicia, could it be her husband tracked her down? , she found herself deeply disturbed with jealousy, then pulled a face as she caught her distorted reflection on the numbers board. 'Green eyed monster.' she said out loud and then smiled as she heard the double ring warble. She composed herself when she heard Alicia's voice. No way would Sammy let on to her lover she was so upset, but Alicia did think something was wrong.

'Sammy darling are you alright?'

'Of course I am, I'm frantically cold though. I'm in a draughty phone booth in Sutton Coldfield shivering my nipples off.'

'Ha, listen can you get up here?'

'Why, what's happened?' Sammy asked hoping she wouldn't have to abandon a work day, she didn't need to lose her job.

'It's August, Graham has been to visit, and thinks we ought to go.'

'Well I don't think I can make it now darling, but why don't you go?'

'On my own?'

'Sure, if you want to go now, I can't get there unless you want to go this evening.'

'Oh Sammy if I wait, I will chicken out for sure, could you make it for lunch time?'

'Darling I can't, I have some calls I have got to make.' The pips started to threat. 'I haven't got anymore change, I'll see you later.'

The line purred empty and Sammy shivered again as she hung up the receiver. She dashed back to the car. There she sat staring at the passers' by hunched up in their heavy coats, hands deeply trenched in pockets, scarves to guard their ears from the cold. She turned on the engine to power the heater. Her long polished finger nails tapped the steering wheel, she was so angry about the telling off. Every month she had hit her target sales, and so they pushed her more. All the extra hours she had worked, the nights away from home, a useful ingredient to destroy a relationship as she had found out. Sammy thumped the steering wheel now, snatched on her seat belt and headed out of the urban skirts of Birmingham and toward the countryside of Derbyshire.

Robert had just made the breakfast sitting. He had just rid himself of jet lag the previous day, but his metabolism was still uncertain from too many gin and tonics last night. He really felt like taking breakfast in his room, but didn't want to miss out on any available women, ten days wasn't that long for conquering. Most tables in the dining room were empty, and the feeling of 'must try harder' overwhelmed him. He ordered the biggest English breakfast to put a lining on his stomach, and whilst he waited made a bet with himself. He decided that, no less than three different women should be his conquest, that shouldn't be a let down, but at least one of them should be a native Chinese. He felt happier now with his own challenge than he did with his Chinese English breakfast.

CHAPTER FIFTY FIVE

The sofa in the flat was draped with clothes. Alicia moaned in front of the mirror with her blonde wig on, then off. She studied her own sharp features framed with soft short wisps of brown and ash hair. Her grey blue eyes searched her reflection for an answer. 'Oh damn! this is worse than the Guy Fawkes ball, do I go as Ali or Alicia, think, think…Ali, go as Ali….after all darling,' she said winking to herself, 'Alicia is a high class whore.'

The decision was to be Ali to August, but to use the Golf car, she didn't want Alicia to be associated with the BMW. She changed the car over and drove around the town calling at a small newsagents' for some magazines to take to the hospital. She scanned the titles for a minute or two, her thoughts were more of trepidation of the visit more than anything else. She then chose three quickly, wanting to get away from the man hovering in a very lived in leather jacket who smelled of cigarettes. He seemed to be more interested in her than the magazines his nicotine stained fingers were flicking through.

Dennis Roebuck couldn't believe his luck. When the woman in the sheepskin coat left the shop, he replaced the magazine back on the top shelf and went to the window. He watched the woman get into a black Golf GTi and took out a tatty piece of paper from the ripped lining of his pocket. The registration matched. He waited impatiently for the black car to pull away before scrambling to his own scruffy car to follow her.

He was thoroughly pissed off when she turned into the hospital car park, and now he wished he had bought the magazine, it could be a long wait. Still he was used to it. He lit a cigarette and selected one of the dog eared 'Playboy' mag's from the back seat and settled himself. The leather of his jacket creaked softly into it's well-honed creases, and his knees left empty humps of denim as he stretched his legs over the passenger seat.

The clip caulk of Alicia's stiletto boots sounded louder and faster than anyone else in the chrome yellow corridor that seemed longer to Alicia than the passages of time. She was charged up to get to

August, but then in a flash of disdain, dreaded it. She stalled her pace slower and slower until she stopped. She found herself leaning against a vending machine staring into an open doorway counting a pile of bedpans. Somehow, she felt like all of them, a convenience to be pissed and shit all over, towering one moment teetering to spill the next. Alicia looked all ways, they all looked the same. Long clinical corridors all seemingly endless. Her brain felt the same, caught en-route, without direction.

Alicia took a deep breath, straightened herself, then subsided again. Her torment was with August's feelings. If she didn't want anything to do with her, then why should she force herself upon her?. How could she be so arrogant?. Her Father entered her mind just then. She could remember him telling her once he had helped a blind man with a white stick waiting to cross the road, to cross safely. The blind chap had taken exception to his aide. Her Father then said, 'at least I knew he hadn't been knocked down when I got him to the other side of the road, and I still know that.'

This time when she squared her shoulders, she marched on, the magazines rolled in her grip. The door to August's room appeared more like an obstacle, but still she opened it, more with a gloved spirit than a thrust hand.

She was in the room, staring at August, who had raised her pale face to her visitor. Both of them seemed a little battle weary, and across the empty space between them was not a void, but an overwhelming armistice. August looked at her without doubt, and as Ali moved closer, August slowly raised her arms like she did when she needed love and comfort from her Mum. They silently hugged each other before incessant explanations spilled out.

'I'm so sorry I shouted at you,' August blurted out, 'I was horrible to you and I'm so sorry.'

'Let us forget what happened and start again shall we?' Alicia smiled, and August nodded. 'Thank you for all the presents.'

'Don't mention it Sweetie, but, I want you to tell me all about yourself. You have been an enigma to me ever since I met you.'

August was just getting used to unburdening herself now. It was a strange but good feeling, after all that time when she had no friends, even poor Cruickshank had died on her.

Sammy was so angry about having a reprimand. She was talking to the windscreen only saying, 'All the bloody hours I've put in,' she seethed, 'I've tripled the turnover for them, Christ I wish I could tell them where to stuff their bloody job!'

Driven by temper, it didn't take her long to reach the hospital. She pulled into the familiar packed car park and scanned the lanes for a space. She was panicking a little because she wanted to catch Alicia there. Everywhere seemed full, then she spotted a parking space over by the entrance, and whizzed through the maze of cars to beat anyone else to it. She was pleased to get there until she found herself facing a sign 'SPACE RESERVED FOR DR LIN' She slammed into reverse and crunch. The metal to glass sound came from her rear end and the front of a silver Mercedes, out of which was emerging a gentleman of Chinese origin.

'Dr Lin I presume,' said a very embarrassed Sammy.

CHAPTER FIFTY SIX

August had finished her tale and had started on a chocolate as Sammy gingerly stuck her head around the door. It was a pale but pleased face when she saw August and Alicia chatting away and laughing together. 'Hi you two.'

'Sammy, you made it dar..dear.'

'Dear?' Sammy winced, 'and how is our patient dear?'

'She's a lot better, but you look awfully pale.'

'Yes, you look worse than me,' chimed August taking a cheek kiss from Sammy.

'Well I've just bumped into Dr Lin, well his car really.'

'Oh no, are you alright darling?' Alicia forgot herself.

'Yes, the car's not though. Buggered the back lights, and I hate driving without stop lights and indicators. I shall have to somehow get it fixed today.'

Alicia held her car keys out to Sammy. 'Here take my car back to the flat. The mechanic's number is in my book. Peter is his name, he's a friend, give him the details and he will get the parts here and fix it, tell him it's for me.'

'Great, if I could use your phone too, I really need to make some calls, then I shall return and catch up with you both properly.'

Dennis Roebuck was studying the page of rubber goods and clothes, when a throaty exhaust roared away from him. He looked up to see the back end of a black Golf getting smaller. He threw the magazine into the back seat, bucking and scrambling back into a driving position. The Golf was way ahead of him and was turning off before he had got into third gear. He followed the car around town, always a turning behind unable to catch up, then he lost it. 'Shit.' He swore, and circled the area. Giving up, he turned to go back to the office, it was then he saw it, parked outside a large house. He pulled up opposite, guessed the premises to be flats, like most of the houses around that area. Roebuck wrote down the address and went away. A job for Nigel his watcher, a young youth he paid peanuts for surveillance work, a job he couldn't stand to do himself.

'Have they told you when you can leave?' Alicia asked August.

'No. I'm not sure I'm in such a hurry now. At least while I'm in here I get fed and I am warm. Now I have no job to go to and I am not looking forward to living in that fridge of a room.'

'August, you cannot possibly go back there.'

'I've got to, I don't have any choice.'

'Oh no you are not!, you will never be better. You, young lady are going to convalesce at Brockley.'

'Where?'

'Brockley House, my parents', well my Mother's, well it's mine really I suppose.'

August looked and felt unsure about this. 'But I can't Ali.'

'Look, you will love it there, there's plenty of room, and Nancy and Tom will take care of you.'

'Who?'

'Nancy and Tom, the housekeepers.'

CHAPTER FIFTY SEVEN

When Nancy heard the pompous voice of Mr Holland on the other end of the phone, she screwed her face. 'I will see if she's in,' Nancy said letting the receiver clatter down on the table on purpose, which turned his face sour until he heard Brigitte's polished tones.

'Aah Brigitte, how are you my dear?'

'I'm very well, are you back in town?'

'Not yet,' he lied, 'but tomorrow, I'll be passing through. I was due to take a flight up to Newcastle, but being as I don't have to be there until tomorrow, I wanted to take you out to dinner, that is if you're free?'

'Why, I'm flattered Donald, that is so thoughtful of you.'

Brigitte Heyhott <u>was</u> flattered, and informed Nancy that she would be going out the following evening. 'Isn't it so charming of him, and he's such a busy man?'

'Charming.' Nancy said, but with a lilt of sarcasm only she knew was there.

Don Holland was so pleased with himself. He desperately needed to keep the coals burning, but neither wanted to stoke up the fire or burn his fingers raking it. Not only had he wormed in an excuse not to stay the night, but she will think he's a romantic for putting himself out of his fictitious busy schedule, just for her. He was always amazed at what a pocket full of lies could buy. Time was really ebbing away, his means of revenue would soon dry up with no rents coming in. 'Fancy all the bastards leaving,' he grumbled to himself, 'As if they expect the rents to stay static forever! Well they can all go without a receptionist then, I'll give that ugly girl her cards tomorrow,' he smiled, 'that's another wage saved.'

As soon as Dennis Roebuck got back into his office, he phoned Nigel. He seemed to be in the middle of a yawn. 'You awake aren't you Nigel?'

'Only just, I was up till three o' clock watchin' that Smith bloke.'

'Leave him for a bit. Right now, I want you to go and check this out. Pick the details up at the office pronto, I want to see you here in ten minutes.'

Within forty minutes, Nigel 'the watcher' had the black Golf in view, not too close, not too far away. He didn't have to wait long, but was surprised when a woman with shoulder length blonde hair got into the car. He checked the registration number again, checked the photo. 'Shit, looks like the almighty king of fag ash has given me the wrong photo. I'll tell the silly twat tomorrow.'

'Are you sure you weren't still asleep Nigel?' Roebuck muttered, a cigarette still in his mouth. Nigel didn't answer, but slouched down into a chair. He looked at Roebuck, a halo of smoke hung around his head. 'Fuckin' arsehole,' Nigel thought to himself as Roebuck drummed his fingers on the desk, before saying, 'you did go to the right address?'

'Of course I did, and it was the right car, but a different woman to that photo, unless she had her hair done since it was taken.'

'No, no, I saw her myself only this morning. You say you followed her?'

'Only to the hospital.'

'So did I.' Roebuck crushed his cigarette stub, disturbing the mountain of ash, and then lit another immediately.

'Well maybe she went back for her wig,' Nigel said with a sarcastic sneer.

'Check it out! I want the information for next week when her old man gets back.'

CHAPTER FIFTY EIGHT

Don Holland made sure he was twenty minutes early. Brigitte was on the phone when Tom let him into the hall. She was obviously ready and acknowledged him with a smile. He kissed her hand before strolling into the drawing room that Tom was holding the door open to usher him in. He declined a drink that Tom was offering and trying to home in on the conversation Brigitte was having. When Tom left, he crept closer to the door to get a better audio of what Brigitte was saying.

''No Bradley,' Brigitte sounded cross, 'I don't want to complete just yet, not until she's divorced, besides Alicia said she wants to make some changes to the draft.'

Tom was hovering around the hall pretend tidying and opened the door of the drawing room for Brigitte to meet her visitor. He heard Holland saying, 'I'm so sorry I'm early my dear, I just couldn't wait to see you again.' Tom grimaced, 'Nancy is right.' he thought, making his way back to the kitchen before he heard anything else more sickly.

In the drawing room there was a limited but friendly embrace, and when Brigitte offered him a drink, he accepted. 'I hope you don't mind me being early?'

'Not at all, it's rather nice of you to dash off when you have only just arrived home.'

'Yes, but I caught you in the middle of a phone call, that's what unpunctuality does,' he was hoping for enlightenment, and he got it.

'Oh that's alright. It was Bradley, the family solicitor.'

'You see, I intruded on family business, I do apologise.'

'There's really no need. It's the estate I want to sort out, I was saying last week that I wanted to transfer some funds, well most of the estate really. I would like to get it all ship shape and in my daughter's hands. The last thing I want to leave her with is a huge capital gains tax demand.'

'Quite,' Don said, feeling a sick knot tightening in his gut, especially with that word 'tax'. He had the urge to sling the sherry down his throat in one go and fill up with a large brandy. Brigitte feeling that Donald was a man of standing, allowed herself to continue opening up about her estate matters. 'I was saying to Bradley, I didn't want to transfer anything to Alicia until she's divorced, I don't want her husband to have the riches any more than the Inland Revenue.'

There were those threatening words again. Don nervously stroked his goatee beard, it appeared he would have to act faster than he thought. 'Do you mind if I smoke a cigar Brigitte my dear?'

'Not at all Donald, I love the smell of a good cigar,' she said reminiscing immediately about Peter. '

'As I said before Brigitte,' he paused to suck on his much needed comforter, 'if there's anything I can do.'

'Thank you for saying that Donald, it will be somewhat of a burden lifted when it's all done. It is in hand, but I think Bradley is just impatient, I don't think he likes her husband at all.' Her voice rang with a girlish smicker, which Don found attractive of her. 'You have a lovely giggle Brigitte,' he said quite honestly. Brigitte nearly blushed, she liked this attention.

Don didn't want to lose this thread of the conversation, and looking as laid back as possible asked, 'Will you retain Brockley House?'

'Nooo. I think it would be a little bit foolhardy of me. I shall stay of course, ha, unless Alicia decides to throw me out, but that would be unthinkable. I shall just have as much as I need, a substantial amount to spend as I wish, I wouldn't want for anything.'

Don Holland tightened his punishing hold on his glass, Brigitte seemed to be getting poorer by the second. 'And, what about that wonderful art collection you've talked about? surely you would want to keep those as a memory of your husband?'

'Oh my daughter has plans for that, it really was a passion they both shared, well especially the horsey ones. She has a good eye, and buys well, as Peter did. My daughter earns far more than her salary, much more in fact making very good investments in art. There are some of paintings already pegged for auction. Every so often she will let a painting or print go to raise money for one of her charities. I think the next one is the 'Watson Wood', she's sold all the ones with boats in them,' Brigitte let another giggle escape, 'that reminds me, there's the boat, oh my goodness I completely forgot about her, must do something about it.'

Don Holland was struck dumb and as Brigitte advanced with the decanter, he silently accepted by holding up his glass. She seemed to be lost in thought so he prompted her. 'Boat?'

'Peter's boat, it's a cruiser, you know the sort of thing, six berth. It is sea going, but never has been. Alicia was never keen on water and boats, oh well it has been forgotten on the papers, I may as well sell it. I could treat myself to a painting that I like. My weakness is modern art, I shall keep the few we have, I know that Alicia would sell those first if she had a choice.'

'My dear, you should keep the things that make you happy.' Don was fast growing a hatred for Brigitte's daughter.

Later on the way home, when he had used the Champagne trick to loosen her tongue, Brigitte confided to tell him that she did have a special painting that she would keep, and when she informed him it was a Hockney, he could have wet himself.

CHAPTER FIFTY NINE

When Sammy left the flat on Monday morning, she wasn't too happy. Over the weekend Alicia had found out what was troubling her. Sammy was not content at work because of the pressure the new Sales Director was piling on her. In fact it was more like gunning for her, now he would have more ammunition as Dr Lin had insisted on going through all the channels of insurance companies. Now the Sales Director would know she was where she wasn't supposed to be.

Sammy was worried about losing her job because she had just taken on a hellish mortgage after the break-up of her last relationship. This didn't upset Alicia, but fuelled her thoughts. She opened up her diary. The third of December, no appointments. 'Good, I shall need every minute today,' she smiled to herself.

Back at the hospital, the weekend had seen August relapse. It was more a mental melt down than physical, though she was pretty weak, she was hardly eating. August was concerned that she didn't know what was beyond the walls of the hospital room now. She lay in the lagoon of primrose walled nursing, where the undertow of bad tide couldn't reach her. She was a grown up orphan and the thought of leaving felt like having to wade through a deep current of despair that even God couldn't handle, but then again, hadn't she given him up.

The lack of appetite wasn't a pretence, it was natural worry. What did she have to look forward to, the only thing on offer was the hovel in winter, or Ali's offer of this Brockley place wherever that was. Living with strangers didn't really appeal to her, but trying to survive in the freezer compartment of a Victorian loft space, with no income was worse.

In a predominantly white bathroom, Robert Simpson had become familiar with over the past few days, he sat straddled over the bidet. He cupped his testicles in one hand and guided a tepid jet of water over his sore penis. He closed his eyes with the comforting feeling, then they jarred open as a deep Austrian voice shouted, 'Yu Kom back hier!'

Axel the rich was in his bed and he knew he had made a big mistake this time. His dick felt like a boy scouts tent peg on a good 'ging gang goolie' weekend. She looked like a sack of broken paving slabs with gold bracelets and the gin was wearing off.

'Robort! Yu kom hier, me go again,' the cement mixer voice called again.

'Oh shit,' he whispered. 'Have I made a mistake or what.' He had spotted the gold on every finger and wrist. She had looked fairly attractive from a distance. After several drinks, and no other available talent, she looked pretty good and wealthy. The huge swell of her breasts must have obliterated the huge swell of everything else, and before he knew it he was being Axel battered by Everest in the flesh. What a switch round for him, he had been horny for it, now he had no escape from it.

Nigel, 'the watcher', drove slowly past 4 Hyland Way and saw his target get out of the black Golf parked on the drive. He pulled up a couple of houses down where he still had a view in his mirror. He checked the photo, now he had the right lady. Nigel played his usual time wasting story game of why he was there. Sometimes it made him feel important, sometimes it made him feel he was doing something worthwhile. Mostly it made him feel like a peeping Tom with a license, a sort of sergeant with shit for stripes. Today, he reckoned it would be something to do with divorce, and he wondered why any bloke would want to divorce a woman like her. 'Must be loads o' blokes after that one mind,' he thought.

CHAPTER SIXTY

When Graham walked into August's hospital room, he was very pleased to find the patient chatting to Alicia. He did find himself disappointed that Sammy wasn't there, not just because she was wonderful to look at, but the atmosphere her and Alicia created together was fabulous and amusing.

I'm sorry I can't stay long he said dragging a chair forward to sit on, 'I promised Pam I wouldn't be late home again.'

'It's good of you to come Graham,' Alicia said, 'mind you, you do look a little down in the mouth, is everything all right?'

He sighed heavily, 'Oh we've been ordered to get together for a staff meeting at work. Everyone to attend on Friday, it doesn't sound good does it. Apparently he sacked the receptionist today.'

August felt half pleased she, herself didn't work there anymore.

'Don't worry,' Alicia said calmly,' it probably won't be that bad.'

Graham made a clicking sound with his mouth and formed an upside down smile, showing how unsure he was. Alicia patted his broad knee, 'don't worry,' she said again, and will you try and convince August that she is not going back to that awful room above the flat.'

On Thursday at 10.45 am, Alicia was trying to comfort Sammy on the telephone. 'Calm down, calm down, oh Sammy darling where are you?'

'At bloody Portsmouth and I'm stranded. They were going to let me keep the car for a week, but I told them to shove it up the Sales Director's arse and set fire to it. Oh Alicia, I don't know what to do, I have no job and…and..' Sammy's words dissolved into a burst of crying and anger.

Alicia managed to calm Sammy by giving her strict instructions to take a train back to her house. Pack a large suitcase and wait for Alicia to pick her up, she had something important to discuss. When Alicia replaced the receiver it was only for a few seconds. She was dialling the familiar numbers of the hospital and begun the task of trying to discharge August.

By 1.30pm, August was dressed for the first time in ages and being pushed along the hospital corridors in a wheelchair by Alicia. August was quiet, she couldn't put up a good argument for not being released because she didn't have one. Alicia on the other hand was talking as fast as she was careering the wheelchair along.

'You don't drive your car like this do you?' August winced at a near miss with a laundry trolley.

'Oh no, I'm much faster!' Alicia laughed and went rattling along pre introducing Nancy and Tom. 'You can't not like them, they practically brought me up, and I didn't turn out so bad did I?' August was nearly silenced for good as she dodged a fire extinguisher. The silence made Alicia think, 'well did I?' she asked again. August, concentrating on oncoming victims, shook her head. Alicia screeched to a halt and August grabbed hold of the arms to stop her ejection. Alicia crouched down beside the wheelchair and with a serious face close to August now asked again. 'I did..didn't I?' she whispered.

August peered into those steel blue eyes with the huge dark pooled pupils. They were looking at her for the comfort of a credence that a good willing person would search for. The unreal thing for August was that she couldn't believe that a successful person like Ali could be asking her. August smiled and released her white knuckled grip of the arm rail and covered Ali's hand. 'You are lovely Ali.' There was a moments silence and then Alicia said, 'You're not just saying that to make me slow down are you?' They both laughed, August shaking her head. Alicia grabbed August by the hand and squeezed it, 'Darling you will love Brockley, and Tom and Nancy they are the kindest people. They will adore having you there.'

She bounced up again and sped along talking all the time. 'Nancy is so cuddly, and what a cook, the most unbelievable pastry, and oh what a meat and potato pie. When my parents were throwing a dinner party serving prawn provencal, smoked salmon and things stuffed in vine leaves, I would eat in the kitchen with Tom and Nancy, and enjoy much nicer food and company as far as I'm concerned. Now Tom's service is second to none, he loves the Aristocrat to a point but cannot stand snobbery and boorishness. 'Well dressed with interest,' he says and, 'Too formal to be normal,' is his saying, a good guide don't you think?' August nodded with closed eyes as they burst through the doors into the December daylight.

The fresh air was wintry without a doubt. For the first time since the hovel, she saw her own breath pearl before her, which assured her she was going to a better place. A place where seeing her own breath wasn't a matter of fact or even evidence that she was still breathing, just a better place.

In the car, the narration of Alicia and her childhood carried on throughout the journey. Tom and Nancy became such huge characters. August wondered where Ali's parents must have been all the time.

When the car entered through huge stone pillars and crunched along a gravel drive, August's thought control went dormant and accepted only what she was seeing. A most magnificent cedar tree stood amongst an island of shrubs. The pebbled driveway ran around this island. The house, Brockley House was unveiled from countless shrubs and trees, it's stonework embraced by ivy did belie how large the building was. Brockley was much larger than the house August had lived in that was converted into flats. The doorway, they drew up at, had a large pitched door, like a pointed arch. It was taller and wider than a normal door, it was black stained and protected by a canopy of the same shape, held up on thick timber legs, August likened it to a lych-gate of a church. Just as they stopped a remote sunbeam reached through the pillared supports as if to greet her. August turned and looked at the cedar's open armed boughs and then at Ali. Alicia winked as if she knew what she was thinking, and then nodded indicatively toward the sun washed porch. August looked back to find a plump woman battling her way to be in front of the smart slim man who could have been an aged Groucho Marx. The car door was opened and a smiling round face filled the gap. 'You must be August,' the round pink face said taking hold of her arm, 'Miss Alicia told us you were coming, and we're very pleased to see you aren't we Tom, this is Tom.'

CHAPTER SIXTY ONE

The slim smiling man was trying to help Nancy ease August out of the car, with much instruction from Nancy. 'Easy Tom, easy, the poor child has just come out of hospital Tom. Tom I said easy..easy. By the attention she was receiving, August thought she had just come out of intensive care. The smile and a wink from Ali was assuring.

Beyond that heavy oak door didn't seem so welcoming. It was dim and cool. August half expected to be wading ankle deep in shag pile carpet, but instead there was a stone floor, and despite a good dressing of pictures and oak furniture, it didn't seem homely. It was rather echo touched when they spoke. There were lots of coats, hats and even wellingtons, which August didn't expect, because, despite the coolness, it was very grand and officious.

There were a lot of doors and what took August's eye was a glimpse of a heavy gallery of banister rail. As they moved along the hallway it revealed a large landing over a door at the end. Around the corner was the tail end of the banister trail. A magnificent staircase elbowed in a broad sweep and was lit by sunlight from a tall leaded window that no church would be shy of.

Despite Nancy fussing, August took the stairs slowly taking in every detail. She stroked the heavy drapes each side of the window, they were as thick as an eiderdown that she had on her bed as a child. The last time she had seen curtains like that was in a castle somewhere she went on a school trip. August was in awe of the many paintings she saw that galleried the staircase. Alicia leading the pack stopped occasionally to look over the banister to watch bemused and quiet, not that she could have got a word in edgewise as Nancy was giving a running commentary on whatever August was looking at.

Tom at the back of the troupe, smiled up at Alicia, they knew Nancy was so happy to be in charge of August. They both knew what it meant to Nancy, childless, grand childless, even though August was grown up, Nancy was adopting already. Even though August was an adult, and so was Alicia, Nancy found it hard to let go of the nurse in her, and the naivety of the recent patient, Alicia felt that she might be let go to finally grow up and fly the nest.

'Miss Alicia said that you were to have the best guest room and I agree,' Nancy said opening one of the many doors on the vast landing. August followed her and stopped just inside. Alicia squeezed past her, wanting to see the reaction on August's face, it was worth it, she was awe struck. 'This is just my room?' August's voice was no more than a whisper, 'it's massive,' August said, slowly moving forward.

'I like this room,' Alicia said following her, 'do you like it?'

August nodded, making her way over to one of the windows. A galaxy of shrubs and trees spread out before her, the ones that were copper shredded of autumn were mobbed by the evergreen myriad of rhododendron, elders, privet and shiny spiked holly showing the birth of red berries.

August started to cry and Alicia rushed toward her, followed at close quarters by Nancy. 'Darling, are you all right?' Alicia warbled, Nancy was stood behind them, she was upset, because August was upset. Alicia hugged August, who was snivelling and trying to speak. 'I'm so alright, so..so alright Ali, I can't believe it…is it alright for me to be here?'

Alicia nodded, almost in tears herself, then Nancy took over. 'Come to me child,' it was a Mothering voice, 'you will be comfortable here my love, I will look after you. Let me show you properly. Nancy guided her over to a door off the room. 'Look here, you have your own bathroom, 'Nancy led August through the door. As the two disappeared into the en-suite, Tom looked at Alicia, 'she loves her already,' he whispered.

'Good, I knew it would happen,' she smiled back.

When Nancy reappeared with August, Alicia eased herself back into the frame, 'Nancy, Mother as you know won't be back until this evening, and I would like a few minutes with August before I nip off. Could you organise a light supper for three tonight, something nice and simple in the dining room about 7.30? Meanwhile, I know you will look after August, but remember, her appetite hasn't been awfully large.' Alicia emphasised 'large' knowing that Nancy would knock up a smorgasbord bigger than Germany, and a pudding to stodge ten people.

'Don't you worry yourself,' Nancy said already in charge of unpacking August's small case. Alicia held out her hand to August and led her downstairs and into the lounge. August's other hand was on her skirt which was slithering downwards.

'Don't let Nancy bully you into eating if you don't feel like it,' Alicia whispered.

'She keeps calling you Alicia, it seems strange.'

'You can still call me Ali, it's ok you know.'

August scrunched down into a leather club chair and stared around the large room.

'The sofas' are more comfortable,' Alicia said flopping down on one herself. August followed suit. The sofa was beige and soft and deep. Alicia got up and went over to a beautiful carved table supporting a weight of crystal decanters. 'Would you like a drink sweetie?'

August, who was pinched up like an un-blossomed bud, shook her head.

'I'm going to pour you one anyway, I want you to learn to relax.' Alicia poured a sherry, and strolled over to August, who now sat on the edge of her seat.

'Relax,' Alicia more ordered than spoke. August sat back as if she had a seat belt on.

'I said relax.' Alicia sat down beside her guest and put an arm around her, she sipped the sherry, then held the glass in front of August, hugging her at the same time. 'It really is a very good sherry,' she smiled. August smiled and took the glass and sipped. She sipped some more and Alicia felt her tension subside. 'That's better, I want you to be comfortable here. Think of Brockley as your home, I will show you around and you can wander around as you like. Mother is still a little precious over Father's study, so just avoid that room. I'll take you through the grounds in the morning, you will love the place. Your room is your own territory, your retreat, your space. If you want to eat up there, you can raid the larder, Nancy will show you where that is, and she will also cater for raiding as she did for me.' August managed a smile, and finished the glass, Alicia filled it. 'I think that should thaw you out in more ways than one.'

August was then introduced to the many rooms, as Alicia explained that she was going to pick Sammy up, who would be sharing supper with them, which would also be a meeting. Alicia had something important to discuss with them both. August was glad it was Sammy that was making up the 'three', she was nervous of meeting Mrs Heyhott.

August followed Alicia to the door like a puppy, she didn't want her to leave. Although Alicia had shown her around and made it quite clear she must feel at home, it was still a big strange house. Even despite Nancy and Tom waiting on her, they were still strangers. Alicia sensed this and hugged her again. 'You will be fine, you are a lovely person and deserve to be here,' she said warmly, and then more officious said, 'August can you drive?'

'Err no.'

'Wouldn't you like to?'

'Err..yes.'

'It's necessary Sweetie. Tom!'

Within two seconds, the door under the gallery landing opened and Groucho himself popped out. 'Tom, our girl here doesn't drive, but she would like to.'

Tom made his way toward them, a smile under his droopy moustache, he took August from Alicia saying, 'I'm just the man you're looking for young lady.'

CHAPTER SIXTY TWO

Sammy was so upset when Alicia arrived. She had a yawning suitcase on the bed and clothes sprayed all around, but none in the suitcase. 'I don't know what to pack,' Sammy agonised.

'I do,' Alicia said launching herself toward the wardrobes, 'everything!'

While Sammy poured out her sob story with frequent angry bursts, Alicia packed. In the car, Alicia explained that they were going to the flat, and then on to a business supper meeting at Brockley, where August now was. Sammy was miffed into silence, her 'but whys' were answered with only 'you'll see'.

They stopped off at the flat, where Sammy in neutral surroundings asked more questions than being upset. Alicia easily arrested both, by showering and getting into bed. It didn't totally stop the inquisition or solve Sammy's problems, but it was good for both of them.

Back at Brockley in the kitchen, August was listening to Tom. He was sat in a well-worn chair nursing a pipe, only occasionally sucking on it. She was sitting on a chair opposite that soaked up the heat from a well stoked fire. She strolled back and forth from the large table that Nancy was working lots of bowls on. August picked at the plates Nancy had laid there for her, of chicken, prawns and fresh baked granary loaf. There were curls of butter, a selection of jams and fingers of ham.

'I made the jams myself,' Nancy said nodding at the collection of jars with hand written labels, 'and Tom grew the fruit.'

'That I did,' Tom joined in, 'I will take you around the garden tomorrow, just before I give you a driving lesson.'

'Driving lesson?' August asked.

'Yup, you're going to have a driving lesson. Just in the grounds'.'

'But..but..I've never driven a car before in my life.'

Nancy chuckled, and said, get some prawns down you, shellfish are good for you, brain food.'

August was really beginning to relax, then Tom looked at his watch and stood up saying, 'Ahh, half past four, better get the fire up in the lounge, her ladyship will be back at six.'

August tightened up again, she felt like a yoyo inside, the release and then the bounce of freedom being reeled back up again. Tom butted his pipe, and sauntered off. August went quiet and slowly picked at the prawns. The throbbing of Nancy's pounding in one of the bowls stopped, and a sigh took it's place. 'You're quiet love, is anything the matter?'

August nursed a prawn, not knowing whether to put it into her mouth or masticate it in her fingers. 'Is her ladyship..well..err.. what is Ali's Mother like?'

'Oh take no notice of Tom, he calls her that. Mrs Heyhott is alright, a proper lady of course, but nice.

August was beginning to churn up inside again. 'Is she real snooty?..I mean posh?'

Nancy laughed, a sweet chuckle, and began beating hell out of another bowl. 'Oh child, I've told you she is a real nice kind lady. I mean, well, look at our Alicia, aah, isn't she a nice girl?' Nancy looked at the warm fire and seemed far away at the same time, smiling at something that August couldn't see, but knew.

'Yes..yes she is…is she like her Mother?'

'Yes and no, I suppose Miss Alicia is more like her Father I reckon, but she does have a lot of her Mother's ways even so.'

August plopped the squashed prawn onto her mouth and swallowed it whole. 'She doesn't talk much about her Mother, in fact, she talks more about you and Tom.'

'Ooh, isn't she lovely. They are both very good to us, and so was Mr Heyhott. It seems such a pity they only had one child, but as Tom says, you can count the seeds in an apple, but you can't count the apples in a seed, and I reckon Miss Alicia got all the good fruit.'

No matter what favourable things Nancy said about Mrs Heyhott, the thought of meeting her, terrified August. A sudden wave of tiredness drenched her, she felt a lightness in her head, a giddy rush which made her sit down heavily.

Nancy was quick to question, 'are you alright my child?'

August could only nod, not meaning it and tried to swallow the giddy sensation away.

'I think maybe you should go and have a lie down, it's been a busy day for you really. I shall take you up,' she fussed.

'It's alright, Nancy, I think I can find it.' She made her way slowly. She had lost the colour in her cheeks the sherry had flushed her with earlier.

Back in her room, she lay on one of the beds, staring at the ceiling. It was very different from the hospital and the hovel. This room was bigger than the whole of the flat. She dozed off with the events of the day, it had exhausted her and she still had the supper meeting with Ali and Sammy.

August did not attend the meeting. When the girls arrived at Brockley, August was sleeping like a dead person, and Nancy strongly voiced that they let her get her strength back.

She slept through till morning. When the soft knock on her door roused her, she thought she was still in hospital, and stuck her head under the covers. It was strange, she didn't feel pressed linen, but a fluffy quilt, and neither was she in a nighty, but her clothes. There was no rattle of trolleys either, but a soft sweet chuckle, rasping with a shortness of breath. August peeped out of the quilt, it was momentarily confusing and then wonderful.

There was Nancy, holding a tea tray, and trying to let her lungs subside. 'Ooh, those stairs seem to be getting longer every day.'

August heaved herself up in bed, 'You shouldn't have Nancy, I can come down for supper, is Ali and Sa..but it's day light!'

'Yes it's tomorrow already.'

'But the supper meeting!' August looked frayed and felt dilapidated.

'Don't you worry yourself,' Nancy soothed, 'Miss Alicia is going to have breakfast with you instead.'

CHAPTER SIXTY THREE

August didn't begin to feel better until she had had a soak in the bath, but even then she was bothered that she had slept through. Her thoughts were all over the place, 'I bet Mrs Heyhott thinks I'm really rude now and we haven't even met yet.' She was grumbling to herself all the while she was getting dried. 'It's a nice way to treat Ali, the first evening here and I fall asleep! when I should have been at a meeting.'

She wondered what the meeting was about, which made her all the more angry and embarrassed for missing it. As she dressed, she realised that her bra was now too big, she had gone from a under pressure first row of hooks and eyes to the last row, and still it was loose. This she hadn't noticed at the hospital in the rush that Ali had endorsed. August became a little downcast as she realised that there were a few things she needed now, like new under clothes, but had no means of livelihood anymore. There was still the debt at the bank, that hung over her like a giant curse. Every day at the hospital, she half expected a visit from the bank manager or a bailiff. 'Now that would be amusing,' she thought, 'a bailiff taking all my worldly goods.'

August dressed the best she could, a belt helping to keep her skirt up. She made her way down to the kitchen, fearful all the time of bumping into Mrs Heyhott. It was 8.30am and the kitchen was already warm with a roaring fire and the smell of toast and bacon cooking. Nancy was rattling around the big range cooker, and Tom was laying out a breakfast tray, destined for her ladyship. There was a big warm smile from them both. Nancy slipped two rashers of bacon next to scrambled egg. Tom set down a silver teapot, matching sugar bowl, milk jug ,a jam dish and croissants. Tom took the laden tray on it's delivery.

'What would you like for breakfast my dear?' Nancy called to August, there's bacon, mushrooms, eggs, toast, marmalade, croissants..'

Just then Alicia arrived, 'I could eat all that, good morning,' she sang. August felt embarrassed at falling asleep and missing the meeting and slightly embarrassed because she knew how Ali had got her appetite.

'How are you this morning darling? I'm sorry I didn't wake you, but you were so asleep, and I think Nancy would have smacked my hand if I had disturbed you.'

Alicia apologising for not waking her, made her feel better.

'Shall we have breakfast in here, I usually do,' Alicia sat down so familiar and easy.

Tom popped his head around the door and called, 'Mrs Heyhott would like to know where you two ladies are eating?'

'In here Tom.' Alicia called back and he went away, only to return promptly with the tray, still untouched. Your Mother would like to take breakfast with you,' He said.

August felt a panic belt through her, she wasn't ready, and a 'ooh eck' came out. Alicia laughed, 'Don't worry sweetie, it's only Mother, she wants to meet you.'

All the warm air of the kitchen seemed to be in August's head right now, and she had a blush of pink about her. When Brigitte Heyhott entered the room the air about her was alive and impressive, and August wanted to shrink.

She strode in wearing a smart plaid suit and had her hair tucked up at the back in a French roll. As she neared the table, August had the urge to stand to attention, but just sat there feeling plain and common.

'Good morning girls,' she said smiling and sat down.

'Good morning Mother, this is August.'

'Hello my dear, I'm very pleased to meet you, I do hope that you are settling in alright?'

August said rather quietly, 'thank you very much, I am thank ..' Nancy took over, 'August is settling in fine, aren't you my dear? how would you like your eggs, poached, fried or scrambled?, and how do you like your bacon?' Nancy was hovering for an answer.

'I'll have it how Ali has her's..if that's alright?'

Brigitte giggled, 'gosh it's ages since I've heard you called Ali,' she turned to August, her laughter lines growing each side of her pale blue eyes, 'her Father used to call her that when he got angry with her.'

'He hardly ever got angry with me!'

'Oh Ha,' Brigitte flipped a hand at her daughter, 'she was no angel was she Nancy?'

Nancy, who was still hovering, shook her head. Brigitte said, 'you will have to tell Nancy how you like your food, she doesn't like it if you don't enjoy your meal. If you have your bacon cooked like Alicia, it will be frazzled so much, you can snap it in half. And don't let her talk you into having banana and maple syrup in your croissant because it is very fattening and it turns Nancy green.' Brigitte laughed, August thought how sweet and laid back she was. She could see the likeness of Mother and daughter easily.

August didn't eat much. Her appetite had changed over these past few weeks, which she was pleased about. After breakfast, Alicia took August on a tour of the grounds, and August wished that her Mum could have been with her. They sat in a summer house.

'This is where I spent a lot of my childhood hours. It was sort of my Wendy-house.' Alicia smiled as she spoke, filling her nostrils with the damp air that smelled of weather licked timber and creosote. 'Still smells the same,' she sighed, 'come on let's walk and talk,' she hooked August by the elbow, 'I have so many things to go through with you.'

'Like what?'

'Like, how much do you know about the box making business?'

They talked the morning through, and after lunch, Tom gave August a driving lesson, round and around the loop, down to the garages and back around the island. It was hard for August to concentrate after all that Ali had proposed, but it had made it more important for her to be able to drive. Tom must have thought she'd done ok, as he said she should organise a provisional licence. By mid-afternoon, August was beginning to get jaded again, and Nancy ordered her up to bed for a nap. She went without argument, but with instructions to wake her if she hadn't surfaced by 5pm.

CHAPTER SIXTY FOUR

Graham Topps was pleased when the staff meeting had been cancelled, but angry that he had travelled all those miles to be handed a memo instead. Mrs Charlton looked tired and miserable handing out the memos' each one read, 'NEW STREAMLINE POLICIES MAY HAVE TO BE PUT INTO OPERATION. UNFORTUNATELY THERE MAY BE JOB LOSSES. HOWEVER IF A PROFITABLE SURGE IN TURNOVER IS ACHIEVED THIS WILL NOT BE NECESSARY.

It was a typical blunt memo, the style of which could only have been authored by Don Holland. Graham though felt, as sales, kind of pointed at, in an unflattering account, but he had only just started, he knew it had to be some mismanagement of the company that had caused this.

Every memo was received with a groan, there was no Don Holland to talk to so Graham decided to mosey on down to the factory floor. He had not been down there since he started work there, which just seemed like a spit of time. Fred had forgotten who Graham was, he didn't have much time for the reps, his experience of Simpson was enough. This chap seemed different though, and Fred didn't mind talking to him. Morale was low on the factory floor, wondering if they would have a job by Christmas.

It was a fact that Fred had always blamed the sales rep for, not getting the work in. He was just about to have a jibe at Topps about it when Graham mentioned August. Fred sighed at the mention of her name, 'Now there's a lass I miss bein' around.'

'Yep, it's a shame she was treated like that when she was so poorly.'

'Poorly?'

'Yes, oh yes, she's been in hospital.'

'Good 'eavens, I didn't know she'd been poorly, 'ospital an'all, is she all right?'

'She seems alright now, she's staying with a friend, I'll give her your regards if I see her,' Graham said sauntering away. Fred nodded, but was distant and sad with the news. He had hoped August would be back, but now. He stared at the paper work mounting up in his tray, he wondered if he would ever be able to clear it, now she wasn't here.

As the evening closed in on 6.30, Robert was getting ready to go down to dinner. He had started taking dinner early to avoid Axel the ball basher. He was pleased that he had scored his quota of screws, but one had not been a native Chinese, and time was running out. As he ate, he thought about finding the red light area, to make his holiday complete. The idea of paying for it though, went against the grain. He smiled though as he realised Alicia was really paying for it. He had already blown some credit on the card and wondered what would happen when she found out. He would have to act fast when he returned home, so he decided he would buy a postcard, fill it with 'dearest darlings' to Alicia, to tell her 'how sorry he was, she couldn't be here with him', and 'how much he missed her, and loved her'.

CHAPTER SIXTY FIVE

Alicia was proposing a letter through Bradley. It was to Robert, informing him of her intention to start divorce proceedings. Although she had other business with the solicitor, she made her visit brief. There was so much she had to do. Her next meeting was with her Bank manager and her accountant. Armed with a financial focus of elastic purse strings, she dashed off to pick Sammy up from the flat.

On the way to collect the BMW, neither of them could decide which car they would prefer.

'Alicia, I don't think red is my colour, maybe I should have the Golf.'

'I didn't think black was really your colour either.'

'You choose, they are your cars.'

'Company cars now darling.'

When August got up, she made her way directly to the kitchen where Nancy was prepping vegetables at the table and Tom was stoking up the fire.

'Hello my love,' Nancy sang, 'I bet you need a nice cup of tea.'

'I'll make it Nancy, you're busy.'

'Oh no you won't, anyway, you have to ring Miss Alicia at the flat, I'll mash, while you call her.'

August padded through to the cool hallway and dialled the familiar number, a pang of resentment tinged her as she pulled the last four digits. All the burning hatred for Shaun flared back up as she remembered the trial he had put her through because of that slip of the tongue.

'Ali, it's me August.'

'Hello darling, hope you feel better for your nap?'

'Yes thanks, it seems weird going to bed in the afternoon though.'

'You need it, besides I want you to keep all your energy for tomorrow.'

'What's happening?'

'Tomorrow darling, we are going shopping, clothes shopping, we are going to kit you out.'

'But Ali, I don't have any money!'

'No darling, I'm taking you shopping.'

'You can't..I.I can't afford to pay you back.'

'August calm down, we are going shopping, any way the clothes you have don't even fit you anymore. If you are working for me, then you will look the part, now that's all there is to it, no arguments.'

August blew a distraught sigh, but resigned herself to Alicia's overwhelming expedience, after all, she had become her drawbridge, her protector and her future.

'Oh and August, I hope you don't mind if Sammy and I don't come over tonight, only it's frightfully icy on the roads, will you be alright?'

'Yes I'll be fine.'

'Alright darling, we will see you in the morning.'

August replaced the hand set, it slightly echoed in the large hallway and she felt alone. Her feelings were so mixed up, she felt important and small all at the same time. She was drawn back to Nancy and Tom in the kitchen. 'Is our Alicia home for dinner then?' Nancy asked as she humped a large wad of dough.

August shook her head. Just then Mrs Heyhott breezed into the kitchen. She politely asked if August was feeling alright, before announcing that she wouldn't be home for dinner.

'There'll not be many dining tonight,' Nancy said.

'Is Alicia not in for dinner?'

'No, I just phoned her.'

'Oh dear, I don't want you to be on your own, you're our guest, I'll ring and cancel my dinner date and keep you company.'

'Oh don't do that,' August said, 'I'll be fine, honestly.'

Tom butted in now, 'August could come home with us this evening.' Nancy beamed at the idea, 'Of course she can, Tom can walk her back, make sure she's safe and sound.'

All three faces were staring at August, and she felt like she'd sat on a hot spot. There was a silence and Nancy filled it, 'What do you say my dear, why don't you come and have an evening with me and Tom?'

'Well it would be nice, if you don't mind that is.'

'Don't mind!, it will be a pleasure child.'

'Well that's settled then,' Brigitte Heyhott smiled, 'I'll leave you to deal with the alarm Tom, leave the key in the usual place, so that I can find it.'

August was comfortable with the evening, it was like having Grandparents she had never had. It was strange she thought, that Tom and Nancy had this lovely bungalow that the Heyhotts had bought for them to live whilst ever they drew breath, yet their hearts and minds were always at Brockley. It became apparent that although, they both could have retired years ago they would not give up their 'positions' as Nancy called them. August reckoned that they would have worked for the Heyhotts for nothing, Brockley House and the Heyhotts was like a drug to them. She had a hot toddy that Tom made specially, and she knew where Ali had learned to make it for sure. These 'housekeepers' were home makers, and August could sense their disappointment of not being able to have children. It made her more comfortable to be called 'child' by Nancy, even though she was an adult.

Tom walked August back to Brockley about 10.30pm, it was bitterly cold and she really appreciated the sheepskin coat that Mrs Heyhott had given her. Tom unlocked the huge door to Brockley House and chortled as he went about the burglar alarm. 'Some system, when you have to leave the key handy.' Before he sent August up to bed, he showed her where the sensors to the alarm were.

'You have a clear way down the stairs if you keep tight to the banisters that side, Nancy and Miss Alicia had them set like that, so that Missy could slip downstairs for a pantry raid, midnight snack.' He kissed August on the cheek and said, 'it's done Nancy the power of good having you here. She'll look after you, so will the rest of the family.' He winked and sent her upstairs before setting the alarm and left.

On the other side of the planet, Robert was feeling smug that it was Alicia's money he had spent on a Chinese prostitute, because he wasn't too pleased with the event. Tiny breasts didn't do anything for him. It was only her willingness to use her mouth sucking abilities that made it worthwhile, something that Alicia would never do. His pleasure was short lived when in the middle of the night he woke wildly scratching his pubic area. 'The filthy bitch', he shouted into the familiar bidet.

CHAPTER SIXTY SIX

August didn't think she would feel comfortable in this great house alone, she had this underlying dread all the time she was at the bungalow, but it was easy. Brockley House had a way of embracing you, it felt safe. She thought about Tom's words, 'the rest of the family', and it was like being in a family. She felt no fear and lay in her comfy bed drifting into calm sleep. Just as she was dropping over into the unconscious brink, she heard a thud and voices coming from the hallway. They were distant and she recognised Mrs Heyhott's voice. Then she heard a man's voice, which shot a crooked shiver down her spine. Her eyes opened wide and a chilling desire to find out who it was, took her out of bed.

Quietly she opened her door. There was a faint light that filtered up the staircase. Mrs Heyhott's voice was more clear now, and she was giggling, 'that's the wretched alarm off, now, should we have a drink?' The man spoke now and a sickly sourness stung August.

'I don't think I should Brigitte,' he was saying, 'I have to drive.'

The voice caused August to frown, her heart begun to pound and she crept out of the bedroom, Mrs Heyhott was speaking again. 'Oh Donald, you can stay if you like.'

The frown deepened and August felt nauseous, Donald!, the voice, now she felt panicked, he spoke again.

'Brigitte, my dear, another time, tomorrow I will be so busy.'

'But it's Saturday, don't you ever have a break?'

'Not yet my dear, I have things I must do.'

August slowly approached the landing gallery, she hoped the voice wouldn't belong to... there he was!, Don Holland, embracing Ali's Mother! Oh no. She stole back, listening to his sickly retreat.

'Until tomorrow my dearest.'

'Shit.' August whispered, 'I don't bloody believe it.'

Back in her room, she heard Mrs Heyhott tread the stairs and pass her door and wanted to rush out and tell her what an ultra shit Don Holland was. But, she stayed there leaning on her door, staring into her own dark room. When her eyes became accustomed to the dim, she made her way back to her bed, but it was a long time before sleep took her.

Driving back on the frozen roads, don Holland's grip tightened on the steering wheel, and he gritted his teeth with the knowledge that he didn't stand a chance of selling the bloody Bentley to bloody Brigitte. The financial hell that he had got himself into would only be solved by selling Ruban Co. and or wedding the Heyhott treasures. He was so angry, because he would have to buy an impressive Christmas gift to help woo his way. What do you buy a woman who owns a Hockney!.

The other thought that that pestered him, was at some point, he would have to make love to the woman. The thought frightened him. He couldn't ever remember ever making love to a woman he respected. The strange thing was that he did have respect for Brigitte. All he had ever done in the past though, was to have sex. Sex with high class whores and trinket laden tarts who would do it just for more trinkets. He smiled now at some of his memorable exercises, and wondered, if he could keep those thoughts as a fantasy to make it work with Brigitte. His biggest fear was, could he get it up in the first place.

CHAPTER SIXTY SEVEN

When August woke the following morning, all she could think about was last night's visitor. She must tell Ali. As she left her room she found herself sharing the landing with Mrs Heyhott.

'Good morning August, I hope you had a nice evening with Tom and Nancy.'

'Yes thank you, I had a lovely evening, I ..hope you did too, oh and thank you for the sheepskin, it kept me nice and warm.' She wanted to say different things, but they just couldn't come out of her mouth. They sauntered downstairs together as Brigitte carried on talking. 'Is Alicia coming over today?'

'Yes, we're going shopping this morning.'

'Oh that will be nice, and don't forget to wrap up warm, remember you're not long out of hospital.'

Before they reached the kitchen, August heard a car pull up outside, she knew it was Ali and waited in the hall. Sammy and Alicia burst in the hall and August was pleased to see them. They brought in such a festival atmosphere and as they both hugged her, she was overpowered by their distinctive perfumes. Alicia checked August's face like she was an infant, 'You have more colour today sweetie, have you had breakfast yet?'

'No, only just surfaced actually.'

'Great, let's have a business breakfast in the dining room before we go shopping, need to build your strength up for that!'

First on the agenda was who was having what car. Sammy had the Golf and Alicia had the BMW. August actually couldn't believe that faced with a choice of amazing breakfast menu, she still didn't have much of an appetite, and was shocked when Alicia said, 'We will have to get you a car for when you pass your test August.'

'But I haven't had a proper lesson yet, I haven't even got a licence.'

'Sammy can get the ball rolling on that one, could you get the appropriate forms darling.'

'But Ali, what if I don't pass?'

'You will, how do you feel about a week away, on one of those intensive courses that promises a pass at the end of it?'

'I don't know,' shrugged August, 'I suppose so.'

'That's that then, now the other thing is…I think..we have our company premises. Sammy how far have you got with the art materials side of things?'

'I've contacted most of the sources, and I have meetings lined up with practically all of them for next week.'

'Good,' she looked at August now, 'What I would like you to do August, if you feel up to it, is to help me log all the paintings that are going to make up the gallery. I would also like you to be in a meeting with Graham. I'll organise for that to be either here, or lunch somewhere. I am going to ask Mother if she minds me using the study, we need a temporary office. I need to get my drawing board out of the flat, it's hardly usable there with Sammy's bras' and dressing gown draped over it.'

Sammy merely dramatically fluttered her eyelashes and laughed, asking 'What time are we going shopping?'

'As soon as we finish breakfast my little darlings, and the first stop is the beauty parlour.'

August just sat there and took it into her head that this was really happening. She accepted it now, as before she had been without a rudder, and her sails were all tangled up. But now she had quite literally 'a steering wheel'.

Since August had found out what an accelerator and gears were, her life seemed to have taken on a speed and direction she could have only dreamed about. Her tiredness was being replaced by excitement which fed her energy. The biggest buzz she was about to enjoy, was to see a transformation of herself.

She still felt awkward in her belted up skirt and tent of a blouse, but the gown at the parlour covered that, so she looked like all the other clients in this posh garage of hair, makeup and nail mechanics. She was sat in front of a mirror with Sammy and Alicia hovering each side, a hair dresser flouncing her unruly shoulder length mousey hair. August argued, that if her hair was to be changed, she would like to be blonde. Alicia, Sammy and the hairdresser won. Her hair was darkened and trimmed into a neat bob.

The next service was the makeup. The expert worked an array of different tiny pans and little brushes, all the time telling August why and what she was putting on her face, and to take it on board as August would be taking home the tools and materials to create the same look herself. August listened, and when she saw her own reflection, she was glad she had. She stared at the mirror not believing her own image, even she thought she was beautiful.

'Oh, you look fabulous darling, doesn't she Sammy?'

'Gorgeous August,' Sammy said, planting her hands on August's shoulders, looking at her in the mirror, 'Well..what do you think?' Sammy squeezed her shoulders, 'Well?'

'I can't believe it's me, it doesn't look like me.'

'Oh yes it does, do you like it?'

'I love it,' August smiled a wide red lipstick happy smile. The reflection had a defined cupid to her lips, the eyebrows were perfect arcs over a tint of bronze to amber shadow that showed off amber eyes framed with long black lashes. A light blush of ochre defined her cheeks. 'I just love it!' she repeated and could not stop smiling.

There was another big treat in store for August. In the past, clothes shopping for her, had been a pain. The clothes she liked, was never available in her size, if it was, her proportions always spoiled the look. Clothes shopping before had definitely been a depressing outing.

August only now realised how much weight she had lost. The stores and departments Ali was taking her into, she had never been in before, had never even looked beyond the sign over the door which signalled 'very expensive'. The clothes were very expensive, but oh did they look good, and feel good. Sammy and Alicia filtered through rails of clothes and August tried on whatever they held out for her. She would parade each outfit in front of them, they would either nod approvingly, or if they both even slightly disliked it, it would be rejected.

After the tenth outfit, August was tiring slightly, and Alicia noticed, 'Keep that one on darling, it is lovely, I think you have had enough for one day.'

August was pleased, she liked that Alicia had chosen this suit, and was pleased with the new under clothes too. What she didn't realise was that, all four of the outfits they had approved were bought for her to take. When all three women marched out of the boutique together, August didn't at all feel like the ugly duckling trailing alongside two beauties, they made a good looking team. When a wolf whistle followed their march past a dirty ditch of workmen, August even wondered if it was aimed at her.

They hovered for a moment at another shop window, August thought she would faint if she had to do another, she said so. Sammy laughed, 'Oh August, you are certainly not the little girl lost I found in a toilet. You are a classy lady!'

'I know what we'll do,' announced Alicia, 'Let's have lunch at 'The Conservatory.'

CHAPTER SIXTY EIGHT

August went along on this roller coaster. This time, when the waiter ushered her to a table, she didn't feel out of place, or ill. Then she remembered James, and she recalled that this was where she first began to feel really poorly. She had shooed him away because she had felt embarrassed at being ill, and then he had got lost somewhere in her memory. Those following weeks, she had not cared whether she lived or died, and he had been kept out of her thoughts on purpose. It would have been unthinkable to August for him to see her bedraggled in a hospital bed. An unemployed, debt ridden, no hoper. She had shut him away, and now, she wished he was here with her.

Alicia began to giggle, 'Gosh, Sammy, can you remember the last time we came here and bloody Robert was sat over there. August it was so weird, I had my wig on, and makeup and he didn't recognise me, it was frightening and hilarious all at the same time.'

'The last time I came here,' August said as if she was a regular visitor, 'was when I first became ill. It was terrible, it took me ages to struggle back to work, and then I got into trouble for being late, and it was a business meeting.'

'Yes, and then that miserable bugger sacked you!' Sammy said, also still stinging from her treatment.

August pulled a tight smile, more of a grimace, 'Ali, I have something to tell you.'

Robert, made his way along the main drag of market stalls, there was a pungent smell of cooking from vendors offering rice dishes, noodles and unidentifiable fried specimens of fish and meat. An aroma of burnt oil and ginger cranked through the air heavy with aniseed and spice. Simply dressed Chinese sat at tiny tables scooping noodles in a continuous stream with chopsticks.

He tried to follow the scribbled directions, having to hold out the crumpled paper to stall holders to decipher the bits noted in Chinese. He had been directed to a narrow street. Robert strode fast now fighting the urge to scratch himself in public. He showed the note to someone else, who pointed to one of the many shops down the claustrophobic street. It was a dull shop front, with just a heavy deep green curtain filling the window, it looked closed. There was some Chinese symbols embroidered on the curtain alongside a dragon shouting fire from an angry mouth.

Inside, the smell from outside was insulated, but another aroma took it's place. He couldn't put a name to it, but it wasn't unpleasant. It was small space inside with a dark wood glass topped counter displaying long fine needles and small round glass pods. Behind the counter was a backdrop of dark wood shelves loaded with glass jars containing substances he didn't care about. He focussed on the part drawn dark green curtain over a doorway. A small Chinese man in a white doctor's coat appeared through this doorway and stood behind the counter. His beady eyes seemed to examine Robert before he spoke. 'Du.utch?, Engleesh?'

'English,' Robert answered, dying to have a good scratch.

'What a problem is?'

Robert felt embarrassed about the problem, but that is why he was there, no one knew him, and now the itch was so unbearable he didn't care.

Half an hour later, he thought he might have preferred to stick with the itching. The little Chinese chap, shaved him, said a few mixed up words that sounded like, 'shing chong way, long time, short time shin toe.' He also applied some lilac coloured paste, which was immediately soothing and then turned to what Robert could only liken to paint stripper. The pain did calm down after thirty seconds. Robert was then given a small pot of white cream and relieved of a lot of money for his displeasure.

Back at 'The Conservatory', lunch wasn't spoiled by August's revelation, that Alicia's Mother was being courted by the monstrous Don Holland.

Alicia was thoughtful at the revelation, but said, 'I shouldn't have thought he was gold digging, I mean he will have a substantial sum of money when I buy the business from him. Besides, Mother wouldn't put up with anyone shady, she'll soon give him the elbow.'

CHAPTER SIXTY NINE

Saturday continued as one long discussion about the new Company. The only time any of them came out of the Drawing room was to eat or go to the loo. Nancy had not recognised August when she first walked in. Brigitte Heyhott was very impressed. She had just come down stairs, as August came out of the Drawing room. She did have to question at first who this stranger was, and then recognised the honest, twinkling amber eyes of August. 'Perfect, my dear,' she said and made August twirl around, and then put her hands to prayer under her chin, a delighted face said, 'it so suits you August, wonderful!' she giggled. 'By the way are the girls staying with you tonight?'

'Yes, but I would be alright on my own, I wouldn't want you to think you had to stay in for me.' August said this, but blasting her head, she thought, 'I know I was fearful of spending time with you, but I would rather you be here with me than that shit Holland'.

'I have planned to go out actually, in fact Donald should be here any minute.'

August cringed at the sound of his name, and disappeared into the loo. She heard the door bell and then his sucky voice, she hovered in the loo, hoping he would be gone when she came out.

As Don held Brigitte's coat for her, the drawing room door opened and Alicia swanned out. Brigitte was facing her daughter, 'Aah darling, I would like you to meet Donald, Donald, this is my daughter Alicia.'

As their hands merged for a handshake, Alicia smiled politely, but she felt a very strong disaffection coming from him.

August now made her move and immediately realised she had timed it wrong, when she heard the voice. Still, she felt strangely confident and carried on into the hallway where the three stood. Alicia turned and smiled at August. 'This is a friend of mine who is staying with us, August, come and meet Mother's friend, Donald.'

He offered his limp hand to August and she took it firmly for the brief acknowledgment. He then looked a little puzzled as his limp hand let go. 'Strange,' he said, 'I would have said your name would have been a rare one, but I'm almost certain I used to have a member of staff....anyway, strange coincidence.'

Brigitte and Don left, and Alicia and August dissolved into a screaming fit of giggles.

Don Holland was in good spirits that evening. Earlier that day, the estate agents had phoned him to say that someone was interested in buying his Ruban Co., lock stock and barrel, and would be making a formal offer the following day. The piano key money he had lined up had gone, but he thought he could afford to splash out to further bait his fortunes. He took Brigitte to a very expensive restaurant and decided his best ploy would be to invite her to spend a weekend at Paris, a sort of Christmas present. That, he thought would delay him having to sleep with her for now, it would impress her, and besides, he liked Paris too. Brigitte loved the idea, and they planned it for the week before Christmas.

Robert had wanted to join the mile high club, and had hoped that on this singleton holiday, it would happen. The only reason he spent so much time in the loo on the return flight was to have a good scratch and employ the soothing potion. The flight was agonisingly long, with stop offs and while other passengers enjoyed the city stops, he couldn't. He felt airport bound, by his loo visitations and pubic essentials.

When he arrived back home at noon, he went straight to bed and slept until the itching woke him at 3am. He marched about the freezing bedroom, he had been so tired when he got home, he had forgot to set the heating. As he rushed through the house to set it, he realised there was no sign that Alicia had moved back. He poured a large brandy, partly to warm him through and partly to numb his awareness of the itching. It was subsiding with the potion, but he was worried that he didn't have much left.

He went to the hallway in search of his slippers, where he found a pile of mail. He smiled as he picked up the postcard from himself to Alicia. Filing through the letters, dismissing some as trash, selecting three officious looking letters out of the bunch to read, he took them to the lounge and put on the gas fire and sat comfortable. He was beginning to enjoy the radiating warmth from the fire and the brandy when he opened the first envelope. The first paragraph made Robert gulp down the remaining brandy in his glass. He read the solicitor's letter twice before pouring another brandy, he was incensed. 'Bloody bitch!, she won't buy me off with the fucking house!, oh no baby, I want more than this. In fact, you bitch! I'll bloody have it all!'

CHAPTER SEVENTY

At 3.30pm Tuesday eleventh December, Don Holland received a phone call from the estate agents. He smiled with pleasure when they informed him that an offer had been made for Ruban Co.. He reached for a cigar, but stopped when he heard how much the offer was.

'That is preposterous!, ..it's..it's only a two thirds of the asking price!'

'Mr Holland, I am only informing you of an offer, it is entirely up to you if you wish to refuse the offer.'

'Well who is it that has made the offer, I'll ring them myself!'

'The offer was made through a solicitor, the client wishing to remain anonymous.'

'See if you can find out who it is..'

'Mr Holland, I am not allowed to do that, the offer is confidential.'

He slammed down the receiver and buzzed Patricia Charlton. She scribbled his barked instructions down on her pad. *'An immediate sales forecast, and an immediate delivery status, and an up to the minute financial statement.'*

Patricia left his office even less content than her last visit, she was beginning to hate coming to work. It wasn't all that long ago she feared losing her job, her wages allowing her and her husband a holiday abroad and some weekends away. Now she was beginning to loath Ruban Co. It wasn't the company itself, it was Don Holland she hated, he was the bad element draining the company of funds, she saw it and could say nothing. He had just got worse and worse, the sales that had always come in wouldn't match the outgoings, and the rents that were an asset, had been plundered and lost because of him. She now worked mechanically, trying to force out of her mind the worries of Ruban Co. and it's staff.

She was still stinging at the way August had been sacked and wondered of her whereabouts. She knew Fred was getting in a mess on the factory floor, August had always been the magic potion that connected the sales to productivity. Her empty space had left a bigger hole that anyone could have imagined. Patricia was realising that August had been a key cog in this business and had not been at all recognised or recompensed for it either. The quiet girl who got on with her work and got on with everyone, well apart from Simpson, but then again who did. When she was there, the factory floor always got the orders out on schedule. Now there was a steady backlog of delayed orders going out creating phone calls from annoyed clients.

Fred's work sheets that he sent up into the office didn't make any sense, and there wasn't anyone that could actually deal with it. Now, with no rents, not that all of it got into the company funds, but they did help toward the vast utility bills. It was Don Holland's fault expecting businesses to pay an increased rent, but did absolutely nothing to improve their services. Nothing had been done to improve the entrance reception for their visitors.

Patricia allowed herself to be glad, that maybe, Don Holland had cut his own purse strings. Ruban Co. though had always been so precious to her, and it grieved her to see it going down the drain.

CHAPTER SEVENTY ONE

Robert Simpson guarded his itching parts with barrier cream before getting dressed to go and meet Dennis Roebuck. The thought of his scaly office made him wanted to scratch all over anyway. When he got there, it was exactly the same, not even Roebucks clothes had changed. The only evidence the ashtrays had been emptied was the overflowing fag ash mountain in the stinking waste bin.

Robert now sat opposite the seventies specimen and tried to supress a grin as he heard the antics of his wife.

'I've made a list for you,' Roebuck said pausing to drag on his cigarette, and then spoke in a balloon of grey smoke. 'It's a strange one this, a disguise, a double life an' all, but, the details are fact, as we do deliver the facts.' It was said in a way to run short the possibility of apologising for the findings.

'I understand,' Robert said getting to his feet, the excruciating need of a good scratch required an exit. Roebuck remained seated and added, 'If there's nothing else you require, I take it we have completed the job.'

Robert understood that meant the fee was due and he counted out the required cash that he had just withdrawn on Alicia's card.

Back in the car, Robert read through the list, incredulous of Alicia's behaviour. 'God, she must be scared of me,' he laughed, 'serves the bitch right, I'll get her sorted.'

He used the phone booth near where he had parked, to ring a couple of clients, and then put them down on his work sheet as real visits. He tapped Alicia's gold credit card on the chipped shelf in the booth, and wondered about abandoning it there. Then he thought it may fall into the hands of someone honest, which would spoil everything. Then he saw the pub down the street where he had met the fat youth and his side kick. An idea crept into his mind and he slid the card back into his pocket.

In the pub he ordered a gin and tonic, while scanning for the dodgy duo. They weren't there. The drink went down fast and nice, and without thinking he ordered another. He was still in holiday and

I'm a rich man in a posh hotel mode. As he was settling up with the barman, his quest appeared next to him.

'Two pints o' bitter mate.' Fat man ordered.

'I'll get them,' Robert offered.

Fat man and side kick turned to look suspiciously at their host. Robert smiled at them. 'Remember me?'

Their ambivalence suited them.

'The dictaphone?' Robert clued them. Fat man gripped the bar rail. Side kick decided he needed the toilet. There was a tumbleweed silence as Robert paid for the drinks.

'What dictaphone?' Fat man said.

'You sold me a dictaphone, remember?, brilliant little machine.'

Fat man relaxed his grip on the rail. 'Yeah, I remember now, yeah great in it?'

Robert picked up his glass and motioned to an empty table in a corner. 'Could I have a word, private?'

'Course.' Fat man smiled, glad now for the free pint, and hopefully more trade. Side kick gingerly walked back from the toilet and saw his mate getting settled with Mr trenchcoat and decided that things were okay and joined them.

'You remember this bloke don't yer Dave, well he's got a bit o' business for us.'

CHAPTER SEVENTY TWO

As the train started into motion, Nancy stood on the platform with Tom, started to wave faster. August watched them get smaller, Nancy even looked a little upset, she saw Tom put his arm around her shoulder. August had to smile, anyone would think, she was setting off for a year in Siberia, and they were her grandparents.

She settled into her seat, she straightened the mint green, pure wool suit she was wearing and opened up the pale grey leather briefcase Alicia had insisted on buying for her. Inside were purchasing invoices of paintings and limited edition prints she would have to list for the new gallery. She would have plenty of time it was an hours' journey to get to the city where the hotel was near the driving centre. Then she would have a week of evenings spare whilst she was down there. August couldn't believe how calm and confident she felt. When the train rushed through a tunnel, she caught her own reflection in the darkened window. She was different now, so smart and even good looking.

The rhythmic throb of the train poached her concentration. She thought about the incredulous happenings over the past weeks, her deliverance, her transformation. She thought about Shaun, 'Bigshit bay, her Mother, her Brother and James. One of the best moments had been yesterday when Alicia had gone with her to see the bank manager. Mr Gordon didn't recognise her, which she couldn't blame him, she hardly recognised herself. Alicia had paid her an advance of a generous salary, and the debt was wiped away, she was solvent.

There were people and circumstances that had vanished. She had friends, a new family. Alicia, Sammy, Nancy, Tom and Mrs Heyhott. Graham was a new friend, and she would never forget Mr Cruickshank, or James. For other reasons, she would never forget Shaun or her Brother. Don Holland also came in the latter allotment, manure came to mind. She so wished her Mum could see her now, she would be so proud.

Nancy was noisily punishing some suet in a mixing bowl. Tom flicked his newspaper, not being able to concentrate on anything with the rattle of the bowl. He had just read the same line for the fourth time when Alicia breezed into the kitchen. 'Good Heavens Nancy, are you killing something in there?'

'Ignore her my dear, Tom said, 'she's worried about August.'

'Oh Nancy, don't worry, August will be fine. I've booked her into a really good hotel, she'll be well looked after.'

'She still looked a touch pale to me,' and she hit the suet again.

'I take it we're not having soufflé for dinner then.' Alicia smiled.

Nancy stopped and stared flush faced into the bowl, 'I just can't bear to think of that girl being all alone, all those miles away, so fragile.'

Alicia let out a giggle and sat down at the table. 'Let me tell you about our 'fragile' August. She may be a waif and stray to you, but to me she is the most resilient person I have ever met. She is the one person that offered me a helping hand. I can hear her now, 'if there's anything that you need just ask', and she meant to help. I then found out that August didn't have anything. Well she did have an abundance of troubles that I couldn't begin to deal with, but, she did. Well she tried, and she wouldn't have failed either if the odds hadn't been stacked against her. God I admire that girl. If I had half her courage and determination I would be proud of it, and stubborn, so stubborn!'

There was a cough from behind the newspaper and an announcement, 'She gets that from Nancy.'

All three enjoyed Tom's silly joke, and Nancy abandoned the suet and decided to make a soufflé for dinner.

When Alicia drove away from Brockley, she knew that the apron strings had been severed between her and Nancy. She was by no means distraught but happy. It was something that had got knotted up before she was old enough to understand. Alicia could remember an odd atmosphere sometimes when her Mother had to gently remind Nancy that she was not her child but hers and Peters' daughter.' Now Alicia was happy that Nancy had a surrogate daughter to replace her.

She drove to the garage, Sammy was to meet her there. Just the thought of being with Sammy made Alicia glad to be alive. 'There's another person who wanted nothing from you but gave so much.' Alicia flushed at the thought. She realised that for the first time in her life she was really and truly in love. When she pulled up at the garage and saw Sammy standing there, she knew it was true.

As much as she loved Sammy, she could have bit her head off for sweet calling her in front of the mechanics. 'Oh Darling,' she started off far too loud for Alicia's comfort, 'I know I was supposed to take you back to the flat, but I really have to dash to go and see Roger about some gear. Peter here said I could use the courtesy car today, so you take the Golf and I'll pick up your car and see you later at Brockley.'

The Golf had the scent of Sammy now, her perfume seemed to fill the car. Alicia had to call at the flat to pick some things up, she would be sorry when they had to give it up.

CHAPTER SEVENTY THREE

Shaun Ratcliffe watched the black golf pull up, he was stood some distance away and was trying to check the registration number. Dave the side kick was struggling to see it too in the fading light. 'Let's get a closer look,' Dave said, 'I can't see it proper from 'ere.'

'Got to watch it mate, I lived with a bird in that place, better keep me distance. 'ad a bit of a fall out, you know?'

'Looks a bit familiar to me an' all, what's the address, yeah I thought so, me sister lives 'ere, Christ I better keep me 'ead down 'an all.'

'What you got to be frit of your sister for?'

'Well last time I saw 'er, she was a bit mad with me, cos I was a bit wrecked if I remember, an' I sort of borrowed some money off 'er without askin' an' I ain't seen 'er to give it back.'

They were stopped in their tracks as a woman came out. Shaun nudged Dave, 'That looks like 'er photo, before she disguises 'erself like he says.'

'Yeah, it's 'er.'

'C'mon then we've got some shopping to do. Ain't it nice the shops are staying open late for us Christmas shoppers, should be really busy, bloody perfect.' Shaun smiled at the plastic card in his hand. 'I reckon we'll catch the next bus and have nearly two hours to shag this rotten.'

On the bus Shaun was practising the card signature. 'Which flat was your sister in then?, I must 'ave seen 'er.'

'Can't remember the number now, I know there were a lot of stairs.'

'No I can't remember any birds on our landing, she must 'ave been on the ground floor.'

'No, our August was definitely upstairs.'

Shaun stopped writing, 'Who did you say?'

'August, I know it's a strange name.'

'I don't believe it.'

'No honest, that's her name.'

'That's the bird I was livin' with!'

'Gerraway!'

Both sat there bemused, Dave slowly shaking his head, 'What did you two fall out about then?'

That wiped the smile off of Shaun's fat face. 'Oh..err..over money..you know..I was there payin' all the rent, she wouldn't chip in, so we 'ad a barny. I left and took a few things to cover my share of the rent..you know.'

Dave nodded in agreement, and Shaun went on, 'Yeah she begrudged me takin' what was rightfully mine, I mean, it's only fair.'

'Women,' Dave said, 'you know somethin' though, that day I met you in the pub, remember we got talkin' an' I bought you a pint?'

Shaun nodded.

'Well, you might be pleased to know, I nicked that money out of our August's purse, so in a way you got a bit more back didn't you mate.'

This information amused both of them for the rest of the journey, then other business took their amusement.

CHAPTER SEVENTY FOUR

That week back screamed by for Robert, He was happy that he had set his plans in motion to become a rich boy, and shared his working days, partly seeing clients, but mostly drinking and chatting up skirt. His nerves were adrenalin pumped with what he had put into motion. He actually didn't care if he achieved his figures or not for Ruban Co., soon he could tell Holland to shove the job up his arse.

August's new confidence had certainly joined her in the drivers' seat, all twenty five hours of it, and most importantly, when she took her test. She stared at her pass certificate as she headed for home. She placed it with all the other paperwork she had put in order in her briefcase. She felt proud. Her little weary spells were beaten back with a buzz of excitement. It was if she had picked up a germ that gave her renewed mettle. August was so grateful for the sturdy ladder that Alicia had provided, but no one else was in that driving seat, she had done it herself. Now the fact was she could hold her head up once again, she could see a future.

Sammy and Alicia were setting off to meet August at the station. They were full of news and couldn't wait to see her. Alicia had wanted to take her out to dinner to celebrate her pass, but Nancy had insisted on cooking a special meal and Brigitte wanted to join them to. She stayed at home, putting off a date with Donald.

When August stepped off the train, she was embraced by Alicia and Sammy, and felt like a celebrity. She also thought they had turned into giggling teenagers as they bustled her through the station and out into the car park, where Alicia planted the car keys into August's hand.

'I can't..I have never driven your car.'

'Well you had better get used to it, because.. it's your company car now!'

'What!' August was stricken with somewhere between fear and elation. 'Mine?, but it's yours!, it's a BMW!'

Sammy burst into a loud laugh, 'Oh August sweetie, Alicia ordered another one the day you left, she was positive you'd pass.'

August took up the driving seat and listened to the nonstop tic-tac information bursting from both of them. Alicia saying now, 'We've had several meetings with Graham, he needs a get together with you now, you understanding how Ruban Co. should work.'

'But I was only admin!'

'Apparently not. August, I have had solid reports back that you were the backbone there, you underestimate what you did, more annoyingly, other people took advantage of your knowledge and work ethic!. Now he needs to work out some deals for customers to make it attractive for them to stall their orders for a couple of weeks.'

'Why?'

'Because that way sweetie, that bastard will be only too happy to snap up our offer for the Company.'

The evening at Brockley was like a party, the only thing that clouded the seemingly raised ceiling, was Brigitte's announcement that she was off to Paris with Don Holland.

The party atmosphere soon picked up again and Alicia waited until it had reached a full swing moment before quietly saying to her Mother, 'Mummy, can I have a private word?' Brigitte didn't hesitate, the last time her daughter had called her Mummy, was when she was to announce her engagement to that frightful Robert.

They slipped away to the study. 'What is it Darling? Are you upset that I'm going away so close to Christmas?'

'No..no..you should get away, Paris is wonderful any time of year it's just,.well..it's who you are going with.' With that out, Alicia rushed over to the drinks cabinet avoiding any eye contact.

'Alicia, Donald is alright, I know you will still feel precious about your Father..I am too..but'

'No it's not that. To be honest with you Mummy, he's not been a very nice man.'

'Alicia, you don't know Donald, he's a very respectable, hard-working business man.'

'Do you know his business?' Alicia slugged back her brandy. There was an empty silence as Brigitte searched briefly in her memory. 'Err, do you know, I don't think I do, oh good heavens, you're not going to tell me he's a drug baron or something are you?'

They both smiled shallowly.

'No, it's nothing like that.'

'Well what then?' Brigitte was impatient now.

'Don Holland's company is Ruban Co..' Alicia waited while her Mother verbally juggled with the name.

'Ruban Co…Ru..u.ban Co….Ruban Co., isn't that where Robert works?'

Alicia nodded. 'and, where August was unfairly fired from.'

'Oh dear,' Brigitte pouted and sauntered over to collect her brandy, 'then I will inform Donald, that he should get rid of his manager that was responsible.'

'Mummy…he was the guy responsible.'

'Oh dear,' Brigitte sighed again, 'maybe there was some kind of misunderstanding.'

'Oh hell, I hate to be the bearer of bad news.'

'Alicia, it may be bad news, and it is hard to take in…but August never said anything..and..well they even met.' At this point Brigitte let out one of her bubbly giggles,

'He didn't recognise her!, oh Alicia darling, you have done a splendid job.'

The tension relaxed a little now and the drinks topped up.

'Will you still go to Paris with him?'

'I don't know, it may be an opportunity to find out more about him.'

'Well, I don't believe he's told you anything about himself, for instance, he's selling his company and I've put an offer in for it.'

Brigitte raised her eyebrows, 'so that's the one?'

'Yes, so if you are still going to Paris, I must say, that I am worried about it.'

'Darling, there is no need to worry about me, if my brain can push out this many silver hairs', it is wise enough to deal with anything. You see Donald has been the perfect gentleman, I mean, I feel as if my life has opened up, I really don't want to feel like it's a can of worms.'

'But Mother, he is not a gentleman!'

'Alicia. You must let me be the judge and jury of my life, after all I let you get on with your life, I have accepted your new partner.'

Alicia was at first white in complexion, and then the colour of something cooked tandoori style. Her speech resumed firstly in a stammer, 'I don't err I mean..you know?'

Brigitte laughed at her daughter, 'Oh Lord Alicia, I've seen paler lobster, calm down, of course I know, I'm your Mother.'

'But when? I didn't say..do anything.'

Brigitte went over to her daughter and kissed her on the cheek. 'You don't have to, I have never seen you so happy. Sammy is a nice person. Listen, I'm not going to say a word. Just let me be my own person and jury. Now let's get back to the party.'

CHAPTER SEVENTY FIVE

The Saturday morning mail at Hyland Way wasn't picked up until lunchtime, when Robert dragged himself out of bed and downstairs. He planted one by one, the Alicia's letters on the already growing unopened pile. One in particular stalled him, he recognised the credit card logo immediately, and knew the shit was going to hit the fan. He wasn't too fazed though, anytime now, it would all be over.

It was a lovely wild weekend at Brockley. August took Tom and Nancy out for a spin in her new car. There was such a relaxed atmosphere, especially between Alicia and her Mother. August spent a lot of time too with Sammy, who couldn't help herself, but tell of her love for Alicia. She was saying how sad she was that Alicia wasn't staying the Sunday night at the flat with her because she had to set off early evening to London, because she had a meeting first thing Monday morning with a broker.

At 3am. Monday morning, Shaun and Dave arrived back at the grim little flat they shared their disgusting habits in. Dave was shivering uncontrollably and Shaun went straight to the dirty fridge from which he took two of the multitude of lager cans. He looked at the unshaven wreckage of skinny Dave shaking in front of the fire, 'ere get this down yer, a good job done.' Shaun was also trying to control his nerves, this was big.

Dave stood practically touching the fire, steam rising from his damp, filthy jeans.

'Watch yer mate, you're steamin', 'aven't pissed yer'sen 'ave you?'

'It was fuckin' wet under that car, and freezin'!'

'Yep, I reckon this lot of rain will freeze, fuckin' good alibi.' Shaun placed his already drained lager can on top of a pyramid of empties on the window sill and belched with euphoric loudness.

Don Holland had been a bit put out when Brigitte had turned down a date with him, however a chance of selling the Bentley had cropped up. A smart young chap had approached him in the golf club car park Saturday afternoon and seemed very interested. . He did offer a substantial amount of cash that would have been useful, but it was way below what he wanted for it. He spoke to Brigitte on the phone that evening, and secured a dinner date for Tuesday.

When Alicia arrived back at Brockley, Monday afternoon she was shocked to see a police car parked on the drive. Her nerves raced her out of the car and into the house. Tom was in the hall and bore a serious expression, there was something wrong.

'What's happened?' She asked cautiously. Tom silently motioned toward the drawing room. Alicia rushed in relieved to see her Mother and August sat there, then a horrible thought possessed her. The uniforms, a Police man and a nervous WPC. Brigitte got to her feet, there was a charged atmosphere.

'Where's Sammy?'

'We don't know where Sammy is,' Brigitte said calmly, 'but it's nothing to do with Sammy.'

'Thank God. What is it then, have we been burgled?'

The Police man and woman were standing awkwardly in front of the sofa, where August was sat. Brigitte went over to her daughter. 'It's Robert my dear, I'm afraid there's been an accident.'

The WPC stepped forward now. 'I'm sorry Mrs Simpson, it happened this morning, I'm afraid I have to inform you that your husband, Mr Robert Michael Simpson, was found at the scene of a fatal motor vehicle incident. There were no other vehicles involved. We will unfortunately have to ask you to make a formal identification, and you will be informed of further information we receive in due course. Is this the best address to contact you at?'

'Yes, but how did you get this address in the first place?

'There was a list of phone numbers and a few names on a piece of paper in his car, this address was on it, and apparently your hairdresser too.'

The Police excused themselves and left. August went over to Alicia who was staring into the fire, August took her hand and squeezed it, Brigitte took the other hand. 'Are you alright darling, would you like some tea?' Alicia shook her head, retrieved her hands to rub her pale cheeks, turned and said. 'If Sammy calls, tell her to meet me at the flat this evening.' With that she left the house and screamed off in the car, washed pebbles spitting away from her spinning tyres. Brockley then hung in silence for the rest of the day.

As Alicia drove, she felt like a hot wire was being threaded through her veins. She had a strange desire to laugh, but had tears welling in her eyes. She slowed down, her emotions were in turmoil, far be it that she wanted to be in a fatal accident. When she finally parked on the familiar drive, the knot in her stomach untwined. Here she sat in the car staring at the house that she had come to despise. It had never really felt like home, just a shell of unhappiness.

In the familiar surroundings where it was so quiet, she gazed around trying to find some kind of tribute, some manifestation of being there, not just now, but ever. It was a dead house. She wanted to unearth some token to embalm and hide away the discontent that it had all been a waste of time. Also she needed a prompt of some sadness that Robert was no longer breathing.

There was nothing in the lounge, nor the kitchen. Alicia wandered into the rarely used dining room and there on a shelf was a photograph of them just married. A buried memory of church bells pealed in her head, her Father so proud, the happiness of the day. A lump grazed her throat and she turned away and went upstairs.

Her bedroom was the same as the day she left it, tidy. Robert's, the way he left it, an untidy heap of clothes, his unmade bed. His wardrobe full of expensive suits he would never wear again.

A real sadness began to creep over her, she peeked in the bathroom and sniffed the air, it was always touched with his cologne. Alicia's throat drew tighter and she hastily withdrew from the bathroom and made to go downstairs. She grabbed the banister and took a deep breath to stop herself from crying. Then before she took the first tread, she decided to take a look in the spare room, it may be the last time.

Alicia was surprised to find it untidy but simply shrugged, she spotted the dictaphone and paused. She knew she would never hear his voice again and tentatively picked it up. Her heart pounded as she moved her thumb over the play button and then she stopped. 'No', she breathed, then as she sharply pulled her thumb back it scored the rewind button and she heard it whizzing and didn't know how to stop it, she fumbled with it and it began to play. She was shocked still for a moment when she heard his voice and tears were threatening to spill when she heard, 'condoms, yes got them, mustn't forget though. Err socks…shoes, suits, hey wait a minute, I bet the cow's taken all the bloody suitcases.' Then Alicia heard scuffling noises on the tape and..'who's a lucky boy then, I bet she's forgot all about this since she got her platinum card' Alicia's face tightened and the tears retreated as she heard him record the PIN number and say..'Oh China should be much more fun now' ..and the hard laugh tore into her heart and kicked out any sympathy she had salvaged. When she discovered her credit card bill, she wanted to screw the coffin lid on personally.

CHAPTER SEVENTY SIX

Back in the grimy flat Shaun and Dave were hitting half phase hangover. Dave groaned with gut rot and Shaun admired the trappings of their previous shopping trip. 'I bet we'll clear this lot inside a week, should make us a few quid eh?'

His partner in crime was silent, dark hair hung in greasy shanks over his gaunt ashen face. His skinny frame hunched over close to the gas fire, arms nursing his stomach. Shaun cracked the silence by belching and asking him what was the matter. 'C'mon you miserable bastard, what's up?'

'I'm shittin' mes'sen for what we done, I ain't never done owt like that before. What did we 'ave to go an' do him for any way, we wasn't suppose to. Not that I wanted to do his missis either.'

'Cos , stupid, he's the twat that could put the finger on us!'

'But we hadn't done anythin' to her yet.'

'Exactly. If we didn't do the job on his missis, he would have dobbed us in for the credit card!'

Dave rubbed his pale face. 'Well I'm not doin' that again. I'm not doin' her car.'

'We don't have to do we, he was the one that had the card and he'd used it, let that slip, stupid twat, now as long as he's copped it proper, we're clear. Keep our 'eads down today, tomorrow we'll know for sure and we're up an' runnin' with the gear.'

All day Brigitte had expected a phone call from Donald to cancel their date in view of the circumstances, but he picked her up as arranged, and under his normal veil of charming, chatted all the way to the restaurant.

Over the meal, Brigitte asked him about his business. 'What is your company Donald?, you've never told me.'

'I'm sorry my dear, I thought I had told you, it's a packaging business situated in town, I'm sure I've told you of Ruban Co.'

'You may have mentioned the packaging, but I didn't know what it was called, it's strange, I thought I read only today, yes I'm sure it was your company in the papers. An unfortunate accident, one of your employees?' she paused to sip her wine and watched Donald as he attacked his veal, and shook his head. 'Yes, most unfortunate incident,' he said placing the meat in his mouth and reaching for his glass, 'Rather good wine don't you think Brigitte?'

Brigitte could not answer, but said, 'it must be upsetting at work?'

'Well it is rather, and do you know, it was a brand new car I had just got him, they don't respect them you know, probably driving like a lunatic. It's just as well I had set another chap on in sales really, more wine dear?'

Brigitte cloaked her glass with one hand and stroked her throat with the other. She knew she could not swallow another morsel or share a drink with the moronic man opposite. The atmosphere changed at their table.

'Are you alright dear?'

'To be honest Donald, I don't feel too well, I hate to spoil dinner, but it may be a good idea if I went home.'

Don Holland set down his cutlery as politely as he could to hide the fact that suddenly he was very pissed off. He knew he would not be able to persuade her to stay as she was already retreating from the table. He was now disturbed that Brigitte was in fact ill, and he was upset because he would have to pay full whack for two meals that were still on the plates. When he counted out the money to pay the bill it almost burnt him.

He was well and truly furious and could do no more than to be gushing and concerned for Brigitte. But the journey back to Brockley was a silent one, and the one time he needed to be invited in he was not.

'I do hope you are alright my dear, I'll phone you about the arrangements for the weekend.'

'No, don't do that Donald, I won't be able to make Paris, I have to attend a funeral.'

In the weak light from the porch, Brigitte observed him. He looked pathetic and nasty at the same time.

'Oh I am sorry, someone close?'

'I suppose, yes, I didn't even like Robert Simpson, but he was my son in law.'

And with that she left him on the doorstep and closed the door on him. He was on the verge of tears, he felt the void in his wallet and sped home in a fit of rage. He couldn't believe the finality in Brigitte's voice, he had blown it. All that money he had spent baiting the big fish, gone.

CHAPTER SEVENTY SEVEN

Don Holland sat in his leather wing chair chasing brandy with brandy. He needed to talk to someone, and phoned Henry.

'Hello old boy, how are you, heard you were getting along quite well with lady Heyhott. Sold her the Bentley yet?'

It was a sore point and Don lit a cigar. 'Bugger Brigitte, I don't need her to buy the car, I think I have a buyer.'

'Oh jolly good, anyone I know?'

'Probably, I met him at the golf club, likeable sort of chap, I haven't seen him around before, young chap.'

'What's his name?'

'Tavistock, pound note chappy, not that he wants to pay the asking price of course.'

'Tavistock, doesn't ring a bell, can't say I've seen a young chap in the club house.'

'It wasn't in the club house actually, he approached me in the car park.'

'Ooh, in the car park hey, young chap with lots of pound notes to offer,' Henry laughed, 'sounds like an Inland Revenue man to me.' He laughed again. Don's glass left his hand and brandy splattered over his shoes and up his trousers. Henry was still laughing at his own joke, Don was trembling. 'You don't think he is do you?'

'I'm only joking old boy, then again one never knows, anyway I'm short of a partner on Saturday how about it…oh no, I forgot your away to Paris, oh well lucky you, look I have to go, my turn to do supper, and I can smell burning, see you old chap and enjoy your weekend.'

Don stared at the purring receiver in his hand. He heard the echo of the words in his head, 'Inland Revenue, Inland Revenue, Tavistock, tax man. How old must he be, twenty eight, thirty, far too much cash to be throwing around. 'Jesus Christ, they're on to me, 'he whispered. He picked up the empty glass and filled it. As he lifted the decanter, he saw the decanters at Brockley, he saw Brigitte, the imagined Hockney, Brockley House. He felt his lifeline draining away. His bottom lip trembled, and as the decanter unsteadily clinked against the rim of the glass, he could only hear the clunk of a cell door, the grating of tin mugs on chipped tables. He could almost smell the gross scent of unwashed men crammed in a confined space with him. Don slugged back the brandy and took the glass and decanter through to the hallway. He put on his overcoat and put his favourite tan leather driving gloves in his pocket. Then he took the glass and decanter with him through the kitchen and the door that connected directly to the garage. In the back of the Bentley, he pulled down a mini walnut table attached to the back of the driver's seat. He set out the brandy and his cigars on there. Then he squeezed around the impressive radiator grill and reached for the garden hose. He trailed it back to the rear of the car and took one of his leather gloves and wedged it in the outlet of the exhaust pipe. Calmly he sat in the driver's seat and started the engine, an act he had always enjoyed, the soft powerful purr. Then his face distorted as he cried, head bowed over the steering wheel. He coughed himself clear of tears, gathered himself and without stalling he pressed the little shiny button that let down the rear window. He got out and fed the free end of the hose pipe and gently trapped it in the rear window, careful not to close the pipe. Don Holland swept his hand along the smooth coachwork, 'You beautiful bitch, you were always going to be the death of me.'

He climbed in the back seat, slammed the door shut and poured a brandy nearly to the rim of his glass. It was quiet, all but for the slight hum of the heater blowing. He took off his overcoat and made it into a back support, bringing his legs across the seat. It was just like his couch. He lit a cigar and felt like a huge burden was lifting from him.

His thoughts drifted to Ruban Co., he hated the business, the buildings, everything about it. There was Patricia Charlton, he smiled, and drank half of the glass of brandy. He had often wondered in the early days, what it would have been like to bed her. After a ferocious tug on his cigar, he stubbed it out feeling very light headed. He was comfortable though, his legs felt heavy but rested and he clumsily poured another brandy, spilling a fair amount on the table which dripped all over the cream carpet. Don grinned, it didn't matter, he snatched at the glass spilling some more, and still it didn't matter.

He took a small swig and waved the glass at his blurred image in the window. He closed one eye to focus, but he was struggling to make anything real sharp. A dull discomfort told him he should have emptied his bladder before leaving the house. He snorted a rebellious half laugh, a crooked grin as the warm sensation spread around his crotch. The grin cooled as did the urine and he felt quite disgusted, it would be the last thought he would have about himself.

CHAPTER SEVENTY EIGHT

If Brigitte felt now she had opened a can of worms, she neither felt capricious nor did she fall back into her cocoon of charity work or the bridge club. In quiet moments, she wondered if Donald really did like her, she would never know. She also knew she would never be young again, the beautiful butterfly as Peter used to call her. She could see everything clearly now, she could see the handsomeness in a silken moth, and she would allow herself to be drawn toward the light, but this lady would not have her wings singed again.

Alicia involved her Mother with the new company and Brigitte was in her element organising the gallery in the room that was once home to Judds Jewellery. Sammy would turn the dull foyer into a vibrant retail area full of artist's materials. Alicia was obsessed setting out her own graphic design department on the top floor. All four women had done the rounds whilst the place had been closed for the Christmas holidays. August had given them a guided tour and a very competent account of exactly what was efficient and an authoritative catalogue where improvements could be made. Brigitte followed August around totally bemused at her knowledge, enthusiasm and knowledge of the nuts and bolts of what appeared to her as a strange business altogether. She gave an approving nod to Alicia who was very proud of August. Meanwhile Sammy had the forthright to nip off with a screw driver and remove Don Holland's name plate before they reached the offices. It was for Brigitte's benefit, it wouldn't have been necessary as it was she, who was in a rush to get there. Once in the office, she asked August to sit in the leather swivel chair behind the desk. Alicia then handed August a large, heavy Christmas cracker. August stared at the three smiling women crowded around the desk. She was then startled by voices coming from the corridor, the door opened and Tom and Nancy bustled in beaming all over their faces. Alicia took one end of the cracker and Brigitte ordered 'PULL!'

The paper tore without a bang and a toblerone shaped brass weight slid out. August picked it up and turned it. Her mouth fell open when she read Miss August Jackson M.D.

There had been much talk and anxiety in the work place, Mrs Charlton had read out a letter to everyone to assure them that it was business as usual and their new Managing Director would be joining them soon. There were apologies for them having to work whilst tradesmen were working in the premises making the new installations and decorating. It relieved tensions a little, but they were all aware that orders had been slow coming in.

The staff worked mechanically, there was a mute atmosphere and Jayne was miserable, she missed August being around, but not as much as Fred. He had managed to catch up a little with the down turn of incoming work sheets, but his paperwork still made little sense. Patricia and Jayne did their best with help from Graham, who seemed confident and kept saying, 'it'll be all right girls, you'll see.'

CHAPTER SEVENTY NINE

On August's first day at the office, she had been up at 6am. and had taken her time getting ready. She was excited, like a child on Christmas morning. She had got her hair and makeup off to a fine art, and had a wonderful selection of smart expensive clothes and gorgeous shoes to choose from.

It was the third Monday in February. It was still dark outside and the lights filtering out from the windows of Brockley House, showed up the sugary frost on the low shrubs outside. By 7am. Everyone was in the kitchen eating breakfast. August was beginning to wonder if Nancy and Tom ever slept, they were nearly always there. The kitchen was glowing warm, Tom in his favourite chair next to the fire, and Nancy was all smiles in total command of her cooking range. The room smelled of bacon, eggs and coffee.

The weekend had been hectic, it had been spent hanging prints and paintings and stocking out the shop. Sammy and Alicia had stayed over at Brockley and there was an excited buzz around the table. August could only manage to nibble a croissant and drink black coffee, much to Nancy's disappointment. She was thankful of Sammy's appetite, but the thought of how she got it, Nancy kept out of her mind.

At twenty minutes to eight the convoy of two BMW's, the Golf and a Rover Coupe set off for town. August couldn't have bought the feelings that ripped through her when she parked her BMW in the spot that had the sign 'RESERVED FOR M.D.'

The four women each went to their own departments with the prior arrangement to join for lunch at 'The Conservatory'. Graham was soon in too knocking on the M.D.'s door, he was the only member of staff to know and sworn to secrecy. The voice that said, come in was familiar, but the person stood by the desk turned him dumb. 'Hey Graham, what do you think?'....'Graham?'

'Wow..it is you?, August?'

August giggled and did a twirl. Graham was stunned, 'bloody wow, you are the business!, I can't believe you, the last time I saw you, you were Miss grumpy in hospital!'

'Yes I was, but thanks to a great friend like you Graham, who made Miss Grumpy open her eyes and mind. Thank you Graham.'

'You Miss Managing Director! are very welcome, and I tell you what, I wish Slime was here to see this, and Holland.'

'Yes, it is sad though,' she looked a little sad now.

'Don't be down now, you deserve this and it would have happened if they were still around, you know that. Anyway, I will catch up with you later, I want to see the rest of their faces when they meet you, see you later. Hey, you look good honey, oh I shouldn't call you that now you are my boss.'

'Graham, you are my friend, it isn't going to be like the old regime was.'

'Catch you later..Guvnor.' he winked and left. He was rubbing his hands as he went down the corridor, he met Patricia on the way to the office, she looked nervous. 'Oh good morning Graham, is the new M.D. in yet?'

'Ohhh yes, bright and early.'

Patricia swallowed hard, and nervously played with her necklace, 'Well I suppose we'll all meet him soon, she said and trotted off to the loo.

At 8.45, August heard the faint but familiar clip clop of Patricia Charlton's heels heading down the corridor on her usual visit to the mirror in the ladies cloak room. August had her briefcase lid open in front of her on the desk when at precisely 8.55 the frail knock preceded Patricia. 'Good morning Sir..oh I do beg your pardon,'

August gently closed the case and smiled a broad red lipstick smile.

'I am so sorry,' the embarrassed secretary stumbled on.

'It's alright Patricia, come on in.'

The familiar voice drew the woman in slowly.

'Come and sit down, we have a lot to talk about.'

Patricia sat, at the same time staring at this new boss, who seemed almost familiar, and the voice, the voice she knew, she was sure they had met before, she felt almost comfortable, her nervousness ebbed away. This, imposing, attractive young lady was friendly and warm. She was sure she had seen her before.

August leaned forward and rolled over the brass toblerone to reveal her identity. She laughed when Patricia silently mouthed her name.

'Yes it is me, shall we have coffee?'

Patricia was still in shock, watching the well-dressed woman glide over to the coffeemaker, lay a tray and bring it back to the desk. August relished the dumbstruck attention. 'Surprised?' she said to prompt Patricia to speak.

'Surprised, doesn't come into it. It is you, isn't it?'

'Yes. August Jackson, Managing director of Ruban Co.'

'Well, I am err .. amazed..how?'

'I should settle for amazed for the moment. I am.'

Jayne, who had just found out she was pregnant began going through names of months she could call her baby if it was a boy, after she was introduced to her new boss. Fred thought it was his birthday and the whole day was over before August wanted it to be.

CHAPTER EIGHTY

All that first week, August was in an hour before anyone else, and left after the cleaners had gone home. She was happy and like a woman possessed. It did get her into hot water with Nancy though and Alicia had to restrain her from working all hours. August gave in though only when she had got production up by twenty per cent. Then she came home at a sensible hour and Brockley was at peace again.

Alicia had put the Simpson estate in the hands of Bradley, the solicitor to sort out. There had been a huge pay out of Roberts life insurance and now the sale of Hyland Way was about due for completion. After several discussions, Alicia decided that the capital should be ploughed into the new company. The dormant area to the rear of the factory should become a printing outfit as August had suggested, and they should have their own delivery van. 'All products and services to be in house and profitable'

The staff at Ruban Co. had a new lease of life, the atmosphere was light and positive, Jayne could not but stare every time she saw August, and was in awe of her until she spoke and put her at ease. This would go on for weeks, and Jayne asked August if she would be a Godmother. This pleased August so much, it was another marker for her growth, for the respect she had for herself.

It was a sunny Sunday in April and August enjoyed the early streams of light that filtered through the white wispy voile that covered her window. It was the first day she had allowed herself from work since her official appointment of M.D. Although she told everyone she intended to have a lie in, she found herself taking breakfast at the same time. It wasn't the same as when Tom and Nancy were there whom had been ordered to take a day off. August was tempted to visit them at their bungalow but stopped herself. She knew full well that Nancy would spring to her feet and start cooking and fussing as if she were at Brockley. She enjoyed just walking in the grounds of Brockley, there was a sensational carpet of snowdrops on the south lawn and buds were starting to fist on shrubs and trees.

Midday, Brigitte found her and asked her if she would like to join her for lunch with some friends. 'They really wouldn't mind August, and they aren't too boring.'

'Thank you, but I am just loving the quiet and restfulness of this house.'

'I know exactly what you mean darling, enjoy, I often do.'

It was early afternoon and August lay on her comfortable bed taking advantage of the solitude. She ran her hand over her flat belly. It gave her a satisfying feeling, it was a far cry from the Sundays she had were she had felt bloated and somehow bullied into eating more than she needed. She was pleased with her weight loss, she had retained a good bust and felt energetic.

She stared at the window and in her mind a ghost memory of a pyramid of beer cans made her sit up. 'I wonder where that bastard is', she said. She thought of that last Sunday, she had lain with him in a similar position. The misery that was that life of going nowhere and worrying about paying the bills. That was the last time she had laid eyes on Bigshit bay, and she wondered where that was too. She was so sad about that, and vowed she would find the painting. She was so, so glad she was rid of Shaun and his control and smiled in the knowledge that it was just a memory.

There was another twang of recall that ambled through her as her hand involuntary travelled through her bush, and her finger caught a sensitive spot. She replayed the spot, it may not have been memorable sex with Shaun, but for the first time she missed the sensation. It was a remote enjoyment that made her carry on, but with the climax, the comfort was short lived and her thoughts turned to James.

Monday morning was just as bright and beautiful, and August was rested and ready for the day. Alicia was to spend most of the day with her as they had scheduled a run of appointments, seeing representatives who were going to try and sell their benefits of printing machines and bolt on products. August invited Fred to be part of the decision making and he loved it. He was buoyant because August was back and the work scheduling was streamlined, and he felt important. He felt like he was part of the company for once, instead of being frightened of getting a bollocking every other week.

The first rep was scheduled for midmorning and the next an hour later. The afternoon had three more booked in. To say that August had the company running like clockwork was an understated fact. She packed twice as much into the time without pressuring the staff. So, half a frantic days work had been done by the time the first rep arrived. He was allocated an hour to do his selling, before the next appointment was due in. Patricia brought in the next rep's business card and Alicia went over to the coffee maker. When she returned to the desk, she found August in a depth of crimson complexion and staring at the card, the business card flittering in her shaking hand.

Alicia stopped, 'darling are you alright?'

'Err..yes..fine, I'm fine,' she said and laid the card down like a fragile piece of parchment. Alicia picked up the card. 'If you don't feel like seeing another rep, I'll deal with it if you like, and I can get Fred to come up again.'

'No,' August said abruptly, and then went quiet as did her pallor. 'No, I'm fine really.'

Alicia wasn't convinced, especially when Mr Blonde walked in, and August sat in a shy silence. There was a long moment as they stared at each other, him at the brass name plate on the desk and then at her bewildered friend who seemed to have an urgency to bounce together all the papers on the desk into a neat order on the desk.

Alicia felt the air charge with a supressed electricity reaching between August and this representative. She couldn't help feeling like a gooseberry. 'Excuse me a minute, I have to nip upstairs,' she said leaving and going instead to the admin office. There was a low toned conversation going on between Patricia and Jayne. Alicia joined them and begun to whisper too. Back in the M.D.'s office, Alicia had left a silence behind, which was broken by James Blonde. 'It is..August, isn't it?'

CHAPTER EIGHTY ONE

August nodded, really knocked a little sideways with the sight of him. Her emotions collided and for the first time since re-entering this building all those weeks ago, she was speechless.

James blew a little pent up air out and said, 'Would you excuse me for a minute too?'

August could only nod, and he left the office. She sat for the first time behind that desk, feeling vulnerable and alone, she twiddled with her pen, readjusted her name plate, stroked his name on the card and wondered if he would come back. She felt the same pang of wanting to be close to him as she did when they first met.

She jumped when the phone rang, 'Yes Patricia,'

'There is a call for you on line two, it's a policeman.'

August wanted to say, I don't want to take the call right now, but the police. 'ok, put him through.' At the same time a knock on the office door was preceded by a peek around it by James, she motioned to him to sit down and in sign language apologised that she had to take a call and stood and turned her back to him.

The policeman was saying, 'I have two lads in custody that need someone to support bail for them, one David Jackson says he's your brother.'

'I don't have any relatives,' August said.

'I have another chap, a Shaun Ratcliffe who claims he is your boyfriend.'

Back in the police station, fat lad and sidekick were stood with a holding policeman, whilst Sergeant Newton a few feet away carried on his quest on their behalf.

'Oh does he now?, 'August said, I do not have a boyfriend. James didn't know whether to run or smile.

'He is quite persistent Miss Jackson.'

'Ask this so called boyfriend what colour eyes I have.'

She heard the faint question being asked, and 'well lad, what colour?

'He says brown.'

'Oh he says brown does he well he's wrong, like I said, he is no boyfriend of mine.'

'He really is quite persistent Miss.'

I have someone with me who can verify the colour of my eyes,' before she could turn around she felt the close presence of James behind her, he placed one hand on her left shoulder and took the receiver from her, snuggled close to her back and said to the sergeant. 'Miss Jackson has the most beautiful amber eyes.. they have a sprinkle of burnt ochre around a deep black saucer of iris. It dilates when you look at her and her eyes sparkle with a kindness and love you only see in one lifetime.'

Shaun was waiting for a response from Sergeant Newton, who was looking quite emotional.

'Well?' Shaun asked.

'Well, lad, you are most definitely fucked, back to the cells.'

August went all weak as James replaced the receiver, she turned into his body, his arms' were already curling to encircle her. She buried her face into his shoulder, closing her eyes, not wanting for this moment to end. He kissed the top of her forehead, saying I have something for you. He let go and went to the chair where he had leaned a brown paper wrapped parcel.

'I have carried this around since our last date..I mean lunch. I tried to reach you, I felt such a swine for leaving you on the street when you were ill. I have rung you here and they said you didn't work here anymore. I just knew I would find you. He handed the big flat parcel to August. She slowly tore the paper away, knowing, yes it was 'Bigshit bay!

''Bigshit bay, Bigshit bay, she was whispering it over and over and then the tears came. James took hold of August and for the first time their lips met. Just then Alicia came in. She stopped, witnessing the most incredible intensity that she had felt and knew only a few months ago. August and James realising they had company pulled slightly apart.

Alicia now on the verge of happy tears said, 'Oh do carry on darling, it seems you may become blonde after all, it certainly suits you.

Printed in Great Britain
by Amazon